RISE OF THE THRALL LORD

TOMB OF THE GODS

BOOK FOUR

F.P. SPIRIT

Thanks to Tim for creating the world of Thac, and to Daniel, Eric, Jeff, John, Mark, and Matt for their roles in bringing the characters to life. Also, thanks to the rest of my friends and family who gave their time and support in the creation of this book.

BOOKS BY F.P. SPIRIT

The Heroes of Ravenford

Ruins on Stone Hill

Serpent Cult

Dark Monolith

Princess of Lanfor

The Baron's Heart

Rise of the Thrall Lord

City of Tears

Protectors of Penwick

Raiders of the Dark Coast

Tomb of the Gods

TABLE OF CONTENTS

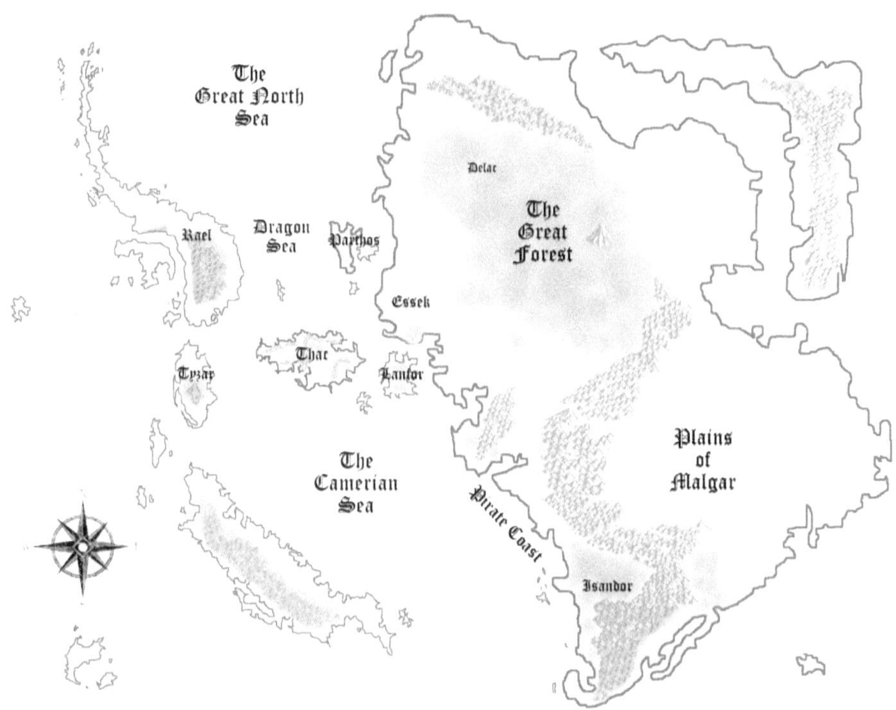

At the beginning of the fourth age, demons arose from the shattered seals of two abyssal chains at once. With the elves and their draconic allies overwhelmed, the storm dragons sought help from the newest of races, humankind. Great heroes stepped forth from their ranks, taking on divine aspects to wage war upon the demons. Chief among these Ralnain gods was Phobas, the Lord of Light. Yet powerful as he was, treachery could still be found even amongst the gods. Tricked into facing a horde led by three demon lords on his own, Phobas fell. Though his body was never found, rumors abound that it is buried somewhere in Thac, along with the mightiest of relics he wielded…

- Lady Lara Stealle, High Wizard of Penwick

1
MOSTLY DEAD

If your body were to thaw out naturally, it might not survive the shock.

The grayness stretched out in all directions as far as the eye could see. No being or thing lay in sight, no other colors marring the emptiness. Not a single sound penetrated the stillness. Nothing seemed to exist here except for the empty void. Closing his eyes, Glolindir gingerly rubbed his temples. When he reopened them though, nothing had changed.

The tall elf floated in the midst of a still gray void with nothing else in sight. Not even a light shone through the dimness, though somehow, he could see in this dull gray gloom.

His memory foggy, Glo shook his head in an effort to clear it. How had he ended up here in the first place? The last thing he remembered was entering the basement of the vampire lord's castle in the Shadow Plane. That chamber had been huge, though thick fog covered most of the floor.

As Glo struggled to recall those memories, something stirred in the emptiness before him. The grayness began to swirl, colors bleeding in, out of nowhere. When the swirling stopped, an oval image had formed in the grayness in front of the flaxen-haired elf.

Glo stifled a gasp. *That's the basement of the shadow castle!*

The vision started to play out the memories at the forefront of his mind.

A sudden chill ran up Glo's spine. Something huge emerged from the mists, towering over him and his companions. It was an enormous skeletal dragon, eerie hollowed sockets staring down at them from where its eyes should have been.

Glo watched in horror as a glacial blast burst from the creature's massive maw straight downward. The wizard felt his chest tighten as he heard himself cast a desperate spell. A split second before the barrage of sleet struck, a translucent globe of shimmering mana formed above them.

The arctic blast slammed into the globe, the force of its sheer power swiftly overwhelming the wizard. Glo's heart raced as he heard himself cry out a last desperate plea.

"Lloyd, get them out of here!" His voice sounded strangely muted, as if traveling over a great distance. Behind him he saw a red blur as the warrior leapt into action.

A second later the barrier broke. The vision zoomed in as a frigid wave of ice and sleet poured over the hapless elf. The image faded after that leaving him alone again in the endless grayness.

Glo floated there feeling even more lost than ever. *What happened once he was gone? Had Lloyd managed to save the others?*

At the thought of his friends, the grayness before him began to swirl once more. Colors filtered in again mixing to form yet another image. A tall red-clad figure came into focus.

Lloyd! Glo gasped in earnest.

The warrior stood against a dark background wearing a gaunt expression. Andrella's head lay upon his broad shoulder, tears openly streaming down her cheeks. The vision widened to show the white-robed Aksel across from the duo. The quiet Xellos stood off to one side, with an uncharacteristically subdued Alys seated on the ground next to him.

Glo breathed a heavy sigh. *They did get away safely.*

A long row of grey tombstones surrounded his companions, stretching off far into the distance. He immediately recognized the place. It was the Olde Town Graveyard in Penwick; the place where the shadow castle first appeared over the city.

It was then his eyes fell on the still form laying in the midst of his friends. Garbed in purple robes, the figure had long flaxen hair with the tip of a pointed ear jutting out from beneath the pale strands.

A lump welled in the back of Glo's throat. *That must be me,* he thought numbly. It felt almost surreal gazing down upon one's own body.

Their eyes fixed on the body in their midst, his friends appeared to be talking amongst themselves. Once again, the sound seemed muted, as if heard through a long tunnel.

Glo strained his ears to hear their words, when a voice abruptly rang in his ear. This one sounded clear as day. "I thought I told you to stay out of trouble?"

The startled elf spun about to find a familiar visage floating in the gray void not far from him. It was a woman garbed in a short red top with a long red skirt tightly affixed around her waist. A matching red hood draped over her black cap which in turn was embossed with a set of yellow stars. A luxurious mane of honey-blonde hair flowed from beneath her cap perfectly framing her heart-shaped face. A sarcastic smile adorned the woman's lips, but he could see the fear hidden behind those striking violet eyes.

Elistra…

Glo's heart melted at the sight of her. The immortal seeress was the love of his life—or had been, he corrected himself. He'd forfeited his life and with it anything that might have been between them. His delight at seeing her shifting to pain, his face contorting into a grimace. "I didn't exactly have a choice."

The seeress' face softened, her eyes filled with understanding. "I know," she murmured.

Down below, the others were discussing what to do next. It abruptly dawned upon Glo that Seth was not among them. Perhaps the halfling was skulking around somewhere invisible, but he still should've been able to see him.

Glo let out a short sigh. Either way, his friends had brought up a good point. *What now? I can't just float up here forever, can I?* He cast a curious eye at Elistra. "Shouldn't I be seeing a white light or something?"

A slight giggle escaped the seeress' mouth. It was not at all the reaction he expected.

A single eyebrow traveled up Glo's forehead. "What's so amusing?"

That wry smile returned to her lips. "Oh, my dear sweet Glolindir. You're not dead."

A wave of confusion abruptly washed over him. He glanced down at his frozen body, his brow knitting into a deep frown. "I'm not? Then what am I doing up here?"

A sudden touch on his shoulder nearly made him jump. Elistra now floated next to him, her eyes twinkling with a mixture of compassion and mirth. "You're in a form of hibernation."

Glo eyed her sharply. During the course of his studies, his father pushed him to research a wide variety of subjects. One of those areas happened to be nature. "You mean like the animals do in the winter?"

Elistra pursed her lips together, her head bobbing back and forth. "Yours is a bit of an extreme case, but yes."

For the first time since he woke in this strange, gray empty void, Glo felt a spark of hope ignite in the very center of his chest. Almost afraid to hear the answer, he tentatively ventured a follow-up question. "Does this mean—I can possibly be revived?"

Instead of answering, Elistra moved closer and placed her hands upon his chest. Though her touch felt warm and calming, he could see the uncertainty in her eyes. "I believe so, but I'm not quite sure of how to go about it." She paused, her gaze falling from his.

Glo had known her long enough to sense there was more to it than she was saying. He put his hand under her chin and lifted her head until their eyes met once more. "What aren't you telling me?"

Elistra let out a soft sigh, a wan smile crossing her lips. "Am I really that transparent?"

For the first time since he found himself up here, Glo let out a soft chuckle. "Only to me."

She fixed him with a piercing stare, then took in a sharp breath and let it out. "Very well. It's just a hunch, but I feel if your body were to thaw out naturally, it might not survive the shock."

Glo arched an eyebrow at her. It certainly wasn't what he wanted to hear, yet she hadn't rung his death knell either. There was still a chance, albeit slim. Gulping down his fears, he put his arms around her waist and forced himself to smile. "Thank you for giving me even the smallest hope. As for the how, there are some extraordinary wizards and healers in Penwick. Perhaps our friends could ask for their help?"

Hope glimmered in her violet eyes as she met his gaze with a firm nod. "I will let them know." Before he could say another word, she stood up on her toes and pressed her lips against his.

Glo's head swam as he lost himself in the warmth and comfort of the only woman he had ever loved.

It was just past midnight in the Olde Town Graveyard. A myriad of twinkling stars dotted the black velvet sky, dimly lighting the expanse of the sacred grounds. The largest graveyard in all of Penwick, it stretched the equivalent of five blocks in all directions. Filled with rows upon rows of gravestones, it was a testament to the death and destruction that had plagued this city far too often.

Now, yet again, death had come to knock on Penwick's door, this time quite literally in the form of the undead. The vampire lord that Aksel and friends had been chasing, summoned an entire castle full of macabre creatures to this very spot. Traveling through the *Plane of Shadows*, the castle materialized over the graveyard surrounded by a giant sphere of darkness. That sphere had begun to fade, and once it did, the undead denizens of the keep would swarm outward and destroy Penwick.

Still, that was not the foremost matter on Aksel's mind. The little gnome cleric had been left numb by all that had recently transpired. Glolindir was dead, frozen solid by the undead dragon, Jinkolothos. Seth was gone as well, disappeared in an explosion he purposely created to deter the dragon. In the end, Seth had saved them, but at the cost of his own life.

"Did that really just happen?" Lloyd murmured, his voice sounding hollow as he gaped at their frozen friend. The tall, muscular, brown-haired warrior somehow seemed quite small at the moment.

"I'm afraid so," Lady Andrella whispered, seeking the comfort of his shoulder as tears openly streamed down her face.

Lloyd brushed back a lock of blonde hair from her brow and gently held her as his own eyes brimmed with moisture. Under other circumstances, the pair would be adorable—Lloyd's crimson red leathers nearly matching Andrella's bright scarlet *Regalia of the Phoenix.*

After Glo's and Seth's sacrifice, Jinkolothos spared the rest of their party. She even transported them all back to the graveyard, including a frozen Glo, a passed-out Alys, and a reticent Xellos. Yet, she had not done so out of the goodness of her non-existent heart. Instead, she laid a task upon their heads along with an ominous threat. She would personally destroy Penwick, before the vampire lord had the chance, if they did not comply with her wishes.

Somewhere deep inside, Aksel knew he should be more concerned about that. Orphaned at a young age, he had been raised in a monastery and instilled with a keen sense of right and wrong. Yet the loss of his family left him with a deep-seated fear, one that had been triggered by the death of his friends. For the moment, that trauma left him paralyzed.

"So, what do we do now?" Lloyd asked, his voice still sounding empty.

"I think we need to find that staff or this city is pretty much done for," came the soft answer from outside the circle of light Andrella had conjured. Barely visible in his green and brown leathers, Xellos had stood there quietly until now. Even his boyish face remained hidden, only a tuft of reddish-orange hair jutting from beneath his hood.

"Staff? What staff?" another voice squeaked before anyone else could answer.

All eyes turned towards Lloyd's friend Alys. The songstress had passed out while trying to hold back the dragon's breath with her sonic cry. Now sitting up, she brushed back the coppery tresses from her brow and gazed around with a puzzled expression.

"And how did we get back to the graveyard?" she abruptly added.

"The Staff of Law," Andrella answered as she held out a hand to help Alys to her feet. "The dragon told us it was hidden beneath the temple before she brought us back here."

"Beneath the temple?" Alys repeated, her comely brow furrowing as she straightened the leather bustier and long coat that perfectly matched her copper-colored hair. "Do you mean the Temple of the Ral…"

Alys' voice abruptly trailed off as her eyes fell upon the frozen figure before them. "Oh my!" Her hand went to her mouth. "Is that Glolindir?"

Everyone fell silent as Alys went to kneel down and touch the icy figure. When she rose back up and turned around, her eyes had misted over. A hand went to her chest as she spoke, her voice sounding very small. "Did he sacrifice himself to save—me?"

Andrella fixed the young lady with a look of keen sympathy. "To save all of us—you, me, and Lloyd," she corrected.

The moisture in Alys' eyes welled into full-fledged tears. She threw herself at Lloyd and Andrella, openly weeping as she wrapped her arms around the both of them.

Still wrestling with his internal demons, Aksel had remained silent this entire time. He knew he could not remain that way though. There was no denying the death of both Seth and Glo laid firmly upon his shoulders. He had been the one to lead them all into the keep, knowing full well their chances of success were slim.

Even so, if he did not pull himself together, the others would get nowhere. They needed some form of leadership before they completely fell apart. Inadequate as he had proved himself, there was no one else to do so at the moment.

A heavy sigh escaped his lips as Aksel opened them to speak. Yet before he could utter a word, another voice interrupted him.

Aksel?

It took the gnome a second or two to realize the sound was coming from inside his head. He knew that voice. It belonged to—*Elistra?*

Yes, came her immediate reply. *I need to talk to you about Glolindir.*

Aksel inwardly cringed. Dealing with the others' grief was bad enough. How was he going to explain to her that the elf she loved had passed on? Still, there was no evading it. She had the right to know.

Aksel grimaced as he formed his reply. *About that...*

He's alive, she abruptly cut him off.

Aksel paused, his heart nearly skipping a beat. *What did you just say?*

Glolindir is alive, she responded emphatically.

Aksel listened carefully as Elistra explained Glo's precarious condition. By the time she finished, Aksel's resolve had been rekindled.

We'll do all that we can, he assured the seeress.

I'll let him know—came her grateful reply—*but do hurry.*

With their friend's life on the line, Aksel swiftly began explaining the situation to the others. Both Lloyd and Alys interrupted him with cries of joy before he could finish.

"That's great!" The duo swiftly curbed their enthusiasm, however, when they noticed the dour expression on Aksel's face.

Lloyd's excitement faded into a frown. "It is, isn't it?"

Aksel took a deep breath and continued with the rest of what Elistra told him. As he did so, Alys went to check on Glo again. This time when she touched his frozen form, she pulled her hand back and yelped.

"I think he's already beginning to melt!" Alys held out her hand revealing a thin layer of moisture on her fingertips.

Panicking, Lloyd ran over to Glo's side. "We need to get him to the temple fast!"

"Wait!" Aksel cried as Lloyd reached for their elven friend.

Lloyd stopped and stared wild-eyed at him. "What is it?"

Aksel returned his friend's stare with keen sympathy. "I know you're just trying to help, but your body heat will only make him melt faster."

Lloyd stepped back, a sheepish grin upon his face. "I guess I didn't think that through."

Aksel rubbed the stubble on his chin as he eyed their slowly thawing friend. "What we really need is a way to keep him frozen and move him at the same time."

Andrella tentatively raised a hand. "I could use a *frost* spell on him every once in a while. It wouldn't last long, but they're of such a low order that I could cast them indefinitely."

Aksel gave her a begrudging smile. "That just might work."

"If we can't touch him, I could build us a makeshift stretcher," Xellos offered. "I've got rope and a blanket in my pack. All we'd need are a pair of stout branches."

The resourcefulness of their little group never ceased to amaze Aksel. His hope renewed, he gave them all a curt nod. "Very well. Let's do this."

2

DISCIPLE OF THE MAD GOD

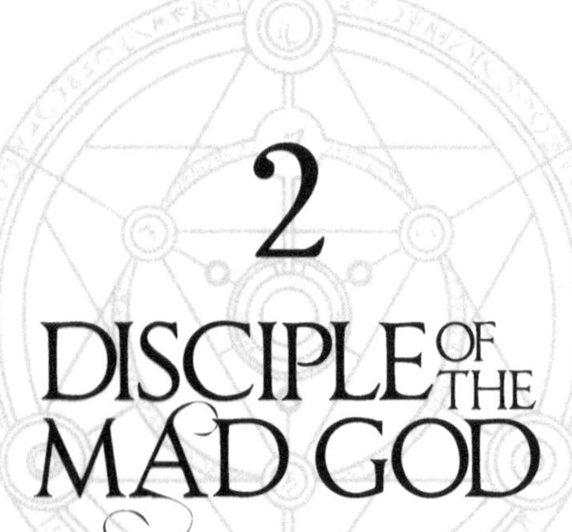

A lopsided grin appeared on the man's face, making him look quite insane.

The streets of Penwick were virtually empty as the determined group rushed across the city. Normally they would have run into folks even this close to midnight. With the impending invasion, however, most citizens had been relocated to the temple grounds or Fortress Hightower. The only people the companions saw were those that manned the blockades.

Makeshift barricades had been set up at strategic points around the city. Boxes, crates, barrels, and anything not nailed down comprised the barriers that obstructed the roads. At one checkpoint, they even spied a piano.

Alys led the way for them, the songstress projecting her voice ahead as they approached each blockade. "Urgent city business! Make way for the Baron's niece and the son of Kratos and Lara Stealle!" Lloyd thought it a bit much, but Alys tended to be more than just a bit dramatic. Still, he couldn't argue with the fact that her ploy sped along their journey.

Before Lloyd knew it, they were passing the Inn of the Three Sisters. The tall, three-story building now stood dark and empty. Ves, Ruka, and the rest of their friends had left to seek out runes of great power—runes that could be used to forge demon slaying weapons.

Lloyd's brother and sister had gone with them, entrusting him with the protection of the city in their absence. Yet, how was he supposed to do that when he couldn't even protect his own friends?

"Where are you going?" Alys blurted, interrupting his sullen brooding. Lloyd stopped and saw the songstress standing off to one side, staring at him with her hands on her hips.

A loud yelp from just behind him interrupted Lloyd before he could respond. "Hey, watch where you're going!"

Xellos stood at the back of a makeshift stretcher, his expression one of horror as the entire thing nearly tipped over. Everyone collectively held their breath as a frozen Glo teetered on the very edge. The elf hung there precariously for a few heartbeats, then finally fell back into the stretcher.

"Whew," Lloyd breathed a heavy sigh. "That was close."

His momentary relief was shattered, however, as Alys planted herself in front of him, her hands on her hips, and a fire in her eyes. "We should be going north."

Lloyd fixed her with a puzzled stare. "I thought the south way would be faster."

Alys grimaced and shook her head. "If you'd been paying attention at the last blockade, you'd have heard that the south gate to the temple is closed."

Feeling suddenly quite foolish, Lloyd met her accusatory stare with a sheepish grin. "Sorry." He nudged his head north across the plaza. "Please lead the way."

Lloyd had known Alys since they were very young. She'd always been mercurial in nature and this time proved no exception. Her anger dissipated in an instant, replaced instead with the brightest of smiles.

"Well, at least you have the good sense to listen when I speak." She grinned at him a second longer, then spun on her heel and marched off northward.

Lloyd started after her when he felt a gentle tug on his arm. The most stunning pair of electric-blue eyes stared up at him from over his shoulder. Framed by a heart-shaped face and perfectly coiffed strawberry-blonde hair, those eyes danced with an amusement he himself didn't quite feel at the moment.

His fiancée, the Lady Andrella, stood on her toes and whispered in his ear, "Don't beat yourself up. I didn't hear about the south gate either."

Lloyd squelched the reply that formed on his lips. He didn't want to talk about what was really bothering him right now, so instead he gave her a grateful smile.

With a quick peck on the cheek, she stood back and said, "Just one minute."

Lloyd winced as she held out her hand and hit Glo with a coating of frost. Though she and Aksel insisted it was the best way to keep their friend alive, it somehow seemed wrong to Lloyd. Still, they knew far more about such things than he did.

With a quick nod to Xellos, Lloyd again took off after Alys. The young lady was nearly halfway across the plaza by now, her hands still waving about as if she were talking to someone. Feeling guilty, he picked up the pace to reach her before she found out she'd been talking to thin air.

They caught up to Alys just as she drew abreast of the Fountain of Lions. Moonlight glinted off the famous Penwick landmark. Recently restored by their friend Calipherous, the three lions that made up the fountain symbolized strength, courage, and hope. The sight was a bitter reminder to Lloyd that he had not lived up to any of those expectations. If only he had, Seth would not be dead, nor would Glo be in danger of a slow, cold death.

"Another blockade?" Alys complained as they approached one more barrier at the edge of the Lord's Square.

"It's standard street warfare tactics," Lloyd explained to the petulant young lady.

Alys glanced back at him, a pout forming on her lips. "But they're slowing us down."

"Trust me," Lloyd responded with a grim smile, "when the

undead come pouring out of that castle, you'll be grateful for each and every one of them."

Alys shrugged, the pout on her face swiftly fading. "I suppose you're right."

The companions deftly passed through that blockade and a second one at the other end of the square. The alabaster spires of Avernos Keep towered over them as they encountered another blockade at the western end of the Lord's Bridge.

Silvery moonlight sparkled on the river below as they crossed the great stone archway over the Penderbun. The twin of the bridge where the river met the bay, it made Lloyd think of the epic battle that had taken place beneath that archway.

Kratos Stealle had been Lloyd's age when he faced and defeated the deadly pirate warlord, Eboneye. He had saved the city with that decisive victory, driving out the rest of the pirate invaders. Lloyd wondered if it had been him in his father's stead, would he have succeeded?

The young warrior continued to brood; his dark mood only broken by Andrella's cry. "There it is!"

Shaking off his somber thoughts, Lloyd focused his gaze upon the brilliantly lit golden-capped spires of the Temple of the Ralnai. The rest of the large temple remained out of sight, hidden behind the great outer walls that surrounded the complex.

The stirring sight inspired Lloyd to make a vow to the gods. *I swear I will protect my friends. I will find a way to get stronger. I will not let them down again.*

A strange tingling touched his brow as the young man finished his silent vow. It felt as if someone was watching him. Lloyd swept his gaze about the area, but saw nothing. The feeling lingered an instant longer, then abruptly dissipated. Shrugging it off as his imagination, he picked up the pace again as they marched toward the temple gate.

Andrella experienced conflicting emotions as they passed through the gate to the temple grounds. Though sick over Seth's sacrifice, she felt a glimmer of hope about Glo. Still, the road to saving her friend and mentor was fraught with peril. According to Elistra, letting him thaw naturally might kill him. However, he would die as well if they kept him frozen for too long.

As if that wasn't enough to worry about, Lloyd had not been quite himself since their friends' sacrifice. Though Andrella could understand his grief, it seemed more than that. She had caught a dark look in his eyes that she had never seen there before. Andrella had been drawn to Lloyd because of his good heart and their shared beliefs in kindness and fairness to all. She silently prayed this terrible tragedy hadn't permanently jaded the young man she'd come to love so dearly.

A second barrier had been erected behind the iron portcullis and thick doors of the main gate. Makeshift tents and temporary shelters littered the wide temple grounds which now housed much of the population of Penwick.

A pair of guards escorted them through the encampment toward the temple at the south end of the complex. Though it was late, numerous campfires still burned bright and folks milled about the tents. Andrella could hear the fear in their voices as they passed. She wished she could say something to ease their minds, but considering their recent defeat, any such words would sound hollow, if not downright dishonest.

A priest met them at the temple doors. After seeing Glo and hearing their plight, he showed them to the cloister off the main temple. The man then hurried to fetch the High Priestess.

A number of visiting clergy folk were camped out in that garden area. Andrella swept her gaze over their sleeping forms, discerning the gods they worshipped by the symbols emblazoned on their vestments. One priest in particular though, gave her pause.

Garbed in a simple brown robe, long shaggy black hair and an unkempt beard hid most of the man's hawkish face. Still, it was the symbol on his chest that unnerved her the most. Two thin lines, one black and one white, swirled around each other in a gradually tightening spiral, until both disappeared at a point in the very center. The pattern tended to be disorienting if one stared at it for too long, but even that was trifling compared to what it represented. That symbol marked the stranger as a follower of the Lord of Madness.

Roleo, father of the Ralnai, went mad after the disappearance of his son, Phobos. That madness spread to his followers, causing them all to go quite insane. Yet despite their insanity, disciples of the Mad God still retained their divine powers. Thus, any dealings with them tended to be a dangerous proposition at best.

It took Andrella a few seconds to realize the stranger was staring back at her. She thought she detected a glint of amusement in those deep penetrating black eyes. She nearly said something in spite of herself, but was saved at the last instant by the arrival of the High Priestess.

The swish of robes preceded Sirus as she marched resolutely into the cloister. Not surprisingly, Lara Stealle strode determinedly by her side. Though both equally imposing figures, their appearance could be likened to that of night and day.

Sirus radiated an angelic air with long, wavy yellow-gold hair draped over her white and golden temple robes. Yet, her tall frame, steel resolve, and intense pale green eyes gave her the countenance of an avenging angel.

Though shorter in stature, Lara Stealle nonetheless exuded authority. While obviously used to wielding power, time had not detracted from her beauty. Long, straight light-brown hair framed her porcelain skin with just a hint of freckles. Royal blue robes accentuated those piercing blue eyes which sparkled with a keen intelligence.

Andrella silently hoped she could be like these women when it came her turn to rule. She would need to be strong to govern her uncle's duchy. As evidenced by these two, as well as her mother, she could do so and still retain her beauty.

Alys practically threw herself at Lara. "Oh Lady Stealle, you need to do something!" The young lady proceeded to regurgitate at breakneck speed everything she had seen or heard about their friend's current predicament. Andrella thought she might miss something in her hysterics, but Alys was amazingly accurate.

Bards, go figure, Andrella thought with mild amusement. They could be the most emotional people in the world, but give them a heart wrenching story, and they'll recite it verbatim.

While Lara listened patiently to Alys, Sirus went to examine Glo.

She ran her hands over his frozen form, her face contorting into all sorts of expressions.

When Alys finally finished, Lara grabbed her firmly by the shoulders. "Calm down, Alys. We'll do everything we can."

Still sniffling, Alys took a step back, a handkerchief appearing in her hand as she did so. She dabbed the tears from the corners of her eyes and nodded. "If anyone can, it's you, Lady Stealle."

Stepping past the weepy Alys, Lara stopped briefly in front of Lloyd. "How are you holding up?"

"Fine," Lloyd declared emphatically. "It's Glo that needs your help."

Lara took a deep breath and cast a sidelong glance at Andrella. Andrella could see the worry on his mother's face. Though tempted to say something, she thought better of it. Instead, she responded with a subtle shake of her head.

Lara gave her a barely perceptible nod, then grasped her son by the hand. "Alright, we'll do what we can for your friend, but afterwards you and I are going to have a talk."

It appeared as if Lloyd was going to object, but instead he dropped his eyes to the ground. "Yes, mother," he said in a soft voice.

"I've never seen anything like this," Sirus declared. The High Priestess had finished examining Glo and taken a few steps back. She turned her gaze toward Lara. "Have you?"

"No, I have not," Lara replied as she joined Sirus. The wizardess took a closer look at the ice. "Hmm, the work of a silver dragon most likely. White dragons are not the brightest and rarely live long enough to be ancient."

Andrella might have laughed were the situation not so grim.

Lara stood back and gently tapped a finger to her chin. "I seem to remember reading about something like this before. I could go and check my library."

A strange voice interrupted her musings. "Ahem, if you wait too much longer, your friend there will go from 'mostly dead' to 'all dead.'"

All eyes turned to see the priest of the Mad God rise from his bedroll. He got up and stretched his arms rather wide.

The unkempt man still made Andrella nervous, but Lara appeared unphased by him. Her eyes bore into the strange priest. "Have you had experience with something like this before?"

"Might have," the priest mumbled as he shuffled across the garden and drew up next to Glo. Everyone took a step back, giving him a wide berth. The shaggy haired priest contorted his body in all sorts of directions as he examined the frozen elf.

"Ah yes…uh huh…I see," he mumbled to himself.

This went on for about a minute until Lloyd finally lost his patience. "Well, can you help him or not?"

The unkempt priest stood back and let out an outrageous cackle. "Me? Oh no. If I were to beseech my god on his behalf, he might as soon kill him as spare him."

Lloyd's eyes went wide at the unexpected response. "Just what kind of god do you serve?"

A lopsided grin appeared on the man's face, making him look quite insane. "Why the craziest of gods—or so they say," the priest replied with a strange lilt to his voice. His eyes then strayed back to Glo. "No, no, it's best for all involved that you do this for yourselves."

Andrella gulped down her fear. Crazy as he sounded, this mad priest might just be Glo's only hope. She opened her mouth to speak, but Aksel beat her to it.

"What do we do?"

The mad priest took another step back and absently scratched under his armpit. "You need to thaw him as slowly as possible. Probably best to apply a bit of heat and just a smidge of cold to slow the process." He held up his thumb and forefinger, keeping them less than an inch apart.

Lara folded her arms across her chest and eyed the priest skeptically. "Is that all there is to it?"

"Oh no, no. You must also apply deep healing to the parts of his body as they defrost. Otherwise, they might just fall off," the priest ended with another outrageous cackle.

Andrella's eyes went wide. *Poor Glo,* she thought. This was not going to be easy, if it worked at all.

Sirus peered past the man, locking eyes with Lara. "What do you think?"

Lara again tapped her chin. "I think it could work, but it will take more than just the two of us."

The odd priest spun about and shuffled toward his bedroll. "Whatever you do, you better do it quick!" He called back over his shoulder.

Sirus pressed her lips together and swept her eyes around the group. "He's your friend. What do you think?"

Aksel furiously rubbed his chin. "I don't think we have much choice."

Lloyd set his jaw. "We have to do something or we'll lose Glo too."

Lara narrowed her gaze at her son. "I thought someone was missing. What happened to Seth?"

"He gave his life to save us all!" Alys began to wail again. She briefly explained what the halfling had done. Andrella was amazed once more at the accuracy of her description, especially considering that Alys had been passed out during it.

Lara responded with a begrudging smile and a nod. "Hm, that's quite a bold move. It wouldn't have killed him though."

Silence fell over the group. Andrella's heart nearly skipped a beat.

Aksel was the first to find his voice again. "Do you mean to say that Seth is still alive?"

Lara nodded her head back and forth. "Most likely swept him off to the astral plane. Not a fun place to be if you don't know your way around—or back for that matter."

Lloyd slammed his fist into his palm. "Then we need to go get him!"

Lara met her son's gaze evenly. "I can send you, but you'll need someone to bring you back."

"I'll…go…" Aksel said simply, his voice cracking with emotion.

"As will I!" Alys added with an overly dramatic flourish.

"Guess I'll go too," Xellos offered in quiet contrast to the songstress.

Andrella wanted to go as well, but Lara cut her off before she could say anything. "We need you to stay here with us. We'll apply the heat and cold while Sirus does the healing."

Andrella felt a momentary twinge of nervousness, but then

quickly pushed it down. Here was a chance to use her newly honed abilities to help her dear mentor—not to mention the opportunity to work side-by-side with two powerful women she truly admired.

Feeling both inspired and honored, Andrella gave Lara a firm nod. "Very well, let's do this."

3
ALIVE AND KICKING

And you all thought it was a good idea to listen to the ramblings of
a mad priest?

Seth felt confused and more than just a bit annoyed. Glo had assured him that placing one portal bag inside of the other would end up in a deadly explosion. Seth had banked everything on it, getting as close as he could to that damn bone dragon before stuffing the two bags inside each other. Though the result had been different than he expected, he had to admit it was nothing short of spectacular.

A rift four times as tall as Seth formed in the air around him. It had been large enough in fact to completely engulf one of the dragon's legs. Still, he had been hoping for something a bit more—explosive. Instead, the rift had sucked him through to this endless gray void before it closed. It had not been a complete loss though. The rift had also pulled the dragon's entire leg with it.

Seth had found that quite amusing at first. His laughter stopped, however, when the dragon leg proceeded to try and stomp him out of existence. It couldn't have just fallen over like a normal severed leg. No, that would have been far too much to ask. Instead, the stupid thing chased him around the void trying to stamp him into the ground—or whatever passed for the ground in this gods forsaken endless void.

"Alright already!" Seth screamed at the stupid leg after rolling away from under it for about the tenth time. "Can't you pick on someone your own size?"

"Well, there's something you don't see every day," a familiar voice sounded behind him.

That sounded like Xellos. Was he hearing things now too?

Still wary of the dragon's leg, Seth cast a quick glance over his shoulder. To his surprise, another portal had formed in the grayness. Even more surprising, Lloyd, Aksel, Xellos, and Alys all stood in front of it. *They actually came looking for me!*

Seth felt like jumping for joy, but it wasn't in his nature to get all mushy. So instead, he responded the way he knew best—with sarcasm. "You just going to stand there all day and gawk?"

A wide grin spread across Lloyd's face. "Nice to see you too, Seth." A second later, he took off into the air, his blades coming alive with flames.

The rest of them rushed forward as Seth dodged yet another attempt by the dragon leg to squash him. Xellos let loose with a barrage of arrows. Normally, arrows would not work against a creature of all bone, but the archer had a knack for pinpointing critical spots in even the toughest of opponents.

As Seth rolled out of the way, Alys hit the creature with one of those sonic shrieks. Such was the force behind the assault that it caused the leg to stop in its tracks and even made its bones rattle. At the same time, a large translucent hammer slammed into the leg. Aksel's doing no doubt.

Above them, Lloyd strafed the dragon leg with his two swords. Made of star metal, his black blade would cut through almost anything. His other blade, a holy sword, acted as an anathema to the undead dragon leg.

Never seeming to run out of breath, Alys held the leg immobilized while the others pounded and sliced it to pieces. When it was over, all that remained of the leg was a large pile of bones.

Seth glared at that pile with a keen sense of satisfaction. "Told you to pick on someone your own size."

As Lloyd landed and the others gathered, Aksel confronted Seth with a hard stare. "So, were you trying to get yourself killed?"

"Tsk." Seth clicked his tongue. "More like I was trying to stop the rest of you from dying."

Aksel folded his arms in front of him and narrowed his eyes even further. "By sacrificing yourself?"

"Well, duh." Seth shrugged. He thought that would have been obvious by now.

Aksel unfolded his arms and stepped forward until his face was mere inches from Seth's. When he spoke, his voice was thick with emotion. "Well don't you ever even think of doing that again."

Aksel's anger over his 'almost' death truly caught Seth by surprise. He had no idea just how much the little cleric cared about him. Still, Seth didn't do emotions very well. So once again, he resorted to sarcasm. He took a step back, clicked his heels together, and gave Aksel a sharp salute. "Yes, sir!"

Aksel glared at him, then sighed and shook his head. "Seth, you're incorrigible."

A wicked grin spread across the halfling's lips. "I am, aren't I?"

"Well, I'm just happy you're still alive!" Lloyd declared emphatically. Before Seth could stop him, the young man grabbed him and pulled him into a bear hug.

Seth blanched at the unwanted attention. "Get off of me, you goon!"

Unfortunately, his complaints just made Lloyd grin even more. "Awe, I missed you too, Seth."

When Lloyd finally put him down, Seth hid any further embarrassment by vehemently brushing himself off. "Thanks a lot, Lloyd. It's going to take me forever to get the wrinkles out."

"Well, I think it's cute how all your friends care about you," Alys practically gushed.

Though Seth didn't dislike Alys, he didn't much care for her emotional ramblings. An interesting thought suddenly crossed his mind, leading to a derisive snort. "If you think it's so cute, maybe you'd like Lloyd to squish the heck out of you instead?"

Alys' cheeks abruptly turned a bright shade of red. She cast a sidelong glance at the handsome young man. "I don't think that would be quite appropriate."

Seth had obviously struck a nerve. Interestingly, Lloyd's face reddened as well. Instead of responding though, he quickly changed the subject.

"Um, yes. Well, anyway, we should probably be heading back. With any luck they've managed to defrost Glo by now."

Seth's breath suddenly caught in his throat. "You mean Glo's alive?"

Aksel quickly explained Glo's situation to him. He finished with what Lara, Sirus, and Andrella were attempting in order to revive their elven friend.

After hearing the entire hairbrained scheme, Seth just shook his head. "And you all thought it was a good idea to listen to the ramblings of a mad priest?"

Lloyd's hand went to the back of his neck. "Well, we really didn't have much choice."

Seth grimaced and shook his head. "I think Glo will be lucky to survive this all in one piece."

Alys fixed him with a curious stare. "Funny, that mad priest said just about the same thing."

Seth stared at them all incredulously. "And you still thought it was a good idea?"

Aksel breathed a heavy sigh. "Anyway, Lloyd's right. We should be heading back." Before anyone could say another word, the little cleric gathered his concentration and traced a pattern through the air. Seth could feel the magic gathering around the pattern until Aksel released it with two words.

"*Planum porta.*"

As soon as the words left Aksel's lips, a glowing blue oval of swirling energy appeared in the grayness before them. Through the portal, Seth could clearly see the grounds of the temple complex in Penwick.

"After you," Aksel said, ushering Seth forward.

He didn't have to tell him twice. Seth gingerly leapt into the portal, glad to leave the strangeness of that gray void behind.

The scene below Glo continually shifted as his friends dragged his body across Penwick. It finally settled when they stopped in the gardens and once again when they moved him to a healing chamber. Elistra hung over his shoulder as Sirus, Lara, and Andrella surrounded his inert form.

Glo turned his attention to the seeress. "I hope that priest knew what he was talking about. I mean, even though he serves the Mad God, I could see a certain logic behind his idea."

Elistra didn't immediately respond, her eyes slightly glazed as if she were lost in thought. Abruptly, her focus settled on him. "Oh, um, yes. I have the distinct feeling that one knows what he's talking about."

Glo's brow knit into a frown. She seemed reluctant to speak once again, as if she were not saying all she knew. She had been that way when they first met. He thought they had put that all behind them after they reunited in Lukescros. He was starting to think he had been wrong.

Below them, Lara applied a mild spell of heat to his body. Andrella immediately followed it with a *Ray of Frost*.

"So, you think this will work?" Glo asked Elistra tentatively.

The seeress met his gaze with a cautious smile. "I certainly hope so. Unfortunately, your future is somewhat cloudy to me."

"Why is that?" Glo asked with more irritation in his voice than he intended. This entire situation was nerve wracking to say the least and the unreliability of the mystic arts didn't help matters.

Elistra's expression grew pained. "Basically, the dearer someone is to me, the less I can see of their future."

A half-smile crossed Glo's lips. "Well, that's both nice and disconcerting at the same time."

"Tell me about it," she responded with a deep sigh.

Below, the ice that encapsulated Glo had begun to melt. The part of his skin that had been exposed shone a dark shade of purple. Though quite unsettling, it swiftly turned pink after Sirus applied her healing powers.

Without warning, Glo felt a strange tug on his astral form. He swept his eyes around nervously, but saw nothing except for Elistra and the grayness that made up this plane. "What was that?"

Elistra floated over to his side and gently wrapped her arms around him. "Calm down. It's merely your body waking up. As it does, you'll be dragged back into it."

Glo had been holding his breath without realizing it. He let it out now, a sheepish grin crossing his face. "Oh. Okay. I guess I should have expected that."

Elistra gazed at him with keen sympathy. "How could you? These are not exactly normal circumstances."

"True." Glo agreed with a simple nod. It suddenly occurred to him that once he was back in his body, she wouldn't be following him. He grabbed her by the shoulders and gazed at her tenderly. "When will I see you again?"

She reached out and touched his chin with her finger, a brave smile on her lips. Even so, he could see the sadness in her eyes. "My body is still recovering from trying to save you and Aksel the other day."

Her chiding brought the memory back to the forefront of his mind. Both he and Aksel nearly perished trying to down two flying stone dragons that chased them while aboard the Remington. Still, something about her answer mystified him. "Then how are you here?"

A small laugh escaped her lips. "My astral body can freely roam this plane even while my material body heals."

Glo thought he understood that. "So, that means you won't be able to come and see me in the material plane for a while."

"I'm afraid not," she responded with a sad shake of her head.

Glo felt another tug, this one quite a bit stronger than the first. Once it passed, he peered into Elistra's eyes. He could see his own love reflected there, but it was mixed with sadness and more than a touch of fear.

A wave of affection washed over him. "Well then, we might as well make the most of it."

He ran his fingers up her neck and behind her head as he gently pulled her closer. Their lips met as he leaned in, sending an array of sparks traveling all across his skin. The two of them continued to trade kisses, their passion growing as they did so.

Suddenly, he felt another tug. This one was so strong it ripped him from her arms and dragged him downward. Glo reached a hand out for her, the words "Love you" trailing from his lips.

Love you too, came the reply in his mind as she and the gray void faded from view.

Butterflies flitted through Andrella's stomach as they proceeded with the process of reviving Glo. It was painstaking to say the least. Lara would apply heat to the elf's body with a spell of *Burning Hands.* Andrella then immediately counteracted it with a *Ray of Frost.*

This back and forth casting continued repeatedly, seeming as if they'd made little progress. Despite that, Andrella forced herself to stay calm. She'd known this would be a slow, arduous process. It also helped that she was working as an equal with these two amazing women.

Finally, a portion of Glo's upper torso defrosted. In spite of herself, Andrella blanched at the sight. "His skin looks so purple."

"Stand back," Sirus commanded. The High Priestess stepped forth, waves of brilliant white light emanating from her palms. Completely engulfing Glo's upper torso, the light was so bright that it forced Andrella to shield her eyes.

When it finally died down, Andrella chanced a peek at Glo. She nearly jumped for joy. The skin that had been revealed from beneath the ice now looked a nice healthy shade of pink.

"Don't get too excited," Lara cautioned her. "We still have a long way to go."

She's right, Andrella chastised herself. Forcing down her emotions, the young lady refocused on her part in the painstaking task still before them.

After what seemed like forever, but only half an hour in reality, Glo's entire body had been defrosted. Sirus applied a major healing, then stepped back with a firm nod. "That should do it."

Andrella held her breath as Glo's eyes fluttered open. The elf seemed extremely sleepy, his lids opening and closing multiple times. Finally, he took a deep breath and softly mumbled, "I guess it worked?"

Andrella couldn't contain herself any longer. She flung herself at her mentor and hugged him tight. "Oh Glo! I'm so glad you're alright! You gave us a real scare."

The tall elf patted her back and chuckled softly. "Trust me, I scared myself as well. It's not every day you get turned into an elven popsicle." His tone grew serious as he addressed the High Priestess. "Sirus, do you think there will be any lasting effects?"

Sirus' response was laced with amusement. "Everything appears to be working fine to me."

Andrella abruptly realized there was something pressing hard against her abdomen. She pulled back and glanced down before she could stop herself. In that moment, she saw more of Glo than she ever intended.

"Oh my," she gasped, her cheeks burning as she pulled away completely.

"What the…" Glo stammered, abruptly realizing he was naked. He covered himself as best he could, his face turning a bright shade of scarlet. He glared accusingly at all of them present. "Where's my clothes?"

Lara and Sirus exchanged a glance, then both burst into laughter. "Simmer down," Lara scolded as she grabbed his robes and tossed them to him. "We had to make certain your entire body was healed— or would you have preferred if we left some parts still frozen?"

Glo blanched as he caught the robes and wrapped them around his lower half. His expression turned to one of chagrin. "No, I guess not."

Andrella had averted her eyes, but caught a glimpse of Glo's posterior as he whirled about to pull on his robes. *Not bad,* she thought to herself. *Almost as nice as Lloyd's.*

Andrella! She mentally chastised herself. *Get a grip, girl. You're engaged after all.*

Once Glo had covered himself, Sirus circled around the elf, her hands hovering just a few inches above his skin. When she was done, she stood in front of him and met his gaze evenly. "Your body is healed, but you just went through a terrible ordeal. Best you should rest, even if just for an hour or so."

Glo took in a deep breath, a wan smile crossing his lips. "I really wish I could, but I don't think we have the time."

Lara cocked her head to one side and peered at him quizzically. "Why not? We still have a few hours before the castle completes its shift into this plane."

Andrella knew why, but before either she or Glo could answer, an acolyte appeared at the door to the healing chamber. "High Priestess," he addressed Sirus, "the others have returned from the Astral Plane."

Sirus gave the man a firm nod. "Very good. Have them brought to my chambers." As the man went off, she turned her attention to Andrella and Glo. "Hold that thought. We can discuss this once we're all together."

"Good idea." Glo nodded his approval.

Sirus and Lara led the way out of the chamber. Andrella started to follow, but noticed Glo appeared a bit wobbly on his feet. The young lady scooted under his arm and wrapped one of hers around his waist.

"Let me give you a hand," she said, smiling up at him.

"Also, a good idea," Glo agreed with a grimace. His expression turned into an embarrassed smile as they trailed the others through the temple. "Sorry about before."

Andrella felt the blood rush to her cheeks once again. Tilting her head, she responded with a closed mouthed laugh. "It's alright. It was basically my fault anyway. I was so happy to see you healed that I sort of forgot myself."

A wry smile spread across her mentor's face. "Thanks." Abruptly his smile clouded over. "Um…we don't have to mention this to Lloyd, do we?"

Andrella nearly choked at the thought. Lloyd was extremely good natured, but with everything else going on right now, this was the last thing he needed to hear. "Um, no," she stammered. "I think it's probably best we keep this between the two of us."

Glo arched an eyebrow at her, then nodded. "Agreed."

4

LONG BURIED SECRETS

It was buried there ages ago, along with the body of Phobas.

Alys thought she had seen everything. As a young teen she'd gone in search of Eboneye's treasure, died, and sang with the angels. After being brought back, she studied music at the Bardic College in Lukescros, and ended up touring with the famous songstress Cassilla Nightbird. After achieving fame in her own right, chance reunited her with Pallas Stealle, the love of her life. Yet since she joined this small group of adventurers, she'd seen and done things she'd never thought possible.

From flying on dragon back, to fighting vampires beneath Penwick, to finding a traveling city right out of legend, it had been a whirlwind ride. As if that weren't enough, she'd been chased by stone dragons, shifted to another plane, and fought an entire castle full of undead. Still, nothing had prepared Alys for facing that gigantic ancient bone dragon.

The apparent death of Glo and Seth had been a shock to them all. Yet, by the grace of the gods, Glo somehow remained alive. Furthermore, instead of being blown to bits, they'd found Seth completely whole on the Astral Plane.

Alys and the others had just returned with the missing halfling when they were redirected to the High Priestess' office. Upon arriving there they were met with a pleasant surprise.

"Glo!" Lloyd cried as they passed through the open doorway. The tall elf sat across from Sirus, looking completely healthy once again. As Glo rose to meet them, Lloyd rushed across the room and caught the elf in a huge bear hug.

"It's good to see you too," Glo managed through gritted teeth, "but can you please put me down?"

"Oh, sorry," Lloyd exclaimed, abruptly dropping his friend. Lloyd's hand went to the back of his neck as he gazed at Glo with a sheepish grin.

"Yeah, I see you're not a popsicle anymore," Seth noted with a slight twist to his lips.

Glo regarded the halfling with a raised eyebrow. "And I see you're back from your little side trip."

Seth fixed the elf with an accusing stare. "Not exactly where I intended to go, but *someone* fed me misinformation about putting two portal bags together."

A closemouthed snort rumbled in the elf's throat. "It wasn't misinformation. I merely noted it wouldn't quite work the way you intended."

Alys found it rather amusing the way the two of them went at each other. She sensed that beneath all that bluster, the two really cared for one another. Before they could continue arguing, however, Aksel intervened.

"Alright, that's enough from the both of you."

Caught by surprise, the duo stopped and turned to face the frustrated gnome. "There will be no more dangerous heroics from either of you," Aksel stated emphatically.

Glo and Seth exchanged a stunned glance. The elf appeared to take his friend quite seriously. He hung his head and replied with a soft, "Sorry."

Seth, on the other hand, had the exact opposite reaction. He snapped his heels together and gave his friend a mock salute. "Yes, boss."

Aksel looked at Seth for a couple of seconds, then let out an exasperated sigh. "Why do I even bother?"

After listening patiently to the amusing banter, Sirus finally spoke up. "Now that we're all here, could we please get down to business? Lara and I have some serious concerns about what happened in the castle."

As they all shuffled to take a seat, Alys studied the layout of the office. It was far more illustrious than she would have imagined.

A large cherrywood desk sat in the middle of the room surrounded by a pair of matching bookcases and a stained-glass depiction of the god Arenor. Religious trinkets lined most of those shelves with a few books scattered here and there. A plush high back chair sat behind the desk with a trio of less opulent chairs lined up on the other side. A long couch with enough seating for three or four more people stood against the opposite wall.

Once everyone had settled in, Alys took it upon herself to describe their adventures in the *Plane of Shadows*. In the interest of time, she tried to be brief, but couldn't help adding a touch of flare here and there. The mood in the room grew tense when her narration brought them to the lowest levels of the keep.

"Around the corner lay a vast underground chamber. Massive carved stone pillars reached aloft to the unseen ceiling above. Dim light filtered down from torches on the walls and pillars, yet most of the chamber lay hidden beneath a layer of thick fog."

Alys continued her tale with the first appearance of the dragon. The room grew deathly quiet as she described the attack that nearly killed them. "A cold blue light appeared in the dragon's chest. It raced up the skeletal neck, forming into a brilliant ball at the back of the dragon's throat. A second later, a glacial blast burst from its great maw and hurtled downward directly at us."

Alys vividly remembered that moment. She had acted on pure instinct, trying to use her sonic cry to protect them all. Yet the dragon's power proved too great and she was easily overwhelmed. Having passed out at that point, she deferred the rest of the story to Aksel.

"After Seth disappeared with the dragon's leg, she stopped her attack," Aksel informed Lara and Sirus.

"You're welcome," Seth interjected, sounding rather pleased with himself.

Aksel chose to ignore the halfling. "She then changed to human form and introduced herself as Jinkolothos. She told us she used to be the mistress of the keep, but had been displaced by the vampire lord's master."

Lara absently tapped her chin. "Jinkolothos? Where have I heard that name before?"

"There's a Jinkolothos mentioned in the elvish ballad *Knights of the Silver Wind*," Alys pointed out. Having led a sheltered childhood, Alys had read almost every book in the Penwick library. Her favorite tales revolved around those of legend, especially the ones put to verse.

Glo raised a single eyebrow. "I thought that sounded familiar. What does the song say about her?"

Alys pursed her lips together as she pictured the words in her mind. "In the ballad, she is the mate of Silverwind, the leader of the *Silver Alliance*. He falls under the spell of the Dragon Thrall Master and is tragically slain by the mad dragon, Yatharia."

"Does it say what happened to her afterward?" Aksel asked.

Alys scanned the rest of the ballad in her mind, but could find no other reference. "No, I'm afraid not."

Glo shifted his gaze to Lara. "Is it possible this is the same Jinkolothos?"

Lara tilted her head to one side as she mulled over his question. "It could be, but if I remember right, this Jinkolothos was also a very powerful sorceress."

A round of nervous murmurs swept across the room. Alys didn't quite understand why until Aksel put voice to their concerns. "So, you're saying that we might be dealing with more than just an undead dragon. She might, in fact, be a dracolich."

Lara's expression grew rather grim. "I think it's more than likely."

Alys felt a cold shudder travel up her spine. She knew at least a couple of works that made mention of a dracolich. None of them ended up well for those that came face-to-face with one. Wrapping her arms around her torso, she nervously blurted out a description of one of those works.

"In the *Vault of the Dragon*, the dragon mage, Xlander, hid all his plunder in a great vault beneath the Fire Mountains. He then proceeded to terrorize the range to keep folks away. When the dwarven army set out to destroy him, the mage cast one last horrible spell. He possessed his own corpse, then wiped out their entire army."

A strangled silence blanketed the room until Seth let out a derisive snort. "Well, that's not foreboding in the slightest."

Sirus sat slowly forward in her chair and clasped her hands together in front of her. "So, what is it that this Jinkolothos wants?"

Aksel took a deep breath before explaining the dracolich's ultimatum. "She told us we'd find the Staff of Law beneath the temple. She said if we did not remove it, she would personally destroy Penwick before the vampire lord has a chance to release his hordes."

Alys shivered again at the thought. A vision played through her mind of the dracolich strafing the city, its ice cold breath raining destruction like some deadly blizzard.

Glo went pale at hearing this for the first time. Seth, on the other hand, responded with a sarcastic click of his tongue. "Tsk. So, now it's a competition on who gets to kill us first?"

Sirus did not answer him though. Instead, the priestess sat back in her chair and exchanged a worried glance with Lara. Alys noted that neither seemed surprised by the mention of the staff, nor its location.

Andrella must have noticed the same thing. She pointed an accusing finger at the priestess. "So, the staff is there!"

Sirus turned back to face her and dipped her chin ever so slightly. "Yes. It was buried there ages ago, along with the body of Phobas."

Alys gasped. She, Thea, and their friends had died searching for Eboneye's treasure. Yet all this time, what the warlord had been seeking lay hidden below this very temple. Alys could just imagine the look on Thea's face when she told her.

Strangely enough, the others did not appear quite as shocked as Alys. Even so, Lloyd let out a low whistle. "Phobos' tomb was right here this entire time?"

Sirus didn't immediately answer, instead exchanging a guilty glance with Lara. Lloyd peered accusingly at his mother. "Mom? You knew exactly where it was?"

Lara calmly met her son's gaze. "I suspected," she corrected him. She then motioned to Sirus. "Might as well tell them the rest."

Sirus held her head high as she swept her eyes around the room. "This entire temple complex was built by the cleric Valgar after returning from the Abyss."

Alys nearly jumped out of her seat. "Valgar? As in the legendary cleric from the ballad, *Assault on the Planes of Shaddonon?*"

"Yes," Sirus confirmed with a slight nod.

Alys snapped her fingers with glee. "I knew it! I knew that story was more than just a legend."

Glo steepled his hands together, his expression pensive. "That's not exactly a happy tale."

Alys fixed the wizard with a curious stare. "You know of it?" It was a rather old work and written in a style that didn't appeal to most modern folk.

"If it's in writing, you can be sure Glo's read it," Seth answered with an impish smirk before the elf could respond.

Glo fixed the halfling with a scathing stare before explaining to Alys. "My father has a rather extensive library. There is an entire text devoted to what little we know about the abyssal planes. It includes the ballad you just mentioned."

Alys peered back at the elf with newfound respect. She made a mental note to find out more about his family library.

"So how does the story go?" Lloyd asked.

Relishing the request, Alys took a dramatic pause before paraphrasing the ballad. "Over five hundred years ago a group of great heroes led an assault on the Planes of Shaddonon. That party included the great Wizard Gaither, the renown warrior Devian, the holy knight Vanalor, the eminent cleric Valgar, the well-known inventor Larketh, and the famed bard Arcus. Their mighty quest was to reseal the fifth abyssal chain which had been broken during the fall of the Baleful Moon."

Lloyd let out another low whistle. "They actually went into the Abyss?"

"According to the poem," Alys responded with more than a touch of delight. She had spent so much time in the last year singing and dancing that she forgot how much she loved oration.

"It didn't end well, though, for them" Glo interjected.

Lloyd sat forward on the edge of his seat. "How so?"

Glo began to answer, then seemingly thought better of it and instead motioned for Alys to continue. She gave him an appreciative nod and cleared her throat.

"Yes, well the party strayed a bit too far into the Abyss for their own good. Caught between a horde of demons and a demon lord, most of the invading forces were slain. The only ones to make it out alive were those heroes of renown—all except for Devian. The valiant warrior single-handedly fended off the demon lord while the others escaped their terrible fate."

A hush fell over the room as Alys finished her chilling narration. It was Seth that finally broke the silence. "Interesting as that is, what does it have to do with Phobas' tomb?"

"It has everything to do with it," Sirus told him. The High Priestess wore a grim expression as all eyes turned upon her. "Apparently, Valgar and company came across the body of Phobas lying beneath the head of the third chain. It had lain there for almost five thousand years since the end of the previous demon war."

Sirus halted as a look of confusion passed amongst the others. It was Glo who first voiced their concerns. "Pardon me, High Priestess, but how do you know that? There's no mention of Phobas anywhere in that ballad."

"That's true," Alys agreed.

"That part was purposely left out," Sirus announced in a soft voice.

Glo exchanged a puzzled glance with Aksel who then took up the conversation. "If I may, High Priestess, our friend Karathralla of the Thul Dunin told us a slightly different version of Phobas' demise."

Sirus seemed unfazed by his statement. "Oh, and just what did she tell you?"

"She said that the Ralnai took up his remains and buried them in this world," Aksel explained.

A strained smile crossed Sirus' lips. "Ah, I see. Yes, that is what the host was led to believe. Otherwise, they would have descended upon the Abyss in full force. Strong as they were, they would have been overwhelmed by the sheer number of demons that live there."

Though Sirus' explanation inherently made sense, it nonetheless appalled Alys. "But how could the gods do that to one of their own?" she blurted out before she could stop herself.

Sirus shifted uncomfortably in her chair, her face contorting into a grimace. "I can't imagine it was an easy decision. Yet were the Ralnai to appear in the force necessary to rescue their fallen kindred, the sheer power unleashed would have backlashed across the chains and torn this world asunder."

Sirus' pronouncement left Alys feeling chagrined at her hasty judgement of the gods. Hanging her head, she said in a soft voice, "Sorry for my outburst, your holiness. I should have known better."

The High Priestess met her gaze with a look of utmost understanding. "That's alright, my child. Much as it pained them, the Ralnai chose to leave the body where it lay, counting on the power of the staff to protect it from the chaotic forces that dwell in the Abyss."

Andrella's mouth hung open in awe. "So all that time the Staff of Law protected Phobas' body?"

"Essentially." Lara agreed.

Lloyd's eyes had been wide as saucers during the entire exchange. "That's incredible. It was this Valgar, then that brought the body back here to Penwick."

Lara corrected him as she rose from her seat. "It wasn't exactly Penwick at the time." She walked around to the back of her chair and leaned against it. "This city was built upon the ruins of a much older one—one that was part of the Naradon empire."

Alys had barely recovered from the truth surrounding Phobas' death when Lara hit them with this new revelation. She'd heard tales of ruins found below ground during the renovations taking place in the old quarter. Still, there had been nothing linking them to the fallen empire.

Glo appeared far less surprised than either of them. The elf steepled his hands together and responded with a deliberate nod. "That makes sense. After all, their sojourn to the Abyss occurred around the same time as the founding of the empire."

Lara eyed the elf approvingly. "You are correct." She paused to glance at the large window behind Sirus. The sky outside had begun to lighten with the first traces of dawn. "Furthermore, the vaults this temple was built upon were created by the mad emperor himself."

Before she could go on any further, Seth let out an exasperated sigh. Lara halted once again and raised an eyebrow at the halfling. "Was there something you wanted to add?"

Seth returned her gaze, the corner of his mouth lifted ever so slightly. "No disrespect, but is there a point to this history lesson?" He gazed outside at the coming dawn. "We don't exactly have all day."

Much as Alys was enjoying their conversation, she had to agree with Seth. They needed to find that staff sooner rather than later if Penwick were to have any chance of survival.

Lara fixed the halfling with a stare one might give a petulant child. Though Seth seemed unaffected by it, the weight of that stare made Alys flinch.

"Yes, well, the point is there are many things hidden in those vaults—some good and some evil," Lara finally continued. "Since the power of Phobas tends to suppress such things, many have used the vaults near the tomb to seal various evil artifacts—dark treasures if you were."

Still unfazed, Seth casually stretched in his seat. "Why didn't you just say so in the first place?"

A sudden flash of intuition struck Alys. "Aha!" she exclaimed, wagging a finger at Lara and Sirus. "That's why Penwick has been invaded so many times. Folks may not have necessarily known about Phobas, but rumors must have spread about these *dark treasures.*"

Sirus met her glee with a wan expression. "That is what we believe. Larketh for certain knew that Valgar had taken the body, but the Parthians and the Pirate Clans were at the very least after those treasures, as you say."

"That might explain the rest of what Jinkolothos told us," Andrella murmured as she absently tapped her chin.

Alys wrinkled her nose at the young wizardess. "Oh, and what was that?"

Andrella's eyes drifted upward as she recited the dracolich's exact words. *"There is something buried there that I seek. Something that belongs to me."*

"Perhaps something that the staff is preventing her from retrieving?" Glo speculated.

Lara met the elf's query with a deliberate nod. "That seems most likely."

After listening quietly to all that had been revealed, Aksel cleared his throat and addressed Sirus. "So, how exactly do we find Phobas' tomb in the midst of all these evil artifacts?"

The High Priestess rose from her seat and walked over toward the shelves. "There is a sealed section down in the catacombs. I can lead you to it, but from there you will be on your own. We still have much to do to prepare for the imminent invasion."

Lara pushed back her long sleeves, her expression dark. "Not to mention that we now need to prepare for the possibility of a dracolich attack."

Lloyd stood as well. "How much time do you think we have?"

It was Glo that answered him. "While we were still inside the castle, it appeared as if it had already started shifting between the two planes." The tall elf pursed his lips together. "Since that took roughly about six hours, I'd say we have at least that much time left."

"I concur," Lara said with a grim nod toward the elf.

Once again, Alys peered out the window. Though clouded over, the sky had lightened further with the impending dawn. If the two wizards were right, that would give them until somewhere around noon.

Aksel cleared his throat yet again, his countenance grave. "Very well. Let's get going."

As they lined up to leave the room, Sirus produced a key from her robes and unlocked a small chest on the shelf in front of her. The priestess palmed the chest's contents and swiftly stuffed it into her robes. From the short glimpse Alys caught, it appeared to be a locket affixed with a large ruby.

In the meantime, over by the doorway, Andrella had placed herself directly in Glo's path. She held up a hand in front of the tall elf. "Whoa, I thought you were going to rest."

Glo halted and grimaced back at her. "I'll rest when this is all over."

Andrella folded her arms across her chest, her eyes ablaze. When she spoke, her voice took on a commanding tone. "Sirus said you should rest *now*."

Glo closed his eyes and winced. When he opened them again, he met her gaze with a single nod. "I promise, if any spellcasting is required, you can do the honors."

Alys couldn't help giggling at the pair. She drew up next to Andrella and nudged her in the shoulder. "He's starting to sound a lot like Lloyd."

Her observation made Andrella laugh. "He does, doesn't he?"

Lloyd had stopped in the doorway ahead of them. He turned and gazed from Alys to Andrella, his face reddening. "Did I do something wrong?"

The last of her anger fading, Andrella threw her arms around the young man's neck. "No, not at all," she replied, standing on her toes and kissing him.

The romantic display drew a longing sigh from Alys. A face similar to Lloyd's appeared in her mind's eye, but this one was slightly older and more mature. After one blissful kiss, Pallas Stealle had left her behind on a quest to save the world. Though Alys knew he had to go, still she missed him terribly.

As the group filed out of Sirus' office, Alys said a silent prayer to the gods to bring her love back safely to her.

5
BEYOND THE BARRIER

I think the whole pure at heart thing has him spooked.

loyd had been relieved to find both Glo and Seth alive. Yet, that didn't change the fact that he hadn't been able to protect them. Even now, the dracolich was threatening to level Penwick if they didn't find the staff in time. Even if they did, the vampire lord still had an entire army of undead bent on destroying the city.

Lloyd silently berated himself as Sirus led them towards the rear of the temple grounds. *I'm useless like this.* Somehow, someway, he needed to get stronger—and fast.

They had nearly reached their destination—a small white circular building near the back wall next to the river—when Lloyd felt a familiar tingling touch his brow. He immediately recognized it as the feeling he had earlier as they entered the grounds. The young warrior swept his eyes around the brightening landscape, yet there was no one other than themselves in sight.

Sirus abruptly halted, turned her head, and fixed her eyes on Lloyd. The young man met her gaze warily, unsure why she had stopped to stare at him.

"Is something wrong?" Aksel asked the High Priestess.

At that same time, the tingling sensation across Lloyd's brow disappeared. Sirus held his gaze a few seconds longer, then slowly shook her head.

"It's nothing," she responded in a soft voice, though her brow remained furrowed.

Resuming their march, they soon reached the small building which turned out to be a mausoleum. A circle of columns rose from its foundation to hold up the domed roof that capped the structure. A short flight of steps led up to a pair of wrought iron doors inside the circle. Inset in the dome above those doors sat a stone with the symbol of Arenor carved into it—a golden circle with six rays flaring out from its center.

At the base of the steps stood a scripted plaque. Alys paused to read the inscription aloud as they started up the stairs. "Herein lies the faithful—those who have chosen to serve the light."

"Any who have ever served in this temple may be buried here," Sirus expounded as she reached the top of the stairs.

Seth stopped just behind her and swept his eyes across the small building. "Must get kind of cramped in there."

Aksel halted next to the halfling and fixed him with an incredulous stare.

Seth peered back at the gnome and shrugged. "What? If Donnie were here, he'd definitely have said it."

The slimmest of smiles crossed Sirus' lips as she led them into the small mausoleum. With a wave of her hand, she sent four globe-like lights spiraling into the air above them. The lights fanned out, peeling back the darkness and revealing a statue in the very center of the building. Six stone coffins fanned out in a circle around it.

The statue itself depicted a man with a muscular frame partially covered in long flowing robes. His face of indeterminate age, a mane of lush hair draped down over his broad shoulders. A radiant circle framed the man's head representing a nimbus of light.

"Oh my!" Andrella's cheeks flushed ever so slightly as she stopped to stare at the striking statue. "Is that supposed to be Arenor? I don't think I've ever seen him depicted quite like that."

Alys drew up beside Andrella, a knowing smile on her lips. "Oh yes, that's exactly how he looks. Thea and I both saw him when we nearly crossed over."

Lloyd was struck with a tinge of jealousy, but immediately caught himself. He could just imagine the chastisement he'd get if either of his siblings found out he was even momentarily jealous of a god.

"That's merely one of Arenor's aspects," Sirus corrected them. "His actual form is far larger and more imposing."

Somehow that made Lloyd feel better. He'd never actually thought about it before, but it made sense that the gods would actually be larger than life.

Sirus motioned them toward a set of stairs at the back of the structure. "This way."

The dancing lights followed overhead as they descended to a landing below. Another flight of stairs continued down in the opposite direction, ending at the bottom at another wrought iron door. On the other side lay a circular chamber similar to the one above sans the statue in its center. An archway on the opposite wall led off into a long tunnel.

The corridor here consisted of the same elegantly carved stone as in the mausoleum above. The walls here, however, had recesses in them for more tombs. A short distance further, they reached an intersection and beyond that a number of others. Sirus led them unerringly through each, sometimes going straight, and at other times turning. Some of the side corridors led down flights of stairs taking them deeper into the earth. Lloyd grew anxious about finding their way back, but noted that neither Seth nor Xellos showed any signs of concern.

Finally, maybe half an hour after leaving the temple, the stairs they descended opened into a wide chamber. This one appeared a bit different than the others. A triple archway split the room in half with a pale glow emanated from somewhere on the other side. Lloyd peered through to see a single archway sitting there behind a glowing translucent purple barrier.

Sirus addressed them as they all gathered in front of the barrier. "Valgar himself put this seal here. Keepers have been watching it for ages."

The High Priestess pulled a pendant from her robes and dangled it from her hand. Affixed in the center of the circular amulet stood a single large blood red ruby. "Here, you will need this."

Seemingly mesmerized, Seth tentatively reached for the pendant, but halted as Sirus cautioned them. "Be warned, only those pure of heart may enter."

The halfling immediately withdrew his hand. "On second thought, nah."

"I'll do it," Lloyd declared emphatically, realizing that time was of the essence. Before anyone could stop him, he grabbed the amulet from Sirus' hand and marched toward the barrier.

"Lloyd!" he heard Andrella cry his name. Still, he did not stop. The amulet felt cool in his hand, but pulsed as he stepped into the barrier. A second later he was through.

Lloyd hadn't realized he'd been holding his breath. He let it out now as he surveyed the chamber before him. It was neither small nor overly large. White light filtered down from the ceiling, falling on a wide circular pedestal in the center of the room.

Lloyd briefly glanced over his shoulder and saw his friends waiting on the other side of the barrier. Although they appeared to be talking, he could not hear anything they said. He waved to let them know he was okay, but no one responded. Apparently, they could not see him either.

Realizing he was on his own, Lloyd took a deep breath and started towards the wide pedestal. He had not gone more than two steps when a booming voice reverberated around the room.

"You who seek to enter must prove you are worthy."

Those words sent a cold chill up Lloyd's spine. *Am I worthy?* He didn't exactly feel like it after what had happened to his friends. Even so, at this point he had little choice. They had to find that staff.

Steeling his resolve, Lloyd called out to the disembodied voice, "How do I do that?"

The voice responded almost immediately. "Stand on the pedestal of light and be judged."

Lloyd gulped. He was about to find out one way or the other if he was indeed worthy. He slowly walked up to the pedestal, noting the footprints he left in the dusty floor. The layer of dust here was so thick that it appeared as if no one had been here in ages.

The young warrior hesitated for a split-second before stepping up onto the pedestal. He moved to the center and braced himself for the worst. In response, the light from above grew brighter and brighter. It became so intense that Lloyd had to shield his eyes. He'd half expected to be burned for his failures, but as it turned out, the light didn't hurt at all.

After about half a minute or so, the light faded back to normal. The voice pronounced his fate with three simple words.

"You may pass."

Lloyd breathed a heavy sigh. Despite his doubts, he had been judged at least somewhat worthy. Even so, he wasn't about to find Phobas' tomb on his own. He pointed a thumb back towards the archway behind him. "What about my friends?"

There was a short pause before the voice answered. "Have them enter one by one. They too must prove worthy."

Lloyd puzzled over the voice's words for a few seconds. "But… there's only the one amulet."

There was another short pause before the voice responded again. This time its tone held the slightest hint of exasperation. "All who have proved worthy may pass freely."

Not wanting to press his luck, Lloyd replied with a simple, "Thank you."

The young man then strode back through the barrier. He found Andrella waiting for him on the other side. There was a slight edge to her voice that made Lloyd feel guilty.

"What happened to you? As soon as you passed through the barrier you disappeared."

Lloyd reached back and rubbed the back of his neck, a sheepish smile across his face. "Were you worried about me?"

Andrella shrugged, then gave him a peck on the lips. "Maybe a little."

"Speak for yourself," Seth corrected her, his arms folded across his chest.

"So, what did happen in there?" Aksel reemphasized as everyone gathered around.

Lloyd briefly explained what had transpired in the *judgement* chamber. When he finished, Sirus gave him a knowing nod.

"You have proved yourself true of heart. You may now pass the barrier unhindered."

"That's what the voice said," Lloyd affirmed.

"Give the amulet to the next person," she instructed him further.

Aksel took the amulet next. Lloyd accompanied him as they traversed the barrier. Just as the voice and Sirus promised, they both passed through unscathed.

Aksel repeated the test and passed it easily as Lloyd expected. Andrella went next, followed by Alys, Xellos, and then Glo.

When Lloyd brought the amulet back for Seth, however, the halfling stood there with his arms folded. "I'll pass."

Lloyd frowned at his friend. "Are you sure?"

"Yeah, I'll just wait here," Seth told him emphatically.

Deep creases formed across Lloyd's brow. If he could pass the test, surely Seth would. Despite the halfling's sketchy background, he had always done the right thing as long as Lloyd had known him. Still, if Seth didn't want to try, there was no forcing him.

Lloyd scratched his head and fixed his friend with a sheepish smile. "Very well. I'll let the others know."

Without another word, Lloyd passed back through the barrier leaving Seth behind.

Aksel waited impatiently on the opposite side of the barrier for Lloyd to come back with Seth. Beyond all hope, their halfling friend and Glo had returned to them. Though no longer paralyzed with grief, Aksel now felt the full weight of the task before them on his slim shoulders.

A good part of an hour had passed since they left Sirus' office, and as Seth already pointed out, they didn't have much time left. If they did not find the staff soon, Penwick would be turned into a frozen wasteland at the hand of the dracolich, Jinkolothos.

When Lloyd finally returned by himself, Aksel knit his brow. He could clearly see Seth on the other side of the barrier, standing there with his arms folded, his face devoid of its usual smirk.

Aksel eyed Lloyd with clear confusion. "Isn't Seth coming with us?"

Lloyd wore a sheepish expression. "Yeah, about that—I think the whole pure at heart thing has him spooked."

Aksel peered through the barrier at the reluctant halfling. During their journeys, Seth had confided in him bits and pieces of his checkered past. Thus, Aksel understood perhaps more than most just how much it tortured him.

The little cleric paused to consider their options. Though their search might prove difficult without Seth's skills, even now Aksel could sense an aura of good emanating from the way forward. If that were indeed Phobas' influence, he would expect it to grow stronger the closer they drew. Furthermore, the dark artifacts buried down here might unwittingly provide them with a roadmap. Much as Aksel had detected the presence of vampires in Ravenford, he could do the same thing here to steer them past anything evil.

After mulling it over, Aksel shrugged and let out an exasperated sigh. "Very well. I guess we'll just have to do this without him."

His mind made up, Aksel turned his attention to the way forward. A wide archway stood opposite the barrier, the corridor beyond disappearing into the darkness.

"I'll take the lead," he announced to the others.

"You sure?" Came Lloyd's immediate response.

The tall man's concern touched Aksel. In truth, the corridor was wide enough for two to travel side by side. After giving it some consideration, Aksel turned his gaze toward Xellos. "Would you care to accompany me?" The tracker's uncanny sense of direction had helped them find their way through the fog that surrounded the Marsh Tower.

"Sure," Xellos responded, his hooded head tilting slightly in Aksel's direction.

"And we'll be right behind you," Andrella affirmed, grabbing Lloyd by the arm before he could say anything further.

With a grateful nod to Andrella, Aksel traced a quick pattern through the air while silently praying to his goddess. As mana flowed into the tracing, he spoke two soft words, *"Deprehendere Malum."*

White light filled the cleric's palms and encircled his fingers. Raising his glowing hands, he tilted his head as the mana spread out like invisible "feelers" before him. He then started down the corridor with Xellos beside him. Focused on the sensations provided by the spell, Aksel only half-noticed the torches lining either side of the hallway coming alight upon their approach.

"That's a neat trick," Andrella noted with clear appreciation.

"Maybe they're expecting us?" Alys responded, her voice rising in a nervous lilt.

Glo arched an eyebrow at the anxious young lady. "I would somehow doubt it. Anyone down here should be long dead, and I doubt the undead could survive in the sphere of Phobas' influence."

The elven wizard's words seemed to soothe her nerves. The group grew silent as they continued down the hall. Torches continued to light as they went, revealing other corridors leading off from this one. Many immediately dead ended, while others led off into further darkness.

Nothing evil had reached Aksel's senses so far while at the same time the aura of good had indeed grown stronger. Still, that neglected to give him any sense of direction. He stopped and cast a sidelong glance at Xellos. "Do we continue forward, or try one of the side hallways?"

Xellos examined each corridor carefully, even circling back to the ones they had passed. When he returned, he pulled his hood back and met Aksel's gaze with his keen green eyes. "These halls all look the same, but my gut says we should continue forward."

Aksel remembered the tracker saying something similar back in the marshes. He gave Xellos a solemn nod. "Straight it is."

They continued forth, passing a few more side corridors on the way. At each, Xellos reached the same conclusion. Finally, they came to a split in the main corridor. The right fork continued on while the left led to a flight of stairs going down.

Drawing to a halt, Aksel sensed both paths ahead. For the first time since they entered these catacombs he detected a faint trace of evil. Unfortunately, it was too far away to pinpoint. Once again, he turned to Xellos. "Any idea which way?"

The tracker went a short way down the right corridor, then returned and went to the top of the stairs down the left. After a short pause, he waved them to join him. "This way."

"Makes sense," Glo noted with a wry smile. "If you wanted to hide the tomb of a god, I'd say the deeper the better."

Aksel almost laughed aloud. "Down it is."

As before, torches spontaneously lit along the walls as they descended the stairs. They reached a landing, then continued down a second flight in the opposite direction. At the bottom of the staircase, they found another corridor stretching off into the darkness. More torches sprang to life lighting the way ahead. A few hundred yards or so ahead, the small company reached a four-way intersection.

"Which way now?" Alys asked, a touch of nervousness once again creeping into her voice.

The aura of good Aksel felt earlier had definitely grown stronger. He also noticed more traces of evil, yet could not pinpoint the source.

Xellos spent a few minutes examining each corridor in turn. When he returned, he lowered his hood again, revealing the look of confusion on his face. "I'm getting the sense of 'something' down the hall to the left..."

"Then we should go that way," Lloyd interrupted him before he could finish.

"...and also, to the right," Xellos quickly added, his expression impassive.

Aksel could understand Lloyd's impatience. Time was slipping away with every passing minute and they seemed no closer to finding Phobas' tomb.

Glo stared intently at him. "Can you sense anything down either hall?"

Aksel grimaced. "Nothing specific."

"Process of elimination then," Andrella murmured.

Alys stopped biting her lower lip and studied her curiously. "What's that?"

"Basically, we try one way, then the other," Andrella explained further.

"Oh," Alys responded softly, then resumed gnawing on her lip.

Aksel felt keen sympathy for the young woman. Not only was she still new to all this, but the fate of her entire city lay in the balance. He tried to give her an encouraging smile as he made a swift decision. "Let's try left first."

Aksel and Xellos led the way down the corridor through a number of twists and turns. The further they went, however, the greater his sense of foreboding grew. When they reached the final turn, a blank stone slab blocked the path some distance ahead. His senses practically screamed at some great evil behind that slab.

A touch on his shoulder nearly made him jump. "Are you alright?" Andrella asked in a soft voice.

"F—fine," Aksel managed to stammer.

"You do know you're trembling," Alys pointed out to him, her eyes filled with sympathy.

Aksel gazed down at his body and saw that Alys was right. He was shaking all over. The little cleric wrapped his arms around his torso and took a few deep breaths to calm down.

"I'm going to hazard a guess that's not the door we want," Glo noted sardonically. The wizard's words once again broke the tension.

A closemouthed laugh reverberated in the back of Aksel's throat. "You wouldn't be wrong."

Realizing they had chosen the wrong path, the companions swiftly backtracked to the intersection and immediately continued down the opposite corridor.

6
I DREAM OF DJINNI

The top half of the cloud solidified into the upper portion of a large well-muscled man with bluish skin.

Alys had practically stumbled into "adventuring" this time around. She had been chasing after Pallas during the initial vampire raid on Penwick, but soon found out she could make a difference. She had actually helped save lives that day. Afterwards, she fell in with this little group, a long-stifled part of her still yearning for excitement.

Yet, the dangers of adventuring soon came back to haunt her. Two of her new friends had nearly died, and now the fate of everyone in Penwick, including her father, lay in the balance. The burden felt almost stifling, like a great weight lying on her chest. Yet, just when she found it impossible to breathe, the words of her mentor, Cassilla, reverberated through her mind.

Easy, girl. You've got this—you've got the talent. Just take a deep breath and assume the part. The rest will come naturally.

Of course, Cassilla had given her that advice before her first real concert, but it still applied now. There was a part here for Alys to play—the part of the bardess in the little group trying to save her city. As they wound through the next corridor, she took a deep breath and immersed herself in this new persona.

Instead of ending in a stone slab, this corridor opened to a long chamber. Ornate stone columns held up the low arched ceiling. Two rows of exquisitely detailed sarcophagi lined the center of the room. The path between them led to an alcove containing a pristine stone altar. Murals along either wall depicted epic battles between a host of angels and a horde of demons.

Caught off guard by the unusual sight, the companions stopped and stared in the entrance of the magnificent chamber. After a few seconds or more of gawking, Alys tore her eyes away from the surrounding opulence and fixed them instead on Aksel. Unlike before, the little cleric showed no signs of aversion to this place.

As if on cue, he reported in a soft voice, "There are no traces of evil in this room."

His assurances sparked them all into motion. As one, the group crossed the room, admiring the elegant sarcophagi as they went.

When they reached the altar at the other end, Alys' eyes were immediately drawn to a silver plaque affixed to its front. She bent down and squinted her eyes as she read the inscription engraved there aloud. "Herein lies the servants of truth and goodness."

A number of familiar symbols had been carved into the plaque below the inscription. Alys immediately recognized two of them as the radiant sun of Arenor and the lightning bolt of Alaric. Glo confirmed the rest of them signified more of the gods: the hammer and flames of Caldorn, the winds of Cormar, the scales of Iustatia, the owl of Loric, the radiant crown of Rhea, and the stag of Thena.

Alys spun about and peered at the sarcophagi lined up behind them, her voice filled with a renewed sense of awe. "These must contain the servants of the Ralnai that fell in battle against the forces of darkness."

Lloyd stepped forward and drew one of his swords, saluting the fallen warriors of the gods. "I can only hope when my time comes, I am worthy of such an honorable burial."

Andrella glided up beside him and interlocked her hands around his free arm. "Hopefully that won't be for a very long time," she mildly chastised him.

Lloyd shifted his gaze to meet hers, then sheathed his sword and took both her hands in his. "Hopefully not, as you say," he responded with a weak smile.

Something in the way he said that struck Alys as rather strange. She had known Lloyd for a very long time and he'd always been extremely confident. Overly so, in fact at times. Yet, his statement just now seemed uncharacteristically subdued.

Her thoughts were interrupted by the sounds of prayer. Aksel knelt before the altar reciting a quick supplication. As soon as he finished, Xellos announced he'd spied another doorway leading from this room.

The hallway beyond led to another chamber almost identical to the first. The major difference here was the bronze urn that sat atop the altar. The urn was rather beautiful, its rounded bottom decorated with colorful patterns that seemed to portray blowing winds. A long tapered neck rose from its base to meet with its ornate cap.

Glolindir bent down for a closer look at the urn. "Well, since Seth isn't here, I guess it's up to us to figure out the nature of this thing."

He raised a hand to cast a spell, but before he could do so, Andrella caught him by the wrist. The wizard arched an eyebrow as he met the lady's disdainful gaze.

"Um, what did we agree upon back in Sirus office?" Andrella reminded him.

A foolish smile replaced Glolindir's surprised expression. "Oh, yes. Right." He took a step back and ushered her forward. "You cast the spell."

Andrella gave him a perfunctory nod. She then proceeded to make a great show of stepping forward and rolling up her sleeves before casting the spell.

Alys did her best to stifle a laugh. Lady Andrella could be nearly as much a drama queen as she herself. She'd have to compare notes with her when they got the chance.

Andrella's spell revealed a dim aura around the urn, signifying it to be magical. Glo peered at it closely before declaring, "It's some sort of conjuration magic."

Andrella took a step back and eyed the urn warily. "Do you think it might be some sort of trap?"

The elf's brow knit into a frown. "It's possible, but I somehow doubt it."

"I agree with Glo," Aksel affirmed. "It's unlikely that whoever built these chambers would include something that might desecrate them."

The more she stared at the marvelous work of art, the more curious Alys became. "What do you think is inside?"

"There's one way to find out," Lloyd stated as he walked up to the urn.

A thin smile crossed Alys' lips. Now there was the self-assured young man that she knew.

Lloyd grabbed the lid with one hand and tried to yank it off. Unfortunately, it would not budge.

"Oof," Lloyd grunted, "that's on tighter than I expected."

Rubbing his hands together, this time he grabbed it with both of them. A harsh groan escaped his lips as he pulled on the stubborn cap.

All at once, the lid came free with a sharp *pop*. Lloyd nearly toppled backwards, but caught himself at the last instant.

In the meantime, a blue mist had risen from the mouth of the now open urn. The mist swiftly coalesced into a large cloud about five feet above the altar. Everyone stepped back and took up defensive postures—all except for Alys who stood mesmerized by the strange sight.

The top half of the cloud solidified into the upper portion of a large well-muscled man with bluish skin. Garbed in a fancy gold trim vest, long jet-black hair draped down those broad shoulders framing an exquisitely handsome face. Deep eyes the color of coal settled on Alys making her knees go weak.

Somewhere in the back of her mind, she remembered reading about such creatures. This was an air djinn based on its skin color and the markings on the urn. Possessing great magic, they were supposed to grant a wish to those that freed them. However, djinn were tricky beings, ofttimes granting wishes that caused more harm than good.

A warm smile spread across the djinn's attractive features. "Oh my. What a beautiful sight to behold after all my many years of solitude."

Alys felt her cheeks grow hot as the blood rushed into them. This djinn was certainly smooth, but she was no novice to this game. In fact, she might just be able to use it to turn the tables against him. Damping down her emotions, she fixed the djinn with a winsome smile. "I see all that time has not dulled your senses."

The djinn smile widened as he bowed towards her in midair. "Fair lady who hath freed me, doth thou have a name?"

"I freed him," she heard Lloyd complain over her shoulder.

"Shh, let Alys handle this," Andrella chastised him.

A gratified smirk momentarily crossed Alys' lips at the lady's admonition of faith. Determined not to let her down, Alys drew in a deep breath and resumed the role she was playing.

Drawing herself up to her full height of 5 foot 7 inches, Alys placed a hand on her chest, her eyes widening as if in surprise. "Moi? Why I am none other than the Lady Alicia Lynde Dunamal, only daughter of Penwick's Master of Coin."

She waited to see if the djinn had been impressed by her title. If he was not, he did a rather good job of faking it. Satisfied she had made an impact, Alys lightened the mood by placing the back of her hand beside her mouth and speaking in a conspiratorial tone, "but you, my handsome djinn, may call me Alys."

"Al-ys", the djinn rolled it around on his tongue. "Simple, yet elegant—a fitting name for its ravishing owner."

"Why thank you," Alys replied, trying hard not to blush any further. *The Stealle boys could learn a thing or two from this djinn,* Alys thought wryly. Aloud she said, "Tell me, good sir, how may I address you?"

The question seemed to puzzle the djinn. He placed a large finger on his chin and hummed softly to himself. "Hmm, it has been a long while since anyone addressed me. Nonetheless, my true name might be hard for you to pronounce—it being a series of whistles after all—so you can call me *Zantillis.*"

"Zan-tillis," Alys repeated. "A handsome name for a handsome djinn."

Zantillis' cheeks reddened ever so slightly. "Thank you, kind Alys. So then, since you have freed me from my confinement, I believe I owe you a wish."

Finally, Alys stifled a sigh. Much as she enjoyed this little flirtation, time really was of the essence. Batting her eyes at the handsome creature, Alys made her dramatic pitch. "Oh kind and noble Zantillis, we are on a mission of utmost importance and must find the Staff of Law before great tragedy strikes. We would be most appreciative if you could help us."

Zantillis continued to smile at her warmly as it spread its arms in either direction. "Well, my fair Alys, that is an easy request to fulfill. The staff is right here within these catacombs."

Alys turned her head slightly and dipped her chin, letting her long hair partially cover her face. She then fixed the djinn with a coy smile. "Do you think you could lead us to it?"

Her demure pose had the desired effect. Zantillis' eyes sparkled as he bent down closer to her. "Ah, for that dear Alys, you will need the key."

Alys played up the shy role further by clasping her hands together and twirling back and forth. "And just where would that be?"

Zantillis drew even closer, his eyes now practically glued to her. "Why, in the Fount of Tears, of course."

Alys reached up and gently brushed her fingertips along the Zantillis' handsome cheek. "Would you be kind enough to lead the way?"

The djinn abruptly pulled back, his large face clouding over. "I can, dear Alys, but be warned—you will be tested along the way."

"What else is new?" she heard Andrella murmur over her shoulder.

Alys stifled a laugh and waved a nonchalant hand at the companions behind her. "Do not worry, kind Zantillis. That is what my entourage is for."

For the first time since he appeared, Zantillis tore his eyes away from Alys. He scanned the group behind her, then grunted. "They look to be adequate enough."

"Just adequate?" Lloyd grumbled behind her.

"Shh, let it go," Andrella admonished him yet again.

"Very well then," Zantillis said with a wave, "follow me."

He started to float away from the altar, then halted and peered down at Alys. "Would you be kind enough, fair Alys, to bring my urn?"

"Why, of course," she gushed at the handsome djinn.

Keeping in character, she peered back behind her and waved a nonchalant hand at Lloyd. "Be a good man, and fetch the urn."

Lloyd stared at her dumbfounded for a few seconds, then marched over to the altar. The tall man grabbed the urn and hefted it up off the altar with one hand.

"Fetch the urn," he grumbled under his breath. "When did I become her man-servant?"

The rest of the company appeared amused by Lloyd's sudden discomfort. It was the first time Alys had seen any of them smile since Glo's and Seth's return.

Andrella slid up alongside Lloyd and placed a gentle hand on his arm. "Just play along for now—unless you rather not save the city."

Lloyd let out a deep sigh. "You're right." Swallowing his wounded pride, he lifted his voice and called out to Alys, "I've got the urn as requested, your ladyship."

Smothering a sudden pang of guilt, Alys gave him another nonchalant wave. "Very good. Now follow us."

She turned her gaze back to the djinn and gave him another winsome smile. "Whenever you are ready, kind Zantillis."

"At your service, fair lady." Zantillis beamed back at her, then floated off again, leading the small group through the catacombs.

7
FOUNT OF TEARS

"Let me see if I have this straight—you want us to drink acid?"

lo experienced a moment of trepidation when Lloyd first uncorked the urn. Visions played through his mind of their encounter with a group of djinns beneath the Inn of the Three sisters. Yet this one was of the air variety—far less hot headed than its fiery cousins. Still, any djinn could be difficult, unless you knew how to handle one.

Thus, he found it quite amusing to watch Alys verbally fence with this Zantillis. She handled herself masterfully in fact, in the end getting him to "grant a wish" that involved no magic on its part. In Glo's mind that was a huge win. He knew perhaps better than most just how easily magic could go awry.

Zantillis led them back to the intersection and from there further into the catacombs. They followed the djinn on a winding path down side corridors and through more intersections until finally reaching their destination.

According to Glo's internal clock, another three quarters of an hour had passed when they entered this new chamber. It looked almost identical to the two where they found Zantillis with one exception—the altar here had an iron rod embedded in its very center.

Zantillis led them up to the altar and proffered his hand to the rod in question. "This is your first challenge. Remove the rod." Though his tone was somber, Glo detected a hint of amusement in the djinn's eyes. There was obviously more to this challenge than he let on.

Glo trained his eyes on the object of the challenge. For all intents and purposes, it appeared to be a simple iron rod with no markings of any kind.

"This should be easy," Lloyd exclaimed. Before anyone could stop him, the young man walked up to the altar and grasped the rod with both hands.

"Lloyd, I don't think that's a good…" Andrella tried to warn him, but stopped as he braced himself and heaved.

The warrior's face turned a bright scarlet as he pulled on the rod with all his might. His efforts were for naught, however. The thing would not budge from its spot in the altar.

Lloyd finally let go, his face still red and covered with beads of sweat. "What's—that—thing—made of?" he panted, trying to catch his breath.

"That is indeed the question," Zantillis responded to his query, doing very little to hide his amusement.

While Lloyd recovered, Glo stilled his mind and peered beyond the veil of this plane. He could definitely see a distinct aura of mana circling around the edges of the rod. Shifting his gaze to meet Andrella's, he gave his apprentice a knowing nod. "Would you care to do the honors?"

"Certainly," she affirmed. The young lady gently pushed Lloyd back out of the way, then once again made a great show of rolling up her sleeves before casting her spell. Her antics definitely drove the point home.

A sheepish smile crossed Lloyd's lips as he reached back and rubbed the back of his neck. "Sorry. Guess I got a bit carried away."

Andrella cast him a brief smile before invoking her spell. A pale aura appeared around the iron rod, revealing to the naked eye what Glo had seen beyond the veil.

Now that the aura was visible, however, Glo could determine what kind of magic was involved. Squinting his eyes, he quickly noticed a familiar pattern. "There appears to be some sort of illusion at work here."

"I'll take a look," Xellos declared. The agile archer leapt upon the altar and ran his hands along the rod. When he reached the top, he announced, "I think there's something here."

An audible click rang out across the chamber. The illusion faded revealing a button on the top of the rod.

"Aha!" Glo cried out triumphantly. "Try pulling on it now."

Xellos shrugged, then yanked on the iron rod. It easily slid out of the altar. The archer stood there holding the bar in both hands, an expression of mild surprise on his face. "Now that's something you don't see every day."

Andrella's eyes burned with curiosity as she peered from the rod to her mentor. "What exactly is that thing?"

A thin smile spread across the wizard's lips. "It would be easier to show you." He held out his hands towards Xellos. "May I?"

"Sure." The archer knelt down on the altar and handed the rod off to Glo. Despite its appearance, the bar was rather light to the touch.

Glo took a few steps back, then held the iron rod over his head. He then pressed the button and let the bar go. Instead of falling to the ground, however, it stood there hanging in midair.

"Woah." "Cool." "Neat." Came the various comments from their little company.

Glo ushered Lloyd forth. "Go ahead, try moving it now."

The young man gave him a sidelong glance as he walked up and grabbed the bar. Once again, it would not budge.

"Now press the button on the end," Glo instructed him.

Lloyd did so and the bar abruptly fell into his hands. He gaped at it in wonder. "That's really cool."

Andrella fixed the elf with a questioning stare. "Is that what they call an *immovable* rod?"

Glo touched a finger to his nose and smiled. "Exactly."

"What are these two buttons?" Aksel stood next to Lloyd and pointed at the opposite end of the rod.

Glo's brow creased into a frown. How had he not noticed those before? The elf shook his head in puzzlement. "I have no idea. I've only ever read of such rods with a single button."

"Guess there's only one way to find out," Lloyd declared. As soon as he pushed one of the buttons, the rod began to grow. It stretched out across the chamber to nearly ten times its normal length.

"That's certainly different," Aksel noted with mild surprise.

Equally amazed, Glo silently nodded his agreement.

Lloyd pressed the button again and the pole retracted to its normal size. He then pressed the button next to it, but nothing appeared to happen.

"I guess that button doesn't work," Alys remarked.

Lloyd met her gaze with a perplexed expression. "Oh, it definitely did something. You all froze in place for about ten seconds."

Andrella's mouth fell open. She tugged on the sleeve of Glo's robe. "Is that a time stop spell?"

Glo met her gaze with an arched eyebrow. "It certainly sounds like it, but that is a spell of the ninth order." At best Glo could cast spells of the fifth order.

Aksel held his hands out toward Lloyd. "May I see that?"

Lloyd proffered the rod to Aksel. The little gnome took it in his hands and pressed the third button again. This time nothing actually happened. A wry smile touched Aksel's lips. "I surmised that. It probably needs to recharge its mana before it can use that spell again."

At that point Alys cleared her throat and addressed Zantillis with a bright smile. "So, did we pass?"

Zantillis nodded. "Indeed, you did, fair Alys." The djinn swept his eyes over the rest of the group. "Your entourage is perhaps more adept than I originally thought."

Before anyone could comment, however, he floated off towards an archway behind the altar. "Ah, well then, on to the next challenge."

The next chamber turned out to be yet another room like the

last, again filled with the sarcophagi of fallen servants of the gods. This time though, a crystal goblet sat upon the altar. Strange looking runes were carved into the bowl and stem, and the contents appeared to be a sickly green liquid.

"That doesn't look appealing at all," Andrella murmured under her breath.

An acrid smell rose from the vessel as they approached. It also became apparent that the greenish liquid inside the goblet was bubbling.

Alys eyed the djinn with uncertainty. "Pardon me for asking the obvious, but what is the test here?"

Zantillis' brow rose in surprise. He hesitated before proffering a large hand towards the goblet. "Why, you must drink from the cup, of course."

Gasps erupted from among the group. To her credit, Alys managed to maintain her composure. "Let me see if I have this straight— you want us to drink acid?"

Zantillis cocked his head to one side. "Well, that's entirely up to you."

The companions began talking among themselves. Lloyd sounded incensed. "He can't be serious."

"It does sound a bit dangerous," Xellos agreed.

"There has to be some trick to it," Andrella insisted.

In the meantime, Glo bent next to the goblet and examined the runes. Something about them looked vaguely familiar.

Aksel poked his head next to Glo's. "We've definitely seen these before," he said, mirroring Glo's thoughts. "The question is, where?"

Glo's mind raced through every time they'd seen runes in their travels. It amazed him how often that had been. In the monolith alone, they'd seen approximately three different sets of runes. All of a sudden, it struck him where they'd seen these before.

"The monolith!" Glo and Aksel cried at the same time.

There had been a wheel atop the Golem Master's monolith with three sets of runes on each ring: one in the Common tongue, one in Dwarven, and the third in the language of the *Titans*.

Donnie had sketched the rings before the monolith had been

destroyed. He'd made a copy of that sketch for Glo before he departed for the Pirate Coast. The wizard now doffed his pack and rummaged through it for that diagram. Finding it, he laid it out on the altar next to the bubbling goblet.

As the others gathered around, Glo swiftly explained what they were looking for. After a few minutes of back and forth, the group deciphered the meaning of the runes on the goblet. The inscription denoted it as a *Goblet of Transmutation.*

Glo stood and raised a hand to invoke the goblet, but immediately thought better of it. He cast a wary gaze at Andrella. "Care to do the honors?"

A satisfied smile slipped across the young lady's face. "See, you're learning."

As Andrella stood in front of the goblet, Lloyd grasped her by the shoulders, his voice laced with concern. "Are you sure it's safe?".

Andrella reached back and patted him on the cheek. "It will be in a moment."

The young lady drew in her will, then waved her hands over the goblet. *"Mutare Liquidum."*

As the words rolled from her tongue, the goblet began to glow. As it did so, the bubbling stopped. When the glow faded, the color of the liquid had changed from a sickly green to crystal clear.

"You're amazing," Lloyd cooed in Andrella's ear.

Her cheeks reddening, Andrella spun about, and threw her arms around his neck. "Thank you, kind sir."

As the two of them kissed, Glo decided to take matters into his own hands. He reached behind the pair, grabbed the goblet, and downed the contents before anyone could stop him.

The entire room went silent as everyone stopped what they were doing and focused their attention on the tall elf. Glo removed the goblet from his lips and grinned back at them all. "Ah, that was refreshing."

Aksel sighed and shook his head. "You and Seth are going to be the death of me someday."

A boisterous laugh caused them all to turn and gaze at Zantillis. "Very clever," the djinn commended them. "You have now passed test two."

Alys peered up the djinn with just a hint of irritation. "Alright then, now what?"

Zantillis met her gaze with a hurt expression. He put up his hands before him and exclaimed, "Just one more test, fair Alys."

Regaining her composure, Alys instead fixed the djinn with a sweet smile. "Very well, lead on then," she urged him, shushing him forth with a wave of her hand.

Andrella felt quite proud of herself. Though she had to remind him, Glo had deferred to her for spellcasting throughout these catacombs. More so, her spellcraft had been impeccable. There had been no slip ups on her part like when she blew the heads off those practice dummies at Vermoorden Keep.

Nonetheless, despite her sense of inner accomplishment, Andrella still felt the pressure of time slipping past. They needed to find the Staff of Law soon and somehow contact Jinkolothos before it ran out. She just hoped the handsome djinn was telling the truth about this being the last test.

Zantillis led them further into the catacombs, through more intersections, flights of stairs, and down side corridors. Finally, after what seemed like forever, they entered a hallway which ended in a solid bronze door.

The metallic yellow-brown door had a number of carvings inset up and down its length. They were the same markings that appeared on the plaques in each of the burial chambers—the symbols of the gods. Besides that, the door evidenced no form of entry, no handle nor keyhole.

Finally losing patience, Alys huffed at the djinn. "Is this the final test?"

Zantillis faltered, his expression one of embarrassment. "The test lies beyond the door."

Alys placed her hands on her hips. "You mean, the door without a handle or even a keyhole?"

Zantillis hung his oversized head. "Yes, that door," he mumbled beneath his breath.

"What do we do now?" Lloyd asked, angrily sweeping his eyes between the djinn and the door blocking their path.

Andrella placed a gentle hand on his arm. "I'm sure we'll think of something. We always do."

Lloyd folded his arms and grunted. "Well, it better be soon."

Andrella couldn't blame him for being disgruntled. His entire city, including his parents, was in danger, and they were stuck down here solving enigmatic puzzles.

Her own frustration building, she cast a pleading glance at Glo and Aksel. Both now stood before the bronze door with their "thinking hats" on, Glo with his hands steepled together and Aksel gently stroking his chin.

Noticing her stare, the little cleric raised a finger into the air. "I might have an idea. Give me a moment." Aksel then clasped his hands together and bent his head in obvious prayer.

They all stood there in agonizing silence for a minute or so until he once again raised his head. Without a word, Aksel plucked the holy symbol of his goddess from his chest and strode up to the door. Holding it firmly in his hand, he took the symbol and inserted it into a shallow inset with the picture of the owl.

Everyone held their breath.

Would that even work? Andrella wondered. The Soldenar was not of the Ralnai, though one could argue her closest equivalent might be Loric, the Master of Knowledge.

A few seconds passed before her supposition was met with an answer. The inset where Aksel held his holy symbol began to glow. A loud grinding sound ensued and a second later the bronze door swung open of its own accord.

Lloyd rushed forth and lifted Aksel off the ground. "Aksel, you're a genius!" the young man exclaimed as he spun the gnome around.

"T-thanks," Aksel stammered, "but can you please put me down now?"

Lloyd stopped mid-swing, his face reddening as he gently returned his friend to the floor. He stepped back and murmured, "Sorry," his hand once again going to the back of his neck.

Aksel gazed at him with keen understanding. "Forget it. Let's just move on already."

Beyond the door stood a bare chamber decorated with only two suits of armor. Each armor held the pommels of a great sword in its gloves, blade down touching the floor.

Having had prior experience with animated armors, Lloyd drew his own swords and went in first. Xellos followed with an arrow nocked and drawn. When nothing happened, the others filed in behind them.

Before anyone could ask, Andrella cast the spell to illuminate magical items. Sure enough, each sword began to glow. Given time she could surely have identified them herself, but Glo was extremely adept at such things.

After a slight pause, the elven wizard identified both weapons. "The one sword is made of cold iron and the other is a holy blade."

Andrella saw Lloyd's ears perk up at the words 'cold iron.' Back in Lukescros, the Thul Dunin had confided in them that cold iron was a bane to demons.

Andrella traded glances with Glo. "That could come in handy."

The elven wizard responded with a reticent, "We'll see."

Zantillis had floated into the near empty chamber with them. Alys once again addressed their secretive guide. "So, what are we supposed to do here?"

Seemingly startled, the djinn executed a mid-air bow to the young lady. "My apologies, fair Alys. You must pray to your gods."

Taking his cue, Aksel knelt and prayed. In answer to his prayer, one of the armors began to move. It lifted its sword off the ground and stepped forward.

Lloyd immediately moved to intercept it, but Aksel motioned for him to halt. "Wait, Lloyd. Let's see what it does."

The armor lumbered forward and held out its huge sword toward Aksel, pommel first.

"Of course, it's the holy sword," Glo murmured ironically.

Andrella met his gaze with a knowing expression. "Of course."

"Lloyd, would you do the honors?" Aksel asked.

Letting out a deep breath, the young warrior sheathed his swords and took the proffered blade from the waiting armor.

The instant he did so, the other armor came to life. It rushed forward at an alarming rate, sword raised high over its head.

Thankfully, Lloyd was ready for it. Bracing himself, the young warrior raised the sword in his hands and blocked the vicious attack.

Andrella had been worried at first, but soon realized her concerns had been unwarranted. Though she'd never seen him fight with such a large blade, Lloyd appeared rather adept with it. He easily blocked the armor's attacks and returned them with ease.

Even so, she decided to lend him a hand. Tracing a mildly complex symbol through the air, she released the mana that filled it with a single word. *"Accelero."* The mana rushed forth and enveloped her fiancé, speeding up his movements and reactions.

Lloyd laid into his opponent with a rain of heavy blows, forcing it back step by step. After one particularly resounding blow, the armor took two steps back and lowered its greatsword.

Lloyd held up and eyed the armor warily, but it merely bowed then took up its original position. Behind it, on the other side of the room, a section of wall retracted upward revealing another archway.

Cautiously weaving through the two now stationary armors, the small company passed through the open archway. They now found themselves inside a large circular chamber encompassing a gorgeous white stone fountain. Numerous angelic statues adorned the fount in a variety of poses. Across the chamber stood another stone door with a single large keyhole in its very center.

On approaching the fountain, they found it to be dry. Alys spun about and fixed Zantillis with an accusatory state. "I thought you said there were no more tests?"

A hurt expression crossed the djinn's face. "You passed all the tests, fair Alys, and as promised, here is the Fount of Tears."

Alys folded her arms across her chest, her foot tapping against the floor in an angry rhythm. "In case you haven't noticed, the 'fount' is dry."

A smile sprang across the djinn's lips, replacing his hurt expression with a mischievous one. "Ah, but you have everything you need to find the staff, my dear Alys."

His response only served to irritate Alys more, but something in his words sparked an idea in Andrella's mind. Placing a hand on Glo's arm, she said, "Can I have the goblet?"

The wizard arched an eyebrow at her, but then nodded. "Certainly." Pulling the goblet from his pack, Glo handed it over to her. As soon as he did so, it immediately refilled to the top with clear liquid.

Andrella strode to the dry fountain and held the goblet over it with one hand. She then waved her other hand across the top and incanted the spell set upon the crystal. *Mutare Liquidum.*

As the words rolled from her tongue, the goblet began to glow once again. The glow faded from the stem, but the bowl was now filled with a shining white liquid.

"Very clever," Glo commended her.

Andrella beamed back at him as she poured the contents into the fountain. Lloyd joined her and marveled as the goblet refilled with more glowing liquid. "What is that, exactly?"

"It's Angel Tears," she said with a grin. "They call this the Fount of Tears and it's decorated with angels."

"Still, this is going to take forever to fill," Andrella complained as she emptied another goblet full into the fountain.

Alys waltzed up beside her and wrapped her hand around the one holding the goblet. "What if we do this instead?" The young lady then turned both their hands over.

The contents of the goblet began to pour out at an incredible rate. It practically gushed into the fountain as the magic continually attempted to refill the cup.

Andrella exchanged a triumphant glance with Alys. "Never underestimate girl power!" she declared emphatically.

"You know it!" Alys agreed with a broad smile.

About twenty minutes later according to Glo's internal clock, the fount had been filled to the top. The waters began to bubble and spray out of the mouths of the angels at its top. At the same time an indentation appeared in the basin of the fountain.

Leaning forward, Andrella squinted at it through the waters until she was struck by another epiphany. Reaching backward, she held out a hand towards Lloyd. "Can you give me that amulet from Sirus?"

"Sure," Lloyd replied. "What do you want it for," he asked as he placed it into her waiting hand.

"Watch and see," she told him with a cryptic smile.

Swinging one leg and then the other over the edge, she waded out into the fountain until she stood over the indentation. Rolling up her sleeve, she reached down into the waters and pushed the amulet into the open slot. As soon as she had done so, a golden key appeared over the top of the fountain.

"Lloyd, can you be a dear and grab that for me?" she called out to him over her shoulder.

A bemused smile crossed the young man's lips as he too waded into the fountain. He reached up and grabbed the key from the top of the fount, then scooped her up in his arms and kissed her soundly.

"You never cease to amaze me," he whispered once their lips parted.

She smiled back up at him playfully. "Well, if you keep kissing me like that, I'll have to think of more ways to do so."

The two of them waded out of the basin together, then strode over to the waiting stone door. Once they reached it, Lloyd held out the key to her. "I think the honor should be yours."

"Why thank you, good sir," Andrella responded in a courtly voice, executing a perfect curtsey.

Their lighthearted antics were in direct contrast to the nerves they felt inside. With any luck, behind this door they would finally find the Tomb of Phobas and the Staff of Law therein.

Andrella took the key from his hand and inserted it into the waiting lock. It was a perfect fit.

"Wish me luck!" she exclaimed as she gave it a turn.

In response, a loud click reverberated across the circular chamber. Everyone stood back as the stone door slowly rumbled open.

8
TOMB OF LIGHT

The boy sat atop the sarcophagus wearing a forlorn expression.

Alys held her breath as the heavy stone door slowly slid aside. After their frantic search of these seemingly endless catacombs, they might have finally found Phobas' tomb. Nonetheless, she'd dared not breathe. With so much riding on them retrieving the staff, it almost seemed too good to be true.

The same as with the rest of the catacombs, torches affixed to the walls came alight as the door the chamber opened. Long stone braziers also sprang to life, their bright reddish-yellow flames dancing up and along the walls. Together they revealed a huge stone chamber.

Thick elaborately decorated columns stretched upward to meet the high ceiling barely visible above. Between those columns, stood suits of armor similar to the ones they previously encountered. These armors were far larger than the others and further embossed with the emblem of the sun upon their chest. Moreover, in place of a greatsword, each held within its metallic gauntlets a rather menacing, long-handled war hammer.

All that swiftly fled Alys' mind though as her eyes fell on what lay in the very center of the chamber. Atop a wide raised stone dais sat a giant sarcophagus. Whether a trick of the flames, or something else entirely, a subtle glow appeared to waver around the edges of the great stone coffin.

"It is rather impressive," Zantillis murmured in a low tone, "but perhaps you'd like to follow your friends inside?"

Alys had been so awestruck by the sight that her feet had remained firmly rooted to the spot. The others, in the meantime, had already filed through the now open doorway. Feeling rather foolish, she covered her embarrassment with an impish smile. "One must know when to make an entrance."

She held out her arm to the djinn. "Care to escort me?"

"Of course, milady Alys," Zantillis replied in a serious voice, though his eyes danced with mild amusement.

The djinn led her inside to join the others as they climbed up onto the broad dais. After clambering up behind them, Alys spied a sun symbol embellishing the chest area of the sarcophagus. The emblem matched the ones on the surrounding suits of armor—a golden circle with eight rays fanning out from its center.

As they approached the stone coffin, multiple lines of glowing characters flared to life along its side. Alys recognized the beautiful flowing script as Celestial—the language of the gods, angels, and the like. Intrigued, her mind immediately set to the task of translating it, but Glo proved far more fluent than she.

The elf ran a finger along the glowing lines as he relayed the meaning of the inscription. "This passage details Phobas' final battle. It states that he took the essences of the demon lords and bound them to him with the staff. He then apparently used that power to break the fifth Abyssal chain."

Lloyd let out a low whistle. "Phew! Talk about using your enemy's own strength against them."

"Yes, but at the cost of his own life," Aksel reminded the young man.

Despite Aksel's attempt to dissuade him, Lloyd's face remained lit with admiration. It was a stirring tale, one filled with epic glory as well as tragedy. Alys had found herself drawn to such stories in her isolated youth. The truth be told, she still found the tale quite rousing.

A sudden glitter caught her eye. The air had begun to shimmer above the sarcophagus.. Wary of the strange phenomenon, Alys pointed it out to the others. "What's that?"

All eyes followed her finger as the shimmering intensified. A few seconds later, the glittering faded revealing the form of a dark-haired young boy garbed in a black jacket and shorts. Appearing perhaps ten years old, the boy sat atop the sarcophagus wearing a forlorn expression.

Andrella took a step forward and called up to the lad. "Who are you?"

His head in his hands, the boy's dark eyes shifted to fix on her. His response sounded as despondent as his expression. "I don't know."

Something in his tone tore at Alys' heartstrings. Andrella must have felt it as well. "Oh, you poor thing," she crooned as she reached up to console the forlorn lad.

The boy stretched a hand down to meet hers, but before they met, Lloyd pulled her back. Andrella spun about and regarded him stiffly, but the young man merely shook his head.

Meanwhile, Glo addressed the boy. "What exactly do you remember?"

The boy's expression instantly changed, a look of terror creeping over his face. "A—all I remember is a big scary man approaching me."

Before Glo could respond, Aksel interrupted him. The gnome stood a few paces behind them, his hands glowing a distinct white. He wore a deathly pale expression as he waved for everyone to fall back.

Alys' heart raced as she hastily retreated from the sarcophagus. *Could this innocent looking child be something other than what he appeared to be?*

Aksel confirmed her suspicions as they all gathered around him. His voice hushed in an insistent whisper, he proclaimed, "That kid is evil."

"How evil?" Glo asked in a voice to match Aksel's.

"Very," the little cleric responded grimly.

Goosebumps now forming on her arms, Alys chanced a look at the 'boy.' He had not moved, still sitting on the sarcophagus looking forlorn.

Abruptly, the air next to him started to glitter. Just as before, the shimmering gave way to another form. This time it was a young blonde girl with pigtails wearing a plain short black dress. The girl peered down at the boy, the corner of her mouth upturned slightly. "They may be rubes, but that old ploy will never work."

The boy glanced up at her and stuck out his tongue. "Well, it won't now that you've given it away."

The girl folded her arms, her smirk broadening into a smug smile. After a bit of gloating, she turned her gaze towards the onlookers. "Have you come to take the staff?"

"And what if we have?" Glo responded churlishly to her question.

While Alys intrinsically understood his reaction, she didn't think it a good idea to antagonize this pair. There was a fairly good chance these were the demons Phobas had bound with the staff. Though constrained, they obviously had enough power to appear to them in these forms. That given, who knows what else they could do.

Erring on the side of caution, Alys placed a hand on Glo's arm. Meeting his gaze with a subtle shake of her head, she then turned and smiled at the girl. "Don't mind him. He died recently and it sort of left him grumpy."

A wicked laugh escaped the girl's lips at Alys' explanation. "I can understand that."

The malevolence behind that laugh unsettled Alys. Taking a deep breath, she forced down her nerves and resumed smiling at the girl.

"So, what's your name?" she asked in as congenial a tone as she could muster.

The girl placed a hand on her chest. "You can call me Lily"—she paused and motioned towards the boy— "and you can refer to this clod as Jack."

"Lily, that's a pretty name," Alys said as if talking to one of her best friends.

An actual smile crossed Lily's face. She snorted at the boy. "Well at least this one has nice manners."

Jack rose and wiped off his clothes though they didn't look dusty in the slightest. "Manners? What do manners matter down here?"

Lily made a face at the boy, then peered imploringly at Alys. "See what I have to deal with?"

A wave of sympathy washed over Alys as faces from the past played through her mind. Dom, Vic, and especially Cole had been difficult companions at best. The latter had constantly needled her about every little thing she did.

Alys nearly said as much, but then caught herself. *Am I crazy feeling sympathy for a demoness?*

Thankfully Glo stepped in before the silence became too awkward. "My apologies, Miss Lily," he stated with a slight bow. "I have been rather grumpy"—he paused and gave Alys a pointed stare—"as of late. If you don't mind, though, we'd like to have a short conversation amongst ourselves." He finished by gently grasping Alys by the arm and tugging on it.

A pout formed about Lily's childish lips. "And just as we were getting to know one another."

Jack, on the other hand, waved them off. "Let them go. It's not like we're going anywhere, anyway."

Not wanting to lose what little headway she'd already made with the demon girl, Alys backed away with the best smile she could muster. "I'll be right back. I promise!"

Lily smiled back, but the look in her eyes chilled Alys to the very bone.

Gulping, Alys took another deep breath to calm herself. This role she was playing required stern resolve. She prayed this little interruption didn't dampen her determination.

Feeling a bit peevish, she placed her hands on her hips as they all gathered once again. "Now what is it?"

His expression pained, Aksel responded in a soft voice, "My apologies, but we really need to get a look inside that sarcophagus…"

"…and you'd rather do it without those demons staring over your shoulder," Glo finished for him.

Alys suddenly felt horrible for lashing out at the little cleric. She nearly said so, but Andrella interrupted her before she could.

"Wasn't there supposed to be a third one?" Andrella hissed, her brow knit into a frown.

Glo gazed around the room before bending closer and whispering an answer to her question. "I wouldn't be so sure there isn't. It might just choose not to manifest itself like the others."

Andrella peered back at her mentor with a wan smile. "Point taken."

In the meantime, Alys had been puzzling over how to distract the demon children. Chancing a glance over her shoulder, she nearly jumped out of her skin. Lily still stood on the giant coffin, her eyes fixated on Alys.

Gulping again, Alys gave her a half-hearted wave. As she turned about, however, an idea abruptly struck her. She felt rather pleased with herself as she addressed the others, "I think I can manage that."

Glo eyed her skeptically. "And just how do you intend to do that?"

Feeling rather smug at having one over on the intelligent wizard, Alys pointed a finger in the air and affected a bright smile. "Watch and learn."

"This I have to see," she heard Glo exclaim as she spun on her heel and sauntered back across the chamber. She only wished she felt half as confident as she acted.

Aksel didn't know what to believe. He felt the strong vibrations of evil emanating from the innocent-looking children. Furthermore, their very presence here professed them to be the demon lords Phobas had bound to the staff. And yet, something seemed off. The vibrations coming from the pair were not quite as strong as he'd come to expect.

The strongest of demons, a demon lord rose far above the rest, usually through carnage and slaughter, though sometimes through trickery and deceit. Ruling over their own layer of the Abyss, each lord had hordes of lesser demons in their service. Some even had mortal worshippers to whom they granted power and as such were treated as demigods.

These two "children", however, did not give off nearly the power of that vampire lord they'd faced in the recent past. Their evil, in fact, paled in comparison to the dracolich, Jinkolothos.

Perhaps the staff is muting their powers, Aksel mulled over silently. *Or, their powers have faded altogether due to their extended confinement,* he mused further.

While the little cleric puzzled over this apparent enigma, Alys had set to the task of distracting the youthful-looking pair. In a clever maneuver, she convinced Lily that her outfit needed "just a touch more color." After a bit of magical fashion manipulation, Alys persuaded the girl to relocate to the wall near the head of the sarcophagus where, in her words, the lighting was "far more flattering."

Once there, Alys then artfully turned Lily's attention towards Jack. It only took mild prompting to get her to pester the sullen lad into joining them. Poor Jack's fate was sealed once he begrudgingly leapt down from the lid of the coffin.

Glo had stood nearby the entire time watching the entire exchange, his face a mask of astonishment mixed with trepidation. Andrella, on the other hand, had an entirely different reaction to the scene playing out before them.

Hard pressed to contain her amusement, the young lady kept her mouth covered the entire time. As the cajoling continued, she gently nudged Lloyd in the arm. "That girl is quite the con artist. Has she always been like that?"

"Always," Lloyd said with a grimace that hinted of personal experience with Alys' machinations.

Lloyd's discomfort notwithstanding, Alys had achieved what she set out to do. The sarcophagus now stood unattended. With any luck it would remain that way until they had a chance to retrieve the staff.

As an added precaution, Aksel whispered to Xellos, "Would you mind keeping watch for us?"

"Sure," Xellos responded.

Without another word, the tracker padded off to the edge of the dais and slipped away into the shadows below. Raising a finger to his mouth, Aksel then urged Lloyd and Andrella to follow him. He led them to the foot of the stone coffin directly opposite from where Alys and Lily continued to fuss over a reluctant Jack.

Though Alys seemed quite adept at distracting the pair, she could not keep it up forever. They needed to get into the sarcophagus as quickly as possible.

Aksel took a few moments to assess the situation. The stone coffin was huge, about twenty feet long and half as wide in his estimation. The base met the lid about a foot above Aksel's head with its top rising nearly three feet beyond that. Considering its size and stone composition, the lid should prove extremely heavy.

Lloyd chimed in right on cue. "Do you want me to try moving the lid?"

Aksel absently tugged on his chin. Lloyd was perhaps the strongest person he knew. His strength had been even further augmented by those bracers the Thul Dunin had given him. Even so, that lid had to weigh more than a ton.

"I'm not certain you could," Aksel finally answered with a rueful expression.

"I might be able to help with that," Andrella interrupted, rolling up her sleeves. Tracing a pattern through the air, she touched Lloyd's arm as she invoked her spell. *"Taurus Vires."*

A brief image of a bull appeared over the young man's head, then disappeared. Lloyd glanced at both his biceps with a wondrous expression. "Wow, I feel ten times stronger."

Andrella touched his bulging bicep with a single finger, both eyebrows rising as she did so. "I think you might be right." Almost immediately thereafter the look faded, her expression serious once more.

"Just remember, it only lasts a few minutes," she cautioned him.

Lloyd grinned at her as he rubbed his hands together. "Well then, I better get to it."

With his new found strength, the young man braced himself against the side of the lid and heaved. His muscles bulged and his face reddened until gradually, but inexorably, the huge stone lid began to move.

Aksel's eyes widened with astonishment. He hadn't expected it to even budge.

The stone lid slowly, but quietly moved under Lloyd's continued efforts. Unfortunately, he swiftly reached his limit. His face beet red, he finally let go, huffing deeply as he pushed back to access his handiwork. The expectant look upon his face abruptly faded into a frown.

"Is that—all?" he panted with clear discouragement.

Lloyd had moved the lid maybe a foot in total. Though more than Aksel had actually expected, it was still not enough for even him to squeeze inside.

Andrella placed a hand on Lloyd's back and tried to console him. "You did good, hon. In fairness, that lid probably weighs two to three tons."

Lloyd's eyes narrowed into a look of fierce determination. "Let me just catch my breath—and I'll give it another try."

Though Aksel admired his tenacity, they were running short on time. As if out of nowhere, an idea struck him. Doffing his pack, Aksel pulled out the immovable pole they had found earlier.

Lloyd wore a puzzled expression. "What are you going to do with that?"

"I have an idea," Aksel explained as he held up the rod as far as he could above his head. Lining it up so it pointed towards the lid, he pressed the button on the end that fixed it in place.

Andrella's face lit up with understanding. "Oh, I see." She gave Lloyd a gentle shove. "Get ready to give him a hand."

A broad smile swept across Lloyd's face as he glanced between Andrella and Aksel. "I get it now." The young man leapt up and placed his hands back on the stone lid. His eyes fixed on Aksel, he gave him a curt nod. "Ready, when you are."

I just hope this works, Aksel thought gingerly.

Running his hands along the pole he found the two buttons at the opposite end. Pressing one, he hissed at Lloyd, "Go."

At the same time Lloyd began to push, the pole started to extend. The end shot out until it butted up against the stone lid about a foot from where Lloyd heaved heavily against it.

Aksel took a few steps back and held his breath. Slowly, but inevitably, the heavy lid began to slide.

"They're doing it!" Andrella exulted in a hushed voice.

Stone ground on stone as the heavy lid continued to give. At the same time something unforeseen happened. The immovable pole had begun to bend. The longer it pushed against the stone lid, the more it bowed from the strain.

Not knowing what would happen, Aksel leapt forward to retract the pole. Unfortunately, he was just a second too late. With a sharp *twang* the pole retracted and fell to the ground at his feet.

His heart racing, Aksel peered at the stone coffin. The lid had moved another two feet.

"It worked!" Lloyd cried with glee just before slapping his hand over his mouth.

"It's alright, Lloyd," Aksel assured him. "I'm sure all that grinding of stone on stone has alerted the demons by now anyway."

"Woah." Andrella's gasp brought Aksel's attention back towards the sarcophagus. A brilliant glow now emanated from the small opening they'd managed to create.

Totally intrigued, Aksel had Lloyd give him a boost up onto the edge. A triangular gap now stood below him with just enough room for Aksel to squeeze through.

Exchanging a quick glance with Lloyd and Andrella. "Wish me luck!" He told the pair, then leapt down into the gleaming hole below.

Glo had learned a lot about the art of diplomacy from watching both Elladan and Andrella. Yet, Alys had a flair for it all her own. Where Elladan flashed that charming smile, Alys acted coy. While Andrella focused on the other party's desires, Alys instead played on their weaknesses.

Even so, a demon did not become a lord without some measure of cunning. Thus, Glo had to assume at some level Jack and Lily knew they were being manipulated. Still, they both chose to play along and therein lay the beauty of Alys' scheme. She didn't necessarily have to fool the demons—she just needed to keep them preoccupied.

The entire charade came to an end though when a loud grinding noise reverberated across the chamber from the other end of the sarcophagus. Jack, now dressed in a bright red jacket and shorts, spun about with a maniacal grin.

"Twelve seconds," the boy called out.

Lily, garbed in a lavender dress, answered him with a cry of her own. "I give them sixteen."

Alys cocked her head to one side, her comely brow crinkling. "What are you two going on about?"

Still wearing an evil grin, Jack gave her a nonchalant wave. "Oh, just how long before your friends are splattered against the wall."

Alys blanched, then placed her hands on her hips and narrowed her eyes at the frighteningly cheerful lad. "And just why would that happen?"

Lily answered her this time. The young girl strode over to the suit of armor nearest them and patted it almost affectionately on the leg. "See this little ole thing? If someone tries to remove the staff, they tend to take offense—"

Jack spun back around and rubbed his hands together. "—and then it's hammer time!" he finished for Lily with clear relish.

The glee on both of the children's faces made Glo tremble inside. These demons had finally revealed their true nature.

Fighting down a rising panic, Glo focused on the more immediate problem. Those huge hammers the armors carried were no joke. He needed to warn the others before it was too late.

With the demons still reveling in anticipation, Glo covertly signaled Alys. A momentary spark of fear flashed in her eyes, but then disappeared. Feigning interest, Alys asked the pair to share their tales about the armors' previous assaults. To her credit, the young lady didn't bat an eye as they related the gory details.

Seeing his chance, Glo slipped away and swiftly scrambled across the chamber. He'd just reached the others when Aksel's head popped out of the coffin. His heart in his throat, Glo frantically spun about expecting to see the huge armors bearing down on them. To his surprise, none had moved.

"What's going on?" Lloyd cried anxiously.

Glo breathed a heavy sign and wiped a hand across his brow. Either the demons had been trolling him or Aksel hadn't yet retrieved the staff. He quickly explained what he'd been told to the others, then listened intently as Aksel reported what he had found.

As evidenced by the size of the sarcophagus, Phobas was indeed a giant. Furthermore, he'd been buried in full regalia—garbed in armor and holding his staff which turned out to be giant-sized as well. That explained why Aksel had not yet retrieved it. The thing would have been far too unwieldy for him to handle.

"The entire thing is covered in glowing runes," Aksel went on to explain further. "They appear to be suspended above the staff and spiral around it in an ongoing pattern."

"Do you know what language they are in?" Andrella asked, clasping her hands together excitedly.

Aksel shook his head. "I tried focusing on them, and some came to the top, but I couldn't quite decipher them." He paused and peered at Glo imploringly. "I was hoping you might be able to."

Glo eyed the small aperture into the sarcophagus with a single eyebrow raised. There was no way he could fit his whole body through there. Perhaps if he cast the fly spell upon himself though, he'd be able to hover upside down and poke his head inside.

Clasping his hands behind his back, he addressed both Lloyd and Andrella. "I'll take a look, but I left Alys all alone with that gruesome pair."

Andrella raised a hand in front of her. "Say no more. We'll go keep an eye on her—"

"—and those armored guardians, too," Lloyd added, his hands straying to his sword hilts as he swept his eyes around the chamber.

"Don't forget to warn Xellos as well," Aksel advised him.

"Will do," Lloyd waved as the pair strode off towards the other end of the chamber.

With the other's gone, Glo took a few seconds to mentally prepare himself for what would come next. He didn't exactly relish the idea of hanging upside down in midair, but it couldn't be helped.

With a short sigh, he traced the pattern through the air that would enable him to fly. Less than a minute later, the tall elf's body hung suspended in the air while his head peeked inside the coffin.

Glo blinked and rubbed his eyes to make sure he wasn't seeing things. Encased in armor with a silver-sheen, Phobas' giant form took up most of the inside of the casket. The brilliant glow emanating from the runes along the length of the staff reflected off that armor, lighting up the entire casket.

The runes across the staff appeared to be Celestial, but for some reason Glo couldn't quite make them out. Squinting his eyes, he noticed something strange. There was actually more than one layer of runes here. In fact, there were several overlaid atop each other.

No wonder Aksel had trouble deciphering these, Glo thought wryly. Between the swirling and the multiple layers, it was almost impossible to isolate a specific rune, let alone identify it.

Glo's head began to ache. Rubbing his temples, he realized he'd need a bit more help with this one. An ironic smile crossed his lips. *Andrella would probably be mad at me for casting another spell, but then again, she's not here to scold me.*

Still somewhat amused with his own thoughts, Glo traced a little used pattern through the air. Once finished, he invoked the spell with the words, *"Ibis Sapientia."*

Had Phobas not been lifeless, he might have noticed the brief visage of an owl appearing over the elf's head. All at once, the runes around the staff became crystal clear in Glo's mind. It was as if they had stopped twirling and separated from each other as well.

Swiftly perusing through them all, Glo noticed a pattern emerge. All the runes were somehow related to law versus chaos—hence the *Staff of Law.* He noted many spells of varying orders, but even the lower ones would be cast with the vast power of the staff.

Pulling the pack from his back, the elven wizard set it down in the coffin below him. Retrieving a quill and a piece of parchment, he scribbled at incredible speed until he'd deciphered nearly every rune. In the end only a very few escaped the elf's heightened awareness.

Aksel did his best to remain calm as Glo hung upside down with his head buried inside the coffin. They'd come so far to find Phobas' tomb, passing many tests along the way. Yet all that mattered little if they couldn't even remove the staff from its resting place.

There had to be a way, he kept telling himself. Some trick perhaps of the staff that would allow them to take it.

Realizing it would do no good to dwell on the matter until Glo had finished, Aksel tried to keep himself preoccupied. Sweeping his gaze around the chamber, his eyes settled on one of those armored guardians. The huge warhammers they held in their hands appeared quite daunting. He had no doubt a single hit from one of those would kill him. He doubted even Lloyd could take more than a couple of shots from the great weapon.

Not wanting to dwell on it further, Aksel ripped his eyes away and took a few steps back from the sarcophagus. Across the chamber, Jack and Lily carried on an animated discussion with Alys, Andrella, and Lloyd. From the pallid looks upon their faces, he assumed the pair were doing their best to intimidate his friends.

Finally, after what felt like an eternity, Glo rose back up out of the sarcophagus. Righting himself, the wizard floated downwards and held out a rolled parchment to Aksel.

Aksel grasped the pale-brown paper and anxiously unrolled it. "You were able to decipher it?"

"With a little help," Glo admitted, swirling his finger through the air to mimic the casting of a spell.

"Good thing Andrella wasn't around to see that," Aksel noted wryly as his eyes swept over the parchment.

The paper listed dozens of spells. Many lay outside the realm of his goddess' domain. Others were far more powerful than any of them could currently cast.

Glo pointed out a specific spell closer to the top of the list. "I think you'll find this one in particular rather interesting."

Aksel had initially passed over the relatively minor spell. Looking at it now, his eyes went wide. *This would alter the size of the staff!*

The little cleric breathed a heavy sigh. This is the break they'd been looking for. And yet, now that they could shrink the staff, they wouldn't be able to take it without fighting those armored guardians. Furthermore, he still wasn't convinced that those demons couldn't interfere in that fight.

"This does make things easier," Aksel finally said aloud, "but I'm still not sure what to do next."

Glo admitted to being stymied as well.

Aksel lowered the paper and shook his head. "I wish Seth were here. He's far better equipped to deal with these devious demons than any of us."

A puff of smoke exploded in front of them, almost making Aksel leap out of his skin. Zantillis appeared from out of the fumes and gazed expectantly down at Aksel. "Did I hear someone use the word wish?"

Aksel hadn't thought about it up until now, but the djinn had disappeared not long after they entered this chamber. Yet here he was and apparently willing to grant them another wish.

Aksel exchanged a hopeful glance with Glo. Perhaps there was a way out of this dilemma after all.

9
DEAL WITH THE DEVIL

I don't think we have the time to take them to court.

Seth sat cross-legged on the floor just outside the glowing purple barrier. It had been nearly two hours since his friends had passed through with no sign or word from them since. Sirus had left right after they disappeared, leaving him alone to his own devices.

The recalcitrant halfling had tried to while away the time by sharpening his knives and checking through his other weapons. True he had quite a few things hidden on him, but not even that could keep him busy for this amount of time.

Seth rose from where he sat and stretched after being seated for so long. He then proceeded to pace back and forth in front of the translucent barrier.

"Maybe I should have gone with them", he muttered to himself. Still, after hearing Sirus' pronouncement about having to be pure of heart, he had been reluctant to test his luck beyond the barrier.

Seth had a checkered past at best. Hailing from a long line of thieves and charlatans, he'd learned to pick his first lock by the age of five. By the time he was ten, he could unlock almost any door or safe.

Despite that, Seth tried his best to stay out of the family business. He'd even clandestinely pursued a career in a type of martial arts suited to his small frame. Unfortunately, when his family found out, they killed his teacher. To this day, Seth carried the burden of his former master's death on his small shoulders.

The tormented halfling halted in front of the barrier and eyed it speculatively. *Maybe it wouldn't really fry me. Maybe it would just singe me a bit.*

True Lloyd had taken the amulet with him, but Seth had come across enough magical obstacles to know there was always a way around them. He moved in for a closer look, when a large puff of smoke abruptly appeared in the air next to the barrier.

Jumping back, a pair of knives immediately appeared in the halfling's hands. Crouching down, Seth spied two dark shapes within the smoke. One looked vaguely familiar—at least familiar enough to stop him from throwing his daggers at it.

Seth let out a barely audible sigh when the smoke began to clear. One of the dark shapes was most definitely Lloyd. Next to his friend floated a blue-skinned half-man, half-cloud garbed in a fancy vest. He immediately recognized it as a djinn.

The corner of Seth's mouth lifted upwards ever so slightly as he straightened from his crouch. "Hey Lloyd, who's your friend in the fancy pajamas?"

Lloyd pointed a thumb at the djinn. "This is Zantillis."

Zantillis executed a deep bow in mid-air. "Master Seth, the Cleric Aksel has sent me to procure your services."

Intrigued, Seth slipped both knives back up his sleeves and folded his arms across his chest. "Oh really? What for?"

Despite no one else being around, Zantillis leaned in closer and put a hand to one side of his mouth. "It appears they are dealing with a pair of demon lords. Cleric Aksel thought you might be best equipped to handle the situation."

Seth eyed them both as if they were daft. "A pair of demon lords? What've you two been smoking?"

"They were bound by Phobas to the staff," Lloyd explained further, "but Aksel isn't completely convinced they can't cause trouble."

"Well why didn't you just say so in the first place?" Seth chided his good-natured friend. "So, when do we leave?"

"How about now?" Zantillis answered, his eyes twinkling. Before Seth could respond, the djinn snapped his fingers and the world around them disappeared in a puff of smoke.

In the blink of an eye, Seth, Lloyd, and the djinn reappeared in front of the biggest coffin he had ever seen. Glo stood next to it, a haggard expression on the wizard's face.

Quickly taking in his surroundings, Seth spotted Andrella and Alys at the other end of the sarcophagus talking with a couple of young children. Putting two and two together, he immediately realized those must be the demon lords.

Seth shook his head. Leave it to Lloyd to leave out important details. Unable to resist himself, he cupped his hands together and called out across the chamber, "Hey where did we get the kids from?"

A lopsided grin crossed the boy's face as he met Seth's stare. He flung his arms out wide in response and cried, "Daddy!"

Not to be upstaged, Seth did the same with a cry of, "Son!"

A thin chuckle escaped the boy's lips, but then his expression turned deathly serious. His eyes grew strangely intense making Seth's skin crawl. "Tell me, have you ever thought of being a vessel of demonic possession?"

The question caught Seth by surprise—not an easy thing to do. Even so, he wasn't about to let this demon know it had rattled him. Holding the boy's stare, he answered with a drawn out, "Yes."

The boy seemed startled by his answer at first, but then turned to the girl with a wicked smile. "This one is more interesting than the rest."

The girl looked Seth over with her dark black eyes sending goosebumps up and down his skin. Finally, she gazed back at the boy and nodded. "I agree."

No longer having any doubts that these were the demon lords, Seth turned his attention to Glo. "So, where's Aksel?"

Glo gestured towards the sarcophagus behind him. "He's inside there."

Seth frowned at the wizard. "By choice?"

Glo scratched his head and sighed. "It's a long story. Probably best if he tells it."

"Whatever." Seth shrugged.

The lid of the huge sarcophagus had been moved somewhat aside. Leaping up onto the edge he found a hole just big enough for him to slip through.

Dropping down, Seth found Aksel seated next to a huge body encased in silver armor. A wooden staff with glowing runes lay between Aksel and the body. The runes were so bright that they lit up the whole interior of the coffin.

Seth drew up next to his friend and paused to look over the huge body. "So that's what a dead god looks like. I thought he'd be taller."

Aksel's expression remained stoic. "Very funny, Seth."

Unperturbed, Seth gestured towards the staff. "Is that it?"

"Yeah," Aksel sighed.

Seth would've expected a much more enthusiastic response from his friend. There was obviously more going on here than met the eye. Placing a hand on his chin, he pretended to appraise the staff. "It looks impressive, but isn't it a bit small for Phobas?"

"It wasn't a few minutes ago," Aksel responded blithely.

"Neat trick," Seth acknowledged. His attempts at levity had gotten him nowhere, so instead he decided to get down to business. "Want to tell me why you're hiding in here and what's with the weird demon kids outside?"

Seth listened attentively as Aksel brought him up to speed on all that had happened since they found Phobas' tomb. Once he'd finished his incredulous story, Seth tried his best to sum things up. "Let's see if I've got this straight. As soon as you take the staff, these guardians are going to come and splat you."

"Essentially," Aksel agreed.

"But if you don't take it, Penwick gets turned into an icy wasteland and overrun with undead," Seth added for good measure.

Aksel pressed his lips together and nodded. "That pretty much sums it up."

Seth sat down next to the gnome and crossed his legs. "Alright. What's the plan?"

Aksel breathed a short sigh. "Well, before we take on those guardians, I'd like to do something about these demons."

Seth leaned forward and placed the back of his hand on Aksel's forehead. It felt cool to the touch. "You don't have a fever. Did you hit your head or something?"

A sour look crossed Aksel's face. "I'm aware of what we are dealing with. Just one of them could probably crush us all. However, one of the spells on this staff is a *Binding Agreement*."

"Tsk," Seth clicked his tongue. "I don't think we have the time to take them to court."

Ignoring Seth's sarcastic response, Aksel plunged on with his idea. "That's the beauty of that spell. The court comes to us."

"Sure it does," Seth agreed, putting his hand on Aksel's forehead again.

Aksel swatted his hand away this time, but before he could answer, Glo's voice echoed from outside the coffin. "The spell summons an *Inevitable*."

Now Seth had heard of those. They were powerful creatures, metal constructs from another plane with the single-minded task of hunting down their quarry. Before Seth left home, one of his uncles had broken a contract with the *Inevitables*. Slippery as he was, they eventually hunted him down and killed him.

Seth glanced dubiously at Aksel, then sat back and stared in the direction of Glo's voice. "Let me get this straight—you two want to make a pact with these demon lords and if they break it, they get hunted down by *Inevitables*?"

"Sounds like fun," a different voice said, this time from behind him. That definitely did not sound like Aksel.

Seth spun about to find Lily now seated on the opposite side of Aksel. She hadn't been there a moment ago and he definitely would have noticed if she had climbed past him. Therefore, she must have materialized herself inside the coffin.

Not wanting to show his surprise, Seth instead snorted at her. "Glad you think so."

"So what's the deal?" a third voice said from outside the coffin.

The sound of stone grinding on stone echoed around them as the heavy stone lid shifted farther open. As soon as it stopped, Jack jumped through the now wider crack and slowly strode over towards them. Plopping himself down, the demon did his best to act casual, though Seth caught him glancing nervously at the staff in front of Aksel.

So it does scare them, Seth noted to himself. *Good to know.*

With the lid shifted far enough over, Glo's face now appeared just outside the sarcophagus. An instant later, Andrella and Alys showed up on either side of the wizard. As predictable as ever, the elf's cheeks flushed with discomfort.

Seth couldn't resist poking fun at him. "Nice and cozy in here, ain't it, Glo?"

The wizard fixed him with a withering stare. "Is this really the time for that?"

"It's always the time," Seth responded with a light chortle.

Alys batted her eyes at the uncomfortable elf. "Are you really going to complain about being surrounded by two beautiful women?"

Glo's face reddened even further. "I—I wouldn't dream of it," he sputtered awkwardly.

Andrella and Alys exchanged a glance and giggled at the wizard's discomfort. Chortling along, Seth found himself liking this Alys more than ever.

Once the laughter had died down, Alys bade Aksel to continue. The little cleric cleared his throat and addressed both Jack and Lily in turn. "Ahem, well then, the deal is we free the both of you from the staff. Afterwards you are banished forever to your home plane."

Still playing the child, Jack stuck out his tongue at Aksel. "That's no fun. How about we make it banished for a hundred years instead?"

"How about we make it for a thousand?" Seth countered firmly.

Jack raised his hands and made a warding gesture in the air in front of him. "Okay, okay. I get your point."

"How about we make it six hundred and sixty six years?" Lily interjected coyly.

Seth smirked at the demoness. "Very cute."

Lily responded with a sly smile of her own. "So I've been told."

Eww, Seth thought to himself. *Definitely not my type.*

Thankfully, Alys chose that moment to interject her thoughts. "Pardon me for asking, but aren't we missing a golden opportunity here?"

All eyes turned to the songstress.

Having everyone's attention, Alys went on with her thoughts. "Couldn't we have them take out that demon tower you've all been going on about, and then banish them?"

"We could definitely do that," Jack agreed, leaping to his feet and rubbing his hands together enthusiastically. An evil smile crossed his face as he locked eyes with Lily. "Just think of all the souls we could feast on." He ended by rubbing his tummy and eliciting moans of pure delight.

"Wait—what?" Alys stammered at the twisting around of her well-meaning idea.

Seth was not surprised in the slightest. Demons were not to be trusted, period. On the other hand, they faced overwhelming odds between that dracolich and the vampire lord's undead army. Further, he doubted even demon lords would want a line of never ending *Inevitables* chasing after them. Sooner or later, they'd both end up dead.

Seth finally understood why Aksel had sent for him. The rest of them were ill equipped to deal with such devious creatures. Seth, to the contrary, had grown up around liars and cheats. He knew quite well how to handle them.

Folding his arms across his chest, he fixed Jack with a hard stare. "Yeah, that's not going to happen."

Jack's face fell. "Killjoy," he muttered as he resumed his seat.

"Always," Seth snorted as he in turn rose from his seat.

Whirling about, he backed up and casually leaned against Phobas' armored leg. The others might have seen that as a bit irreverent, but somehow he doubted the dead god would mind. Also, it made the desired statement that he had little respect for gods or demons—an implicit point he wanted to make before starting his pitch.

"Now, let's get serious," Seth said in a no nonsense tone. "We free you. No mind control, no mind reading, no killing, maiming, rending, or eating of souls," he ticked off on his fingers as he spoke. He let that sink in, then added, "Not unless Aksel tells you to."

Jack and Lily both held his gaze, but neither seemed to balk at what he'd said so far.

"Good," Seth declared firmly. "On top of that, if Aksel tells you to fight or kill something, you must obey. Finally, once Aksel tells you it's time to go, you to go back to your home plane for six hundred and sixty six years."

When Seth finished, Jack and Lily traded a furtive glance.

"Oh, and just so you don't get any ideas," Seth paused until both demons again stared at him, "upon Aksel's death this agreement passes to Glo."

Both Jack's and Lily's faces went blank. Based on their lack of reaction, Seth knew he had guessed right as to the kind of loophole the pair had been considering.

"Excuse us," Jack finally responded. He got up and went to sit on the opposite side of Lily. The pair began whispering in a tongue that Seth had not heard before. From the harsh sound of it, he guessed it to be Infernal, the native language of demons.

"Thanks for the vote of confidence," Aksel whispered.

"You're welcome," Seth responded without missing a beat.

As the intense discussion continued, Seth decided to take things up a notch. "And upon Glo's death this agreement passes to..."

"I'll take it!" he heard Lloyd call from outside the sarcophagus.

Seth stopped to consider that. He had originally thought about taking on the burden himself, but that would be tantamount to suicide. Much as he hated to admit it, Lloyd was probably the next best candidate after Aksel and Glo.

"...Lloyd," Seth finally finished.

Jack and Lily whispered back and forth a bit more before Lily spoke up for the pair. "We need to discuss this in private." With that the duo disappeared from sight.

Seth let out a deep breath, then pushed away from the body of Phobas. "Cozy as this is, I'm not waiting in here."

Glo, Andrella, and Alys backed out of the way as Seth climbed out of the sarcophagus. Aksel followed him to the edge, but stayed there instead of climbing down after him.

Glo glared at him as his feet touched down outside the coffin. "Thanks for volunteering me, Seth."

"You're welcome," Seth responded to the wizard without so much as batting an eye.

Before Glo could say anything further, Andrella tugged at the wizard's sleeve. "Do you think they'll agree to it?" she asked him in a hushed voice.

Glo cocked his head to one side as he mulled over her question. "Probably, considering they've been stuck in here for a thousand years or so."

Lloyd scanned the chamber around them anxiously. "I wonder where they went to discuss it."

"They're up there." Xellos climbed up from the shadows at the edge of the dais and pointed towards one of the armored guardians towards the back of the room.

Seth peered where Xellos indicated and saw Lily sitting on the guardian's head. In the meantime, Jack paced back and forth, disappearing from one shoulder and reappearing on the opposite one. The pair appeared to be arguing between themselves.

"I wonder how long that will take?" Alys asked, mirroring Seth's thoughts.

Surprisingly it didn't take nearly as long as Seth had expected. A few minutes later, the arguing stopped. An instant later, both Jack and Lily disappeared again only to reappear right in front of them.

Seth folded his arms in front of his chest. "So, do we have a deal, or what?"

"Deal," Jack said simply.

"Yes," Lily agreed.

Seth carefully studied the pair, but couldn't detect any sign of deceit. Though he knew they would eventually try something, it would have to do for now.

"Go ahead," he told Aksel with a nod.

Aksel scurried back into the sarcophagus and reappeared moments later at the edge holding the staff in hand. A swift glance around the chamber proved that the guardians hadn't reacted just yet. Seth was almost certain their trigger would come when the staff left the confines of Phobas' coffin.

The little cleric lifted the staff up in front of him and invoked one of its many powers. The head of the staff glowed a brilliant blue matching the colors of the runes along its length. The energy coming from it grew so intense that it made Seth's skin crawl.

In answer to the spell, a wide oval portal opened above Phobas' sarcophagus. A large humanoid creature lumbered out of the portal and onto the lid. Encased in metal from head to toe, it held in its hands a long parchment and a strange looking quill.

"Give me a boost," Seth prompted Lloyd.

The young man interwove his hands together and bent down creating a makeshift foothold for the halfling. Seth stepped onto it and Lloyd launched him upward. Flying upward, the halfling executed a midair flip, then landed gracefully upon the lid.

The Inevitable towered over Seth as he strode up to it and held up his hands. With nary a word, the metal creature handed over the parchment and the quill to him.

Quickly scanning over the parchment, Seth was surprised to find their entire agreement written out on it verbatim. Thoroughly impressed, he peered up at the Inevitable. "Going to show this to my partners."

The creature responded with a curt nod.

Leaping down, Seth showed the details of the agreement to the others. Once everyone agreed, he handed it over to Lily and Jack. The duo scanned over the document intently, going over it at least half a dozen times.

After the last time, Jack took a deep breath and grimaced. "Let's get this over with."

He took the quill from Seth's hand and drew it across the parchment.

The point of the strange quill lit up with a brilliant light as it burned the demon's name into the contract. Smoke rose from the point of contact and a distinct burning smell wafted through the air.

"Cool effect," Seth noted to no one in particular.

"Very," Glo agreed.

Jack then handed the quill to Lily who did the same. The demoness then passed the quill over to Lloyd who also signed. Glo followed suit. Lastly, they gave the parchment and quill over to Aksel. As soon as the little cleric signed the agreement, it and the quill disappeared from his hand and reappeared in the hand of the Inevitable.

A gong sounded from somewhere on the other side of the portal. The Inevitable then backed into it and the portal swished shut with a loud *whoosh*.

10
HAMMER TIME

The guardian charged in and swung its giant hammer at the little cleric.

Xellos Runell stood off to one side quietly contemplating how things had gone so far astray. What started out as an innocent visit to Hagentree ended with him being cursed. He had one year to find three rare Arcarion seeds or forfeit his life. When the companions offered him passage on their airship, Xellos thought it might help his search. Unfortunately, from there things went swiftly downhill.

First, he'd been dragged off to fight a crazed sorceress with an undead army. Next, he'd been teleported to Penwick only to find more undead invading that city. From there they'd traveled to the shadow planes where a deranged dracolich nearly killed them all. Now he'd helped them desecrate the tomb of a god and make a questionable deal with a pair of demons.

Though the thought made Xellos cringe, he understood the fate of the world lay in the balance. Even so, this all seemed far beyond him. In truth, he was little more than a forest dweller, living off the land and nurturing it in turn. His people tended to avoid the types of conflicts that involved the other races. Unfortunately, at this point he'd already seen too much and there was no going back to that simple life.

While Xellos ruminated on his reluctant indoctrination into the hero business, the others planned on how to deal with the guardians of the staff. Seth kicked things off by first confronting Jack and Lily. "We won't be needing your help on this one."

Jack rubbed his hands together. "You mean we get to watch you get smooshed from the sidelines? Sounds good to me."

Lily pushed a lock of hair off her brow and haughtily regarded Aksel. "What does our 'boss' say?"

Aksel stared back at the duo with a stony expression. "I agree with Seth."

Seemingly unperturbed, Lily waved a nonchalant hand in the air. "Very well then."

Without another word, the two of them disappeared. Seth gave Aksel an approving nod, then motioned for everyone to gather around. "Okay then, here's what I'm thinking…"

Twenty minutes later everyone was in position. An extra-large, blurry, metallic-grey skinned Lloyd stood with weapons readied on one side of the giant casket. Andrella, Alys, and Glo had fanned out across the lid facing in the other three directions.

Xellos hovered above them all thanks to the enchantment on his cloak. Though not quite sure how effective his arrows would be, he nonetheless held one nocked and ready.

With everyone in place, Aksel then disappeared into the casket. What emerged shortly thereafter looked more akin to a wavering dust cloud than the gnome cleric. Within the cloud's hand hovered a long exquisitely carved staff inscribed with brilliantly glowing runes.

As soon as the cloud exited the coffin, the guardians creaked to life. Hefting their warhammers into the air, the large armored creatures set forth on a direct path towards Aksel.

A sudden movement caught the corner of Xellos' eye. Chancing a glance below, he was just in time to see Glo and Andrella release simultaneously spells. In answer to their incantations, two thick veils of shimmering scarlet rose up on either side of the chamber. The flames curved around the casket, their ends meeting to enclose it in a wall of fire that reached almost to the ceiling.

Sadly, the hot flames did little to deter the charging juggernauts. On one side, two of the guardians plunged straight through the flaming wall with seemingly no concern for the char marks it left on their armor. Thankfully, the companions had planned for such contingencies.

Now equal in size to the guardians, Lloyd stood between them and Aksel. Yet, neither attacked the warrior. Instead, they both tried to push past him.

Swords ablaze, Lloyd launched a fierce offensive against the two armors. Moving faster than his heavily laden opponents, his flashing blades sliced through each of their armor. His unrelenting assault brought the guardians to a halt despite their single-minded obsession with the staff wielder.

On the opposite side of the chamber, another guardian burst through the flames. It had only taken two steps forward when a piercing cry filled the air. A wave of pure sonic energy rushed forth from Alys' open jaw. It slammed into the armored figure, knocking it back into the fire.

As the last guardian slipped through the flames, Alys turned her sights upon it. Yet before she could let loose another cry, Seth appeared between them. Tracing a swift pattern across the ground, the crafty halfling released a spell.

The sound of thunder erupted from the symbol he had drawn, buckling the very earth before him. The undulating ground swept forth, passing directly beneath the guardian's feet. The resulting wave knocked it off its feet and sent it flying back into the fire.

Not bad, Xellos had to admit. Their plan worked better than he had expected. Despite their sometimes erratic behavior, when the need arose this group could function like a well-trained pack.

Unfortunately, his admiration was short-lived. Effectively cut off from their target, the two guardians shifted their focus to Lloyd. Working in tandem, the pair hammered away at the warrior.

As talented as Lloyd was, those hammers were far too heavy to parry. Thrown completely on the defensive, he could only avoid them for so long before one connected. Though a glancing blow, the force behind it was still enough to throw him off balance.

In an amazing display of resilience, Lloyd spun about and resumed his impromptu blockade. Regrettably, it was not fast enough to prevent one of the guardians from slipping through.

Now with a clear shot, Xellos pelted the rushing guardian with arrows. The adept archer fired off one, two, three, four, five rounds in rapid succession. The sharp headed shafts ripped through the heavy armor, embedding themselves deep into their target. Nonetheless, it did little to slow the juggernaut's progression.

At the same time, two brilliant red beams of light lanced across the chamber from the top of the sarcophagus. Each struck the charging guardian square in the chest with a sharp sizzling sound. Nevertheless, the creature merely shrugged them off and continued its mad rush forward.

"Watch out!" Lloyd's cry rang out across the chamber, but it was too late.

Coming within striking distance of its prey, the guardian hefted its huge weapon. Xellos held his breath as it unleashed a devastating blow.

Wincing as the hammer connected, he half expected to hear a sickening crunch. Yet instead, it merely passed through the cloudy figure. Xellos breathed an audible sigh as the dust that had been swept away in its wake swiftly reformed into its original shape.

Before the guardian could recover, Lloyd caught up with it. Dropping his one sword, the warrior leveled an incredible two-handed blow at its unprotected back. The flaming black blade sang through the air as it connected with the creature's midriff.

The screeching sound of metal scraping against metal echoed throughout the chamber as the black blade continued relentlessly along its arc. It passed clean through the other side, cleaving the armored guardian in two.

As the severed halves crumbled to the ground, Andrella cried out in warning, "Lloyd, behind you!"

At that very same moment, Xellos spied the second guardian hurtling at the warrior's exposed back. The deft archer unloaded three arrows in rapid succession. Once again, they all hit their mark, embedding themselves deep into the creature's armored hide.

Another ray of sizzling-hot red light caught the guardian square in the chest. Still, neither Xellos' barrage nor Andrella's spell slowed the thing down in the slightest.

Using the momentum of his previous attack, Lloyd spun about barely in time to face the charging juggernaut. Amazingly, it blew right past him and instead headed straight for Aksel.

A shrill cry split the air as a sonic wave slammed into the creature's side. Between the force of that blow and its own momentum, the guardian hit the ground and skidded off sideways back into the firewall.

That's gotta sting, Xellos noted wryly to himself.

Shifting his attention to the other side, Xellos saw the other two remaining guardians burst back through the ring of fire.

Seemingly unperturbed, Seth aimed a spell at the first with a quick swish of his fingers. In response, a pool of black liquid appeared beneath the creature's feet.

Suddenly unable to maintain its balance, the guardian's legs slipped out from under it. It slammed to the ground with a resounding crash.

Xellos did his best to refrain from laughing as he targeted the armor beside it. As if planned, Glo launched a simultaneous barrage of purple projectiles.

As Xellos' shafts buried themselves in the guardian's hide, those translucent missiles connected with an audible *thud*. Sadly, the synchronous bombardment barely slowed the creature down.

With no one else standing between it and Aksel, the guardian charged in and swung its giant hammer at the little cleric. Once again, the weapon passed through the cloud leaving it seemingly unharmed. Still, Xellos' sharp eyes couldn't help but notice that the dust didn't look quite as thick as it had before.

A loud shriek split the air as a sonic wave smashed into the guardian. It fell backward nearly careening into its counterpart floundering in the nearby pool of grease.

Seth again swished his fingers through the air. In answer, the dark pool expanded until it reached beneath the second creature's feet. As with the other guardian, this one too lost its balance. It fell to the ground with a loud crash.

Taking advantage of the situation, Andrella launched a fist-sized ball of flame at the two floundering creatures. The ball rocketed across the chamber and struck the ground between the pair.

The angry red orb exploded on impact sending a storm of blazing fire sweeping over the surrounding area. It was so hot that Xellos could feel the heat all the way up by the ceiling.

When the flames finally winked out, all that remained of the guardians were two piles of melted slag.

Back on the opposite side, Lloyd had managed to get behind his opponent. With a mighty swing, he cleaved it clear down the center with his black blade.

Everything went quiet after that. Not daring to breathe, Xellos swept his gaze around the chamber. The walls lay empty of armored figures. All the guardians had either been melted or split in twain.

The silence was ultimately broken by the sound of a slow clap. Jack and Lily reappeared, the former applauding their efforts with mock admiration.

"Not bad, not bad at all," Jack said blithely. Even so, Xellos thought he caught a glimpse of grudging respect in the creature's eyes.

Ignoring the pair, Seth went straight over to Aksel. The little cleric had resumed his solid form, though he looked pretty roughed up.

"You doing okay there?" Seth asked with genuine concern.

"I've been better," Aksel admitted. He held up the glowing staff in his hands. "Still, we got what we came for."

The little cleric abruptly winced, dropping his arms and nearly the staff as well. Seth was immediately at his side.

"Why don't we worry about that after you heal," Seth admonished.

Holding his friend by the arm, Seth helped him into a seated position with his back up against the casket. Alys leapt down from the top of the sarcophagus and the two of them took to healing the little cleric.

As Xellos touched down nearby, his keen ears picked up Lily's whisper to Jack. "That's one tough little gnome."

Jack responded with a subtle nod. "Yeah. This is not going to be as easy as we thought."

Andrella nearly jumped for joy when the last guardian fell. They had won and now possessed the staff—the thing needed to save Penwick from Jinkolothos' wrath. The battle had not been without cost, however. Aksel had taken a brutal beating. Furthermore, Glo now looked more haggard than ever.

Andrella had warned her mentor against using spells. Though, if she were being honest, they wouldn't have succeeded without his help. On a brighter note, Lloyd had not been hurt. Between the spells she had cast on him and his own "Stealle Skin" ability, he managed to shrug off the worst of the guardian's blows.

That left them with one more issue to address before satisfying the dracolich's request. They needed to free the demons as promised. The question now was how to go about that. It's not like the Staff of Law came with an instruction manual.

While Seth and Alys helped to heal Aksel, Andrella gathered with the others to discuss their next steps. Jack and Lily sauntered over to them, the latter wearing a smug expression. "You're going about it totally wrong you know."

Andrella met the demoness' dark-eyed gaze warily. "What do you mean?"

Lily did not immediately answer, apparently relishing the idea of keeping them in suspense. She paused to brush back a lock of hair before responding, "We're not technically bound by the staff."

Andrella felt her jaw go slack. If it wasn't the staff binding the demons, then what else could it be? She glanced at Glo, but her mentor appeared lost in thought.

A wicked laugh escaped Lily's lips. She seemed to truly enjoy playing these games with them—even at her own expense.

Lloyd had lost all patience at this point. He railed at the demoness, "Are you going to tell us what is, or do you like being stuck down here?"

Lily folded her thin arms across her chest and regarded him with a lofty stare. "Oh my, aren't we testy."

His face reddening, Lloyd took a step towards the demoness, but stopped as Andrella grabbed him by the arm. Meeting her gaze, the anger in his eyes swiftly dissipated. Lloyd squared his shoulders and took a step back, his expression now stony.

With Lloyd calmed down, Andrella returned her attention to the smug little demoness. "What is binding you here then?"

Still wearing that insufferable expression, Lily leaned back on one leg and tapped a finger to her chin. "My, my, isn't it obvious? Do you really think the god of light would only have one artifact on him?"

"The Crucible of Souls," Glo exclaimed as if having an epiphany.

Lloyd slapped his forehead, his face lit up with recognition. "Oh, right. That's one of the holy relics my sister said Phobas carried on him."

"At least someone in your family has brains," Lily taunted him further.

Thankfully, Lloyd chose to ignore her this time. Just to be sure though, Andrella motioned for him to accompany her. "Give me a boost, would you? I'd like to see what else is in that sarcophagus."

Once inside, Andrella cast a rudimentary identification spell. In response, Phobas' boots, gloves, helm, and pendant all began to glow from the mana surrounding them. Andrella felt a momentary twinge at raiding the god's tomb further, but immediately pushed the guilt back down. If they were to save Penwick, it couldn't be helped.

Realizing there was no way she could retrieve all these giant-sized items herself, she called out to Lloyd, "Could you give me a hand in here?"

"Sure," came his immediate response. A few seconds later, the young man leapt into the coffin next to her.

Not long thereafter, they stood outside with all the god's paraphernalia spread out before them—all except for the pendant. Andrella had already handed that off to Glo. The elven wizard spun the pendant around in his hands, scrutinizing it from all angles.

"Do you have any idea how it works?" Andrella asked in a hushed voice.

Glo shook his head, not taking his eyes off the pendant in his hands. "I'm not sure just quite yet. I'll need to study it a bit further."

While Glo went off on his own to further examine the pendant, Lloyd stooped down to examine the rest of the items spread out before them. "Do you have any idea what these things do?"

The corners of Andrella's eyes crinkled as she rolled up her sleeves and squatted next to him. "Let's find out, shall we."

Knitting her brow, the young wizardess touched each item in turn. First, she placed a hand on the soft brown leather boots. In her mind's eyes she saw herself pulling them on. Standing, Andrella took a step forward and the world abruptly shifted around her. She found herself surrounded by a sea of fire and flaming volcanoes. Wincing from the imagined heat she backed up a step and the world shifted once again.

Andrella now found herself in a frozen tundra. Before any imaginary shivers set in she stepped forth and the world changed yet again. This time she was surrounded by total darkness. Gulping, she took another tentative step. The world shifted one last time and she found herself back in Phobas' tomb.

"Stride of the Gods," Andrella repeated, the words entering her mind as the vision faded.

Next, she went over to the horned helm. Closing her eyes, she envisioned herself placing it on her head. Everything around her grew clearer as its single large purple gem shone brightly upon her brow. When she looked at Jack and Lily, however, their childish frames were overshadowed by huge demonic forms.

Andrella involuntarily shuddered. *Is that what they truly look like?*

"Helm of True Sight," she said aloud as the words popped into her head.

Lastly, Andrella placed a hand on the soft white leather gloves. Shutting her eyes, she saw herself pulling on the left one first. She nearly jumped out of her skin as her body morphed into a bolt of lightning. That bolt lashed out across a field of evil creatures, striking down each one as if with the wrath of the gods.

As the vision faded, Andrella paused to catch her breath. As she did so, the name of the magical handwear appeared in her mind.

"The Hand of Retribution," she intoned aloud with firm conviction.

Moving her hand to the other glove, Andrella pulled it on in her mind's eye. All at once, a strange power coursed through her body. Her muscles bulged with incredible strength. A huge scale appeared before her carrying a mountain in either pan. She reached out and lifted the scale with almost no effort, watching with keen exhilaration as the twin peaks balanced against each other.

Still feeling flush from the incredible rush of power, she took a moment to reflect on the true name of this last incredible item.

"The Hand of Justice," she repeated as it came to her.

A fire burned in Lloyd's eyes as they fixated on those gloves. "Not that I want to raid the tomb of a god, but considering what we are up against, we could use all the help we can get." He sounded more like he was trying to convince himself more than anyone else.

Jack held a hand to his chin as he scrutinized Lloyd more closely than Andrella cared for. "I like the way you think," the little demon finally said.

Andrella wanted to warn Lloyd, but Seth and Alys rejoined them at that point. Back behind them she could see Aksel still sitting with his back up against the sarcophagus. The little gnome appeared to be fully healed, but Andrella imagined he was still in the process of recovering.

Alys placed a hand on Lloyd's shoulder. "All joking aside, I don't believe the gods would mind us putting these things to use—for a righteous cause," she finished with a pointed stare at Jack.

"Yeah, yeah," Seth scoffed as he pushed past Alys and Lloyd, "let me see those gloves."

The halfling picked up the left glove and shoved his arm as far into it as he could. It was so large on his diminutive frame that it fit all the way up to his shoulder. Before their eyes, the glove then shrank to fit perfectly on Seth's hand.

The halfling pressed his lips together into an appreciative smile. "Nice fit."

Without warning, sparks appeared all over his body. Those sparks turned into arcs of electricity that danced across his small frame.

All of a sudden, Seth took off at an incredible speed. In mere seconds he made one, two, three laps around the chamber.

Andrella's neck hurt from trying to follow him with her eyes. As she reached back to rub it, Seth finally came to halt.

"That…was…fun!" the halfling exclaimed in between trying to catch his breath.

"It looked like it," Lloyd answered, eyeing the glove on the halfling's hand ruefully.

The corner of Seth's mouth lifted ever so slightly as he picked up the second glove and hurled it at the wistful young man's feet. "Here, take it."

Deep creases formed across Lloyd's brow as he hungrily eyed the glove in front of him. "Are you sure you only want the one?"

"Yeah, I'm sure." Seth lifted the glove on his hand and twirled it back and forth in front of him. "Actually, it's kind of stylish."

Lloyd's face lit up like a little kid getting a present at Festivus. He picked up the glove and pulled it onto his right arm. Just like what had happened with Seth, the glove immediately resized to fit his hand.

A deep red glow enveloped Lloyd's arms and upper torso, then swiftly disappeared. The young man's eyes went wide as he lifted his arms and flexed.

After her prior vision, Andrella had an inkling of what Lloyd was feeling. Lloyd met her gaze with a childlike grin. "I feel like I could move a mountain."

Andrella leaned in close and whispered in his ear, "I know the feeling."

His grin widened as he swept his gaze around the chamber until it finally settled on the sarcophagus. "Watch this."

The young man strutted over to the casket and grabbed the lid. Without so much as a grunt, he easily moved it back into place.

Aksel had gotten up when Lloyd began to move the lid. He now stood behind the young man looking over his handiwork. "Now that's impressive."

In the meantime, Xellos had knelt down to examine the boots. "What did you call these again?"

Andrella strode over to stand next to him as she answered, "Stride of the Gods."

Alys knelt beside the archer and rubbed her hand across one of the boots. "I've read about these before. I believe you can also use them to teleport somewhere within the same world."

"That's interesting," Xellos said softly.

Though he tried to downplay it, Andrella caught the hint of excitement in his voice. Knowing of the young man's plight, she imagined such boots would come in handy. He could go anywhere in the world instantaneously to search for Arcarion seeds.

"Though I daresay they might take a full day to recharge," Alys cautioned, "depending on how far you go, that is."

Based on what Andrella knew of magic, Alys' statement made sense. Upon invocation, magic items spent the mana stored within them. Afterwards it would take a while for the mana around it to seep back into the object, thus "recharging" it.

Xellos watched Alys mindfully as she continued to stroke the soft leather boot. "Did you want them?" he asked her quietly.

Alys pulled her hand back and stared at the soft-spoken archer. She placed that same hand on her chest, her expression incredulous. "What, me? No," she replied with a dramatic flourish. "Anyway, they would clash with my outfit," she added.

Though her performance was perhaps just a bit too theatrical, Alys' heart was definitely in the right place. Andrella gave her a knowing smile as the timid young archer took the boots and pulled them on. Just like the gloves, they resized to fit him perfectly.

That left Phobas' helm. Andrella pointed it out to Alys. "I don't suppose you'd be interested in this?"

Alys chuckled softly. "I'm not sure I could even lift it."

"I could lift it for you," Lloyd offered.

Alys gave him a warm smile. "Thanks, but the purple would definitely clash with my outfit."

"Suit yourself then," Seth snorted as he strode past them.

Stopping in front of the helm, the halfling flipped up into a handstand. He then walked on his hands over the headpiece and slowly lowered himself to the ground. As soon as his head touched the helm, it shrank to fit over his brow.

Andrella stared at the halfling in wonder while Alys clapped with glee. "That was quite clever."

Lloyd shared a broad grin with the two of them. "Leave it to Seth."

11
CRUCIBLE OF SOULS

Two dark "seeds" shot out of that hole, swirling about each other as they raced from the crucible.

Before taking up the staff from Phobas, Aksel had prayed to his own goddess for a means to protect himself from the guardians' wrath. In a totally uncharacteristic move, she had provided him with a new spell without so much as a single riddle. That had caught Aksel completely by surprise. The Soldenar prided herself on the devoutness and intellectual prowess of her followers. In order to become her servant, one needed to prove themselves worthy in both areas.

Perhaps his recent accomplishments had earned Aksel a pass this time, or maybe she truly believed in the importance of his cause. Still, he somehow doubted she would continue her generosity without testing him again. In truth, though, the spell had not come without a cost. Despite being fully healed, he still ached all over. Yet, he had to push that pain aside. There were far more pressing matters at hand, not the least of fulfilling their end of the bargain with these demons.

Aksel had known the contract to be foolhardy and would not even have considered it under other circumstances. Sadly, they didn't know enough about how the demons had been bound to do otherwise. Just removing the artifacts from Phobas' tomb ran the risk of accidentally freeing them. Conversely, leaving them here for someone else to find was also out of the question.

"Aksel!"

Lloyd had just finished displaying his new found strength when the gnome heard his name echo across the chamber. Glo stood at the other end of the sarcophagus, holding the Crucible of Souls in his hands. The wizard had distanced himself from the others to study the powerful artifact, but now motioned for Aksel to join him.

A wave of hope washed over the little cleric. Perhaps Glo had found the key to their dilemma. Forcing his aching body to move, Aksel strode the length of the sarcophagus to meet with his elven friend.

The wizard's eyes were alight with excitement. Between his palms sat a burnished gold circular pendant with intricately carved celestial runes traced across its entire length. An iridescent jewel sat in its center that shimmered with the colors of a setting sun.

Glo held the pendant with profound reverence, his voice hushed with awe as he spoke. "This object is infused with an incredible amount of light energy. I believe that's what fuels its ability to bind dark souls in place."

The wizard carefully held out the artifact for Aksel to take a closer look. The little cleric placed his hands over the crucible and let out a sharp breath. Glo was right. He could feel it radiating tremendous waves of positive energy.

Aksel wondered how it was even possible to infuse any object with that much power. Nonetheless, that wasn't something to dwell on at this moment.

Ripping his gaze away from the crucible, he locked eyes with Glo. "Do you have any idea how to release what's inside?"

Glo's face twisted into a rueful grimace. "Unfortunately, no. I think I'd need at least a month to begin to understand the workings of a magic of this order."

That was not at all what Aksel wanted to hear. If they could not keep their end of the bargain, he, Glo, and Lloyd would all become targets of the Inevitables.

Ignoring the shooting pains from his still recovering body, Aksel absently rubbed his chin. "Then what do you suggest we do?"

Glo threw up his hands and shrugged. "Pray?"

Again, that was not what Aksel wanted to hear. He had just asked his goddess for a boon. He'd be pushing his luck asking her for help again so soon—especially with something of this magnitude. Yet Glo was right. At this point, they had little choice.

If Aksel were to do this, however, he would need as much solitude as possible. It would also be best if he had the crucible with him. Holding out his hands, he said to Glo, "May I?"

The look of remorse on the wizard's face spoke volumes. Glo must have felt like he'd failed them all at this crucial juncture.

Aksel forced himself to smile at his friend. "Don't worry just yet. I'll see what I can do."

Taking the crucible from Glo's outstretched hands, Aksel shuffled off to the nearest edge of the sarcophagus. Seating himself down on the stone floor, he closed his eyes and focused his mind. It proved difficult with the jabbing pains that continued to plague him. Nonetheless, he persisted. After what felt like forever, he finally reached the deepest level of prayer-state.

Soldenar, Goddess of all Gnomes, I beseech you, he began his usual prayer. *Please…*

Before he could continue further, the lilting voice of his goddess interrupted him. *Yes, yes, lad, I know what it is you seek. I just have one question for ya. Are ya daft?*

Aksel mentally winced. In truth, he'd been asking himself that very same question. Refocusing his thoughts, he responded, *I don't see as we have any choice.*

For the first time ever, he heard his goddess sigh. *Lad, there's always a choice…but I suppose at this point, ya have chosen yer path.*

A long pause followed as the Soldenar fell silent. Though loathe to push her any farther, Aksel tentatively prayed once more. *So, do you think you can help us?*

Her response was immediate. *That all depends on the kind of help ya seek. Are ya wantin to free these demons or save the city?*

Aksel grimaced. Again, he had asked himself that very same thing. *I don't see how we can do one without the other,* he answered.

Ah, and therein lies the riddle, the Soldenar declared to Aksel's chagrin. *How do ya propose to solve it?*

Aksel's head began to ache. The Soldenar hadn't needed to test him this time. The predicament they'd put themselves in was more than enough of a test.

Aksel mulled over the entire situation in his mind before answering. *No matter how I look at it, I still think it safest to free the demons first, here where they're at their weakest.*

Is that really safe, though? The Soldenar asked in a tone rife with insinuation.

The question gave Aksel pause. These were not just any demons. These two were demon lords, the most powerful of their kind. It took the power of a god to bind them. Even with all their combined talents, what chance did he and his friends stand against them?

Probably not, Aksel admitted.

Ah, good, now yer using yer head, the Soldenar derided him.

Ouch, Aksel thought to himself. Perhaps he deserved that, but it still stung, nonetheless. He had discovered at a young age about the Soldenar's biting wit, but hadn't been the target of it in quite a number of years. In a sudden epiphany, it struck him why he felt so at home with Seth.

Well then, now that you see the truth of it, we can get down to business, the Soldenar declared.

Relief flooded through Aksel. If they stood any chance, it would be under the guidance of his goddess. The little cleric listened from there on as the Soldenar advised him on how to proceed.

Lloyd felt keen exhilaration at the new found strength provided to him by Phobas' glove. That stone lid he could barely budge before now moved with ease beneath his hands. If only he'd been wearing this glove earlier…

The sobering thought quickly dampened Lloyd's spirit. If he'd been strong enough to stand his ground, those guardians would never have gotten past him. It almost pained him to think of it. It was nothing short of a miracle that Aksel had not been fatally injured.

Nonetheless, Lloyd wasn't certain they'd make a difference in what lay ahead. That dracolich was far tougher than those guardians. And she had hinted that the vampire lord served a being even more powerful than she herself. If that were the case, he might need something even more powerful than these gloves.

A gentle hand brushed against his arm. Lloyd looked down to see Andrella peering up at him with a frown across her brow. "Is something the matter?"

The concern in her eyes made him melt inside. He grabbed her hand gently in his and forced himself to smile. "It's nothing," he lied. He lifted his other hand encased in Phobas' glove and made a fist with it. "I just can't wait to put this new found power to good use."

Andrella placed her other hand atop his glove, her eyes filled with quiet understanding. "I'm certain you will," she said softly.

Lloyd nearly choked as the depth of her compassion swept over him. This was exactly why he needed more power—to protect her—to protect everyone he cared about. He nearly broke down at that point and confessed to her how he felt, but before he could, Aksel rejoined them.

The little cleric posed an impressive sight with the shining Staff of Law in his hand and the shimmering Crucible of Souls now hanging on a chain around his neck. Glo stood on one side of him, the wizard looking rather tired. Seth stood on the other side warily eyeing the demon kids.

Jack immediately confronted the pair, wringing his hands together impatiently. "Have you figured out how to free us yet?"

Lily strode up to him and shoved the demon boy in the arm. "Don't get your hopes up, halfwit. This level of magic might take these rubes a while to figure out."

"Hey, watch it!" Jack protested, pushing her back.

Lily's face reddened with anger, an inhuman growl escaping her lips. She hauled off to hit Jack back, but before she could, Aksel interrupted them.

"We have, actually."

Lily paused in mid-strike and stared at the gnome with obvious disbelief.

"You have?" Both she and Jack said simultaneously.

"Yes," Aksel answered simply.

Though Aksel remained reserved, Seth seemed to revel in holding this kind of power over the demons. The halfling pointed to the floor in front of them and barked an order at the pair. "If you want this done, then the two of you sit down and be quiet."

Without another word, the pair scrambled to the floor and seated themselves cross-legged in front of the trio. Lily, however, couldn't resist sticking her tongue out at Jack before sitting still. Jack, of course, responded in kind, then also finally settled down.

"Alright then. Now don't move if you want this to work," Aksel stated firmly.

Despite his warning, Jack and Lily continued to fidget like the kids they emulated.

In the meantime, Aksel grasped the Crucible of Souls with his free hand. He then lifted the Staff of Law into the air and began to chant words in a language Lloyd had never heard before. Whatever it was, it had a beautiful, yet unearthly tone to it.

Alys, standing next to Lloyd, murmured under her breath, "I believe that's Celestial."

That made sense. An object that could bind demons would probably use the language of the gods and angels, Lloyd reasoned.

A soft light began to emanate from the gem in the center of the crucible. It swiftly intensified in brightness, bathing the entire chamber in vivid white. The light grew so bright in fact that Lloyd had to shield his eyes.

Peeking out between his fingers, Lloyd noticed a hole had appeared in the center of the crucible as if a door were opening. Two dark "seeds" shot out of that hole, swirling about each other as they raced from the crucible. They streaked through the air finally coming to rest just above each demon child.

Without warning, the seeds expanded into a pair of ghostly demonic forms. Though translucent, they emitted a sheer malevolence that made Lloyd's very skin crawl.

The ghostly figure that overshadowed Lily had tall horns sprouting from its thick mane of long black hair. A scant outfit matching that mane barely covered the important parts of the sultry pale-skinned figure. The apparition superimposed upon Jack had similar tall horns along with thick batlike wings that sprouted from its powerfully built red-hued body.

The ghostly apparitions hung there atop the children until a sucking sound filled the chamber. Lloyd watched in unabashed horror as the ghostly forms were drawn down into the bodies of Jack and Lily.

As soon as it was over, the light from the crucible faded and the chamber around them returned to normal. Even so, Lloyd could tell something had changed. First, his skin still tingled from that sense of malevolence. Furthermore, both children's eyes had turned completely black.

His throat felt dry as the duo swept their dark eyes around the chamber. Lily proceeded to yawn and stretch, the sound having a strange echo-like quality to it. When she finally spoke, it sounded as if multiple voices were speaking at once. "You know, I like it here. I think I'll make this my home plane."

An array of gasps echoed around the tomb at her incredulous declaration. *If Lily makes this her home plane, she won't have to leave once their contract expires,* Lloyd reasoned. That meant she could remain in their world to wreak havoc for all eternity.

Realizing she had to be stopped, Lloyd stepped in front of the others and drew his weapons. "Over my dead body," he declared vehemently.

Lily turned her dark gaze upon him, a smug smile on her lips. "That can be arranged," she answered his challenge, her voice practically dripping with malice.

The tension in the air grew almost palpable as Lloyd prepared for the fight of his life. Yet before either of them could make a move, Aksel's voice cut through the tension like a knife.

"That won't be necessary," he said almost too calmly.

Aksel slowly raised the staff and began to speak again in that same beautiful tongue. The crucible on his chest flared to life in response. Brilliant rays emanated out from within, bathing Lily in its pristine light.

Lily flinched at first, but then began to laugh—a cold, heartless sound that made Lloyd involuntarily shiver. "Do you really think you can bind me, little gnome? The last time it took a god."

"And so, it shall again," another voice rang out across the chamber.

A feminine voice with a strange accent, it practically resonated with power. At first Lloyd thought it belonged to Alys, but a peek at the songstress proved her to be as surprised as him.

The powerful voice joined in with Aksel's perfectly harmonizing with his chant. In response the light from the crucible exploded outward, reaching and wrapping itself around Lily's childlike form.

"No, no, not again!" Lily shrieked in terror.

Her small body swiftly expanded into the dark form they'd seen hovering over her. The demonic creature railed against the light, but to no avail. Slowly, but inexorably it was pulled towards the waiting vessel.

An inhuman cry escaped Lily's throat as she struggled in vain against the power of Aksel's goddess. It was quickly drowned out by a loud sucking sound as the creature was drawn down and into the Crucible of Souls.

What had once been Lily completely disappeared along with the light that had drawn her into the crucible. The sucking noise ended as well, punctuated with what sounded like a huge door slamming shut.

Afterwards the chamber went completely still.

By the grace of the gods, or more aptly the Soldenar, Aksel had sealed Lily back in the Crucible of Souls. Even so, that still left Jack to be dealt with.

Shifting his stance to face the remaining demon, Lloyd found a positively pale Jack. The boy looked as if he'd seen his entire life pass before him.

Realizing that all eyes were upon him, Jack swiftly recovered, his lips curling into a smirk. "I told her that was a stupid idea."

A mock sigh escaped his throat. "Ah well, her loss."

Seth folded his arms and snorted at the demon kid. "Right. Like you won't try to exploit some loophole the first chance you get."

Jack waved him off with a negligent flip of his hand. "Me? "I'm too lazy for that." He paused and stretched, a loud yawn echoing across the chamber. "In fact, I could use a good rest right now."

Lloyd remained wary as the boy turned his gaze upon him. "Say, how'd you like a better weapon than those pig stickers you're using?"

Those words caused all Lloyd's former doubts to boil back to the surface. He did feel the need for something more with which to protect his friends, but this kid was a demon and not to be trusted. Still, would it truly hurt to hear what he had to say?

Trying to get a grip on his wavering emotions, Lloyd eyed the boy warily. "What did you have in mind?"

A thin smile spread across Jack's lips. "This," he said with a snap of his fingers. A thick puff of smoke enveloped the boy. When it dissipated a few seconds later, a huge black blade hovered in his place. The color of night, the sword practically glowed with a darkness blacker than even his star metal sword.

As the blade began to fall to the ground, Lloyd instinctively reached out and grabbed it. It felt strangely warm to the touch. He was in for another surprise as he hefted it.

"Wow, this thing is super light!" he exclaimed. His brow furrowed as he examined the blade more closely. "I wonder how sharp it is?"

Spying the remains of a guardian nearby, Lloyd strode over to it. Lifting the huge blade over his head he brought it down in one swift strike. The black blade sliced right through the guardian's armor as if it weren't even there.

Duly impressed, Lloyd pulled the blade back and examined the edge for nicks or dull spots. As far as he could see, it remained just as sharp as before. Lloyd pressed his lips together and nodded to himself. *This might just be the thing I need to protect my friends.*

A light touch on his arm brought him out of his reverie. Andrella peered up at him, her brow furrowed and her eyes filled with uneasiness. When she spoke, there was a hard edge to her voice. "Lloyd, I don't think it's a good idea for you to use that thing."

While Lloyd understood her concern, he just couldn't contain his excitement. "Did you see what it did to that guardian?" Alas, his argument did little to assuage the disquiet in her eyes.

Still holding the black blade in one hand, Lloyd reached out and took her hand with his free one. Pulling her closer, he tried once more to explain how he felt. "Look, Andrella, this thing is power-ful—and right now we need powerful."

A slight grimace passed across her features, then swiftly faded. She tightened her grip on his hand and pulled him down even closer to her and wrapped her other hand around the back of his neck.

"Alright, but I still have a bad feeling about this. You better promise me not to get caught up in all that power," she told him emphatically.

It warmed his heart how much she cared about him, but Lloyd wasn't worried. He could handle this.

"I promise," he replied with all sincerity, then leaned in and kissed her.

"Alright with the lovey dovey stuff you two," Seth taunted them. "We have places to be."

"I'm afraid Seth is right," Aksel agreed. "I think it's time we head back up to the temple."

Andrella reluctantly pulled away from Lloyd and fixed Seth with a mock angry stare. "Killjoy," she said to him, turning one of his fa-vorite words against him. She then shifted her gaze toward Aksel and added, "I'll do the honors."

Alys' nerves still felt jagged. She had thought the dracolich scary, but this last near encounter with those demons set a whole new bar for purely terrifying. In truth, she'd expected one, or both, demons to try and pull something. Thankfully, Aksel had been prepared for such contingencies or they'd all be dead right now.

What truly resonated with Alys, however, was the voice of this Soldenar. It had such a wonderful timbre to it and the power behind it was beyond imagining. She promised herself to read more about this amazing and wonderful goddess when all of this adventuring was said and done.

Other than that, Alys hadn't quite decided how she felt about Lloyd's new sword. Jack was a demon and by definition not to be trusted, but it did appear to be quite the powerful blade. As long as she'd known him, Lloyd had a weak spot for such weapons. The demon probably had sensed that as well. Thus, Alys felt certain that some sort of catch would eventually materialize itself.

"*Planum porta.*"

Andrella's spell opened a glowing blue oval of swirling energy in the midst of Phobas' tomb. Alys could clearly see the grounds of the temple complex beyond.

As the others funneled through the portal, Zantillis reappeared in a puff of smoke. The tall djinn took Alys by the hand and executed a deep bow. "You still have one wish left, my good lady."

Alys felt her cheeks warm just a bit at the handsome djinn's attention, but a sudden thought made her frown. "How long have you been stuck down here?"

A puzzled expression crossed Zantillis' face. He grabbed his chin and hummed softly to himself. "Honestly, I don't know how long it's actually been. Since Phobas' body was interred here to be certain."

That meant he'd been down here at least a thousand years. A wave of compassion washed over Alys.

"That sounds awfully lonely," she responded in a hushed voice. Alys knew only too well what it felt like to be alone. She'd spent most of her childhood locked away until she met Thea and the rest of the Stealles.

"Alys, everyone else is through," Andrella interrupted them. "We need to go."

"Okay, just one sec." Alys held up a finger towards the lady wizard before shifting her gaze back to Zantillis. "Tell me, can I use my one last wish to set you free."

The djinn's eyes went wide with astonishment, his voice cracking as he responded. "Y—you would do that for me?"

"Yes," Alys murmured as she thought it over. "I believe I would."

"Well then, yes," Zantillis answered, still appearing shocked at this unexpected turn.

Her mind made up, Alys set her jaw. Folding her arms in front of her, she made her wish in a firm voice. "I wish for you to be free."

Strong magic filled the air in response to her wish. A brilliant golden glow enveloped the tall djinn transforming him before their very eyes. When it faded, Zantillis had shrunk down to normal size and his bluish skin had changed to a deep tan.

Taking a step forward, Zantillis once again took her hand, and knelt down before her. Softly kissing the back of it, he whispered, "Lady Alys, I am forever in your debt."

Alys felt her cheeks grow hot this time. The former djinn was even more handsome now than before. It took her a moment to find her voice, and when she did, her throat felt thick. "No—no one should be alone."

"You can use our portal, if you wish," Andrella interjected once again.

Zantillis rose to his feet and gave Andrella a grateful nod. "Thank you, but that won't be necessary. I still have some magic of my own."

Letting go of Alys' hand, he took a step back. "Until we meet again," he told her in a gentle voice, then snapped his fingers and disappeared in a puff of smoke.

Alys stood there mesmerized until the last vestiges of smoke had disappeared. *If she hadn't already been in love with Pallas...*

"That's a nice thing you did," Andrella interrupted her thought.

Alys whirled towards the lady wizard and saw the knowing smile on her face. Straightening her outfit to cover her embarrassment, she stated a bit more firmly than she intended, "As I said, no one deserves to be alone."

Seeing right through her, Andrella chuckled, but had the good grace to let the subject drop. The lady wizard then offered her an arm and the two of them strode together through the portal.

12
BATS IN THE BELFRY

The huge bat-like shadows were like something out of her worst nightmares.

Glo held major reservations concerning the deal they'd made with the demons. The contract had been risky at best as evidenced by Lily's attempt to circumvent it. Considering all that lay at risk though, he hadn't seen any other way. Even so, he couldn't stop himself from imagining what his father would say about the matter. He could just hear the old man's scathing critique now:

Thought you were clever, didn't you. Well, you and your so-called friends have really done it this time. A demon lord of all things! Do you really think that paltry contract will keep it at bay? It's already got your gullible friend wrapped around its finger with that stupid sword. You and your little gnome friend better watch your backs. Bah! I thought I taught you better than that.

Glo mentally cringed at the blistering analysis. Though a construct of his own mind, he couldn't quite shake the feeling of dread that came along with it. The old man was right—they had been foolish. They'd allowed desperation to cloud their better judgement. The young elf resolved then and there to keep a close eye on Lloyd and that demon sword. There was no telling what kind of influence it might exert on their far too trusting friend.

Despite Glo's misgivings, they had managed to retrieve the staff from Phobas' tomb. At the very least, that should save Penwick from the dracolich's wrath. Yet, as they stepped out of the portal, things appeared far from quiet. Guards and clergy folk rushed around the temple grounds with an urgency bordering on panic.

Deep creases formed across Lloyd's usually unfurrowed brow. "Are we too late?"

Alys waylaid one of the priests as he hurried by. "What's going on, father?"

The priest paused, his eyes wild as they swept over the group that had just emerged from the portal. "Not long after daybreak, dark creatures started to pour from that castle hanging above the graveyard."

Glo wrestled with mixed emotions at the dire tidings. Though not the best of news, at least the city hadn't suffered an attack from the dracolich.

Aksel placed a reassuring hand on his fellow cleric's arm. "Where's the High Priestess?"

The man's eyes darted about before settling on a specific direction. He pointed back along the path he had just come. "She's at the front gate preparing for an imminent attack."

Lloyd grabbed the priest by the other arm. "What about Lara Stealle?" The man winced under Lloyd's firm grasp. Not realizing his newfound strength, he'd unintentionally hurt the man. Lloyd swiftly let loose his grip, a sheepish smile crossing his face. "Sorry."

The priest gingerly rubbed his arm as he answered. "That's alright, my son. There were reports of a great winged creature in the vicinity of Fortress Hightower. She teleported over there to investigate."

Lloyd gave the man a grateful nod, then grasped the end of his cloak. "I'm heading there too then," he told the others before speaking the word that invoked its magic. *"Fugere."*

"I'll go with you," Glo practically blurted out as his friend prepared to launch himself skyward. If the creature the priest mentioned was what he assumed it to be, then Lloyd would be in for the fight of his life. Though Glo felt weary to the bone, he couldn't just let his friend face that terror on his own.

Before they could say another word, Andrella grasped Glo by the arm. "We'll go with you," she amended his statement placing emphasis on that first word. Her expression hard, she glared at the two of them as if daring either to contradict her.

Glo and Lloyd exchanged a knowing glance. They had learned better than to argue with her when she got like this. Lloyd slowly rose up into the air, motioning for the two of them to follow. "Well hurry up then."

Glo began tracing the symbol for the fly spell when Andrella swatted his hand away. "I'll do it," she told him bluntly before proceeding herself.

Glo arched an eyebrow at the feisty young lady. She'd really been mother-henning him as of late. Though thoughtful to a certain degree, it had become quite annoying.

"I'm not a child," he grumbled at her as she cast the spell on the both of them.

"Then stop acting like one," she countered loftily as they rose into the air.

Glo was all too familiar with that tone. His mother used it whenever his father was being especially pig-headed. The thought of acting like his old man quickly sobered the young elf. He clamped his mouth shut and let it go as the three of them soared up and out across the city.

The sounds of battle reached them from the streets below, but Lloyd paid them little heed. Though uncharacteristic of his gallant friend, Glo intrinsically understood his urgency to reach the fortress. He would have done the same thing if it had been his mother in peril.

It didn't take too long before they drew in sight of the great stone fortress. Easily a quarter mile in length, a massive grey tower rose from the center of the huge structure. Taller than the city's outer walls, the tower stood as the cornerstone of Penwick's northern defenses.

As they drew closer, Glo's keen eyes spotted a pair of dark-winged creatures circling the tower. Though somewhat indistinct, they looked like two giant shadowy bats.

A number of figures stood at the very top of the great tower. A bolt of lightning flashed up from one of them causing the shadowy creatures to disperse. As the nearer creature swung about it abruptly veered off in their direction.

"What are those things?" Andrella hissed as the shadowy form rushed to meet them.

"A Nightwing," Glo responded, not quite succeeding at keeping the dread out of his voice. It was just as he feared. These were a type of Nightshade, a creature of pure darkness that could drain the life from you as easily as any vampire. They needed to deal with these things fast, before they had the chance to strike.

Before Andrella could stop him, Glo traced a spell through the air and let loose the most destructive force he could currently muster. *"Pessulum Electrica."*

In response to his words, a spark appeared at the very tip of his fingers. It hung there for a fleeting moment, then erupted into a bolt of lightning that arced across the sky ahead. In the blink of an eye, the bolt struck the dark shadow speeding towards them.

Thunder echoed across the sky as the nightwing came to a screeching halt. Arcs of electricity danced across its dark frame as the creature shuddered from the fierce attack.

Unfortunately, the effect lasted for far less time than Glo had hoped. Not a second later, the Nightwing stopped trembling and retaliated with a spell of its own. In response to its raised claw, a monstrous dark hand appeared in the air before him.

Paralyzed with fear, Glo couldn't move a muscle as a cruel-looking finger reached out and touched his chest. The pain that followed was nothing less than excruciating. It wracked his body, his muscles jerking in uncontrolled spasms of agony.

In his weakened state, Glo could barely mount a defense. The world around him started to spin and everything went black.

Andrella thought of herself as battle-hardened after her experiences in Ravenford and thereafter. From vampires to wraiths to banshees, she'd faced a whole assortment of undead. She stood with her friends against the necromancer Empress as well as the fearsome dracolich, Jinkolothos. She hadn't even balked at the horrific forms of the two demon lords. Yet, these huge bat-like shadows were like something out of her worst nightmares.

Cloaked in an eerie shadow of darkness, it was impossible to see their true form. Andrella sensed it was more than that though. Much like a dragon, she believed these creatures exuded a palpable aura of fear. Perhaps that's why both she and Lloyd froze as Glo was brutally knocked from the sky.

Though Andrella had never seen it cast before she immediately recognized that spell—it was called the *Finger of Death*. As deadly as the name implied, it could easily kill an unsuspecting target.

"Glo!" Both she and Lloyd cried as their elven friend fell away towards the ground below.

Jolted from her momentary paralysis, Andrella acted on pure instinct. Tracing a quick symbol through the air she practically spat the words, *"Pluma Ruina."*

Leaping from her fingertips the magic raced downwards and swiftly encircled her plummeting mentor. Glo's descent immediately slowed to mimic the speed of a falling feather.

At the same time Lloyd spurred into action. He disappeared from the skies only to reappear in a flash behind the nightmarish creature. Flames burst from the great black blade as he mercilessly slashed at the great shadow.

An unearthly scream erupted from the darkness as the blade bit into the creature's concealed hide. Yet, instead of swiping back or trying to escape, the nightwing once again lifted its claw.

A portal opened up just behind Lloyd revealing a place of total darkness. Yet this was no mere transport spell. Black tendrils shot from the rift and wrapped themselves around the unprepared warrior.

Lloyd struggled mightily against them, but to no avail. Despite his best efforts, he was inexorably drawn back towards the dark portal.

"Lloyd!" Andrella screamed as the cold reality of the enemy's plan dawned upon her. The creature was trying to send him into the plane of shadows. If it succeeded, he might be lost forever in endless darkness.

An unabiding anger welled up from somewhere deep inside of her. She was not about to let that happen, not as long as she could still draw breath. That unfettered rage coursed through Andrella's body as she traced the most potent spell she knew.

"Pessulum Electrica."

The words had barely left her lips as the bolt leapt from her fingertips. Lightning flashed across the sky striking the dark shadow where it hung in mid-air. Thunder echoed loud in her ears as electricity danced over the bat-shaped shadow.

Behind it, the portal that held Lloyd began to waver. Seeing his chance, the young warrior heaved against his bonds. The tendrils stretched farther and farther until they suddenly snapped. Its grip broken, the dark portal and its tendrils burst into sparks that swiftly disappeared.

"Take that!" Andrella cried out in triumph. Her exuberance was short-lived, however.

The nightwing swiftly shrugged off the effects of her spell. Once again, a dark claw emerged from inside the shadow, this time pointed directly at her.

Andrella braced herself. She recognized the spell the creature now drew in the air. It was the same one that had felled her mentor. Unfortunately for the nightwing, it had made one critical error in judgement. In retaliating against her, it had forgotten about Lloyd.

The young spiritblade now rushed the shadow. Just as it was about to let loose its spell, Lloyd flashed out of existence. A moment later he reappeared in front of it, his momentum carrying him directly beneath the unsuspecting creature.

Spinning about in mid-air he drew his black blade along the length of the shadow's belly. The blade sliced through it like some kind of giant knife through butter.

An unearthly scream shattered the heavens as the shadow burst into dozens of black sparks. Strangely, instead of fading like the dark portal, those sparks seemed to be drawn to the black blade.

Andrella cocked her head to one side, puzzled as to what she had just witnessed. *Did the blade just absorb the essence of the nightwing?*

Her confusion swiftly faded as Lloyd came rushing over to her. He gently grasped the sides of her face and met her gaze with those soulful steel blue eyes. "Are you alright?"

Andrella nearly melted when he looked at her like that. He was so damn handsome it almost hurt. Still, this was not the time for those kinds of thoughts.

"I'm fine," she told him, "but poor Glo isn't."

They peered down in unison to see the elf's body lying on the cobblestones of the street just below. Thankfully there were no un-dead in sight, but Glo's body remained there unmoving.

Andrella went cold inside as she realized he might very well be dead this time. Before either of them could move a muscle, another crash of thunder rolled across the sky.

Over at the tower, the other nightwing continued to strafe the people at its top. Lara stood there like a storm goddess out of the Ralnai fending the dark creature off. Furthermore, she'd now been joined by a warrior on a flying steed.

Andrella paused to marvel at the sight. She had never seen a live Pegasus before, let alone a Pegasus knight. Yet, even with the flying knight's aid, they still had not been able to vanquish the shadow.

Lloyd peered between the tower and the ground, his fists clenched as he cried out in anguish. "What do we do? We can't just leave Glo there, but my mom needs our help."

Andrella's heart went out to the tortured young man. It was truly unfair to make him pick between his mother and his friend. If Glo was even somewhat conscious, she could've helped get him to safety, but as it stood there was no way she could lift him

Not knowing what else to do, Andrella said a silent prayer to Arenor.

Dear God of Light, Please shine your guidance upon us in this darkest of hours.

As if in answer to her prayer, a solitary figure appeared in the sky coming from the direction of the temple. As it drew closer, Andrella recognized the figure. It was Xellos!

Andrella breathed a quick sigh as the archer closed in on them. With renewed hope, she turned to Lloyd. "You go down and get Glo. While you bring him back to the temple, Xellos and I will go help your mom."

It appeared for a moment as if he were going to protest, but then Lloyd merely nodded. "Alright, but please hurry."

Drawing her to him, he gave her a quick kiss, then launched himself downwards towards their unmoving friend.

Andrella and Xellos sped through the air as the battle waged on over Fortress Hightower. Though they were actually moving quite fast, it wasn't fast enough for Andrella.

Come on, she berated herself, her fingers itching to draw in range of a spell.

Thankfully Xellos had no such limitations. They had come within maybe two hundred yards of the battle when the archer let loose with a lightning-fast volley of arrows. Despite the great distance, each arrow struck home disappearing into the shadows surrounding its target.

"Yes!" Andrella cheered him on, ecstatic that at least one of them could make a difference.

Not two seconds later, Lara fired off another lightning bolt. Taking advantage of the enemy's momentary paralysis, the Pegasus knight swooped in and slashed her gleaming blade across the creature's shuddering torso.

Xellos followed her attack up with another triple volley. Much as its companion, the shadow let out an unearthly scream before bursting into a multitude of black sparks. Those sparks quickly drifted away, scattered by the winds that whipped around the top of the tower.

Andrella gave the archer a grateful smile. "Thank you, Xellos."

She could just see the hint of a shy smile beneath the archer's white cloth hood. "At least I got some target practice out of it."

Andrella hadn't quite figured him out as of yet. While deadly in battle, outside of it Xellos rarely interacted with any of them. Even when he did, his words were few. Most of the time he wore that hood making it hard to read his facial expressions. Even so, he'd proven to be a valiant ally time and again.

Landing atop Fortress Hightower, they found a nearly exhausted Lara Stealle. Andrella went over to her future mother-in-law and helped her to a seat along the parapets.

"Are you alright?" she asked as Lara sat down.

"I've been—better," Lara responded, her wry smile in stark contrast to the dark circles beneath her eyes. "Where's Lloyd?"

Andrella briefly explained what had happened to Glo.

Lara grasped her by the hands, her expression one of keen sympathy. "I'm sure he'll be alright, dear. Sirus is one of the finest healers this side of Lanfor—and your friend Aksel is quite adept as well."

Andrella squeezed her hands gratefully in return. "Thank you, Lady Stealle." She hesitated as Lara fixed her with a hurt look. "I mean, mom," she quickly amended.

Though still tired, Lara's countenance brightened markedly. "You're welcome, my dear."

Andrella swept her gaze around the tower. "Where's Kratos?"

"Still out trying to hold off the enemy," a gentleman in a Penwick uniform answered her query.

A tall muscular man with chiseled features strode up to meet them. Aside from his dark hair speckled white at the temples, he was the spitting image of Lord Lagerie Hightower.

Andrella's eyes crinkled as she rose to meet the man. "Lord Hightower?"

A friendly laugh escaped the man's lips. "You must have met my father." He took her hand and bowed. "Lagrange Hightower, at your service."

That makes far more sense, Andrella thought wryly as she curtsied in turn. "Andrella Avernos, at yours as well."

Lagrange's eyes widened ever so slightly at her introduction. "Ah, the Lady Andrella. I'd heard that you recently arrived in town."

He shifted his gaze towards Lara, a smile curving his thick black mustache upwards. "Wherever have you been hiding her?"

Lara fixed him with an irritated stare. "Is this really the time for pleasantries, Lagrange?"

The middle-aged lord's grin swiftly faded. "No, I suppose not." Returning his gaze to Andrella, he went on. "To better answer your question, young lady, a large crowd of undead began spilling out of the graveyard a few hours ago. Kratos took a contingent of spirit-blades and went to see if they could hold them off."

"And there's been no word of him since?" Andrella pressed.

"Unfortunately, no," Lara answered with a heavy sigh.

Andrella could see the worry in her eyes. Between that and all the spellcasting she had done, no wonder the woman was tired. It abruptly struck her that Lara was the only mage atop the tower. She found that quite strange considering the number of wizards she'd seen at the magic school.

"Pardon my asking, but where are the rest of your students?"

A wan expression spread across Lara's face. "I sent the novices away to their home towns. They wouldn't be much help anyway," she continued with a dismissive gesture.

Though Andrella could understand her motivations, it still didn't completely answer the question. She leaned in closer. "What about the rest of them?"

A flicker of annoyance passed through the mage's eyes. It was also reflected in her tone as she spoke. "The rest are busy protecting Avernos Keep."

Andrella sat back and raised both eyebrows. "All of them?"

"At the Baron's specific request." Lara nodded, no longer even trying to hide her irritation.

"That sounds just like Caverinus," Lagrange agreed, "putting his own safety above everyone else."

Andrella was livid. She had been raised on the tenets of *noblesse oblige*, that the obligations of a noble took precedence over their own needs. She always thought it a Penwick concept. Her family firmly subscribed to it as did the Stealles almost to a fault.

Andrella put her hands on her hips and fixed Lara with an

incredulous stare. "So you decided to take it upon yourself to defend the fortress?"

Lara shrugged, a half-laugh escaping her lips. "I guess it's obvious where Lloyd gets his impetuousness."

Any further conversation halted as the lady knight swooped down towards the top of the tower. The Pegasus glided onto the stone roof, its magnificent white wings spread to slow their descent. The clip-clop of its equine hoofs punctuated the flying horse's graceful landing.

Once they came to a stop, the lady knight swung down out of the saddle. After taking a moment to doff her shield and pat her mount, she turned and strode in their direction.

Andrella marveled at the strength and grace of the tall warrior. Clad in a gleaming set of fullplate she nonetheless moved as if she wore a courtly gown. The armor itself looked quite familiar, each piece adorned with pale roses and intricately carved ruins. This woman was none other than a Knight of the Rose.

A brief moment of melancholy washed over Andrella. Sir Craven and Dame Alana had been Knights of the Rose and good friends. Unfortunately, both had fallen during their expedition to the Marsh Tower.

The lady knight drew up before them and brushed a lock of reddish-blonde hair from her hazel eyes. Though her countenance was quite stern, she nonetheless had the face of an angel. Her perfect nose and high cheek bones were accentuated by creamy smooth porcelain skin without evidence of the slightest blemish.

"Dame Aura Coventry at your service," the knight said with a slight bow.

Lara rose to introduce herself. "Lady Lara Stealle, High Wizard of Penwick." She motioned towards Andrella. "And this is Lady Andrella Avernos, the baron's niece and wizard in training."

Lagrange bowed in turn to the lady knight and introduced himself.

Aura responded with a curt nod to them all. "Well met."

Andrella touched a finger to her chin as she eyed the knight with unabashed curiosity. "Not that we're complaining mind you, but how exactly did you end up in Penwick?"

Aura took a deep breath as she ran her fingers through her hair. "It's a bit of a long story, actually. With Sir Nigel away, I was left in charge of the Wind Tower. When we got word of the undead outbreak, I led a contingent of knights to Twin Oaks and Three Forks."

Andrella pursed her lips together and nodded. "Yes, we heard about that from our druid friends and Lord Hightower"—she cast a quick glance at Lagrange and amended—"the other Lord Hightower, that is."

A touch of amusement passed through Dame Aura's eyes. "Funny you should mention him. He's the one who alerted us to the trouble here in Penwick."

"That sounds like father," Lagrange agreed. "Always strategizing and marshaling forces where they're most needed."

"Much needed qualities in a leader," Aura agreed with a deferential nod before going on. "As soon as we cleaned up Three Forks, I headed straight here. Unfortunately, my troops are not airborne like myself. They are probably still a day or so behind me."

Andrella let out a short sigh. "While we appreciate any help we can get, I'm not sure we have another day or so."

Aura's countenance resumed its former grim expression. "From what I've seen here, you may be right. There are definitely more of those nightwing creatures circling the castle above the graveyard."

"Hmm," Lara murmured to herself. Deep creases forming across the wizardess' brow as she absently tapped her chin. "I believe there might be another alternative. We could close the rift between the planes with the power of an artifact—if we had one." She ended her musings by leveling a penetrating stare at Andrella.

Andrella responded with a noncommittal smile, her voice dropping to a whisper. "We do have one—we found the staff."

A flicker of hope sparkled in Lara's eyes. "That's excellent news. Where is it now?"

"Aksel has it back at the temple," Andrella confided in her, "but he's still learning to use it."

Lara took a deep breath and rolled up her sleeves. "Well, then we should go and help him." Her brow furrowed once again as she raised a hand to trace a spell, but she had to halt as a yawn escaped her throat. Covering her mouth, her face reddened with embarrassment. "Oh my. Excuse me."

Andrella couldn't help but grin at her impulsive mother-in-law to be. "Beg your pardon, Lara, but I think you need to rest a bit first."

"Plus, we could use you here if more undead show up," Lagrange chimed in with a sly wink Andrella's way.

Andrella gave him a grateful look before adding, "Besides, between Glo, Aksel, and Sirus, I'm sure they can figure it out."

Lara gave them both a long stare, but then finally shrugged and sighed. "I suppose I am needed more here." She plopped herself back down and fixed Andrella with a pointed stare. "I just hope you're right about the rest, my dear."

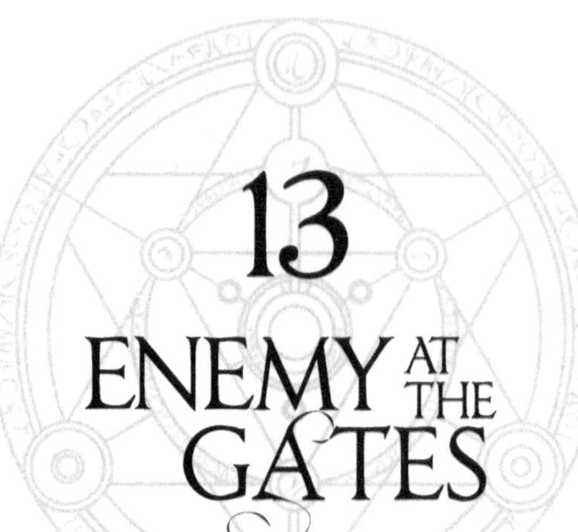

13
ENEMY AT THE GATES

The sonic forces slammed into each other sending an earsplitting cacophony of sound in all directions.

Lloyd struggled with mixed emotions as he flew Glo back towards the temple. On the one hand he was glad to have found his friend alive. On the other, he felt frustrated that he'd been unable to protect him. Even with his newfound sword and glove it had made little difference.

I need to be even stronger, the young man silently berated himself. If only he could have stopped that thing from attacking Glo in the first place, the three of them would now be at the tower helping his mother.

Lloyd's thoughts shifted to Lara and Andrella, the two women he loved the most in life. He prayed to Arenor that they would both be alright fighting that last shadow bat.

Stop that, Lloyd chided himself after a moment's reflection. *Your mom is the most powerful wizard on the east coast of Thac and Andrella has proven herself time and again. Plus, they have Xellos and that Pegasus knight with them.*

"That shadow creature doesn't stand a chance," he told himself aloud. Despite his vehement declaration, he couldn't quite stop the gnawing feeling in the pit of his stomach.

The temple grounds opened up before him as he passed over the northern wall. As luck would have it, he found Aksel a short distance from there beside Alys and Sirus. Lloyd landed and gently placed the unconscious Glolindir on the ground before them.

"What happened this time?" Aksel exclaimed as they all rushed over to them.

Lloyd hesitated as a keen sense of guilt washed over him. Grimacing, he forced it down and described their encounter with the shadow creatures.

"Nightshades," Sirus hissed. "I should have guessed."

As Aksel and Alys stooped down to examine Glo, Sirus motioned to a nearby priest and priestess. "Please take Glolindir here back to the chamber of Arenor to heal him."

Lloyd, Aksel, and Alys all frowned in unison at the high priestess. Aksel fixed her with a pointed stare. "Why do that when we can heal him right here."

Sirus knelt down and placed her hands upon the gnome's, her expression one of heartfelt sympathy. "I am quite sure you could, but he'll heal much faster in that holiest of chambers."

Lloyd took a moment to dwell on that. He had been in that chamber himself many times over the course of his eighteen years. One could definitely feel the raw power of spirit inside, but strangely, he had never associated that with healing until now.

Alys must have experienced a similar realization, her brow raising as if having a likewise epiphany. The two of them exchanged a knowing glance before Lloyd addressed Aksel. "She's probably right, you know."

"Probably?" Sirus' tone was ripe with offense as she arched an eyebrow at him.

Lloyd's cheeks grew hot with embarrassment. One did not typically question the healing knowledge of the High Priestess of the

Temple of Arenor. Gulping, he swiftly amended his words. "I mean, of course she's right."

Sirus regarded him stonily before also addressing Aksel. "Besides, if there are nightshades about, the sooner we close that rift to the shadow plane, the better."

Alys motioned to the staff laying on the ground next to them. "Which translates to, the sooner we unlock the secrets of the staff, the better."

Sirus reached over and picked up the staff, her eyes traversing its length as she spoke. "Indeed. This artifact might be our only hope."

The three of them rose and backed away as the two clerics lifted Glo off the ground. It wasn't until they had carried him off that Lloyd realized someone was missing from their ranks.

"Where's Seth?"

"He went to check out the front gates," Alys explained. She drew closer, placing a hand on his arm as she practically waltzed around him.

"So, you killed a nightshade with that sword?" Her hand still touching his arm, she leaned in for a closer look at the great black blade now strapped to his back.

"Well, yeah," Lloyd admitted sheepishly, his hand going to the back of his neck.

Alys' sudden close proximity made him feel rather uncomfortable. Meeting her gaze, he noted the look of amusement in her eyes. She seemed to be enjoying his discomfort just a bit too much. Ever since he had known her, she seemed to love teasing him.

Without warning, a portal opened in the air a few feet from where they stood. Gently pushing Alys behind him, Lloyd fell into a defense stance, his hand grasping the hilt of the sword on his back.

A moment later, Andrella and Xellos spilled out of the magical gateway. Seeing the two of them, Lloyd breathed an audible sigh. His relief didn't last too long though as his thoughts turned to his mother and that shadow creature.

"What happened?" he couldn't help blurting as he rushed forth to greet them.

"Everything's fine," Andrella assured him as she slipped into his arms. She gave him a brief hug before continuing. "Between Xellos, your mom, and Dame Aura, we blew that thing out of the sky."

Lloyd felt the tension drain from his shoulders. Both Andrella and his mom were safe—at least for the moment. Still, one thing puzzled him. "Is that the Pegasus knight we saw?"

"Yes," Andrella affirmed as she slipped from his embrace. "She's actually the head of the Knights of the Rose in Sir Nigel's absence. Also, the younger Lord Hightower is with them."

Lloyd's brow rose in surprise. "You mean Lagrange?"

Andrella nodded. "Looks just like his father, but with less gray."

"That's great!" Lloyd exclaimed, feeling even more relieved. "He's one tough old coot—was captain of the Avenger before Pallas took over." He wavered as something nagged at the back of his mind. It only took a few seconds before it came to him.

Spinning about, he peered intently at Alys. "Wasn't he heading your dad's merchant fleet or something?"

Alys wrinkled her nose. "He was until all these undead started cropping up in town. Father said it was 'bad for business'"—she mimicked his voice—"so he called him back to town to help deal with it."

Lloyd shook his head, a wry smile forming on his lips. Leave it to Alburg Dunamal to weigh things on the welfare of business over people. Even so, Lagrange was an excellent tactician, nearly as good as his father.

The thought brought Lloyd back full circle to his own family. Andrella had made no mention of Kratos being at the fortress.

"Any sign of my dad?" he asked her.

Andrella briefly explained how Kratos went out with a group of blades to hold back the undead. She tried to sound upbeat about it, but Lloyd detected a note of worry in her voice.

"If anyone can handle themselves in this mess, it's my dad," Lloyd assured her.

"You're right," she agreed, though she didn't sound completely convinced.

Lloyd had been on the receiving end of his dad's blade too many times to think otherwise. The man was unparalleled when it came to swordplay. It would take more than an army of simple undead to bring him down. Lloyd was sure of it.

He wanted to say as much to Andrella, but she had already moved past him to address the others. "Lara says our only chance might be to use the staff to seal the rift between us and the shadow plane."

"We were just discussing the same thing," Aksel told her.

"It needs to be done carefully though," Sirus cautioned. "The staff is extremely powerful. If used incorrectly we could make things worse."

"They're already worse!" Seth's voice echoed across the temple grounds. They all turned to see the halfling running towards them from the main gate.

"There's a group of undead outside with some heavy hitters. The gate ain't going to hold much longer."

Alys couldn't believe she had the opportunity to work with Sirus and Aksel. Though both were far more experienced with magic, nonetheless she was determined to prove herself. After all, she had studied at the Bardic College in Lukescros and knew Celestial, the language of the runes on the staff. Having Glolindir's notes didn't hurt either. By some technique not quite clear to Alys, the runes represented multiple layers of spells, the most powerful beyond Aksel and even Sirus.

As one might expect, most of those spells centered around what was considered lawful, or order based, magic. That type of magic would be most effective against creatures like demons who thrived on chaos. The only order to a demonic society was survival of the fittest, where the strongest, or the most devious, rose to the top. Undead, on the other hand, did adhere to an actual code. The lesser creatures faithfully followed their masters, forming a warped society of sorts.

Against such enemies the power of the staff would seem useless, though Jinkolothos did appear to be deterred by its presence. Alys wondered what made the dracolich different in that respect from other undead. Perhaps more study into undead culture would be required to understand. Either way, with a group of undead currently at the gates, they'd have to take them on the old-fashioned way for now.

"Don't worry, we'll take care of them," Lloyd said, once again grabbing the edge of his cloak.

After all these years she thought he had matured a bit, but something had changed since the near death of Seth and Glolindir. More and more he seemed to be falling back into his old reckless ways. It was almost as if he felt he had something to prove.

Alys nearly said something at that point, but Andrella beat her to it. "Lloyd, stop!"

Poised to take off, the young warrior halted to stare at her.

"Let's be smart about this," she told him in a matter-of-fact tone.

Seth exhaled an irreverent snort. "You want Lloyd to use his head?"

Alys couldn't help chuckling at the savage remark. "There's a first time for everything," she pointed out with a dimpled smile.

"Ouch," Lloyd winced, his face visibly reddening. "Am I really that bad?"

"Yes," Seth and Alys replied in unison.

"Sorry," Lloyd mumbled. His gaze dropped to the ground and his hand went to the back of his neck.

He looked so miserable that it made Alys regret poking fun at him. It was like kicking a puppy.

Andrella, on the other hand, was far more diplomatic than either of them. "I was merely going to suggest that I open a portal out in the street a short distance from the gate…"

"…so, we can take them by surprise," Lloyd finished for her, his eyes raising and his face brightening.

"Exactly," she responded warmly.

Alys marveled at the way she handled him. Though she herself had mastered the art of flirtation, Andrella appeared far more adept at actual relationships. Maybe she could learn a thing or two from her.

"That's an excellent strategy," Aksel agreed.

As Andrella opened her portal, Sirus placed a hand on Aksel's shoulder. "Perhaps you should stay here to study the staff. I can send one of the temple clerics with your friends."

If Alys had learned anything at all about Aksel these last few days, it was that he valued his friends over all else. Sure enough, he turned down Sirus' offer.

"Here," he said, holding the staff out to her. "You can keep studying it while I'm gone."

Sirus sighed, but did not push the point further. "Very well," she responded, taking the staff from his hands.

Alys' world was shattered as she stepped from the portal. It looked like a warzone out here. The beautiful, purple-flowered trees that had once lined the temple boulevard all now lay felled upon the ground. Every window and door in the buildings across the street had been smashed. An acrid odor accompanied the smoke that rose above the city to the north. Similar plumes could be seen across the river to the west and out towards the bay to the east.

Butterflies fluttered through Alys' stomach at the sight. Her home sat on a small isle at the mouth where the river met the bay.

Father! An image flashed through her mind of him in their house surrounded by a wall of turbulent flames. For a moment she almost panicked, but then caught herself. Alburg was far too smart to get caught like that. If she knew him at all, he'd be safe at the keep along with the Baron.

As for Alys, she reminded herself she still had a part to play in all this. Taking a deep breath, she once again immersed herself in the persona of the bardess in the group trying to save her city.

"There they are," Seth whispered as the last of them filtered through the portal.

A short distance down the boulevard a group of ugly creatures had gathered around the temple entrance. Alys counted mostly animated skeletons among them, but spied a pair of black knights prodding two large creatures against the gates.

"You weren't kidding when you said heavy hitters," Aksel hissed. "Those are phantom armors goading skeletal drakes."

Alys shivered, feeling as if a palpable darkness swept over them at the mention of those creatures. Phantom armors were the cold spirits of slain knights bent on death and destruction. Drakes were the smaller wingless cousins of dragons, though tough and fierce, nonetheless.

"Not to mention those wraiths and banshees," Seth murmured, pointing toward the air above the other creatures.

Alys' skin crawled as she followed his gaze. A few dark-robed shadows hovered there. The malevolent remains of beings of pure evil, those soulless shades could drain one's life with their very touch. A pair of ghostly apparitions floated next to them, their wild white hair whipping about their skeletal heads. Even worse than wraiths, those hideous phantoms could utter a wail that would kill anyone within earshot.

"We're going to have to play this smart…" Aksel began.

Anything further he had to say was drowned out by a loud crack of thunder. A lightning bolt had shot from the midst of the pack of skeletons and felled a pair of guards at the top of the parapets.

All hell broke loose after that. Seth disappeared. Xellos let loose a volley of arrows that dropped the mage who fired the bolt. Lloyd grabbed his robe and took off into the air straight at the line of undead.

"Lloyd, wait!" Andrella called after him, but to no avail.

As Alys feared, he'd regressed back into the reckless youth she'd known since childhood. Things had never ended well for him back then. She could only pray he didn't get himself killed this time.

As Lloyd hurtled towards his certain demise, a brilliant circle of white light surrounded the rest of them. Aksel had encased them within a *magic circle*. Nothing malevolent could enter the area and all inside were protected from dark influences.

With her attempt to rein Lloyd back in vain, a determined Andrella resorted to magic. Her brow furrowed with deep concentration as she spat the words, *"Murum Ignis."*

In answer, a thick veil of shimmering scarlet rose up amongst the undead in front of the gates. The resulting flames caught most of the creatures inside, but did little to deter Lloyd if that was her intent.

The single-minded warrior flew right through the wall and sliced one of the drakes clean in half with his shiny new demonic blade. Not stopping, Lloyd banked around again and barreled through the rest of the undead.

Caught off guard, the wraiths and banshees clawed at him, but Lloyd proved too agile. Expertly weaving through their midst, he shot out into the open and clear away from the temple grounds. With cries of frustration, the hovering undead took off in hot pursuit.

That's rather impressive, Alys had to admit. Perhaps that had been his plan all along, to draw off as many undead as he could away from the gates.

As she had feared though, his recklessness nearly led to his undoing. As luck would have it, most of the skeletons carried bows. About two dozen were drawn and trained in Lloyd's direction as he sped away from the temple.

Thankfully, about half that number collapsed as the heat of the firewall took its toll. The rest, however, let loose a tremendous volley, their arrows swiftly closing the gap to the retreating warrior.

Without thinking Alys stepped forth and drew in a breath, at the same time pulling mana in through her diaphragm. That energy traveled up her lungs, into her throat, and coalesced around her vocal chords. Those chords vibrated faster and faster and within moments reached a fevered pitch. Opening her mouth, she let it loose with a high-pitched cry.

The resulting force lashed out through the air creating a sonic wave in the space just behind the fleeing warrior. As the volley of arrows hit that wave, they merely bounced off as if hitting a solid wall.

Alys felt rather pleased with herself until a cone of snow and ice shot forth from the mass of skeletons. The blast was so thick that it swept around her sonic barrier and caught up to the soaring warrior.

"Look out!" Andrella screamed at the top of her lungs.

Between her warning and his own swift reflexes, Lloyd somehow managed to avoid the worst of the freezing blast. Banking at the last moment, it clipped him sending the warrior spinning through the air end over end.

Luckily, his pursuers did not fare much better. The cone of snow and ice washed over them freezing at least one of the wraiths solid. Encased in a block of ice, the dark shadow fell to the ground and shattered into a million pieces.

Uncaring about their hapless companion, the rest of the airborne undead resumed their pursuit. Alys, held her breath as they closed in on the tumbling Lloyd, but somehow at the last moment he managed to right himself and the chase began anew.

Her heart still thumping in her chest, Alys wiped a hand across her brow. *Phew, that was close.*

Though Lloyd had drawn the attention of most of the undead, the phantom armors still goaded on the remaining drake. Even from here Alys could see the gates bowing inward from the pressure. It didn't appear as if they could take much more before reaching the point of complete collapse.

Fortunately, Aksel had seen it as well. The little cleric traced a symbol through the air ending with the words, *"Columna Lucis."*

In answer to his spell, a pillar of blinding white light shot up from the ground engulfing both armors and the drake. It only lasted for a few seconds, but when it winked out. All that remained of the knights was two piles of armor.

Steam rose from the drake's hide, but somehow it had managed to withstand the divine onslaught. Bellowing in pain, the creature shambled away from the gates, spewing acid all over the place. In a fit of rage, it decimated the rest of the skeletons in its path.

In the meantime, the lead wraiths had drawn uncomfortably close to Lloyd. If one were to touch him, it would be his certain undoing.

Alys took in a breath for another sonic blast when a red-hot ray leapt from Andrella's fingertips. It was so hot, in fact, that Alys could feel the heat even from a few feet away. The beam raced across the sky and connected with one of the shadows nearest Lloyd.

Bursting into flames, the wraith stopped in mid-air and arched its back up towards the sky. An unearthly shriek erupted from beneath its hood just before the creature exploded in a burst of black smoke.

"One down," Andrella intoned grimly as she prepared yet another spell.

Before either of them could let loose their magic, Lloyd executed a brilliant maneuver. Banking and spinning in mid-air, he slashed the nearest shadow as it passed over him with his demon blade. Just like the previous wraith, it shrieked and disappeared in a burst of black smoke.

Unfortunately, his maneuver brought him within shrieking distance of the banshees. In unison the pair of hideous phantoms wailed at the flying warrior.

Alys' heart leapt into her throat. *If those hit him, he'll be dead in seconds.* Her heart still pounding, the fiery songstress unleashed a powerful scream of her own.

The force of her sonic blast slammed into the wail of the banshees resulting in an explosion of sound that brought the ghostly apparitions to a halt. Their efforts unexpectedly thwarted, the hideous phantoms then turned their unearthly gaze upon Alys.

Alys' body went cold with dread as both banshees charged, their renewed wails now directed at her. Fighting down a rising panic, she forced herself to take in another deep breath and meet their screams with one of her own.

The sonic forces slammed into each other sending an earsplitting cacophony of sound in all directions. Unfortunately, her wave began to give way to the force of the twin wails.

Alys had never been so tested in all her life. These creatures were strong, each nearly as strong as her.

Moisture welled up in the corners of her eyes as she faced certain death for the second time in her life. A vision of Pallas flashed before her eyes repeating the last words he said to her before he left.

"I won't be gone that long. Once I get back, we can take up where we left off."

Those words sparked a fire deep inside Alys' gut. She wouldn't give up that easily. She couldn't, not before she reunited with the man she so desperately loved.

Steeling her resolve, the fiery songstress drew in more mana than ever before. Bringing that energy up to her throat, she put everything she had into her cry. In answer, her sonic wave expanded to almost twice its width.

The banshees halted in their tracks. Try as they might, they couldn't close any further.

Though relieved for the moment, Alys knew she couldn't keep up this kind of power for very long. Thankfully she was not alone.

A blinding ray of white light lanced across the sky striking one of the banshees square in the chest. Its torso smoldering, the creature lost concentration and stopped wailing for the moment.

With only one wail to contend with, the force of Alys' cry pushed back the two ghostly apparitions. At the same time an angry red ball shot from Andrella's outstretched palm.

The fist-sized ball streaked across the sky as Lloyd swept past with the last wraith on his tail. The red ball reached them just as the dark shadow and ghostly apparitions came together, exploding into a giant raging sphere of flame.

When the fire dissipated a few seconds later, all three creatures were gone. Only Lloyd remained, albeit looking quite singed.

Catching her breath, Alys was surprised to see one last skeleton still standing. She watched in amazement as a volley of arrows caught the creature in its bony chest. In retaliation, the skeleton sent a bolt of lightning careening down the street directly at Xellos.

With no time to dodge, the archer took the full brunt of the bolt in his face. Falling to the ground, Xellos lay there shaking as arcs of electricity danced across his body.

Though still winded, Alys tried to draw in a breath, but suddenly halted as Seth appeared behind the skeletal mage. Glowing white knife in hand, the halfling stabbed upward catching the creature in the middle of its back.

Its bony jaw rattling, the mage flailed wildly as it tried to reach behind its back. It stopped cold when a couple of arrows embedded themselves next to the first three. Somehow Xellos had risen to his knees and managed to fire off a couple of shots.

As the last skeleton fell to the ground, the remaining drake charged at Seth.

"Look out!" Aksel cried.

Seth leapt and rolled to the side as the large creature trampled the remains of the skeletal mage. Before it could swing around and give chase, a pair of white and red rays lashed out catching the beast directly in its bony snout.

A roar of pain escaped its skeletal maw before the drake fixed its attention on Aksel and Andrella. Setting its claws into the ground, it prepared to spit a stream of acid their way.

Still trying to catch her breath, Alys prepared for the worst, but in its anger, the creature had forgotten all about Lloyd. The flying warrior dove in from behind and strafed the skeletal drake with his demon blade.

Like the previous drake, the black blade cut through the large bony torso as if it were thin air. Cloven in two, the skeletal drake collapsed with a loud rattle.

14
THRILLER

All the undead gyrated in formation as if controlled by some giant unseen puppet master.

Though cheers went up as the last drake fell, Andrella didn't quite share the other's enthusiasm. First and foremost, Xellos had sustained serious injuries. Furthermore, Lloyd had been both burned and frozen, Alys' voice had begun to crack, and she herself found it difficult to concentrate.

The budding wizardess slowly rubbed her temples to relieve the dull ache that had surfaced across her brow. With Glo still out of commission, it fell on her shoulders to hinder any large groups of enemies. On top of that, she'd had her hands full protecting Lloyd.

No wonder I feel fatigued, she thought wryly to herself.

The young man was becoming increasingly reckless, especially since he'd gotten that demonic sword. In truth, Andrella didn't trust Jack at all. She wondered if he could somehow be influencing Lloyd even in the form of a sword.

A vision flashed through her mind from earlier when Lloyd had killed that nightshade. It appeared almost as if the sword had absorbed the creature's dark essence. Still, it hadn't done anything like that during this last battle. Perhaps it was afraid to do so with everyone watching? Either way, she resolved to keep a close watch on that sword.

As soon as the battle finished, Aksel went running over to Xellos. After that last shot, the archer had passed out and now lay unmoving on the ground.

As the rest of them gathered around their fallen comrade, the temple gates flew open. A group of guards came rushing out, some forming a line around the gate while others rushed to their side.

"Quick, bring him inside," one of the approaching guards directed them.

Kneeling over Xellos, Aksel fixed the woman with a grim expression. "He needs immediate attention," he told her definitively.

A look of keen sympathy spread across the guard's face. "I understand, but it's not safe out here."

As if to confirm her statement, the moaning sounds of undead rose up all around them. Andrella swept her gaze across the surrounding streets and buildings. Though no new undead had appeared as of yet, those sounds had come from every direction except for the temple grounds.

Grimacing, Aksel rose to his feet and gave the guard a curt nod. "I suppose you're right, but be careful with him."

The guard gave him a solemn nod. "You have my word."

She directed two other guards forward who carefully lifted Xellos' body. The rest of them fell in behind as they carried the fallen archer back towards the gate.

It was then that Andrella realized Lloyd had not joined them. Peering upward, she saw the young man hovering in the air a short distance from the gate. Exposed skin shown through tears in his armor, both blackened from burns and bluish from freezing. Yet, he seemed oblivious to both, his attention fixed on scouring the empty streets around them.

"Lloyd!" she called out to him.

It took a moment before he turned his steel-blue gaze upon her. "Yes?"

Andrella had to bite her tongue to stop herself from chewing his head off. Taking a deep breath first she instead said, "Are you coming with us?"

It took a moment for her words to register before comprehension dawned upon his face. "Oh, right," he finally responded, then floated down to land by her side. Andrella grabbed him by the arm and firmly yanked him along with her as they passed through the gates.

As soon as they reached the other side, Aksel had the guards lay Xellos down. The little cleric then bent over him, his brow knit with concentration as he flooded the archer's body with divine white light.

Only a few seconds passed before Sirus rushed up to them with dire news. "I just heard from Lara. Kratos returned in pretty bad shape."

Alys gasped. "What happened to him?"

Sirus' winced as she relayed what she'd been told. "Apparently he and his team had been holding off a huge group of zombies. That group now has Fortress Hightower surrounded."

"Then we'll just need to even the odds," Lloyd said in a voice as cold as ice.

Andrella stared at him incredulously. She'd never heard him so deathly calm before. She nearly said something, but Seth interrupted her before she could speak.

"You go get your dad," the halfling told him emphatically. "I'll take care of those stupid zombies."

As if to punctuate his words, sparks appeared around Seth's body. Before anyone could stop him, he took off at blinding speed, passing through the temple gates moments before they clanged shut.

Without a word, Lloyd gazed upward and rose into the air. Though her head still ached, Andrella wasn't about to let him go on his own—especially in his strange state.

Leaping up after him, she wrapped her arms around his neck. "I'm coming with you," she declared in a tone that brooked no quarter.

Grabbing onto her, Lloyd peered down to meet her gaze. Emotion returned to his voice as he spoke. "But Andrella, you've already cast a lot of spells today. Are you sure you're alright?"

It warmed her heart to hear him sounding like himself again. It nearly made up for the fact that she was indeed growing quite tired. Still, she wasn't about to show any signs of weakness. She'd be damned if she gave him any excuse to leave her behind.

Hanging on to his neck with one hand, Andrella pulled back the other. She then cheated just a bit by subtly drawing power from her *Regalia of the Phoenix*. In response, a ball of flame burst into life in her open palm.

"I've still got plenty of juice left," she informed him with a satisfied smirk.

Lloyd's brow raised in response, but otherwise he said nothing.

"Just don't do anything reckless," Aksel called out to them, not taking his eyes off the white light he pumped into Xellos.

Alys walked up just below them, her hands on her hips and her expression stern. "You heard the man." Her expression quickly softened and her voice took on a gentler tone. "Be careful you two."

The level of caring in her voice truly touched Andrella. A warm smile graced her lips as she nodded to the fiery young woman. "We will. I promise."

Something profound passed between the two women at that moment. Growing up, Andrella had always wanted a sister. Between Thea and now Alys, she might just be gaining two.

Feeling suddenly much better, she gave Lloyd a firm nod. "Let's go."

The couple then shot up into the sky and arced onto a path towards the waiting fortress.

The streets of Penwick whooshed by as Seth raced towards Fortress Hightower. The rapid pounding of his feet against the cobblestones filled him with an incredible sense of exhilaration. He was easily moving as fast as any dragon. Had the situation not been so dire, he might have whooped with delight. Unfortunately, things were far from alright.

As if an undead invasion weren't enough, that demon sword was obviously affecting Lloyd's mind. The way he'd thrown himself into battle was easily as reckless as when they first met.

Seth imagined it to be a subtle loosening of his friend's inhibitions. *Not that it would take much,* the halfling snorted to himself.

Even so, Seth doubted that Jack would let Lloyd get killed. If he did, Aksel would banish him and the demon lord didn't seem quite ready to go back to the Abyss just yet.

Seth found that fact quite telling. If he had to guess, the demon's time in the crucible had sucked away much of his power. In his weakened condition Jack would be easy prey for any demon with a grudge against him.

That actually suited Seth just fine. As the old saying went, *keep your friends close and your enemies closer.* Even so, in his current state he wasn't about to let Lloyd fly off to take on a small army of zombies by himself.

Seth screeched to a sudden halt as he entered the great square where the fortress sat. A wide swath of creatures in tattered clothes crowded around the front of the fortress. The air around them was permeated with the stench of their rotting skin.

Seth had to clamp down on his lips to keep himself from gagging. The sight and smell brought back memories of one of their first encounters at Stone Hill. Their group had faced about a half dozen zombies back then. There were easily a dozen times that surrounding Fortress Hightower. Luckily, he was far more accomplished now with spells. It also didn't hurt that zombies were inherently stupid.

"Well, here goes nothing," Seth murmured as he adjusted his white glove. Arcs of electricity danced across his skin as he once again took off at blinding speed.

Swiftly reaching one end of the zombie horde, Seth traced a quick pattern with his finger through the air. Mana rushed into the lines he had just drawn filling the symbol with a strange glowing light. The moment the pattern had been completed, Seth released the spell with the words, *"Multi Susurri."*

The magic of the spell swept over a good third of the crowd. Any zombie it touched immediately stopped shuffling forth. All then slowly spun about to gape at Seth.

Yet, Seth no longer stood in that spot. The halfling had already taken off like a shot towards the other end of the horde. Stopping and tracing that same exact symbol, he cast the spell once more. Again the mana fanned out over the crowd with similar results.

Not waiting, Seth had already dashed off to the center of the square and repeated the process. Once the magic had fallen over the rest of the horde, every zombie in the square stood expectantly watching the nimble halfling.

Seth now had them all temporarily distracted from the fortress. The question was what to do to maintain that distraction.

A sudden movement at the back of the crowd nearly made Seth jump. Near the front gate stood about a half dozen creatures unlike the rest. They were pale, almost skeletal-looking figures with glowing red eyes, each encased in armor and carrying a sword. Some of those creatures had spotted Seth and began pushing their way through the throng in his direction.

Seth had to think quickly. He needed to do something to hamper their approach or the respite he'd brought those inside the fortress would swiftly come undone.

A sudden idea brought a wicked smile to the halfling's lips. "Follow my lead," he mouthed to the waiting horde, then Seth began to dance.

Lloyd held Andrella firmly by the waist as they sped through the sky over the beleaguered city. The young wizardess felt quite grateful that he hadn't questioned having to carry her. That would have been an awkward conversation indeed.

With her concentration all but gone, the best Andrella could hope to muster would be the most basic of incantations. The only exception to that would be fire spells that she could supplement with the power of her regalia. Even so, it would be all worth it if she could keep Lloyd from putting himself in harm's way. His sudden disregard for his own safety had her worried beyond measure.

A strange sight awaited the couple as they passed over the last buildings surrounding the fortress. A huge group of zombies spread out across the square below. All the undead gyrated in formation as if controlled by some giant unseen puppet master.

Lloyd pulled up in mid-air as the both of them stared at the macabre performance. Her mouth agape, Andrella pointed at a diminutive figure at the forefront of the crowd. "Is that Seth?"

"I believe so," Lloyd answered, sounding equally astonished.

It took Andrella a moment or two to realize the zombies were mimicking the halfling's movements. He appeared to have them all enthralled except for maybe a half dozen pale armored figures. Those few attempted to push their way through the throng towards him, but seemed to have little luck as their dancing brethren impeded their progress. Quite obviously frustrated, the creatures began to hack away at their zombie cousins.

Their friend's imminent danger triggered Lloyd. "We need to do something about them before they reach Seth," he declared with just a bit too much enthusiasm.

It was as Andrella had feared. Lloyd seemed ready to leap into battle like a kid let loose in a candy shop. She needed to nip this in the bud right now.

"I'll take care of it," she told him decisively before he could move a muscle.

Wincing inwardly, Andrella pushed her free hand forward. Instead of tracing the familiar pattern though, she mentally drew upon the power of the regalia. In response, a small ball of flame appeared before her palm. It swiftly grew to the size of a fist and shot from her hand with a single word. *"Augue."*

The ball of flame rocketed downward, striking the ground in the midst of the creatures stalking Seth. The fiery orb exploded on impact expanding into a half-sphere that engulfed in flames everything within about two dozen yards. When the fire finally winked out, nothing remained of those creatures or the zombies around them.

Lloyd peered at Andrella with clear admiration. "That was some handy work."

Andrella did her best to smile through the pain that lanced across her brow. "Thanks," she managed.

Lloyd must have noticed something at that point. He eyed her uncertainly, but was interrupted before he could say anything.

Not stopping his macabre dance, Seth shouted up at them, "I've got this. You two go take care of your parents."

Lloyd eyed Andrella a moment more, then saluted the halfling with his free hand. Without another word, he sped them across the remaining distance to Fortress Hightower.

Atop the tower they found Lara and Kratos surrounded by a small group of gravely wounded spiritblades. The former sat upon the ground with the latter's head resting in her lap.

Andrella gasped as they landed next to them. Kratos looked years older, much like the time Lloyd had been drained by a vampire.

Lloyd's expression was aghast as he knelt beside his parents. "What happened?"

At the sight of his son, Kratos' dull eyes sparked to life. "Lloyd!" he croaked, his voice sounded dry and cracked. Reached out, Kratos grabbed his son's hand, and used it to steady himself as he tried to rise.

Lara grabbed her husband's shoulders, her eyes filled with grave concern. "Kratos, don't strain yourself. You need to rest."

Kratos sat up and gazed at his wife while gently patting her hand. "It's alright, dear. He needs to know what happened."

Lara grimaced, then gave her husband a curt nod. "Very well, but make it brief."

The love between the two was almost palpable. Andrella hoped that she and Lloyd would care for each other that much when they reached their age.

Kratos sighed, the lines around his eyes creasing as he turned to face Lloyd. "A huge group of undead poured from the graveyard castle just after daybreak. We fought a pitched battle through the streets, but their numbers were too great and we had to fall back."

The weary gentleman paused to catch his breath. Lloyd leaned forward and grabbed his father's hand, clasping it with both their thumbs pointed upward. Andrella could see the heartbreak in his eyes as he murmured, "Take your time, dad. I'm listening."

Andrella had to fight back the tears. She had nearly lost her own father not so long ago. It was hard to see someone who had been strong and vibrant your entire life suddenly look so frail and withered.

Kratos fixed his son with a wizened smile before continuing. "We made our last stand in the Lord's Square. We held them off as long as we could, but they eventually broke through our ranks."

A sadness glazed over Kratos' eyes as he relayed the next part. "Carenna and her troop gave their lives so the rest of us could escape. Taliana retreated with what was left of the town guard into Avernos keep while the rest of us fell back across the river."

A hush had fallen over the tower top. Andrella had only briefly met Carenna, but she was a valiant woman. The Protector of Penwick, she had given her life doing just that.

Lloyd's face has gone ashen. "Does Lagrange know?"

Kratos responded with a barely perceptible nod, his gaze dropping to the floor. Lara leaned forward and wrapped her arms around her husband, tears openly streaking down her face.

Andrella's heart wrenched in her chest. Carenna had been Lagerie Hightower's granddaughter. That would have made her Lagrange's daughter.

"Where is Lagrange?" Andrella asked softly.

Lara wiped the moisture from her eyes before meeting her gaze. She looked even more exhausted than when Andrella had last seen her. "He took his troops down to protect the gate if they should break through."

Andrella merely dipped her chin to signify she understood. She couldn't even begin to imagine what the man must be feeling. Even losing a parent paled in comparison to losing a child.

After a short silence, Kratos resumed his story. "We fought them all the way across the bridge, but finally had to retreat to the fortress."

"We whittled them down as much as we could, but they just kept coming," Lara finished wearily for her husband.

The sadness in Lloyd's eyes was suddenly replaced with a trace of anger. He stood and swept his eyes around the top of the tower. "What happened to that Pegasus Knight in all of this?"

Lara gave her son a reproachful look. "Now don't go blaming

Dame Aura. She'd already flown off to the graveyard before all hell broke loose here."

At the mention of the graveyard, Andrella shifted her gaze out over the city towards the southwest. A castle hung over the Olde Town Graveyard, still partially shrouded in a spinning sphere of darkness.

Andrella's eyes went wide as they fell on a huge black shadow at the forefront of that sphere. Even at this distance, the shadow appeared immense. She pointed a finger at it and gasped, "What in all Thac is that?"

Everyone turned their heads to see where she was pointing. Whatever the thing was, it was growing larger by the second. Tensions mounted as a small white winged figure darted across the face of the sphere to intercept the growing object.

All at once, the thing burst through the darkness. Though thick clouds still covered the sun, they illuminated it enough to see that the thing they'd been watching was an airship.

Andrella let out a huge sigh, not realizing she'd been holding her breath this entire time.

Lloyd had helped Kratos to his feet. His father now squinted at the approaching vessel and declared excitedly, "I know that ship. That's the *Remington!*"

As the ship drew closer, Andrella spied a large number of figures gathered at the prow. Two in particular looked extremely familiar.

Lloyd traded a knowing glance with her. "That's Martan and Kalyn!"

The words had barely left his lips when a barrage of arrows flew from the deck of the vessel. They rained down on the horde below dropping zombies like flies.

Cheers went up all across the top of the tower.

"...and they've brought a troop of Deepwood Snipers with them!" Lloyd shouted gleefully.

It was then that Andrella spotted a familiar white haired figure on the main deck. The tall man was surrounded by a troop of people all dressed in Penwick uniforms. "Not just that, but I believe that's Lagerie Hightower—and he's brought a troop of spiritblades with him," she cried exultantly.

Andrella and Lloyd grabbed onto each other as did Lara and Kratos. The two couples watched on with clear relief as the *Remington* flew in and decimated the remaining zombies.

15
DEEPWOOD SNIPERS

Leave it to these three to make a deadly encounter into a contest.

Martan Folke had spent a tension filled fortnight traveling to and from Deepwood. Five years ago, he had been accused of murdering his foster father, Old Man Coran. With a lynch mob on his tail, he'd fled Deepwood for his very life. His only regret had been leaving behind Kalyn.

The wild, spirited girl with her quick wit and strange sense of humor had been his only true friend. Kalyn swore she'd caught the actual murderer and the charges against Martan had been dropped. Yet, on his first return to Deepwood in years, he narrowly escaped being thrown in the dungeons.

Martan had little desire to return to Deepwood after that. Unfortunately, Kalyn continued to badger him until, against his better judgement, he went back to clear his name. The tribunal had been a lengthy, nerve wracking process, but even Kalyn's brothers stood up for him this time. In the end, much to his surprise, he was found innocent.

"Zombie in overalls," Kalyn called the shot as she let an arrow fly. The shaft sailed through the air toward the square below, deftly piercing her target in the forehead. The flames swiftly spread out from there and completely engulfed the brainless creature.

A smug expression crawled up her lips. "That's three," she drawled, not waiting for the inevitable outcome.

Turning away from the ship's rail, Kalyn drew another arrow from her quiver. Pausing to brush away a loose braid of her long, wavy, reddish-brown hair, she dipped the edge in a nearby brazier in preparation for the next shot.

"Fat zombie," Decon called from the rail on the opposite side of Kalyn from where Martan stood. The resemblance to his sister was uncanny with the exception of their eyes—where hers were a storm-gray, his were a deep chocolate brown. The *twang* of his bowstring was followed shortly thereafter with the declaration, "Three for me, too."

"Four!" Daer announced from the other side of Decon.

Both Kalyn and Decon stopped to stare incredulously at their other sibling. Short and stocky, Daer's blue eyes peered innocently back at them from beneath a shock of tousled straw-blonde hair. Had Martan not known the family he would never have guessed the three to be related.

"What?" Daer practically flinched from the weight of his sibling's combined stare.

"That's troll dung," Decon accused him heatedly.

"Ain't no way either of you orc lovers got more than me!" Kalyn added with clear irritation.

Due to his hard life, not much amused Martan. The predictable bickering between the Rhans, however, did make the corners of his mouth inch upward. *Leave it to these three to make a deadly encounter into a contest.*

Still, they were Deepwood snipers and therefore some of the best archers in all of Thac. In mere minutes, the twenty or so snipers at the bow of the Remington had picked off close to five dozen zombies. When they were done, the only figure left standing in the square below was Seth.

The halfling had been engaged in some sort of eerie dance with the zombie horde. Either he had somehow bewitched them all or someone else had and Seth thought it funny to dance along. Knowing Seth, Martan would have believed either to be true. Anyway, it had made the creatures easy pickings.

After the last zombie had fallen, Seth gave the Remington a short salute. Sparks then appeared around his small form and he took off at an incredible rate. Within seconds he'd disappeared from sight.

"Well, that's new," Martan murmured, wondering how the halfling had acquired such incredible magic.

"Probably stole it." Kalyn practically read his mind as she nudged him in the arm and guffawed with that awkward laugh of hers.

"You're probably right," Martan admitted, her infectious sense of humor causing him to break out into an uncharacteristic smile.

With the zombie horde dispatched, Lord Hightower ordered the Remington to dock at the fortress. Martan let out a short sigh. Their long journey was nearly at an end.

It had taken them the good portion of a fortnight to travel the roads from Deepwood to Penwick. In fact, they'd only made it to Lukescros late last night. Upon reaching the town, Kalyn insisted they first check in with Lord Hightower. That's when they learned of the dire situation in Penwick. Hightower wasted no time recruiting their entire squad and they all set out together at first light aboard the Remington.

The navigator expertly brought the airship to a stop within a few yards of the great central tower. Ropes were thrown over the side to moor the Remington. The crew then rolled out a cleverly built retractable gangplank that stretched down over the parapets. Once everything was in place, Lord Hightower bade them to follow as he disembarked.

They had barely set foot atop the tower when a pair of familiar voices bellowed their names. "Martan! Kalyn!"

Martan's eyes went wide as a blonde-haired beauty practically barreled into Kalyn. Garbed from head to toe in scarlet, she wrapped her arms around the Deepwooder and pulled her into a tight embrace. "Kalyn, it's so good to see you!"

The expression on Kalyn's face was priceless. Lady Andrella had caught her completely by surprise. Unsure how to react, she gawked helplessly at Martan while awkwardly patting Andrella on the back.

Martan felt a grin forming on his lips when he was unceremoniously grabbed around the waist and hoisted into the air. "Martan! You're back!"

Finding it hard to breathe in that vice-like grip, he stared down into the youthful face of Lloyd Stealle. The young man seemed as exuberant as ever, yet Martan caught a hint of something different about him. There was a sadness behind his eyes that Martan had not seen there before.

"It—it's good to see you too," Martan managed when Lloyd finally put him down.

"You've arrived just in time," Andrella went on excitedly.

Kalyn swept her eyes about while wearing one of those quirky grins. "Looks like all hell broke loose around here—literally." Her eyes fell on the dark castle hovering above the graveyard at the other end of the city.

They had gotten a bird's eye view of the structure on their way in. It had given Martan the shivers. There were dark things circling about that castle—evil looking things. Hightower had insisted though. The lord had wanted a good look at what they were up against.

"Lagerie," a wizened voice interrupted his thoughts. An older gentleman in a Penwick uniform hobbled up to them, his aged frame supported by a striking middle-aged woman garbed in royal blue robes.

Lagerie Hightower's eyes widened as if he'd seen a ghost. "Kratos, is that you?"

Martan traded a puzzled glance with Kalyn. Wasn't Kratos the name of Lloyd's father? Yet this gentleman appeared old enough to be Lloyd's grandfather.

Lagerie looked the elder man over. "You look like hell my friend,"—he paused and motioned at himself—"even older than these old bones."

Kratos' eyes twinkled with mirth. "Didn't you always say that with age comes wisdom?"

Lagerie wrinkled his nose at his friend. "Do you feel any wiser?"

Kratos shook his head. "No, not really."

Lagerie leaned in close and placed a hand on the side of his mouth, his voice dropping to a whisper. "Truth be told, neither do I."

The duo chuckled. It was obvious that these two were fast friends.

The woman holding Kratos aloft let out an exasperated sigh. "You two will be the death of me one day."

Guilt flooded Kratos' eyes as he gave her a sidelong glance. "Sorry, my love."

"Forgive us two old fools, Lara dear," Lagerie added, his expression one of chagrin.

This time Kalyn nudged Martan in the arm. "Isn't Lara the name of Lloyd's mom?" she whispered in his ear.

Martan responded with a confused shrug. Considering the age difference between this Lara and Kratos, how could they possibly be Lloyd's parents?

It was Lara that finally solved the mystery for them by explaining what had happened to her husband. The explanation made Martan's stomach queasy.

He leaned in close to Kalyn and murmured, "Remind me again why we came back to fight undead?"

This time Kalyn slugged him hard in the arm. "Because the *Heroes* need us and we ain't no lily-livered goblin lickers."

"O-oh, right," Martan stammered, still not feeling any better about it.

Martan was a simple man. He was neither warrior, knight, swordsman, assassin, wizard, or healer. Other than his meager abilities with a bow, he had no idea why the companions kept him around. Nonetheless, he was here and he would do his best to help where he could.

"Father." A solemn voice interrupted his pragmatic musings.

Martan's eyebrows raised ever so slightly as Lord Hightower's near twin strode up to greet him. The two men looked almost identical except for the streaks of dark mixed in with the newcomer's silver hair. On closer inspection, he also had fewer lines across his brow than his father.

"It's good to see you as well, Lagrange," Lord Hightower greeted his son. "I just wish it were under better circumstances."

Lagrange stiffened, then ushered his father away from the others. "Father, may we talk in private?"

Lord Hightower seemed momentarily taken aback, but then gave his son a curt nod. "Of course. Lead the way."

Martan was typically one to respect the privacy of others, but Kalyn's insatiable curiosity got the better of her as usual. The young woman placed a hand on her chin as she watched the pair stride off together. "I wonder what that's all about?"

Andrella quietly explained about the sacrifice Lagrange's daughter had made. As if on cue, the two men embraced each other and spent a short while sobbing over their terrible loss.

Martan couldn't even begin to imagine what they were going through. Having been orphaned at a young age, he had no family to speak of. Old man Coran had always been gruff with him. Thus, even his loss hadn't affected Martan.

Any further grieving was cut short as the Dame Aura landed atop the tower. The Pegasus knight had been there to greet them when they first arrived in the airspace above Penwick. Yet, she had soon taken off again to scout out the city.

Lagerie and Lagrange pulled themselves together as the knight offered her report. "The undead have stopped pouring from the castle. I think it's safe to say the first wave is over."

Though her words were meant as good news, they gave Martan little comfort. From the air it had been obvious just how much this city had suffered already. He didn't want to even think about what a second wave would do to it.

"Well, first things first." Lara stated definitively. "Kratos needs healing, so let's continue this discussion at the temple."

"Well we got this big old airship," Kalyn thumbed a finger at the Remington behind them. "Why don't ya'll just hop on board."

Martan smacked his forehead. Good hearted as Kalyn was, sometimes her mouth spoke before her brain kicked in.

"Um, Kalyn…" he quietly drew her attention.

The young woman shifted her gaze towards him, but suddenly grew aware that all eyes were fixed upon her. Her normally pale skin turned a bright shade of red. Digging her toe into the ground, Kalyn peered at Lagerie with a sheepish grin. "…if'n that's alright with you, Lord Hightower, sir."

A trace of moisture still in the corners of his eyes, Lagerie nonetheless stared back at her with a bemused expression. "Yes, let's."

16
TIME WARP

Perhaps the overlap with our world is causing time to slow down.

Glolindir's eyelids slowly fluttered open. He found himself staring up at an ornate ceiling covered with an elaborate portrait of winged angels and a blazing sun. The surface he lay on felt cold and hard as if not designed for the comfort of a resting body. Two figures hovered about him, a man and a woman dressed in the white robes of the priesthood.

Upon seeing his eyes open, the priestess grabbed him by the hand. "It's alright. You're safe."

Glo rose up onto his elbows and fixed her with an incredulous stare. "Safe? From what?" His last recollection was of fighting that nightwing creature in the skies over Penwick. He had shot the creature with a lightning bolt and it had retaliated with—a *Finger of Death*!

Cold realization flooded through Glo's body. The creature had used a death spell on him! Glo sat up and ran his hands over his body. He seemed to be in one piece.

"Where am I?" he asked the priestess.

She responded with a calming smile. "You are in the Temple of the Ralnai—the Chamber of Arenor to be precise."

Glo swept his gaze around the room. It was a small chamber with a few rows of short pews in front of the altar on which he sat. Inset into the wall on his left was a tall arched stained glass window. In the right wall stood a warm oak wooden door that perfectly matched the paneling in this vestibule.

The young elf abruptly became aware of how remarkably re-freshed he felt. It was as if he'd spent an entire night at rest. Yet the light flooding through the stained glass window proved it to still be daytime. Puzzled, he queried the priestess once more. "How long have I been out?"

Her expression remained serene. "Perhaps a little over an hour and a half."

One of Glo's eyebrows rose up to meet his hairline. "Is that all?"

The priest and priestess exchanged a knowing glance before she responded. "This chamber has particularly strong healing properties. That is why the High Priestess had us bring you here."

Glo found that fascinating. If circumstances had been different, he would have liked to study this chamber further. Unfortunately, Penwick was still under siege and a lot could happen in an hour and a half.

Glo vaulted off the altar and briefly bowed to the two clerics. "Thank you both."

"It was our pleasure," they replied in unison.

Grabbing up his robes, the anxious elf yanked them on as he rushed out the chamber door.

Glo found himself in the main chapel at the back of the temple. It was crowded back here, so much so that it took him a few moments to get his bearings. Orienting himself, he weaved through the crowd and passed under the archway that led to the temple proper. A huge, raised dais stood before him with hallways arcing around its edge.

Glo scooted through the congested hallway, but came to a

screeching halt when he reached the temple proper. His mouth hung agape as he took in the sheer volume of people here. There had to be close to three dozen rows of pews stretched across the vast chamber. Despite that, each pew was filled to the brim with more folks spilling out into the aisles. The assault on Penwick had forced all these people from their homes.

A wave of utter empathy washed over the astonished elf. He could see the fear on these people's faces; hear it in their voices. They hadn't asked for any of this. All they wanted was to go about their daily lives. Why was it always the innocents that got caught in the middle of these confrontations?

Despite all his studies, Glo had never found a satisfactory answer to that question. Still, it had given him a sense of purpose. The young elf had left Cairthrellon for this very reason—to help those in need. If anyone needed help at the moment it was the people of Penwick.

Steeling himself, Glo wound his way through the terrified refugees while doing his best to reassure them. Murmurs passed through the crowd as he went.

"There's that tall elf."

"He's one of those heroes from Ravenford."

"I heard they worked with the Protectors…"

"…saved a bunch of folks in the catacombs."

Glo felt glad he could give these people some small measure of solace, even if only for the moment. Yet, he also received something in return. Their belief in him fueled his determination. He swore to do whatever it took to protect them, even at the cost of his own life.

Glo reached the temple doors with a renewed sense of purpose. Pausing to salute the folks inside, he exited just in time to see an airship pass overhead.

That has to be the Remington, Glo reasoned. The *Cloud Hammer* had only left two days ago and would barely have made it to Lanfor by now.

Glo watched with keen curiosity as the airship descended towards the temple grounds not far away. He wondered who could be aboard as he hurried to meet the landing vessel.

Winding through a grove of trees, the apprehensive elf emerged on the other side only to find some familiar faces waiting there for him.

"Glo?" Astonishment was written all over Aksel's face.

Alys waltzed up and placed a finger on her chin as she ran her eyes up and down his body. "Hm, you look pretty good for someone who nearly died a second time in one day."

Glo arched an eyebrow at the spirited, yet sometimes awkward, songstress. "Thanks, I think."

"Of course, he looks fine," Sirus stated definitively. "He should be fully rested and recovered after his time in the Chamber of Arenor."

"I think I'll need to visit this chamber once things are done here," Aksel murmured.

"I would like to return there as well," Glo agreed.

While the airship landed, the others filled him in on what he missed. Glo had to admit he was worried for Andrella. Being the only arcane caster in the group was not an easy job. From the sounds of it, however, his concern was needless. She had carried out her role expertly, as well as, if not better than, he might have himself.

Once the Remington touched down, a number of folks disembarked—some familiar and some not. Glo immediately recognized Lord Hightower from Lukescros, but couldn't quite place his near twin that strode beside him. Lloyd followed carrying an old man that might very well have been his grandfather. Lara came next along with Andrella. Both appeared to be supporting each other as if exhausted.

Behind them he was surprised to see Martan and Kalyn. The Remington had originally returned from Deepwood without them. As if not amazing enough, the pair was followed by Kalyn's brothers and a group of archers dressed similar to the Rhans. Glo guessed them to be more Deepwood snipers. The last to climb down the gangplank were an entire platoon of Penwick spiritblades.

What truly caught Glo by surprise, however, was the appearance of the blonde warrior astride a gorgeous white Pegasus. He had only seen such creatures before in books and was excited to see one in real life.

The surprises continued to pile up when they discovered that Lloyd's 'grandfather' was none other than Kratos. "Take him to the Chamber of Arenor at once," Sirus ordered a pair of waiting members of her clergy.

"You should go too, mom," Lloyd urged Lara as he handed Kratos over to the clerics.

Lara let go of Andrella and threw back her shoulders. "I'm—fine," she insisted, though the bags under her eyes attested to the contrary.

"No, you're not," Andrella declared, her hands on her hips as she locked eyes with her mother-in-law to be.

Lara tried to stare the young lady down, but soon realized she was facing someone equally as stubborn as she herself. Glo had found it to be a common attitude among wizards. When one wielded as much as power they did, it tended to make you think you were invincible. He himself might have turned out the same if he hadn't been constantly reminded of his own shortcomings.

After a short staring contest, Lara capitulated. "Very well," she sighed, her shoulders slumping as she gave in to fatigue.

Andrella stood there looking triumphant as another cleric led Lara away—that is until Lloyd interrupted her gloating.

"You should go as well," he told her in a soft, but firm voice.

Andrella glared defiantly back at him. "And just who's going to watch your back then?"

An uncharacteristic look of anger washed across the young man's face. "I can take care of myself," he declared testily.

His unexpected response only furthered Andrella's defiance. "No, you obviously can't. Not since you got that sword," she practically spat the words at him.

Glo had never seen this side of Lloyd before. He'd only ever seen him mad at aggressors like the folks from Dunwynn. The perplexed elf bent down and whispered to Aksel, "Has he really gotten that bad?"

Aksel responded with a barely perceptible nod. "Think Lloyd when we first met."

That did not bode well at all. Lloyd had been quite reckless back in those days. Perhaps Andrella was on to something there. The demon sword might indeed be messing with the young man's inhibitions. Still, Andrella couldn't constantly watch over him without wearing herself out.

Finally understanding the situation, Glo decided to step in. "Pardon me, Andrella…"

The irate young lady halted in mid-argument and turned to face the hesitant elf. As soon as her eyes fell upon him, the anger in them abated somewhat. "Yes, what is it?"

Glo chose his next few words very carefully. "The others filled me in on how well you handled things. I have to say, I am quite proud of you."

The rest of the anger faded from Andrella's eyes and her skin turned a slight shade of red. "Why, thank you, Glo. I had a great teacher, after all."

Having broken the ice, Glo strode over and grasped her by the arm, gently pulling her aside. When he spoke, his voice was barely above a whisper. "I understand your concerns, but you've obviously used a lot of spells. Why don't you rest a bit. I promise to keep an eye on things in the interim."

Mixed emotions played across the young lady's face. Obviously torn, she glanced briefly at Lloyd.

The young man's uncharacteristically haughty demeanor had thankfully faded at that point. His hand went to the back of his neck as a sheepish grin spread across his face.

"I promise to behave myself," he said with obvious chagrin.

Somewhat mollified, Andrella peered back up at Glo. Without warning, a loud yawn escaped her lips. Completely embarrassed, the young lady shook her head at herself. "Oh, very well—but you better call me if something happens."

Seemingly himself again, Lloyd pulled her into a tender embrace and kissed her on the forehead. "We will. I promise."

She gazed up at him fondly, then said in a stern voice, "You better."

Sirus had another priestess escort Andrella after the others. She then bade the rest of them to follow her to her office. Once there, swift introductions were made all around before proceeding.

Glo listened quietly to all that had happened in Penwick, Deepwood, Twin Oaks, Three Forks, and Lukescros. In the end it all fit together except for one tiny detail. Martan and Kalyn said they'd been away for a fortnight, but by Glo's calculations, it had only been nine days.

It was Sirus who came up with a possible explanation. "I understand that time travels differently in the celestial planes. If that is also true for the shadow plane, perhaps the overlap with our world is causing time to slow down for us?"

As Glo mulled that over, Lloyd interrupted them. "I just got a message from Thea. She said they found the scrolls."

Glo exchanged a puzzled glance with Aksel. Deep creases formed across the gnome's brow. "So soon? They only left two days ago."

"They would have just reached Lanfor by now," Lagrange affirmed.

"Unless…time truly has slowed for us," Glo reasoned.

The room grew quiet as everyone tried to wrap their head around what that actually meant. It was Seth who finally broke the silence. "Not that I'm buying any of this, but where exactly did they find them?"

Lloyd closed his eyes, his brows forming into a single line as if he were in deep concentration. A few moments later, he opened them again and said, "In a place called Kaniron."

"Kaniron," Lagrange murmured, "That's well down the coast from Lanfor."

"That pretty much cinches it," Alys noted glibly. "We're in a time warp."

Lloyd gazed at her with obvious bewilderment. "What's a time warp?"

Alys responded with a flippant smile and a nonchalant wave of her hand. "Oh, just something I read about. It's when time is either stretched out to be longer or scrunched up to be shorter than normal. Hence, time is warped."

"Oh, I see," Lloyd nodded solemnly, though he didn't look any less perplexed than before.

Glo opened his mouth to explain further, but Seth beat him to it. "Basically, time's gone all wonky."

Lloyd gave the halfling a grateful smile. "Now that makes sense."

Glo was hard pressed to suppress his laughter. Leave it to Seth to oversimplify things.

"Just one more thing," Seth went on. "How many scrolls did they find?"

Lloyd cocked his head to one side as he thought it over. "I think she said seven. Why?"

Seth snorted. "It would be a real shame if they didn't come back with all of them."

Lloyd absently scratched his head. "Amada was the one who told us about them in the first place. She might know how many they're supposed to be."

Alys literally jumped out of her seat. "Oh, she's here on the grounds. I'll go and ask her."

The songstress practically flew out of the office as she embarked on her urgent mission to find the well renowned blacksmith. While she was gone, the conversation turned to what their next steps should be. Though the attack had died down for now, everyone agreed a second wave would be coming sooner rather than later.

In the midst of this, Sirus received a communique from Avernos keep. Apparently, they had held off the onslaught, but it came with a heavy price. The commander of the town guard, Taliana, had now also fallen.

Lagerie rose from his seat and slammed his hand on Sirus' desk. "Cavernous is a fool for staying at the castle."

Sirus let out a heavy sigh. "I can't say I disagree. We implored him to move his forces to the fortress or the temple, but he wouldn't listen."

Glo had briefly met the Baron of Penwick before. He seemed more of a bureaucrat than a leader. Those types of people were the worst to be in charge during an onslaught such as this. He was probably more concerned about saving his own skin than putting his own people in jeopardy.

Lagerie exchanged a brief glance with Lagrange, then nodded. "Very well. I left half our forces at the fortress. Lagrange, you head back there to lead them. I'll take the rest of them over to the keep to fortify things there."

Sirus eyed the elder Hightower speculatively. "Are you certain about this?"

Lagerie let out an exasperated sigh. "It's the least we can do now."

Dame Aura rose from her seat at that point. "I'll accompany you."

Glo hadn't ever seen the elder Hightower caught by surprise until now. Lagerie's brow rose, but then he took Aura by the hand. "Thank you, my dear. The sight of a Knight of the Rose will do much to raise morale."

Before they left, Lagerie stopped to address Glo and the others. "We'll hold our positions as long as we can, but the best defense is a good offense. Do whatever you need to, to end this once and for all."

Lloyd stood and saluted him. "You have our word, Lord Hightower."

Lagerie clasped Lloyd's hand between his own and shook it gingerly. "Spoken like a true Stealle, my boy."

"Um, Lord Hightower, Sir," Kalyn said in a soft voice. The normally gregarious Deepwooder seemed quite out of her element in this meeting.

Lagerie faced her with an arched eyebrow. "Yes, young lady? What can I do for you."

"Well, um…" Kalyn looked down and dug her toe into the floor. "…if you want…you can take the rest of our snipers with you."

Lagerie practically beamed at the young woman. "Why that's very generous of you, Mistress Kalyn."

She peered up at him, an embarrassed grin on her face. "It's our pleasure, sir."

Martan, also looking quite uncomfortable in this environment, leaned forward and whispered something in her ear. Kalyn appeared annoyed at first and Glo half expected to see her slug him. It would not have been the first time. Yet her anger swiftly faded.

"Oh, right," she nodded to Martan before facing Lagerie once more. "Just ask my brothers to stay behind, if you don't mind."

"Not at all," Lagerie responded, still smiling at the Deepwood duo.

Lagerie, Lagrange, and Dame Aura finally departed. They had not been gone more than half a minute when Alys practically flew back into the room. The young lady seemed out of breath as if she had run across the entire compound and back.

"Alys, what did you find out?" Sirus pressed her.

"Amada said…there are…fourteen scrolls…in all…" Alys managed to gasp out the words in between breaths.

Seth folded his arms across his chest and stared at Lloyd triumphantly. "Told ya so."

Glo eyed the halfling curiously. "How did you know?"

Seth's lips curled sideways. "It's what any good thief would do."

Lloyd gave Alys a grateful nod. "I'll let my sister know."

While Lloyd contacted Thea, Aksel went on to discuss next steps. "Lord Hightower may be right. While we have this grace period, maybe it's time we take the fight back to our enemies."

Glo frowned at the little cleric. "Do you think that's wise? We barely know how to use the staff just yet."

"Oh, he knows it's not wise," Seth interjected. "He's just feeling the pressure is all."

Aksel shrugged. "Neither of you are wrong, but I don't see as we have much choice."

"At least we don't have to worry about that dracolich anymore," Alys added blithely. "By now she must have gotten what she was after."

Alys' words made Glo stop and wonder. Just what had the dracolich been after? What if it was one of those *dark treasures* Lara had mentioned? Had they in fact just made things worse by removing the staff?

As if in answer to his question, Elistra's voice suddenly popped into his head. *"Glo, dear, you might want to check Phobas' tomb again."*

If she had wanted to scare him, her timing couldn't have been more impeccable. *Why? What's happened?*

There was a short pause before she answered. "You do realize that dracolichs tend to practice necromancy, right?"

Her words sent a chill coursing up Glo's spine. How could he have been so stupid?

Still in shock, he said aloud, "Folks, I think we might have an even bigger problem."

17
FOLLOW THAT LICH

You and your friends really did it this time—practically handed the power of a god to that crazed dracolich.

Stupid. *Stupid. Stupid.* Seth silently berated himself as he sped through the dark halls of the catacombs beneath the temple. The moment the words had left Glo's lips, he realized his mistake.

I must be going soft or something. The halfling continued to berate himself as he raced along the path to Phobas tomb. He should have known better than to trust that draco-*bitch*. Now, because of their supreme stupidity, they all but handed her a god to do her bidding.

At his current speed, Seth reached the tomb in a matter of minutes. Just as Elistra had predicted, the top had been completely ripped off the sarcophagus and a quick peek inside proved Phobas' remains to be gone. As to where it had been taken, that was no secret. The entire back of the tomb was now hidden behind a giant swirling portal.

Still, exactly where that portal led remained a mystery. A landscape filled with nothing but clouds was all Seth could see on the other side. Neither Phobas' body nor the dracolich were anywhere in sight.

Cursing himself thrice over, Seth touched the broach on his cloak. "Yeah, Elistra was right. Phobas is gone."

A few seconds of silence followed before he heard Aksel's voice. "Is there any sign of where she took it?"

Seth breathed a derisive snort. "You mean other than the giant portal in the back of the tomb? Nope."

There was another pause before he heard Glo's voice. "Hang on, we'll be right there."

About ten seconds later, another portal appeared in the air not far from where Seth stood. This one was far smaller than the one in the back of the chamber. As soon as the swirling oval solidified, Aksel, Lloyd, Xellos, Alys, Martan, Kalyn, and her brothers came leaping through. Glo followed shortly thereafter and closed that gateway behind him.

In the meantime, Aksel went to inspect the giant portal. The little gnome swept his gaze across the cloudy landscape beyond. "Any idea where this leads?"

"Nope," Seth answered flatly. "Not sure how much longer it'll stay open either."

"Fair point," Aksel acknowledged. The little gnome didn't look much happier than Seth. Knowing him as well as he did, Seth was sure Aksel believed this to all be his fault.

"I should have seen this coming," Glo muttered. The tall elf stood behind Aksel shaking his head.

Seth wasn't about to disagree with him. They'd all been stupid.

For some reason Seth couldn't fathom, Kalyn seemed to have a soft spot for the wizard. She placed a hand on Glo's shoulder and said, "Ain't no use beating yourself up over it at this point."

"She's right," Alys agreed with a mischievous smile. "You can always beat yourself up later."

"I'll even help," Seth offered, unable to resist adding his two bits on top of Alys' subtle slam.

Seth half expected to be on the receiving end of one of Glo's acid stares, but instead the corner of the wizard's lips lifted slightly. "Nice to know I can always count on you."

"That's what friends are for," Seth replied without missing a beat.

"If you all are done," Aksel interrupted them, "I think the portal is starting to close."

Sure enough the giant gateway had begun to waver and the sides had started to shrink.

Lloyd had been peering over Aksel's shoulder this entire time while anxiously fingered the hilt of the giant blade strapped across his back.

"Let's go then!" he bellowed, urging everyone to action before leaping through himself.

Almost as one, the rest of the companions leaped through the gateway and into the cloudy realm beyond. Behind them, the portal slammed shut leaving Phobas' tomb quiet once more.

How could I have been so blind? Glo continued to berate himself as they leapt through the portal Jinkolothos left behind. He could practically hear his father's scathing words concerning their latest debacle.

You and your friends really did it this time—practically handed the power of a god to that crazed dracolich. I told you that you were ill prepared for this sort of thing. Perhaps if you had listened to me and stayed home in the first place, the whole world wouldn't now be facing its inevitable doom.

Glo's entire body shuddered as they exited the other side of the portal. His father's imagined scolding had cut him to the quick. Add to that his anger at himself and it might explain his sudden tremors. On the other hand, it could merely have been from the abrupt drop in temperature. It was bitter cold on this side of the portal.

They appeared to be standing on a cloudy surface. Mists spread around and above them as far as the naked eye could see. With no sunlight or any other source of warmth, there was nothing to heat up the dreary landscape.

The others seemed equally affected. Alys wrapped her arms

around herself to keep from shivering. Martan's teeth chattered loudly. So did Decon's and Daer's.

Shivering as well, Kalyn's breath came out in a thin stream of steam. "Who poked the ice dragon and forgot to shut the front door?"

Decon elbowed her in the arm. "You're one to talk, sis. How many nights did dad have to yell at ya for not closin' the front door and blowin' out the fire?"

Kalyn spun about and punched her brother hard enough in the shoulder to make him wince and laugh at the same time. "Hush up ya goblin licker—we ain't talking about me."

Decon and Daer exchanged a glance, then clamped their hands over their mouths. They ill succeeded in hiding their amusement as snickers and snorts still slipped from behind their palms.

Huddled nearby beneath his cloak, a wicked grin formed upon Seth's lips. "A fire would be nice and toasty," he managed through chattering teeth, "but it's not like there's any buildings here—for Glo to burn down."

The anger on Kalyn's face abruptly drained away as a short laugh escaped her lips. She immediately silenced it as Glo's eyes fell upon her.

Glo grimaced. Kalyn had always cheered him on, but having her suddenly laugh at him hurt more than he would have thought. Still, there was far too much at stake right now to worry about his feelings. Swallowing his pride, he bit back the smart remark on his lips and focused on their current situation. A few moments later, a solution came to him.

"I have something better than that," Glo announced with more than a hint of satisfaction. Holding his staff firmly in one hand, he traced out a simple pattern through the frigid air with the other. Yet he didn't immediately cast the spell, instead allowing the mana to build up within. The symbol almost visibly glowed with power when he released the magic with a slight variation of the words.

"Donec Omnis Glacius."

In response to his spell, a column of sparse white energy rose from the ground around everyone gathered there. It rushed up to the top of their heads, then swiftly disappeared. A momentary white glow surrounded their bodies, but that, too, abruptly faded.

A collective sigh emanated from the group as the warmth flooded back into their bodies.

"That's much better!" Alys squealed with glee.

"Pretty slick," Kalyn gushed as she nudged Seth with her knee. "Wouldn't ya say, short stack?"

Seth fixed her with a dark stare before grudgingly answering, "Yeah, not bad"—his lips curved to one side as he shifted his gaze to Glo—"and you didn't even have to light anything on fire."

Glo eyed the halfling sharply, but otherwise said nothing. By now he was used to Seth's prodding.

"When did you learn to cast protection spells on multiple people?" Aksel quietly interjected.

The question brought an unbidden smile to Glo's face. "Just now, in fact."

"Well then, I'd say that was rather timely," Aksel pointed out with a cautionary glance at Seth.

Seth stared back at him completely unfazed, the silent admonishment having little effect.

With a short sigh, Aksel shifted his gaze away from his recalcitrant friend. "Well, now that the cold is no longer a problem we should probably move onward."

Glo joined in as the little cleric scrutinized the fluffy landscape that surrounded them. Unfortunately, there was nothing to see but clouds in all directions. Not a single landmark of any kind stood out amongst them.

With no other possible recourse, Aksel once turned to Xellos. "Any idea which way?"

Without a word, the silent tracker cautiously padded out into the cloudy landscape.

As he did so, Kalyn nudged her head after him and muttered under her breath, "Some of us are also trackers, ya know. What makes him so special?"

Deep creases formed across Martan's brow as he whispered back to her. "I don't know about you, but I wouldn't know the first place to look in all this mist."

Silence fell over the group as Xellos searched the surrounding area. He circled back a few times before finally stopping almost directly in front of them. "This way," he waved them forward.

"Hmph," Kalyn snorted as they moved out. "I coulda told you that."

The little group fell into an impromptu formation with Xellos leading the way and Lloyd not far behind him. The others fanned out with Seth and Kalyn on one side and Decon and Daer on the other. Glo, Aksel, and Alys stayed near the middle while Martan brought up the rear.

Glo had been leery at first, but the misty surface remained solid below them. He wondered if that would continue to be the case or if they would eventually run into the end of this cloudy surface.

They had only traveled a short distance when Glo spotted a strange object hovering in the dreary cloudscape not far ahead. It was hard to make out at first, but it appeared to have a diamond-like shape to it.

"Anyone have any idea what that thing is?" Alys asked, her voice tinged with a trace of apprehension.

"It looks like some kind of crystal," Xellos answered her. His response, however, did little to allay her nerves.

"I'm pretty familiar with all kinds of jewelry. They don't normally float in midair like that," Alys observed wryly.

"Fair point," Glo admitted. "There's obviously some magic at play here. We'll know more when we get a bit closer."

Alys peered back at him with an ironic smile. "That's what I'm afraid of."

Though she tried to make light of the matter, Alys' caution was well warranted. From what Glo could determine, they had most likely crossed over to another plane of existence—perhaps some sort of pocket dimension created by Jinkolothos herself. Either way, they had no idea where they were or what waited for them beyond this seemingly benign, if frigid, landscape.

The little group continued their trek towards the floating crystal until the clouds finally thinned out before them. They finally parted to reveal a gleaming wide circular platform a short distance below the hovering crystal. A large pentagram had been engraved into the platform's metallic surface. A glowing rune had been inscribed at each point of the pentagram with a sixth one engraved at its very center.

"Now that's something you don't see every day," Xellos noted blithely.

As the others gathered around the edge of the platform, Glo scrutinized the metallic runes. He had definitely seen these symbols somewhere before. Mental images formed in his mind—pages of a book from his father's library. Inscribed on those pages were pictures of runes quite similar to those laid out before him. An instant later it dawned upon him what language he was looking at.

"These runes are in ancient draconic—or elder dragon to be more precise," Glo murmured in a state of awe.

"Elder dragon?" Alys repeated his words with equal amazement. "Isn't that a dead language?"

Glo responded with a wordless nod, his eyes remained glued to the runes around the pentagram.

The young bardess knelt down for a closer look at the nearest rune. "Can you read this?"

Behind them Seth let out a derisive snort. "You're asking an extinct elf if he can read a dead language."

"Extinct elf?" Kalyn repeated with clear puzzlement.

"Everyone thought the Galinthral elves had been wiped out during the third elf-human war—that is until Glo showed up a few months ago," Aksel explained in a soft voice.

"Oh…" Kalyn's voice was filled with horror. "Sorry," she barely squeaked the word out a few moments later.

Glo paused from scrutinizing the rune before him and glanced over his shoulder at Kalyn. Her face had gone completely ashen and her eyes were firmly fixed on the ground. It took a moment before the source of her anguish registered with him.

The Deepwood Snipers had been instrumental in slaughtering elven mages during that war. Many of those had been from the House of Galinthrae. Apparently, Kalyn was aware of that fact. Still, all that had transpired over five hundred years ago. Glo firmly believed that such things needed to be forgiven and forgotten if there was ever to be peace amongst the races.

"You weren't there. You've got nothing to apologize for," he told her in a matter of fact tone.

Kalyn slowly peered up at him, her eyes glistening with traces of moisture.

"Ya meaning it?" she asked while wringing her hands nervously together.

Glo couldn't help but smile at the genuine young woman. It was caring folks like her that would make the difference in the long run.

"I do," he told her emphatically.

Kalyn's entire face lit up. She beamed at him, but was interrupted before she could say anything further.

"Yeah, yeah, we're all one big happy family," Seth drawled. "Now can we get back to finding the dead god we lost?"

Glo had to fight back the laugh that had formed in the back of his throat. The way Seth phrased it made it sound totally insane. Still, he was not wrong.

Deep creases had formed across Lloyd's brow as he scanned the metallic platform. "What do you think this thing does?"

"Maybe it opens another portal?" Alys suggested offhandedly.

"Or it could just blow up in our faces," Seth pointed out, folding his arms across his chest.

Kalyn nudged the cynical halfling. "Well, isn't it your job to check for that?"

Seth fixed her with a foul look. "Maybe you'd like to do the honors?" he said, ushering her forward.

"Nope, I'm good," she responded, not missing a beat. "Get to it already," she insisted, waving him forward with the back of her hand.

Seth stared at her for a few moments before stepping forth and grumbling under his breath, "Remind me again why we brought her along?"

While Seth checked the pentagram for traps, Glo continued to decipher the runes. From what he remembered, Elder runes were not like any others. Each had a name and a specific meaning associated with it. By the time Seth had finished scouring the platform, Glo had managed to decipher three of them. Standing, he informed the others what he had discovered thus far.

"The top rune is *Thaenrathi* which roughly translates to 'Strong Leader' or 'King.' The symbol in the very center is *Zhukaya* which is usually interpreted as 'Cycles of Action.' The rune on the right is *Athihan* which is typically denoted as the 'Dance of Blades.'"

"You sure about those translations?" Aksel asked, absently stroking his chin as he stared at the pentagram.

Glo shrugged. "About as sure as anyone can be who isn't an elder dragon."

Alys stood as well and brushed off her leather pants. "How do you suppose we use this thing? Do we just stand on a rune?"

Glo steepled his hands together in front of his chin as he thought it over. "Perhaps, but the question is which one?"

"Why don't we just try one?" Lloyd stated, his impatience obvious in his voice.

"Suit yourself," Seth chided him. "Just don't blame me if you get blown up."

Lloyd eyed the halfling uncertainly. "I thought you said there were no traps."

"I said I couldn't find any," Seth corrected him.

Lloyd thought that over for a few moments, then shrugged. "Good enough for me."

Before anyone could stop him, the young man leapt onto the platform and ran over to the middle rune.

"Lloyd, wai…"

Glo never got to finish his sentence. As soon as Lloyd stepped on the center rune, the symbol began to glow. A split second later he was blinded by a flash of light and felt a familiar wrenching feeling in his gut. When his vision cleared, they all still stood on the metallic platform. Clouds surrounded them on all sides, but the runes around the pentagram had changed.

Aksel gave Alys an approving nod. "It appears that you were right. That was definitely a displacement spell, though it teleported us instead of opening a portal."

"What's that ticking noise?" Xellos abruptly interjected.

Being at the periphery of his awareness, Glo had initially ignored the soft sound. Now, however, he searched for its source. Peering upward, his eyes fell on another crystal hovering above them. Unlike the previous crystal though, this one glowed. It pulsed in fact in a pattern matching the ticking sound. Both grew ominously faster.

"Somehow, I don't think that's a good thing," Martan observed with trepidation.

A sudden loud *ding* sounded before anyone could react. Another brilliant flash accompanied it along with that same wrenching feeling. When their eyes cleared, the little company found itself once again on a metallic platform surrounded by a cloudy landscape. Yet again, the runes around the pentagram had changed. A quick scan confirmed them to be the same as the runes on the first platform they had encountered.

"Looks like we're back to square one," Seth noted ironically.

Glo steepled his hands together as he contemplated out loud. "Must be some sort of timer set into the mechanism."

Seth clicked his tongue derisively. "Tsk, ya think?"

Ignoring Seth, Aksel stepped over the lines of the pentagram and strode over to join Lloyd at the center rune. Though the young man still stood on it, the symbol no longer glowed.

"Since this teleported us, I think it's safe to say it was the correct choice," Aksel hypothesized.

Glo swept his eyes around the pentagram, recalling the images of the runes on the next platform. "So, we probably need to make the next choice before the timer goes off."

"Or just disable the timer," Seth pointed out the obvious.

Seth's pragmatic observation left Glo feeling quite foolish. "That would make things easier," he admitted, shaking his head with profound chagrin.

Aksel squinted at their halfling friend. "What are you thinking?"

Seth peered up at the dull crystal that hung over this platform. "When we jump again, this time I take a closer look at that flashing crystal."

Agreeing it to be a sound plan, Glo cast the fly spell upon Seth.

Lloyd then stepped off the center rune and back onto it. As soon as he did so, it lit up. Once more they experienced that brilliant flash and the accompanying disorientation. This time, however, Glo had been prepared for it and kept his eyes closed.

Tick-tick-tick.

Seth was already airborne by the time Glo's eyes snapped open. "Yep, there's a switch in here," he called down to those still on the platform a few seconds later.

Seth's arm disappeared into the crystal. Shortly thereafter, his efforts were rewarded with a short *click*. The ticking abruptly stopped and the crystal itself went dark.

Martan wiped his hand across his brow. "Phew, that's a relief. Not sure how much more of that jumping around I could take."

Kalyn cupped her hands together over her mouth and called up to Seth, "Nice going, short stack!"

Seth glared back down at her, but chose not to comment.

Glo scrutinized these new sets of runes and swiftly identified two of them: *Ratanen,* which loosely translated to 'Fog Dream' and *Ihanen,* which could be interpreted as 'Dream Dancing.'

Alys gently tapped her chin as she looked from one rune to the other. "Stepping on the correct one should then teleport us to another pentagram."

"And if we step on the wrong rune?" Martan asked apprehensively.

"One way to find out!" Seth declared as he glided down from above.

Glo instinctively flinched as the halfling landed on *Ihanen.* The rune lit up just like the previous one. Another stomach-churning flash later, the party found themselves at a third pentagram with an entirely new set of runes.

Tick-tick-tick.

"Another crystal?" Kalyn exhaled with exasperation.

"Yeah, this is going to get old really quick," Seth declared as he launched himself upward.

Thankfully, this crystal had the same switch as the last. Just like before, as soon as Seth flipped it the ticking stopped and the crystal went dark.

"Apparently, that was the right rune," Alys noted gaily.

Caught up in her exultant mood, Glo smiled back at her. "Apparently." His smile swiftly faded, however, as he looked over this new set of runes. "It would help though if I could decipher these things better."

Aksel lifted his staff into the air. "I might be able to help with that."

Glo arched an eyebrow at him. They had deciphered quite a few spells on the staff, but there was still much about it they did not know. "Are you certain?"

Aksel responded with a firm nod. "I believe so."

Glo took in a deep breath and let it out again. Aksel had been watching out for them ever since they first met all those months ago. It was not in his nature to harm any living creature. Thus, if he felt he could safely use the staff, Glo believed it was worth the risk.

"Okay," Glo agreed, rubbing his hands together nervously.

"Hold still now," Aksel admonished as he pointed the staff directly at him.

Glo went rigid and held his breath. The latter was probably overkill, but he did it anyway.

The little cleric slowly ran his hands over the Staff of Law. All of a sudden, a purple beam shot out from the head of the staff.

Glo felt a tingling sensation in the center of his brow as the ray enveloped him. The prickling feeling stayed with him even after the ray stopped. Abruptly the world around him grew brighter. Everything appeared more vivid. He could even see colors in the mists where previously there had been only white.

Turning his attention to the runes, Glo suddenly found he understood them all. *Ihanen*, the connecting rune Lloyd had stepped on, still stood in the center. Starting from the left point and traveling around the pentagram counterclockwise he discerned: *Li*, the rune for 'Fire,' *Abanen*, the symbol for 'Sky dream,' *Ninathen*, the elder rune for 'Earth Kin,' *Mah*, the symbol for 'Storm,' and *Waethan*, the rune for 'Frozen Stones.'

Once again Alys tapped her chin as she stood over the pentagram. "Which rune now? It is cold here. Maybe 'Frozen Stones?'"

"Nah. Too obvious," Seth declared from where he hovered above the platform.

"Let's try something different." Before anyone could stop him, the halfling glided down and landed on 'Earth Kin.'

Once again, Glo barely had time to cover his eyes. After experiencing another intense flash, the little group now found themselves at a fourth pentagram. Like the last, this one had a completely new set of runes.

Tick-tick-tick.

Glo narrowed his gaze at Seth after the halfling disabled the crystal timer. "Either that's two extremely lucky guesses, or you can read Elder Dragon."

Seth waved him off as if he were crazy. "Me? Nah. I can barely grunt in regular Draconic."

The slight smirk on Seth's face did not help Glo in the slightest on deciding whether to believe him or not.

"Either way, he seems to be on to some sort of pattern," Aksel pointed out adroitly.

"'Cycles of Action,' 'Dream Dancing,' and 'Earth Kin,'" Alys ticked off all the runes they had chosen thus far. "Does that make sense to anyone?"

"Nope," Kalyn drawled.

"Not really," Decon agreed with his sister.

Martan placed a hand on his chest. "Don't look at me. I'm just a simple archer."

The group grew quiet until Lloyd murmured something out loud. "Too bad these runes aren't simple like the ones back in the monolith."

Glo opened his mouth to agree with his friend, but halted as an epiphany struck him. Instead of concurring with the young man, instead he exclaimed, "Lloyd, you're a genius!"

Lloyd's brows knit into a single line as he stared back at Glo. "What did I say?"

Glo walked over to each rune in turn, talking excitedly and waving his hands as he went. "It's quite simple, actually. While it is true that each rune has a special name and meaning, they are also associated with a letter in the elder language. Depending on how you look at it, these runes are indeed very much like those back in the Darkwoods monolith!"

Seth let out a contemptuous snort. "Sure, leave it to a wizard to pick the most complicated approach possible."

Alys still wore a puzzled expression on her comely brow. "Well then, what did we spell out so far?"

Glo ticked off each rune on his finger as he went. "*Zhukaya* is a 'J,' *Ihanen* is an 'I,' and *Ninathen* is an 'N.'"

"No way!" Seth exclaimed. "No frickin' way!"

Alys appeared equally as surprised as Seth. "Could the key really be the dracolich's name? Wouldn't that be just a little too obvious?"

Aksel threw up his hands and shrugged. "There's one way to find out."

Out of these next set of runes, Glo identified one of them as *Ratanen* which was associated with the letter 'K.' Sure enough, after Seth landed on it, it brought them to another pentagram.

The following group of runes included *Ta'kaya* which symbolizes the letter 'O.' That rune also brought them to another pentagram.

These new runes included *Nanen* which was associated with the letter 'L.' Choosing that rune produced another disturbing flash and teleportation effect. However, once they reappeared at the next platform, they noticed a distinct lack of that now familiar ticking sound.

A stark realization hit Glo as he swept his gaze over these current series of runes. Alys, however, beat him to expressing it. "Isn't this the same pattern as the first pentagram?"

"She's right," Glo affirmed with a sigh.

Lloyd squinted at the both of them. "So, what does that mean, exactly?"

"It means we picked the wrong letter, genius," Seth chastised the young man.

"Did we spell the name wrong?" Kalyn wondered.

Alys ticked the letters off again on her fingers. "No, that would have been correct," she confirmed once she finished.

Lloyd's face had reddened. He appeared to be close to bursting with frustration. "If the answer isn't her name, then why did the first few letters work?"

Unfortunately, no one had a good answer to that question. Nearly half a minute of silence passed until Alys finally broke it. "Actually, if I'm remembering right, Jinkolothos and Silverwind had a son—and that son's name was fairly similar to hers."

Glo gazed at the bardess expectantly. "Do you remember what it was?"

Alys gingerly tapped her chin as she mulled it over in her mind. "I think it was—Jinkisovan. No, wait, that can't be right." She immediately corrected herself. "Make that Jinkosivan."

Aksel pursed his lips together and nodded. "That would explain why the first five letters worked." He swept his gaze around the group. "What do you think?"

Seth snorted. "It's not like we have anything better to do."

"Agreed." Glo shrugged.

They started the entire process all over again. This time when they reached the sixth pentagram though, they chose the rune *Sha'oren* that symbolized 'S.' Everyone held their breath, but this time they indeed reappeared at a brand-new pentagram.

"Yahoo!"

"It worked!"

"Well, what do you know."

They all cried over the ticking of the latest crystal.

"Let's not get ahead of ourselves," Aksel cautioned. "If Alys is right, we still have four more pentagrams to go."

Glo spied another *Ihanen* 'I' rune on the left. After choosing that one, they were whisked to another new pentagram. There they chose *Drakneal* which stood for 'V,' *Athihan* or 'A' at the next, and another *Ninathen* 'N' rune at the one after that.

After being whooshed away one more time, the little company ended up at a pentagram with all empty rune circles. Directly ahead of them they spied four platforms far larger than the one they currently stood upon. The far most platform was enormous in fact. In its very center stood a towering skeletal figure. It was the dracolich, Jinkolothos.

18
A GIANT PROBLEM

Three skeletal giants stood on floating platforms between them and the dracolich.

Alys thought herself ready for anything after all that had happened these last few days. She was sorely mistaken. This ice-cold plane of mist had her spooked even more so than the Plane of Shadows. At least there you could see what was coming. Here, anything could be hiding behind those ominously fluffy clouds.

Furthermore, vampires did not scare her half as much as that dracolich. They all nearly died during their last encounter with the terrifying creature. They would have, in fact, had it not wanted something from them. This time, however, there was nothing stopping it from killing them all.

Upon reaching the last pentagram, Alys' throat grew dry, her heart beating wildly in her chest. On a huge platform not fifty yards ahead through the mists rose the frightening visage of Jinkolothos in full skeletal dragon form. Perhaps only slightly less daunting, three skeletal giants stood on floating platforms between them and the dracolich. Each of those tall figures brandished a giant sword easily twice the size of Lloyd.

"Well, that doesn't look good," Xellos remarked flippantly.

The normally quiet archer had a talent for understatement.

Alys had been so hyper-focused on the dracolich that she missed the huge slab beneath it. Across that slab lay another giant figure. Yet, it didn't belong to just any giant—this one glowed with a light of its own, a brilliant white light, in fact.

"Whelp, looks like we found Phobas," Kalyn drawled, "and that draco-lich to boot." Her face scrunched up as she tapped a finger to her chin. "Though can't say I expected to find her dancing over 'em like that."

Kalyn was not wrong. Despite her great size, Jinkolothos moved gracefully about the slab supporting the body of Phobas. Furthermore, the faint sound of chanting wafted across the distance that separated them. Shaking off the fear that had paralyzed her, Alys realized what was going on. "That's not a dance—that's a ritual."

"She's most likely trying to reanimate him," Aksel further deduced.

Alys felt a cold chill race up her spine. This is exactly what they feared. Jinkolothos was powerful enough as is. With the power of a god at her disposal their entire world would be in peril.

Aksel must have been thinking along the same lines. His voice was hushed as he queried Glo. "How long do you think we have?"

The wizard's expression already troubled, the creases across his brow deepened even further. "That's hard to say. Normally such a spell would take a few minutes at most, but the remains of a god are anything but normal."

"What's your best guess?" Aksel prodded him.

Glo nervously chewed on his lip before answering. "I'd say anywhere from a few more minutes to a couple of hours."

"That's really helpful." Seth snorted.

Glo's uncertainty did little to allay Alys' fears. The sense of urgency it impressed on her, however, made her realize this was no time to think of herself. Like the fairy tales she'd read as a child, this was the hero's moment—the moment where the hero put their life on the line to save others. The question was could she do that?

Gazing about at the determined expressions around her, she already knew how the others would answer. They'd done it before and would do it again. Yet, did she have what it takes? She'd already died once, was she willing to do so again?

A collection of familiar faces abruptly flashed through her mind: the stern countenance of her father, the smirking smile of her best friend, Thea, and the handsome visage of her true love, Pallas. If Jinkolothos had her way, they might all end up dead.

That crystallized things for Alys. She'd do anything to keep those she loved safe. Gulping down her fears, she steadied her voice and asked, "So—what's the plan?"

His jaw firmly set, Lloyd grabbed the edge of his cloak. "I say we ignore those giants and go straight for the dracolich."

"Brilliant, genius," Seth immediately chided him. "How are you planning on getting around that force barrier?"

Alys squinted in the direction of the dracolich. Sure enough, a barely discernible purplish tint hung in the air at the edge of the main platform. Seth was right, a nearly invisible wall of force encircled the entire thing.

Lloyd let out an exasperated sigh. "How are we supposed to get around that?"

Alys found herself wondering the same thing. Her eyes strayed back to the platforms with the giants. That's when she noticed the carvings on them.

"Those giants are standing on pentagrams like this one!" She pointed out excitedly to the others.

"And there's another crystal above each," Seth swiftly added.

Alys glanced upward to see Seth was right. Perhaps they had a chance after all.

Glo seemed to mirror her thoughts. "If we can find the right combination of runes, perhaps it will take down the barrier."

"Not until I take care of those crystals," Seth admonished.

Aksel stepped in front of them both and raised his hands as a signal for everyone to be quiet. "Alright, here's what we'll do. While Seth takes care of those crystals, the rest of us will concentrate on taking out the giants—without landing on those platforms," he quickly added before Seth could complain further.

Aksel's assuredness was just the tonic Alys needed to calm her nerves. Taking a deep breath, she once again immersed herself in the role of the bardess in this little group trying to save their world.

With time of the essence, they swiftly put their plan into motion. Seth disappeared from sight. Lloyd's body took on a silvery sheen as he launched himself towards the giant on the left. Xellos, Martan, Kalyn, Decon, and Daer sent a barrage of arrows flying at the giant on the right.

Alys wouldn't have guessed those arrows would have much of an impact on a creature made of bones. She was wrong. Whether by magic, a trick, or pure skill, that barrage sent the giant skeleton reeling.

At the same time, Lloyd closed in on the other giant. Alys flinched as the creature attempted to swat him with its mammoth sword, but her concern appeared unwarranted as the warrior effortlessly spiraled around the blade in midair. His own black sword coming ablaze, Lloyd sliced the arm clean off the creature as he swept past.

Alys started to *whoop* for joy when all of a sudden, the floor beneath her started to tilt.

"Grab onto the edge!" Glo cried as the platform continued to slip away from under them.

Alys' years of acrobatic study proved useful once again. What had been a lark to improve her stage performance allowed her to knock out that witch back at Redune. Now with practiced ease she executed a midair flip that let her catch the edge of the platform.

Glo's height enabled him to catch it as well, but Aksel was not so lucky. As the little cleric slid away, Alys acted on pure instinct. Tucking her feet over the edge she lunged as the gnome went sliding past. By the grace of the gods, she just managed to catch the hood of his cloak with her outstretched hand.

"Th—thanks," Aksel stammered as the entire platform turned on its side.

Alys hadn't quite thought out how the two of them would get

back up. Luckily, Glo was there to lend a hand. Afterwards they paused to catch their breath as they balanced precariously on the edge of the platform out in the middle of the mists.

Kalyn Rhan had been enamored with the companions since before they met. Tales of the daring Heroes of Ravenford had reached Deepwood Fort prior to her first encounter with Seth. Upon meeting them all she practically gushed, completely losing it when they invited her to join their ranks. Even so, it didn't take long for Kalyn to discover they had faults and foibles just like everyone else. She wasn't about to admit that to anyone though, especially not Martan.

The gloomy archer had been her best friend back in Deepwood until his abrupt departure. That betrayal had left an ugly stain upon her heart. When they reunited Kalyn had been loath to forgive him, but then he went and sacrificed himself to save her from that medusa. She'd all but forgiven him after that right up until she found him in bed with that Ves look-alike hussy.

Kalyn had done her best to decapitate him afterwards. Yet, despite the worst she could manage, Martan stuck by her side. He'd even followed her back to Deepwood despite the fact that they nearly hung him. Even now he chose to stay with her though the thought of hunting the dracolich obviously terrified him.

Martan let out a gloomy sigh. "I still don't know what we're doing here. I don't think arrows are going to do much good against those giant bones."

"Ah, that's where yer wrong, my friend," Decon countered as he and Daer set down their packs. Reaching inside they rummaged around until both simultaneously pulled out a group of arrows.

A wide grin stretched across Daer's roundish face as he held them up in his hands. "Yeah, we brought some of 'dem bone-crusher arrows with us!"

The Deepwood Snipers had long since come up with ways to deal with tough-skinned opponents. The arrows her brothers held in their hands were blunt tipped. Though that vastly cut down their range, they would wreak havoc on skeletal bones.

Martan sighed again as he took the proffered handful. "Guess we might as well give it a try."

Kalyn nudged him in the arm, her lips twisting upward as he nearly dropped the arrows from his hands. "That's the spirit!"

Martan wisely chose not to reply as they all lined up to shoot at the giant.

Kalyn felt right at home with this little squad of archers. They were some of the best she'd ever seen. Xellos had an almost inhuman knack for finding the weak spots in the toughest opponents. His arrows incredulously sheared off sections of bone from the skeleton of the giant. The rest of them were no slouches, either. Those blunt-tipped arrows did their jobs splitting and cracking the giant's bony torso.

"Take that!" Kalyn hooted with excitement. Her enthusiasm proved short-lived, however, as the floor beneath her abruptly tipped sideways.

"Leap for it!" Decon cried as he launched himself across the intervening space towards the giant's platform.

Daer almost immediately followed. Their training in the trees of Bendenwood paid off as each easily landed the rather long jump. Xellos was not far behind, the slim tracker leaping like a gazelle. He effortlessly cleared the distance landing on the other side with room to spare.

Kalyn chanced a brief look down before making the jump herself. There was nothing below her but clouds and more clouds. If she fell, she might be doing so forever.

Steeling her resolve, she cried out as she leaped. "Come on, Martan!"

Stretching her legs as she sailed through the air, Kalyn landed in a crouch just at the edge of the giant's platform. She turned her head to wink at Martan, but blanched as she saw he wasn't next to her. Spinning about, she saw him hesitate as he stood at the edge of the tilting platform.

"He ain't gonna make it if he waits much longer," Decon warned.

Her heart leaping into her throat, Kalyn cupped her hands together and screamed, "Martan Folke, you get your hiney over here now!"

Thankfully her words spurred him into action. Martan closed his eyes and leaped. It was a good jump, but he had waited just a second or so too long. As he sailed across the empty space his body began to arc downward.

Martan's hand just barely caught the edge of the platform as he slammed into it. He immediately lost his grip, slipping away down the side.

Without thinking Kalyn threw herself over the edge and caught his wrist in midair. Though she had managed to slow his descent, she too now began to slip over the side after him.

Martan's face contorted with anguish. "Kalyn, what are you doing? Let go before I drag you down with me!"

"Quit yer belly achin'," she yelled back at him. "I ain't about to let you die. If anybody's gonna kill you it's gonna be me!"

Martan's eyes glistened with moisture as he stared back up at her. What she saw in them nearly made her lose her grip. There was love in those deep brown eyes—love directed straight at her.

Briefly lost in that lasting moment, reality reasserted itself as Kalyn slid farther over the edge. She thought that might be it for the both of them when strong arms grabbed her legs and hauled the two of them back to safety.

Kalyn gulped as they sat at the edge of the platform trying to catch their breath. What she had seen in Martan's eyes left her spooked. She had no idea how to react to such feelings. No one had ever felt that way about her before. So, instead she resorted to what she did best.

"Martan, what were you thinking! You nearly got us both killed," she scolded her pensive friend.

Martan opened his mouth to reply, but never got the chance as Xellos interrupted them. "Guys, I think we have a bigger problem right now. A lot bigger."

Kalyn glanced up just in time to see an artic blast of snow and ice heading straight for them.

Shooting past the skeletal giant, Lloyd reveled at how easily he had lopped off the creature's bony arm. Perhaps he had misjudged this new black blade. Even with Soulbreaker or the Shin Tauri blade he couldn't have stopped that shadow creature from mortally wounding Glo.

I could be so much more.

Lloyd faltered in midair at the sound of the strange whisper. With the one-armed giant behind him and the third giant well out of reach there was no one else around. Was he hearing things?

Together we could protect all your friends if you'll let me.

There was the whisper again. He definitely heard it this time. It only took him a moment to realize the voice was inside his mind. Coming to a halt in midair, he thought, *Jack? Is that you?*

Yes, came the demon's reply. *If you help me to become stronger, none of your friends need ever be in danger again.*

Lloyd gulped. This was exactly the kind of thing he'd been warned about growing up. Never trust a demon. And yet, his friends had already made a pact with it. Furthermore, he wanted to protect them more than anything else.

Struggling with a mixture of fear and desire, Lloyd responded with a tentative thought. *Stronger how?*

Jack's response was decidedly cryptic. *When the time comes, I'll let you know. Right now, your friends need you.*

Lloyd glanced back past the one-armed giant to see his friends were indeed in trouble. The platform they'd stood on had tipped upward leaving Glo, Aksel, and Alys balancing precariously on the upper edge.

Without another thought, Lloyd launched himself back the way he had come. The one-armed giant swung at him as he sped past, but Lloyd easily outmaneuvered the heavy blade.

The rest of the party had all leapt to the platform with the second giant. Lloyd nearly veered off towards them as that creature fired an icy blast from the tip of its blade. Yet, somehow they all managed to dodge out of the way in time.

Lloyd let out a sigh of relief. "Phew, that was close."

His gratitude swiftly faded, however, when he realized that the other giants might be able to do the same. Glo, Aksel, and Alys would be sitting ducks for an icy blast.

Glo must have realized it as well. The wizard cast a spell on himself, then rose from the platform with an arm around Aksel and Alys each. He wobbled as he did so, however, making it obvious he was overburdened.

Lloyd swept in and pulled up in front of them. "Need a hand?"

"Oh yes, please," Glo acknowledged with a weak smile.

"I'll go with you," Alys offered, outstretching her arms towards the hovering warrior.

Just as Lloyd took Alys into his arms, a *whoop* of triumph sounded from the other platform. He spun about to see the head of the giant had been shorn from its shoulders. The rest of the giant skeleton crumbled, tumbling off the platform and into the murky mists below.

As soon as it fell, the pentagram and runes on the platform lit up. A blast of snow and ice then erupted outward engulfing their friends in a blizzard of white.

"Take me over there," Aksel urgently implored Glo.

Glo's expression was grim as he sped off with Aksel. In the meantime, Alys had the same idea as Lloyd.

"Let's take out that other one," she told him solemnly.

Lloyd hesitated for the briefest of moments before responding. "That's going to be kind of difficult with me carrying you and all."

A hard smile spread across Aly's lips. "Don't you worry about that. I'll take care of these stupid things."

Lloyd's resolve hardened as he took off back towards the one-armed skeleton. It was a good thing they did. They closed just as the creature took aim with the point of its blade at Glo and Aksel.

Alys let loose with a deafening scream that slammed into the side of the giant. Caught by surprise, the creature slid to the edge of the platform. It tumbled off into the mists before it could catch itself.

Lloyd wanted to cheer, but there was no time. He swiftly banked and veered away expecting an icy blast from the platform. That blast never came, however. Peering upward, Lloyd noticed that the crystal above them had gone dark.

Good old Seth, Lloyd thought with keen satisfaction.

"Lloyd, the last one!" Alys cried, her voice filled with terror.

Lloyd snapped his head back around towards the remaining giant.

Its sword stood poised in front of it, the tip pointed directly at their friends.

We're too far away! Lloyd thought wildly. They'd never make it in time, unless...

Lloyd started to focus inward. He'd never tried the warp technique while holding onto someone else. He had no idea if he could do it, but he had to try. Time around them started to slow when Alys abruptly broke his concentration.

"Look!" she cried, pointing at the giant's feet.

A dark puddle had appeared beneath the creature and quickly expanded to encompass both its legs. The giant faltered where it stood, all else forgotten as it desperately tried to maintain its balance. In the end, it lost. The last giant fell to the floor with a resounding *crack*.

"You're welcome," a familiar voice echoed down from the last crystal.

Lloyd peered up and grinned at Seth.

The halfling pointed to the still glowing crystal. "I'll take care of this thing. You handle the rest."

Lloyd nodded, then exchanged a glance with Alys.

"Let's finish this," she told him with a devilish smile.

Lloyd flew her over to where the last giant lay in a heap. A short yell was all it took to send the creature sliding off the edge.

"Well, that's that..." Lloyd began, but halted as a gong sounded from somewhere across the cloudy landscape.

Over on the main platform, the dracolich halted in its ritual. It raised its bony head and cast a malevolent glance their way.

Aksel felt a lump in his throat as Glo flew him over to the icy platform. The snow hadn't quite settled yet making it hard to see if anyone had been severely injured by that blast. A picture formed unbidden in his mind of Glo after he'd been frozen solid. The thought made Aksel blanch. Both Glo and Seth nearly paid the price for his recklessness.

Well, he wasn't about to repeat that same mistake if he could help it. Following Jinkolothos into her own domain may have been foolhardy, but that didn't mean they had to fight her to the death. On their first encounter, she hadn't seemed hell bent on destroying the world. In fact, she appeared more desperate than not.

Aksel had no doubt she would have carried out her threat if they hadn't met their part of the bargain. Still, she'd been willing to talk to them back then. If he could only discover what it was she wanted now, perhaps they could resolve things without resorting to further violence. For the moment, however, he needed to make certain that everyone survived that last assault.

The snow had cleared enough as they landed for Aksel to see everyone on the platform. They all appeared somewhat frozen, but by the grace of the gods, no one had died.

"Gather around me," he instructed as he began to pray.

A great surge of magic spread out around him as they all huddled closer. It manifested itself in the form of a bright white aura. It was the same type of aura he had seen Thea emit back when they first met the vampire lord.

Aksel breathed an inward sigh. Those few hours he had spent studying with Sirus had not been wasted.

"Th-that's a n-neat trick," Kalyn managed through chattering teeth.

"Perhaps some heat might help as well," Glo offered. Still standing behind Aksel the wizard conjured up some mild fire magic.

While the two of them healed their friends, Lloyd, Alys, and Seth took care of the other two giants. As soon as the last one fell, however, the ring of an unseen gong echoed across the misty landscape.

The sound seemed to alert the dracolich. She paused in her elaborate ritual and raised her head to stare out at the group.

"Why did you follow me here?" Her voice rang out across the clouds.

The fact that she had chosen to talk filled Aksel with hope. If he could just make her see reason, perhaps they could avoid a deadly battle. Sweeping his eyes around the platform, he saw that his companions were mostly healed.

Leaning towards Glo, he whispered, "Continue warming them. I'll talk to Jinkolothos."

Glo arched an eyebrow at him. He could see the skepticism in his friend's eyes, but all Glo ended up saying was, "Good luck."

Taking a deep breath, Aksel doused his aura and stepped forth to the edge of the platform. He made sure to keep his tone slow and measured so as not to antagonize her. "You took something which did not belong to you. I don't believe that was part of the original deal."

A thin laugh came from the back of Jinkolothos' throat. "I'd say it's a fair trade. The world has taken much from me, so I took something from it in return."

Aksel could almost feel the weight of her suffering in those words. He thought back to their first encounter. She had alluded to losing her family back then. That was something he could empathize with.

"I understand loss," he told her frankly. "My entire family was taken from me."

Aksel almost choked as he said it. He'd never quite admitted that out loud before. It affected him more than he realized.

"I hear the pain in your voice," Jinkolothos responded with uncharacteristic sympathy. "Perhaps you do understand."

It was the first hint of compassion he'd noticed her exhibit. If he continued along this tack, maybe he could get through to her. "I do, in fact," he continued somberly, "but understanding should go both ways. The Gods no longer walk this earth for a reason. The last time they did so, Arinthar was nearly torn asunder."

Unfortunately, that did not go as well as he hoped. The dragon snorted in response, cold steam puffing from her bony nostrils. "I no longer care for this world. Once, long ago, we tried to save it. And what did we get for our trouble? Pain and death." Her head edged forward as if her next words were meant specifically for him. "The path of the hero is a lonely one. In the end it brings nothing but heartache."

Her solemn pronouncement chilled Aksel even more than the cold air around them. Was what she said true? Was he destined to end up alone again like before?

No. He wouldn't believe that. Seth, Glo, Lloyd—they were like family to him. He'd die before he'd let anything happen to them again. Still, despite what she had become, he couldn't help feeling sorry for this lonely, misguided creature. "I realize that you have suffered terribly, but can't you see that what you are doing will only put others through that same kind of pain?"

Jinkolothos cocked her huge head to one side as if mulling over his words. After a short pause, she responded, "Do you not see they are already in pain?"

She turned her empty eye sockets upon Glo. "Some are outcasts and can never return home." She tilted her head down at Seth. "Others will never live down the shame of their family." She then fixed her gaze on Lloyd. "Still others are doomed to lose their soul."

Aksel's brow creased further and further with each subsequent observation. Was Jinkolothos a diviner as well as a necromancer? Her pronouncements over Seth and Glo struck far too close to home. What truly worried him, however, was her prophecy concerning Lloyd. He made a mental note to keep an even closer eye on Jack.

For now, though, he needed to make Jinkolothos see reason. "It doesn't have to be that way. We all carry pain inside us. It's when you give into that pain that you lose touch with all the good the world has to offer."

Aksel spoke from personal experience. After losing his family, he walled himself off from everyone. He never let anyone else get close to him until he met Seth and Glo.

His impromptu attempt at counseling was met with utter silence. Those empty eye sockets gave him no insight as to what Jinkolothos might be thinking.

All of a sudden, she started to laugh. It was soft at first, but steadily grew into a shrill maniacal sound.

An uneasy feeling grew in the pit of Aksel's stomach. He had failed and things were about to take a turn for the worse.

When she finally spoke, Jinkolothos confirmed his fears. "You would dare lecture me about pain—me who walked this world for centuries before you were even born?"

She took a step forward, her head rising up higher as her voice boomed across the clouds. "I—lost—everything: my love, my son, and even my castle. Well, no more. Now I start taking back."

The dracolich emphasized her dark pronouncement by slamming her tail down on the platform behind her. In response, three small discs floated down from the clouds above. A human-sized skeleton in tattered robes stood on each.

"Watch out!" Glo cried out in warning. "Those are necromancers."

Aksel braced himself for the worst as the trio began their dark incantations.

19
LOOK WHAT YOU MAGE ME DO

Great swirls of dark energy spun furiously about the trio.

Seth couldn't get over the fact that he'd let the dracolich make off with Phobas' body. It was not like him to overlook something so obvious. His time with this group had definitely made him soft. If only he'd been thinking straight, they wouldn't be in this mess in the first place—traipsing through these never-ending clouds, solving those overly-complicated puzzles, and fighting off those stupid giants.

As if that wasn't enough, their success had been rewarded with the sound of some unseen gong, alerting the dracolich to their presence. Intent on her ritual over Phobas' dead body, she had ignored them up until now. True to form, Aksel attempted to reason with her. Seth knew it wouldn't work, but at least it kept her busy long enough for him to spy out another set of runes.

This particular set lined the outside of the main platform. From what Seth could tell, they appeared to be more elder dragon runes.

With any luck maybe they'd drop the barrier. Then again, maybe that wouldn't be so lucky. After all, they hadn't exactly fared well against this creature the first time.

"…The Gods no longer walk this earth for a reason. The last time they did so, Arinthar was nearly torn asunder," Aksel tried to reason with the dracolich.

The dead dragon's response was pretty much as Seth would have predicted. She snorted and said, "I no longer care for this world…"

She droned on from there, but Seth blocked out the rest. He cared little for her brand of whining, yet it did keep her distracted long enough to let him fly down to those new runes unnoticed.

Looking them over carefully, Seth spotted one that he thought represented the letter 'J'. He tried landing on it, but nothing happened.

The corner of his mouth upturned ever so slightly. *That would've been far too easy.*

"Others will never live down the shame of their family."

Though Seth had blocked out most of the dragon's droning, that particular phrase caught his attention. He peered up to see her large head staring down directly at him.

Seth froze in place. Despite her moaning, she'd been aware of his movements after all. Even so, he wasn't buying her fortune teller act. He'd seen far too many charlatans in his lifetime, and it didn't take a genius to peg him as some sort of outcast.

Seth's greater concern lay in the fact that she'd caught him red-handed standing on this latest puzzle. His concern turned out to be unwarranted, however, as she swiftly moved her gaze onward to Lloyd.

"Still others are doomed to lose their soul."

Now those words got Seth's undivided attention. He'd thought basically the same thing when Lloyd first picked up that damn sword.

The more Seth thought about it though, the more he realized it was just another trick. With her uncanny senses, the dracolich probably recognized the demon sword for what it was. Again, it didn't take a genius to put two and two together from there.

With the dragon's attention once again elsewhere, Seth's thoughts returned to the puzzle before him. Since landing on the 'J' had done nothing, that ruled out both Jinkolothos and Jinkisovan as possible solutions. So, what did that leave him with?

Maybe Silverwind? He reasoned.

Seth's eyes focused on a nearby rune that he recognized as representing the letter 'S.' Leaping over the intervening symbols, he landed squarely upon it.

Once again, nothing happened.

Any further thoughts on his part were interrupted as the dead dragon's voice boomed overhead. "I—lost—everything: my love, my son, and even my castle. Well, no more. Now I start taking back."

A loud crash followed her dire pronouncement and the platform around Seth began to shake violently. It was all he could do to stop himself from tumbling off the edge and into the endless mists below.

A moment later, Glo's voice rang out across the cloudscape. "Watch out! Those are necromancers."

Seth peered up from where he precariously balanced to see three skeletons in black robes float down from the clouds above.

The halfling let out a heavy sigh. *Give me a break. How many more of these things does she have hidden away in these stupid clouds?*

Martan firmly believed he was cursed. The long-suffering archer thought his luck had finally turned when the young heroes first recruited him. He soon found that to be a mistake. His life had been in a constant state of danger ever since. From serpents and demons to dragons and undead Martan had nearly died twice. And just when he thought it couldn't get any worse, they now stood face-to-face with a huge undead dragon.

Standing on a small platform not thirty yards away from the fearsome creature, Martan silently wondered, *Why do I keep doing this to myself?*

The answer, however, stood not two feet away from him.

Kalyn seemed so enamored with the heroes that he was afraid she'd get herself killed following them around. In all good conscience, he couldn't allow her to walk that path alone. Neither could he count on her brothers. Decon and Daer were just as reckless as the companions. Thus, if Martan wanted to keep her safe, he'd have to do it himself.

Well, if I'm to die, at least it will be by her side, he thought glumly.

That had almost happened a third time now. If Aksel had not stepped in when he did, they would all have at best lost limbs to frostbite. Even so, they were not out of the woods just yet. Aside from the undead dragon, three skeletons in dark robes had dropped out of the clouds moments ago.

Strangely, the undead mages had not done anything obvious since. Perhaps Martan should have been grateful that they weren't throwing around spells yet. Still, that very fact made him all the more nervous.

"What are they doing up there?" he whispered anxiously to Kalyn.

"I'm not waitin' to find out. The only good skele mage is a dead skele mage," she answered as she drew an arrow from her quiver.

Martan's brow knit into a deep frown at her last statement. "… but, they're already dead."

Kalyn cast him a scathing look before nocking her arrow and taking aim at the creatures above. "You know what I mean."

Shaking his head, Martan rushed to draw an arrow and catch up to her. Xellos, Decon, and Daer had already followed suit.

The twang of five bowstrings went off almost simultaneously as each archer fired. Five thin, wooden projectiles sailed unerringly upward towards their unmoving targets.

For a minute, Martan thought the arrows would hit their marks. Yet, each, in turn, bounced harmlessly off some unseen barrier not a foot away from its target.

"Dragon dung!" Kalyn swore. "Must have up some sort of protection spell."

Martan paused to scratch his head. He'd seen the black mage Voltark use a similar spell on his first encounter with the heroes. Such a magical shield was impenetrable by arrows.

Feeling completely useless, he exchanged a puzzled glance with the other archers. "So, what do we do now?"

Kalyn's jaw was set with conviction. "I say we keep on shootin'."

Martan peered at her as if she were daft. "What good will that do?"

Kalyn drew another arrow as she answered. "Maybe not much more irritating than a swarm of mosquitoes in the summer, but maybe it'll distract them if nothin' else."

Once again Martan swept his eyes around the group of archers. True to form, the normally quiet Xellos said nothing and just drew another arrow. Decon and Daer peered at the two for a few moments, then both brothers merely shrugged and followed suit.

"This is crazy," Martan muttered to himself, "but I guess it's better than just standing around and waiting to die."

Drawing another arrow as well, he nearly dropped it as a sharp fist hit him in the shoulder. Martan glanced over to see Kalyn staring at him with that goofy grin of hers.

"That's the spirit!" she cheered him on as she drew yet another arrow for yet another useless shot.

Glo had grown more and more anxious since finding the dracolich with the body of Phobas. He really wanted to know what kind of ritual she was performing, but between that barrier and all the distractions, it was hard to tell. His primary concern at the moment, however, was those three skeletal mages that had just descended from above. Even from down here he could sense them gathering magic, though none as of yet had cast a spell.

His apprehension mounting, Glo floated upward for a closer look as he attempted to peer beyond the veil. His efforts were interrupted, however, as Seth called out, "Anything else that might be important to the dracolich besides what we've already tried?"

His concentration broken, Glo shifted his gaze downward. Seth stood at the edge of the main platform, just outside the barrier separating them from the dracolich. Along that edge Glo spied a line of runes similar to those around the pentagrams.

It immediately struck him what Seth was trying to do. This new puzzle must be the key to lowering the barrier. Thankfully Jinkolothos didn't seem to care. After summoning those skeletal casters, she'd gone back to her lengthy ritual over Phobas' remains.

"Have you tried Silverwind?" Glo responded with the first thing that came to mind.

Seth glared back up at him. "Duh. Do I look stupid?"

"Try Argazephari," Alys called down to him from where she hovered nearby with Lloyd. "That was Silverwind's real name."

"'A—that would be Dance of Blades," Glo heard Seth mutter as he gazed up and down the line of runes.

Glo was duly impressed. The crafty halfling had picked up rather quickly on the Elder Dragon symbols.

Seth swiftly spotted the correct rune and leapt towards it. Just as with the pentagram puzzles, the rune lit up as he landed.

Seth peered up at Alys with the hint of a smile. "Looks like we have a winner." His lips abruptly quirked to one side. "Now, want to spell the rest of that?"

Despite the direness of the situation, Seth's irreverent attitude managed to break the tension. Glo had found that irritating at first. It took him a while to realize that Seth's behavior was his way of diffusing stressful situations.

In this particular case it worked. A touch of amusement crossed Alys' face as she started to spell the deceased dragon's name. "A—R—"

While Alys continued to guide Seth, Glo turned his attention back to the three mages. Focusing his gaze beyond the veil, he spied something that sent chills up his spine. Great swirls of dark energy spun furiously about the trio. Normally such energy would be funneled into a spell, but instead they seemed to be channeling the bulk of it off into the nearby clouds.

Glo's brow knit into a deep frown. *What in the world are they doing with all that?*

Tightening his focus, Glo peered deeper into the dim mists beyond the casters. After a few moments, his eyes detected the vague outline of a large figure. Though big, the figure appeared rather scant.

All of a sudden it dawned on Glo what he was seeing. His heart thumped wildly in his chest as he called out a warning to the others. "They're healing the giants!"

As if to confirm his statement, a giant skeleton dropped down out of the clouds and landed with a loud *thump* on the platform just opposite where Aksel and the archers stood. Not two seconds later, a second giant dropped down and landed on the platform between them and the barrier.

As luck would have it, the pool of grease Seth had cast still covered the surface of that platform. The giant had barely touched down when it lost its balance and slid over the edge. The bony creature made no sound as it disappeared into the mists below.

Glo almost laughed aloud, but the sound died in his throat as the last giant slammed down onto the third platform in the midst of his friends. Thankfully, his last-minute warning paid off.

Already alerted, the archers all spun about and hit the giant with a heavy barrage of arrows. Unfortunately, it was not enough to fell the creature. They all had to dodge out of the way as it swung its giant sword at them.

Sadly, Aksel was not quite as nimble as the others. While rolling out of the way, he drew a bit too close to the edge. Before he could stop himself, Aksel went tumbling over the side.

Thankfully, Kalyn was right there. She leapt after him, catching him with one hand and grabbing onto the edge with the other.

Seeing his friends in trouble, Glo acted on pure instinct. He cast the fly spell on Alys, then shouted to Lloyd, "Go help them!"

Lloyd tentatively loosened his grip on the young lady. As soon as she realized she could float on her own though, Alys pushed him away and reiterated, "You heard the man. Go help them!"

A foolish grin momentarily crossed Lloyd's face. It immediately disappeared, however, as he drew his sword and dove down to help the others.

As Lloyd sped away, Alys suddenly wobbled in mid-air. Her hand shot out and grasped onto Glo, her nails digging deep into his skin. Thankfully, her sudden panic swiftly subsided. Her cheeks reddened as she loosened her grip.

"Sorry," Alys apologized with a doleful smile, "but how in the world are you supposed to balance like this?"

A short laugh rumbled in the back of Glo's throat. The first time he tried to fly it hadn't gone smoothly either. Somehow, he'd ended up hanging upside down in mid-air.

"It does take some getting used to," he admitted wryly. Grabbing her hand, he gently lifted it away from his arm and grasped it with his other hand.

"I'll steady you for now," Glo assured her. "What say we take care of that other giant?"

He nudged his head towards the giant standing alone on the second platform.

Alys followed his gaze, then flashed him a bright smile. "Yes, let's."

Kalyn had just about enough of these "goldarn" giants. First Martan and now Aksel nearly plummeted off into the mists below. The gods only knew if they'd have ever seen them again. Luckily, she'd been fast enough to catch both. Even so, this had to stop before someone fell who she couldn't get to in time.

Fortunately, Aksel was a lot lighter than Martan. Nonetheless, he stopped her as she went to haul him up. "Wait a moment."

Kalyn's brow creased. "What for? Light as you are, I can't hold you here forever."

The little cleric was not listening though. Instead, he seemed to be concentrating on the staff in his other hand. A sudden flash of blue light radiated outwards, momentarily causing spots before Kalyn's eyes. Abruptly, the weight on her arm vanished.

"You can let go now." Aksel's voice sounded devoid of emotion.

"If'n you say so," Kalyn responded, praying the little guy knew what he was doing.

Sure enough, as their hands parted, Aksel did not fall. Instead, he just floated there as if walking on air.

"Neat trick," Kalyn admitted. Under better circumstances she might have gushed at how cool that was, but right now they had a giant problem to take care of.

As Kalyn pulled herself back from the edge, she caught sight of something red out of the corner of her eye. Lloyd dove down from above straight in front of the giant on the opposite platform. Sharply banking at the last moment, the young warrior headed straight in her direction.

Behind him, the giant raised its huge sword and pointed the tip at the retreating warrior. Not a second later, a blast of snow and ice shot across the space rushing after him.

"Watch out!" Kalyn screamed as she flung herself back down against the platform.

She could feel the chill of that blast through her clothes as it passed within inches of her. An involuntary shiver swept through her body threatening to overwhelm her. It had only been a few minutes since they'd all nearly frozen to death. If it hadn't been for Aksel…

Get a grip, girl, Kalyn admonished herself. *This is no time to get all willy-nilly over somethin' that might have been.*

Forcing herself to raise her head, she was just in time to see that Lloyd had somehow managed to avoid that blast. The same couldn't be said for their giant though. The creature had been blanketed in a thick coat of snow and ice.

If things hadn't been so dire, she would have laughed. Sweeping her gaze around the platform, she spied the rest of the archers a short distance around the edge. When her eyes fell on her brother Decon though, a wild thought came to mind.

It was a Deepwood thing—something they'd tried on the occasional large game. However, they'd never tried it on something this big. Even so, she thought it might be worth a shot.

Cupping her hands together, she yelled to Decon, "The bigger they are…"

Decon squinted at her for a moment, then nodded and doffed his pack mimicking her. The two archers swiftly pulled out ropes and attached them each to the end of an arrow.

"Whatever you two are doing, you better hurry!" Martan warned.

Sure enough, the giant had begun to shake the snow and ice from its body.

At almost the same exact moment, the two archers fired. Their arrows flew true passing straight through the shin bones on either of the giant's legs. Both then buried themselves into the platform beyond. Kalyn and Decon then hurried to stake down the other ends of each rope.

Its head and torso now completely clear of snow, the giant raised its sword for another swipe at the waiting archers. As it stepped forward and went to swing, however, the ropes caught between its legs.

The weight of the large creature pulled the arrow heads and stakes out of the platform, but that just made things worse for it. The loose ropes went flying in multiple directions, tangling themselves around the giant's legs.

The creature took maybe another step or two before its legs gave out beneath it. The giant went tumbling forth, causing Kalyn to dive out of the way.

Kalyn felt the platform rock beneath her as she rolled back onto her feet. Taking a moment to steady herself, she then joined in as they hit the downed creature with another barrage of arrows. Aksel finished the volley with a blinding ray of white light and the thrashing skeleton abruptly went still.

As Daer *whooped* for joy, Martan peered quizzically from Decon to Kalyn. "…the harder they fall, I guess?"

"You're darn tootin'!" Kalyn exclaimed with a wink at the broody young man.

Despite Glolindir's assurances, Alys still felt a tad nervous about flying. Lloyd made it look so easy the way he arced through the air. He was like a fish in water while she felt more like a beached whale.

Still, with the handsome elf holding her hand she didn't quite wobble like before. In fact, with his guidance, their descent proved to be rather smooth.

Lloyd had dived down well ahead of them. Instead of going after the giant attacking their friends, however, he buzzed the other one.

"What in the world is he up to?" Alys wondered aloud.

"I believe he's trying to use the one against the other," Glo mused in response.

Sure enough, Lloyd maneuvered around the one giant causing it to spray its companion with snow and ice.

"That's brilliant!" Alys squealed with delight.

That had come out a bit louder than she planned. She immediately clamped her free hand over her mouth.

Fortunately, her boisterous cry had not caught the attention of the giant below. Intent on Lloyd, it didn't seem to notice them at all as they slowly descended behind it.

As soon as they drew within a few dozen yards, Glo traced a spell through the air with his free hand. Alys had become so accustomed to magic that she could actually see the symbol fill with glowing mana.

The handsome wizard released the spell with a single word. *"Arvina."*

The mana rushed forth from the symbol and disappeared as far as Alys could see. Not a second later, a dark pool appeared beneath the giant's feet. The creature struggled to maintain its balance, dropping its huge sword and spreading its legs wide.

Alys fixed the wizard with a mischievous smile. "Taking a card out of Seth's playbook, I see."

A closemouthed laugh rumbled in the back of the elf's throat. "Just don't tell him—it'll go to his head."

Its legs spread wide, the giant somehow managed to maintain its balance. Even so, it appeared unable to move without wobbling dangerously.

Glo's deep blue eyes remained fixed on Alys as he nudged his head towards the compromised creature. "Care to do the honors?"

"Why certainly," Alys responded with an impish grin.

Drawing in a deep breath, she pulled the mana in through her diaphragm. The energy coursed through her body, encircling her vocal cords and vibrating them at a fevered pitch.

Alys opened her mouth and let that force loose with a high-pitched wail. The resulting sonic wave slammed into the barely standing skeleton knocking it over and pushing off the edge of the platform.

When it was over, Alys gave the handsome elf a coy smile. "How was that?"

Glo's blue eyes danced with amusement. "I'm no music critic, but I would rate that performance an A+."

Seth had given some serious thought to taking out those black mages. Still, he was loath to waste any more time on stupid minions. The longer the dracolich kept them distracted, the more likely she'd finish her crazy ritual. Whatever she was planning, Seth knew it wouldn't end well for anyone living.

When Alys' suggestion proved to be correct, Seth made up his mind. *I'm sure the others can handle a few minions by themselves.*

Blocking out everything else, Seth proceeded to leap from letter to letter along the edge of the platform. When he finally finished spelling out Argazephari, nearly half of the runes were lit.

Seth gazed up expectantly at the shimmering purple barrier above him. A satisfied smirk graced his lips as it faded from top to bottom until it disappeared completely.

"Child's play," Seth murmured to no one in particular.

His good mood swiftly faded, however, as the surrounding clouds suddenly rolled in over the main platform. In mere seconds, the entire thing had been obscured from his view.

"Dragon dung," Seth cursed himself aloud for not having seen this obvious turn of events.

Feeling like a sitting duck, he shrouded himself in his cloak of invisibility and lifted off away from the edge of the now hidden platform.

With the last giant fallen, Martan felt lucky to still be alive. In just these last few minutes, he'd been both nearly frozen to death and fallen tohis death. The latter would have certainly happened if not for Kalyn.

When this is all said and done, I'm going to tell her how I feel—before it's too late, Martan swore to himself.

Sadly, they were not out of the woods just yet. Those dead mages were still up there. On top of that, a bank of fog had rolled in, hiding the platform with the dracolich and the dead god.

Dead gods? Undead dragons? Martan thought incredulously. This was all way over the simple archer's head.

With the giants gone again for the moment, everyone regrouped at the platform where Martan stood with Kalyn, her brothers, and Xellos.

"What do we do now?" Lloyd asked while nervously fingering the hilt of the large sword strapped to his back. Martan had overheard Alys confide to Kalyn that the black blade was actually a demon. Though it seemed a bit farfetched to him, he had noticed Lloyd acting more anxious than usual.

"We better take care of those mages first or we'll have to fight those giants all over again," Glo cautioned.

"Arrows weren't exactly working all that well the last time," Xellos pointed out.

The quiet young man was not wrong, but thankfully Aksel had a plan. The little cleric was definitely the most pragmatic of the heroes.

"Lloyd, Alys, and I will take care of those mages," Aksel told the wizard. "You see if you can clear away that fog."

Aksel then swept his eyes over the remaining archers. "The rest of you get ready for battle."

As the others flew off, Martan leaned in close to Kalyn. "And just what exactly does he think we've been doing all along?"

Kalyn responded by elbowing him in the side. "Shush, you know what he means."

Lloyd just wanted this all to be over. They'd been gone from Penwick for far too long and he was worried about his parents and Andrella.

Though both Aksel and Alys were already airborne, Lloyd did not have the patience to wait for the two of them. So, instead he grabbed each by the hand and whisked them up to where the mages still hovered. Neither complained though. In fact, Alys seemed to enjoy zipping through the air at the speeds he was used to.

Once they drew within line of the mages, Aksel lined out a quick strategy. "Lloyd, you take the one on the left, Alys, the one on the right, and I'll go for the farthest one."

Letting them both go, Lloyd hesitated before drawing the black blade. It hasn't said anything else to him since earlier, but its words had unnerved him. Even so, it was the only sword he had at the moment and it did do a ton of damage.

This is no time for thinking. It's time to act, Lloyd chided himself.

With that, he launched forth at the mage on the left. The three mages had ignored their presence up until now, most likely concentrating on reviving those giants yet again.

A piercing shriek cut the air as Lloyd clove his target in two. A quick glance over his shoulder confirmed that Alys had blown her target clean off its floating disc. The two mages fell and disappeared into the clouds below.

At the same time, Aksel had blasted the third mage with a ray of pure white light. Though the beam hadn't destroyed it, it definitely got the creature's attention.

Seeing the last mage still standing, Lloyd angled himself in its direction. Bearing down, he readied his black blade to cleave this final mage in two.

The mage did not go down without a fight though. It pointed a bony finger at Lloyd and fired off a black beam at him.

At this range, Lloyd barely managed to roll out of the way. The beam passed so close to his face that it nearly grazed his cheek.

Unfortunately, the fast maneuver sent Lloyd spinning out of control. By the time he managed to pull himself out of it, the mage had him in its sights again. At this range it could hardly miss.

Lloyd braced himself when the mage suddenly stiffened. It arched its back, its jaw opened wide as if to emit a silent scream. The creature then fell off the disc into the clouds below.

Seth stood behind where the skeletal mage had just been, a glowing white knife in his hand. A smirk adorned his lips as he met Lloyd's speechless gaze.

Unprompted, Seth snorted, "You're welcome."

20
CLOUDY WITH A CHANCE OF DRAGONS

Am I seeing things, or is that a T-Rex?

Glo's anxiousness lessened somewhat as Lloyd, Aksel and Alys took off upward. With little doubt his friends could handle the undead mages that left him free to focus on the bigger problem at hand. Jinkolothos still had Phobas' remains and the gods only knew what she was planning with it.

With each passing moment, Glo's sense of urgency grew. It was imperative to find out what kind of ritual the dracolich was performing. In order to do that though, he would first need to get rid of the fog.

While the archers leapt to the next platform, Glo flew up and over to the one beyond. Stopping just short of the thick cloud bank, he paused as the sound of strange chanting reached his ears.

Eerie as the disembodied voice sounded, Glo took it as a good sign. It meant that the dracolich had not yet finished her ritual.

Heartened by the discovery, he swiftly traced a symbol through the air.

"Impetus de Ventus!" The words rolled off Glo's tongue as he invoked the spell. In response, a blast of wind sprang from the symbol. It rushed forth into the bank and attempted to sweep the mists away.

Glo watched expectantly as swirls developed within the fog, but within seconds those eddies died. The spell had fallen far short of what he had hoped.

Fascinating, Glo thought, arching a single eyebrow. He'd never encountered a fog so thick that a blast of wind couldn't move it. There was obviously more going on here than met the eye.

A sudden realization struck him. Considering the cold temperatures in this plane, perhaps ice crystals had mixed in with the fog. If that were indeed the case, then maybe a different spell might do the trick.

With renewed hope, Glo strapped the staff in his hand to his back. He then traced a slightly more complex symbol through the air. As he did so, a small ball of flame appeared in his open palm. By the time he finished, the ball had grown to the size of a fist.

Bringing his hands together, Glo released the spell with a single word. *"Augue!"*

The ball of flame leapt from his palms to be swallowed up by the wall before him. Seconds later the fog lit up as the fiery orb exploded in its midst. The white bank evaporated before Glo's eyes revealing the main platform beyond. Once again, he spied Jinkolothos performing her bizarre dance over the glowing remains of Phobas.

It worked! Glo exulted in triumph.

Now that he had a clear view, Glo once again peered beyond the veil. As with the mages above, a disc of dark energy swirled around Jinkolothos. This disc, however, was vast in comparison. The amount of mana she was gathering was almost unfathomable.

Still, something appeared different about this particular flow of mana. As he might have expected, an arm of energy encircled the body of Phobas. Yet, there appeared to be another arm reaching somewhere behind the dracolich.

Now more curious than ever, Glo slid through the air sideways as he attempted to trace that second line of mana. His efforts were rewarded as his eyes fell upon a glowing sphere that had been hidden behind the lich's huge bulk. Hovering just a few feet above the platform, the sphere radiated an aura of intense blue.

Glo's eyebrow shot up a second time. *What in Thac is that thing?*

Peering deeper beyond the physical plane, Glo discerned the shape of a large jewel inside that sphere. It appeared to be the source of the powerful blue aura.

In a flash of insight, Glo abruptly realized what he was witnessing. The large jewel was in actuality a soul gem. Further, Jinkolothos was attempting to imbue Phobas' remains with the soul trapped within that gem.

The ramifications of what he'd discerned left Glo stunned. *What could possibly possess her to try something so extreme?*

As if in answer to his question, Andrella's recitation of Jinkolothos words replayed through his mind. *"There is something buried there that I seek. Something that belongs to me."*

It has to be that soul gem, Glo reasoned. *That must be what Jinkolothos retrieved from the catacombs—aside from Phobas remains.*

Furthermore, Jinkolothos had just told them that she'd lost everything, including her love. If that were indeed the case, then could the soul in that gem belong to Silverwind? After all these years, could she be trying to resurrect her mate?

If anyone had ever told Kalyn she'd be fighting against an undead dragon, she'd have told them they were *one meal short of a picnic.* Yet here she was, leaping in between these weird platforms hanging in the middle of nowhere. What's worse is that each leap brought her that much closer to this monstrosity which could kill any one of them with just its itty bitty toe.

Albeit, she did notice this particular dragon was missing one of its legs entirely. From what she'd heard, that had been Seth's doing.

What I wouldn't have given to be a fly on that dungeon wall, Kalyn thought dryly. Then again, that encounter hadn't exactly ended all that well. After all, Glo and Seth had both nearly ended up dead.

This one might not either, she reminded herself.

Kalyn's internal voice fell silent as Glo 'fire bombed' the fog away from the main platform. Her eyes went wide as they fell upon the 'giant bone dragon' dancing crazily about the slab with the 'glowing dead god' on it.

No one back home is ever going to believe this, she told herself. She could just imagine Fran's words now.

"Kalyn, you sure you ain't been in my fire water? Bone dragons maybe, just maybe I'd give ya, but glowing dead gods? I'd have ta have a nugget full o' noodles to believe that one."

In truth, Kalyn hardly believed it herself. Yet there it was, right in front of her.

"So—what do we do now?" Martan's voice cracked as he said it, his vocal chords knotted tighter than the tail on Elfar, her lynx back home.

"We take out our bows and shoot," Xellos responded in a matter of fact tone.

Martan's brow furrowed, the confusion on his face growing deeper with each passing second. "You do realize that our arrows will probably just bounce off that thing?"

Xellos shrugged. "But we'll get its attention."

Martan's face visibly paled, but much to Kalyn's surprise, he did not balk at the thought. "Just to be clear, we're all going to die then."

"Most likely," Xellos agreed as he drew an arrow from his quiver.

Kalyn knew Martan was not wrong, but neither was Xellos. They really didn't have much choice. It was either take on the dead dragon now or let it finish its crazy dance and probably destroy the world afterwards. Either way, they would end up dead.

She opened her mouth to say as much, but her brother Decon beat her to it. He slapped Martan hard on the back and winked. "Hell of a way to go though, eh?"

"Sure…" Martan drawled the word, peering at Decon as if he had rocks for brains.

To his credit though, Martan didn't complain any further. Instead, he merely nocked an arrow and prepared to fire with the rest of them.

Lined up across the front of the platform, the archers all waited for Xellos' signal. On his mark, the archers let their arrows fly in nearly perfect unison. The barrage sailed across the intervening space directly at the dancing dead dragon. As Martan had predicted though, each bounced off some unseen barrier about a foot away from their intended target.

Though none had made the slightest dent, it did indeed draw the dead dragon's attention. She paused her crazed dance once more and swiveled her large bony head towards the line of archers.

Kalyn watched with morbid fascination as a cold blue light formed in the dragon's chest. It raced up the skeletal neck and turned into a large, brilliant ball at the back of the dragon's throat. A second later, a glacial blast burst forth from that empty maw directly at them.

The blast was so huge that there was nowhere to duck for cover. They had the choice of being frozen solid or jumping off into oblivion. Martan had been right all along. This is where they were going to die.

At the last minute, a strong hand grabbed hers and held onto it tight. Kalyn barely had the time to see Martan staring at her with a tear in the corner of his eye.

"I love you!" She blurted without thinking, knowing those would be her final words.

Once the barrier had fallen, Seth decided to lend a hand with those dark mages. With their attention focused on Lloyd and the others it had been rather easy for him to sneak up behind them. He was still feeling rather pleased with himself when he noticed what was going on down below. Glo must have dispelled the fog and for some unfathomable reason the archers had chosen to shoot at the dracolich.

Seth couldn't decide whether they were brave or just plain stupid. He fully expected what came next. The dracolich stopped its awkward dance and sent a torrential stream of snow and ice hurtling from its maw at the hapless archers. With nowhere to run they were all sure to be turned into popsicles.

Seth almost couldn't look, but then Glo actually did something heroic. The wizard swooped in at the very last moment and threw up his own barrier in front of the archers. The torrent of snow and ice hit the translucent purple wall head on.

At first, it dispersed harmlessly against the barrier, but the dracolich was not quite done. Seeing her efforts thwarted, she redoubled them, increasing the flow of the blizzard gushing from her maw.

The wizard held fast against the fearsome onslaught, but even from here Seth could tell he was struggling. Unable to just watch any longer, Seth decided to do 'something stupid.'

Cupping his hands around his mouth, he yelled at the top of his lungs, "Hey draco-bitch! Want to know why all the men in your life left you? It's that icy attitude!"

That definitely got her attention. The dracolich halted her assault on Glo, her large skull swiveling upward to point directly at Seth. Though there were no eyes in those empty sockets, he could feel the malevolence behind that stare. He half expected her to launch another blizzard up at him, but instead she uttered a bone-shuddering roar.

Everything happened at once after that. The dracolich spread her wings and launched herself upwards. Lloyd went whooshing past him in a deadly dive toward the rising dragon. At the same moment, something huge materialized on the platform next to the dracolich.

Not believing his eyes, Seth rubbed them and looked again. "Am I seeing things, or is that a T-Rex?"

The dinosaur opened its huge maw and clamped down on the dracolich's tail, effectively stopping it from rising further off the platform. Shaking its great head back and forth, it backed up and dragged the dragon back down.

As the dracolich spun about to face its new opponent, clouds rolled in once again blocking Seth's view. The last thing he saw was the two behemoths locked in mortal combat.

Aksel had never expected the archers to take on the dracolich by themselves. When he had told them to prepare for battle, he assumed they would wait for everyone to regroup. Thankfully, Glo had been there to protect them, but Aksel wasn't quite sure how long the wizard could hold off the dracolich's wrath.

Somehow, they needed to level the playing field. With no other recourse, Aksel decided to pray.

Soldenar, Goddess of all Gnomes, I beseech you, he began his usual prayer…

Before he could continue any further, the lilting voice of his goddess interrupted him. *Ya know, lad, ya don't have ta start every prayer that way.*

Aksel blinked. In all the years he had been following the same ritual this was the first time he'd ever been told that. Completely taken off guard, he responded rather informally, *What would you like me to say?*

How about, 'Good morning, Soldenar,' or 'Soldenar, I need your help,' came the pragmatic reply.

Still stunned by the irreverent revelation, Aksel merely responded, *I'll try to remember that. In the meantime…*

Yes, yes, I know, she interrupted him again. *And from what I see, you're short on time. So just answer me this one simple query—what do you fight fire with, lad?*

Fire? Aksel responded tentatively.

And there's your answer, the Soldenar said definitively.

As Aksel puzzled over her response, his thoughts were interrupted by Seth blurting, "Hey draco-bitch! Want to know why all the men in your life left you? It's that icy attitude!"

Aksel gulped. If Seth had meant to divert Jinkolothos' attention away from the others, his plan most certainly succeeded. Yet in doing so, his friend had placed himself in imminent danger.

With no time to waste, Aksel forced himself to focus on the Soldenar's riddle. The answer came to him almost immediately. *Fight something huge with something huge.*

Now you're thinking! The Soldenar's voice reverberated through his head.

Along with her words, the image of a new spell appeared in his mind. Aksel wasted no time in tracing that symbol through the air.

The dracolich's roar practically drowned out his words as he invoked the spell. *"Vocare Creatura Tyrannosaurus!"*

The huge dinosaur materialized into being just as the dracolich launched itself upward. His summoning had been just in time to catch the creature and pull it back down.

Grappled by an opponent of equal size and strength, the dracolich now stood vulnerable to other attacks. However, Jinkolothos was far from stupid. She immediately conjured another bank of fog to cover her compromising position.

Lloyd had been zeroing in on her as the fog rolled in. Thankfully he pulled up short just above the top of the thick mists. At the same time, the disembodied roars of both creatures echoed from somewhere beneath that fog.

All of a sudden, the roaring stopped. An eerie chant then broke the silence, though Aksel did not recognize the words.

Alys traded a wide-eyed glance with him. "I know that language. It's definitely draconic."

"Do you know what she's saying?" Aksel asked uneasily.

Alys turned her ear toward the fog and listened a few moments before answering, "I believe she's summoning something."

Aksel didn't like the sound of that at all. With Lloyd down below, he felt like a sitting duck up here.

Alys apparently had been thinking along the same lines. "You summoned that dinosaur, right?"

"Yes," Aksel admitted, uncertain why she asked.

Alys flashed him a winsome smile. "Can't you just summon something else that we can fly on?"

Aksel pursed his lips together and nodded thoughtfully. They would need something fast—fast and powerful. The summoning spell the Soldenar had taught him would fall short of what they needed, but he had an idea to rectify that.

Holding the Staff of Law in both hands, Aksel called upon one of its powers that he had mastered. As he did so he felt a tingling in the center of his brow, as if his mind had been expanded somehow.

Drawing in his will, the little cleric then once again traced the summoning symbol through the air. This time, however, he outlined a more complex variation, and when he invoked it, he made a slight modification to the wording. *"Vocare Creatura Tonitrus Avis."*

A rippling effect appeared in the air before them and quickly expanded outward. The head of a long yellow-beaked creature first appeared within the distorted area. A large golden torso followed, flanked on either side by enormous, feathered wings. A wide flat golden tail fanned out behind the body rounding out the shape of the gargantuan creature. Electric arcs danced about the nearby clouds and thunder rolled as it let out a challenging cry.

Alys clasped her hands together and gasped, "Oh my, that's a Thunderbird! It's absolutely gorgeous."

Aksel didn't disagree, but this was no time to stop and ogle at the bird straight out of the pages of legend.

"Hop on," he gestured to Alys.

In the meantime, Glo had cast another fireball at the fog. As soon as it cleared, Aksel saw that the T-Rex and dracolich had been separated. Furthermore, four huge spectral dragons now surrounded Jinkolothos.

"Well, that's certainly not playing fair," Alys bemoaned. "What are we supposed to do now?"

While Aksel thought it best to take a moment to consider their next steps, Lloyd acted impetuously once again. Hovering just above where the fog line had been, the warrior abruptly dove down towards the ring of dragons.

Aksel froze at the sight, paralyzed at the thought of losing yet another friend.

"Is he crazy? He's going to get himself killed!" Alys cried in terror.

Alys' scream shook Aksel from his petrified state. At the same time, a wild idea popped into his head.

"Hang on!" he warned Alys.

Grasping tight onto the thunderbird's feathers, Aksel mentally commanded the thunderbird to dive. At the same time, Lloyd quickly closed the gap between him and the dragons.

Fast as the thunderbird was, Aksel realized they'd never reach the platform in time. Acting on pure instinct, he commanded the creature to do what it did best.

In response, a huge bolt of lightning shot from the clouds above. It scorched past them on its way towards its target below. The bolt raced past Lloyd forcing him to pull up. It blew past the spectral dragons and struck the dracolich with the unbridled force of nature.

Crack!

Thunder rolled across the clouds as the dracolich shuddered under the weight of the fierce electrical attack. Still reeling from the intense blow, Jinkolothos cried out to her bodyguards in stilted speech, "Get…that…damn…bird!"

As one, the spectral dragons lifted off and sped upwards in their direction. Strong as the thunderbird was, Aksel knew they stood no chance against four dragons.

"Hold on," Aksel cried once more over his shoulder to Alys. He then commanded the gargantuan bird to sharply bank and veer away from the main platform.

Aksel and Alys hung on for dear life as the thunderbird sped across the skies with a flight of dragons in hot pursuit.

Many regrets passed through Lloyd's mind when he decided to sacrifice himself for Seth. Foremost among them was that he would never again see Andrella. The unexpected appearance of the T-Rex staved off his demise for the moment, but things were far from over.

The return of the fog, Glo blasting it away, and the appearance of those ghostly dragons happened so fast it made Lloyd's head spin. Perhaps more unsettling though, was the sudden resurgence of Jack's voice.

What are you waiting for?

Lloyd cringed. Somewhere deep inside he had hoped never to hear the demon's voice again.

They look like ghosts. I'm not sure I could even hit them, he argued with the blade.

Trust me, I can, came Jack's assured reply.

Despite the demon's urgings, Lloyd remained unconvinced. What if it were lying to him? What if it couldn't touch those ghostly dragons? Even if it could, the odds were still stacked against him.

That's still four dragons, Lloyd reasoned with the blade.

Jack's reply was sickly smooth. *You don't have to fight them. Just lead them off so the dino can get back to chomping on the lich.*

Lloyd knew the demon was trying to play him. Even so, their only shot might indeed be to split up their enemies. He'd been willing to sacrifice himself before. If this gave his friends a chance to take out the dracolich, then so be it.

Alright, he agreed.

Gathering his will, Lloyd encircled the black blade with flames and dove down towards the ring of ghostly dragons. He'd only gone a short distance, however, when the largest lightning bolt he'd ever seen flashed down in front of him.

"Woah!" Lloyd cried, barely managing to pull up in time.

The huge bolt slammed hard into the dracolich. Even afterwards electrical arcs still danced across its skeletal frame.

Lloyd glanced upward to see a huge golden bird descending towards them. Astride its back sat the comparatively tiny forms of Aksel and Alys.

Still shuddering from the impact, Jinkolothos stuttered as she ordered her ghostly bodyguards to "Get…that…damn…bird!"

The great bird veered off and sped away at incredible speed. The ghostly dragons immediately took off after it passing just out of Lloyd's reach.

Even with that giant bird, Lloyd didn't like his friends' odds against four dragons. He started to take off after them when Glo's shout reached his ears.

"Lloyd, get the gem!"

Lloyd halted and spun about in mid-air, peering at the wizard with confusion. "What gem?"

Glo pointed downward towards the main platform. "The glowing blue crystal down there is a soul gem. Jinkolothos is trying to put its soul inside Phobas' body."

Lloyd peered down at the platform and for the first time saw the glowing blue gem. It looked tiny next to the great slab holding the body of the god, Phobas.

As he did so, Jack whispered in his mind, *Yes, do it. Touch the gem with me. I'll make sure she can't put that soul into Phobas.*

There was a strange intensity in the demon's words that set off all sorts of warning bells in Lloyd's mind. Still, with the ghost dragons gone, the dracolich was once again busy fending off the dinosaur—and Glo had told him to retrieve the gem.

Deciding to ignore Jack, Lloyd flew down and landed next to the blue gem. It was larger than he expected, nearly the size of a human head. Furthermore, at this close proximity, the glow inside pulsed like a disembodied heartbeat.

The eerie sight held Lloyd transfixed. He silently wondered whose, or what's, soul was contained inside the giant gem.

That's not important, Jack whispered in his mind. *Or don't you want to protect your friends?*

Lloyd balked at the question. *Of course, I want to protect my friends—but whatever's in there is still alive.*

Despite Jack's machinations, he was right about one thing. Lloyd's friends had to come first. For now, he needed to take the gem. They could figure out who, or what, was inside later.

The young warrior reached a tentative hand towards the gem when a fierce roar exploded from across the platform.

"Get away from that or I'll kill you!" Jinkolothos screamed.

Still grappling with the T-Rex, she heaved the tenacious creature away and started towards Lloyd.

Lloyd instinctively fell into a defensive stance, but the T-Rex once again caught the dracolich by its tail.

I'm too weak to help you as is, Jack whispered in his ear. *Let me have the soul. It's the only way.*

"Don't touch it! I swear I'll rip you limb from limb—and all your friends when I'm done with you!" Jinkolothos screamed.

With a titanic effort, the dracolich lifted the T-Rex off the ground and hurled it away. Its eye sockets glowing with a cold intensity, it stomped across the platform towards him.

Lloyd briefly thought about grabbing the gem and making a run for it, but the dracolich was too fast. It would catch him before he could make it back to the others.

Jack's whispering grew more insistent as the dracolich closed the gap between them. *Let me have the soul. It's the only way to protect your friends.*

Lloyd didn't like the idea one bit. It would be sacrificing a living soul to the demon. Yet the dracolich was raving now, hell bent on destroying him and those he swore to protect.

Feeling like he had little choice, Lloyd backed up and turned the great blade towards the glowing gem.

"Don't you dare! I'll grind your bones to dust—yours and everyone you love!" The dracolich shrieked.

She was nearly on top of him now. With no time left to think, Lloyd touched the tip of the black blade to the gem. A sickly sucking sound ensued as the light from the gem was drawn into the blade. In mere moments it was all over, the once brilliantly pulsing gem turned into a cold husk.

"Noooooooo!"

Jinkolothos harsh cry echoed through the air around them. The ground beneath his feet began to shake and gale force winds popped up from nowhere. The wind grew chill and sleet and hail began to fall. It was as if the entire plane shared in her anguish.

Oblivious to her pain, the T-Rex barreled into the dracolich yet again. Her agony beyond measure, Jinkolothos reared her head and breathed a steady stream of snow and ice over the mindless beast.

Though she had already frozen it solid, Jinkolothos raged on unchecked. Spinning about, she slammed her tail into the frozen creature smashing it into a million pieces.

Martan didn't know whether to feel happy or terrified. When it looked like they were going to die, Kalyn had declared her love for him. It had happened so unexpectedly that he didn't get the chance to say he felt the same. Yet since they had somehow managed to survive, he was determined to tell her now. He had tried to speak to her a couple of times since. She, however, had shushed him, seemingly intent on the crazed happenings on the main platform.

Though Martan couldn't see it from this angle, apparently the dracolich had some sort of gem. Lloyd had done something to it which drove the creature into a fit of rage. After eliciting a monstrous cry, the main platform began to shake. The winds picked up and a blanket of snow and sleet whipped across it making it hard to see.

In the midst of all the chaos, Glolindir dropped the barrier he had thrown up to protect them.

"Now's our chance," Xellos declared.

Before anyone could say anything, the lithe archer leapt forth. Despite the traces of snow and wind that swept between the intervening distance, he somehow managed to land safely at the edge of the main platform.

Kalyn and the others prepared to follow when Martan grabbed her by the arm. "You're not really going to try and jump that, are you?"

Pulling her arm from his grasp, she didn't even turn to look at him. "We can't let them fight that bone dragon all by themselves!"

"But Kalyn…" Martan began.

"Not listening! People to save!" She interrupted him before he could say anything further.

Daer had already jumped after Xellos. Decon stood at the edge poised to follow, but paused to eye them both with obvious amusement. "Will you two love birds stop arguing already?"

Kalyn hauled off and hit her brother hard in the arm—harder than Martan had ever seen her hit anyone.

"We are not love-birds you troll brained moron!" she screeched. Before either of them could reply, Kalyn rushed to the edge and leaped over the chasm between platforms.

Martan's heart skipped a beat as she sailed across the intervening space. He didn't take another breath until she finally made it safely to the other side.

The entire time, Decon couldn't stop laughing. He clasped Martan on the back and said in between fits, "She must really love you… to get that kind of rise…out of her."

Somehow, that didn't make Martan feel any better.

In the meantime, over on the main platform, Lloyd had grown to double his height. Now only the dragon's neck and head hung over the top of him. Furthermore, his black blade was encircled by flames.

As Martan and Decon landed on the main platform, Glolindir hit the dracolich with a lightning bolt. As incensed as she was, however, it hardly seemed to slow her down.

Lucky for Lloyd, the giant sword seemed more adept at keeping her at bay. Whenever he connected with the black blade, it elicited cries of pain from the undead dragon.

Once again, the archers lined up and fired a round of arrows at the dracolich. Most of those shots continued to bounce off, but this time Zellos managed to sneak one through. It hit the dragon at the base of the neck, causing it to flinch in pain.

"Nice shot!" Kalyn cried with glee.

Xellos merely nodded and said, "Let's go again."

As they prepared their next round of arrows, Martan's keen eye spotted a group of figures off in the distant sky. They appeared to be headed this way at incredible speed.

He pointed them out to the others. "Look up there!"

Within seconds the figures had drawn close enough for him to make out their shapes. Four appeared to be those ghostly dragons. The fifth, however, was the huge golden bird they saw before.

Just as Martan realized what it was, a huge thunderbolt lanced down from the sky and slammed into the dracolich. The accompanying thunderclap was so loud, they all had to stop and cover their ears.

The enormous bolt had left the dracolich stunned. Lloyd took advantage of its momentary lapse, his black blade biting deep into its bony hide.

Though obviously hurt, its unrelenting rage continued to drive the creature. It leapt at Lloyd and grappled him despite being stabbed in the chest by the black blade.

A sudden blast of snow and ice swirled around the pair making it impossible to see.

All of a sudden, everything stopped. The wind died down and the snow and ice disappeared altogether.

Where Lloyd and the dracolich had been standing, the platform now stood empty. The pair had completely vanished.

21
COLD DAY IN HELL

Icy eyes glared at them menacingly as cold vapors spewed from their frozen mouths.

With four ghostly dragons chasing them, Alys probably shouldn't have enjoyed the wild ride on the thunderbird as much as she did. Even so, she was flying at incredible speed on the back of a creature straight from legend. Under better circumstances she would have whooped for joy. Sadly, their current situation was anything but good.

The horrific scream that rang out across the cloudscape filled Alys with a terrible sense of foreboding. When the dragons turned back the way they came, it only magnified that feeling. Aksel must have sensed it as well. He immediately banked the thunderbird around and sped after their previous pursuers.

Back on the main platform, Lloyd faced off against the dracolich. The others had been trying to help, but nothing seemed to faze the raging creature. Aksel finally managed to slow it down with another huge thunderbolt, but then the dracolich and Lloyd disappeared in a swirl of snow and ice. When the blizzard faded, both were gone.

"Lloyd!" Alys cried out in fright. She grabbed Aksel by the arm, her nails unknowingly digging into the poor gnome's skin. "Where did they go?"

Aksel winced but did not complain. Instead he glanced back over his head, his eyes mirroring her concern. "I don't know, but there's one way to find out."

As soon as the dracolich vanished, the airborne dragons came to a halt. They hung there in midair looking confused.

Aksel and Alys flashed past them swiftly landing only a few yards from where Lloyd had vanished. Glo, Seth, and the others were already there, and everyone was talking at once.

"Quiet!" Alys screeched at the top of her lungs, adding just a tiny bit of force to it.

That got everyone's attention. They all stopped their individual conversations and turned to face them.

Aksel swept his eyes around the group. "Did anyone see what happened?"

Seth tapped the side of his helm, the one Andrella had deemed the *Helm of True Sight*. "I saw it. She plane shifted them away under the cover of that blizzard."

Aksel gingerly rubbed his chin. "Alright, alright. So, is there any way to tell where she shifted them to?"

Alys thought back to the moment when Lloyd disappeared. She abruptly remembered something. "I thought I heard a faint musical note just as they vanished."

Glo grabbed her by the shoulders and stared at her intently, his deep blue eyes boring into hers. "Can you repeat it?"

"Yes, of course," Alys replied confidently, her brow knitting into a frown. "Why, is it important?"

Glo gave her a half smile. "I believe it is. Each plane is attuned to a specific frequency. When you open a portal to that plane, the trained ear can hear it."

Alys nodded her understanding. She, of all of them, heard that sound because of her years of musical training.

"My boots don't make any sound," Xellos commented.

Glo shifted his gaze to the gentle archer. "That's because they're a special artifact. They basically teleport you directly to another plane instead of opening a portal."

"Don't look now, but I think we have company," Martan warned.

The four ghostly dragons had landed on the platform not far from them. They made no moves towards them, however, still looking as confused as before.

Everyone had tensed in preparation for battle, but Alys stepped forward and lifted her hand in a halting gesture. "Don't attack them. I have a hunch."

Before anyone could stop her, she strode over towards the dragons. All four turned to face her, but did not make any threatening movements. Instead they watched her approach with forlorn gazes.

Alys' draconic was more from song and poem, but she knew enough to get by.

"Why so sad?" She asked them in their native tongue.

"We are bound here to this <garbled>," one of the dragons responded.

Alys didn't quite catch that last word, but she understood the binding of creatures and spirits.

Approaching from behind, Glo filled in the rest of it for her. "They say they are bound to this 'stage' below us."

Aksel's eyes grew soft with understanding. "Tell them I will free them after we find our friend."

"We understand common," the original dragon who spoke confided in them, "and that would be greatly appreciated."

"Very well." Aksel nodded before turning to face Alys. "Can you please sing that note now?"

"Can do," Alys agreed. Clearing her throat, she recalled the sound she'd heard just before Lloyd vanished. She then sang it loud and clear for the others to hear.

As the note wafted across the stage, Xellos' feet began to twitch. He peered down at them, then looked at the others with a surprised expression. "I think my boots are responding to the sound. I should be able to take us there."

Aksel waved everyone to gather around Xellos. "Alright, let's go."

Lloyd found himself all alone in the battle of his life. One minute he stood on that platform surrounded by his friends, the next he was in this huge ice cave with just the dracolich. He should have been hyper focused against such a deadly opponent, but he couldn't quite calm his mind or his gut.

He had done the unthinkable in letting Jack have that soul. It went against everything he believed—that all life mattered, regardless of one's race, sex, or station. In doing so he had aided in the taking of that life, an innocent for all he knew. It didn't matter that he did it to save his friends. He had crossed a line—a line from which there was no return.

The dracolich had gone crazy afterwards. She had practically skewered herself on the demon blade to bring them both here. Yet Lloyd couldn't exactly blame her. That soul obviously belonged to someone she cared about. Had it been him in her place, he wasn't quite sure what he would do.

Even now Jinkolothos continued to rage. "You will pay for what you've done!"

She clawed at him with her one remaining forearm, but Lloyd managed to avoid the swipe and pull Jack from her breastbone at the same time.

What a waste, Jack murmured in his mind. *There was no soul in there to suck.*

Even if there was, you wouldn't get it, Lloyd railed at the demon while he parried the dragon's follow up bite.

You won't have another soul if I can help it, he swore as he took a wide swing at the dracolich's neck. His tactic succeeded, forcing the creature to fall back or run the risk of losing her head altogether.

Don't sass me, boy. You're no longer innocent you know, Jack reminded him.

Those words wounded Lloyd far worse than anything the dracolich could've done. Unfortunately, he wasn't wrong. Lloyd no longer considered himself one of the good guys.

The dracolich spun about, attempting to swipe him with her tail, but Lloyd was ready for it. Just before her tail hit, he vaulted over it, then punished his opponent by swiping her flank.

The dracolich cried out in pain as she flinched away and scurried out of his reach. Her close up attacks proving ineffective, the dracolich then took to the air.

Lloyd already anticipated her next move. With the ceiling far overhead, she hovered above him just out of reach and breathed a stream of snow and ice down on him. Thankfully at his current size he was able to block the worst of it with the flaming blade.

Ah, so I am good for something after all, Jack taunted him.

Shut up and act like a normal blade, you filthy demon, Lloyd fumed.

Knowing it had hit a nerve, the demon blade merely snickered.

By stopping Jinkolothos from proceeding with her plans, Glo and his friends had probably saved the world. But at what cost? He and Seth might have been the only ones to see it, but Lloyd sacrificed the soul in that gem in order to save them all. Though Glo understood why he did so, he couldn't even begin to imagine the effect something like that would have on his friend's psyche. Someone like Lloyd, who prided himself on doing the right thing, might be shattered after such an act.

Glo only hoped he could hold it together long enough for them to reach him. His mental state notwithstanding, Lloyd's spiritblade abilities and Glo's spells should help him survive against the already wounded dracolich—at least for a while. Unfortunately, the growth spell Glo had cast on him would be running out soon. Lloyd wouldn't stand a chance after that. They needed to find him as soon as possible.

The plane they appeared in was covered with snow as far as the eye could see. Icy peaks rose in the distance and thick flakes fell from the cloud covered sky above. They made for a cave entrance Xellos spotted in the rise ahead. Once inside they found themselves in a huge cavern whose walls shone with a phosphorescent quality. Sculptures of dragons carved in ice filled the cave in all directions. At the very back of the cavern, however, they spied the object of their search.

"Lloyd!" Alys cried, her shout echoing throughout the huge cavern.

Though obviously battered, their friend appeared to be in one piece. Jinkolothos hovered just above the giant-sized warrior, breathing a steady stream of snow and ice down upon him. Luckily, he was able to fend off most of it with his giant flaming blade.

As soon as the dragon's breath stopped, Lloyd retaliated with a mini-fireball from the tip of his sword. The ball of flame caught the dragon directly in the chest causing it to falter and fall from the air.

Cheers went up among their group, but they were short-lived. Their excitement turned to horror as Lloyd suddenly shrank before their eyes.

"That's not good," Xellos commented.

"We have to help him!" Alys cried with mounting fear.

As one they all started forth, only to come to a screeching halt as the dragon statues came to life. The icy sculptures slid across the cavern floor cutting them off as they closed ranks. Icy eyes glared at them menacingly as cold vapors spewed from their frozen mouths.

Glo's immediate reaction was to put up a wall of fire.

"Eww, those things are uglier than a troll's butt," Kalyn exclaimed as she and the other archers chimed in with a flurry of arrows.

"It could be worse. They could be snakes," Seth taunted as he approached one of the sculptures. Apparently, she held an irrational fear of the legless reptiles.

Kalyn fixed him with a dark stare. "You just had to say it, didn't ya short stack?"

"Yup," Seth responded with an evil grin as he traced a spell on the ground before him. As he invoked it the ground swept forward in a wave that shattered the ice statue into pieces.

Mimicking the halfling, Alys stepped forth and wailed at another statue shattering that one as well. "We've got this, you all go ahead," she called over her shoulder before moving on to her next target.

Glo did not have to be told twice. Dropping his firewall, he and the others sprinted through the hole the pair had made in the statues' ranks.

The icy sculptures glared at them, spewing more cold vapors as they passed. Even so, they could not move fast enough to close the gap.

Meanwhile, Jinkolothos had risen back to her feet. A cold laugh emanated from her skeletal mouth as she regarded the normal-sized Lloyd.

"You don't look so tough now!" She cried in a shrill voice. "I'll squish you like the bug you are." Supremely confident, the dracolich started for him, not even bothering to take to the air.

Looking cold and worn, Lloyd stood his ground. Unless he was planning some last minute spiritblade trick, it looked for certain that he would be trampled.

They still had quite a distance to cover to reach the pair, but the archers took shots on the run nonetheless. A few even hit the mark, but merely bounced off the lich's magic protective aura.

Glo had one spell he could use from this distance that might deter the enraged creature. Screeching to a halt, he swiftly traced a symbol through the air and released it with a quick word.

"Augue."

A fist-sized ball of flame shot from his outstretched palm and rocketed across the intervening space between them. It caught the dracolich a few dozen yards from Lloyd, exploding into a fiery half-sphere that completely engulfed her.

When the fire winked out, the dracolich had stopped moving. Tendrils of smoke rose from her skeletal frame. Under normal circumstances that spell wouldn't have fazed her, but in her weakened condition it had definitely hurt.

Now angered beyond reason, she completely forgot her original target. Turning she focused those empty eye sockets on Glo. A feral growl escaped her maw.

"Don't look now, but I think ya got her attention," Kalyn commented dryly.

Glo found the situation anything but funny.

A sudden panic rose from his abdomen as the dracolich abruptly charged straight for him. His concentration all but shredded, he somehow managed to fire off a couple of sizzling rays. Neither, however, seemed to deter her in the slightest.

The archers joined in, their arrows now hitting the mark, but with little effect.

All of a sudden, a red blur streaked across the cavern. Lloyd flew over the dracolich, his black blade biting deep into her bones.

As he passed, her tail caught him and slammed the warrior to the ground. Lloyd lay there in a patch of cracked ice, unmoving.

A chill ran up Glo's spine. *Is Lloyd dead?*

As the dracolich's empty eye sockets focused back on him, he thought, *Am I next?*

Aksel was mortified. Lloyd had been taken down hard, and might, in fact, be dead. What's worse is that Glo could be next. Unfortunately, the wizard looked completely flustered. Another fireball might have finished the dracolich, but all Glo could manage was a couple of fire rays. That would not be nearly enough to stop the creature.

In an act of bravery, the archers stood by the wizard while continuing to bombard the dracolich. Their arrows were now taking their toll, but it wouldn't be enough to stop it in time.

Aksel felt the need to do something. He couldn't just watch another friend die. Yet what could he do? The dracolich was too close to summon another beast without endangering his friends. Even in its current state, his best spell would not be enough to fell the creature. He really had only one good option—the staff.

Sadly, Aksel could barely control it. He certainly hadn't mastered any spells that might stop the dracolich. With no other recourse, the little cleric turned to prayer.

Soldenar, Goddess of all Gnomes... he began before catching himself. *Soldenar, I need your help,* he immediately amended.

Aye, lad, she answered instantly. *Use the staff.*

But... Aksel stammered.

There's no time. The Soldenar interrupted him. *Do you trust me lad?*

Of course, Aksel responded without hesitation.

Then use the staff. I will guide you, she declared emphatically.

The dracolich had closed to within a few yards of his friends. With only a matter of seconds left, Aksel raised the staff aloft. A pair of unseen hands laid themselves atop his as he invoked the first spell he could think of.

"Sanctus Percutiat."

The staff flared to life with a light so bright that Aksel had to avert his eyes. Divine power rippled through the air far greater than anything he could have mustered himself. Taking the form of a huge hammer of pure white light, it came down on the dracolich in the blink of an eye.

A tremendous crunching sound echoed throughout the cavern as it smashed the unsuspecting creature into the ground. A moment later the hammer flashed out of existence, leaving a heap of broken bones where the dracolich had just been.

22
NEEDLE IN A HAYSTACK

I would have had just as much luck searching for it on my own.

Seth and Alys finished off the last of the ice sculptures just in time to see the dracolich pulverized by that tremendous hammer.

"Woah…" Alys gaped, "talk about meting out justice."

"And with that, ladies and gentlemen, court is adjourned…" Seth snorted. It might have been funnier if Lloyd hadn't also been plastered, but Seth never learned to face adversity with anything less than a heavy dose of sarcasm.

With the dracolich down, everyone went running to check on their fallen friend. Seth did not join them though. If Lloyd were still alive, Aksel was far more capable of healing him. Seth's talents would be better put to use finding the lich's phylactery. If it were allowed to remain intact with Jinkolothos' soul inside, she'd be back to haunt them again someday. That was something they could do without.

Scouring the cavern, Seth spotted an indentation in the wall that didn't look natural. On closer inspection, he confirmed it to be a hidden doorway. After a bit of feeling around, he discovered an invisible keyhole in the ice.

Seth had never picked an ice lock before. "First time for everything," he murmured to himself as he got out his picks.

This particular lock was a bit trickier than your normal pin and tumbler. Two rotating cylinders had to be turned in the right direction at the exact same time. Add to that the difficulty of not chipping the ice and it became a real challenge.

After three failed attempts, Seth finally got it. The ice door swung open to reveal another large cavern. Tall piles of gold glinted in the pale phosphorescent light of this second cave. Chests, baubles, and other trinkets lay randomly scattered amidst the staggering array of wealth.

"Well, I think we found Jinkolothos hoard!" Seth announced over his shoulder.

"Good thing, too. Somebody has to pay for all the damage to Penwick," Lloyd's voice echoed from behind him.

Seth was more than a little surprised to see his friend standing there, albeit being supported by Martan and Decon. Even so, he appeared to be in one piece. Though secretly pleased, he wasn't about to broadcast that fact to anyone else.

"Tsk," Seth clicked his tongue to cover his welling emotions. "Wasn't sure we'd see you again after that last stunt you pulled."

Lloyd's response was not at all what he expected. A haunted look passed through the young man's eyes as he answered, "Yeah, well I'm not exactly proud of what I did."

Seth narrowed his gaze at his friend. He'd seen what Lloyd had done with that soul gem. If it had been him in his stead, Seth would probably have done the same exact thing. Still, he already had innocent blood on his hands. His mentor paid the price with his life because of Seth's selfish desire to change his fate.

Pushing down the nightmarish memories, Seth folded his arms across his chest. "Trust me, I've seen a lot worse."

Lloyd responded with a feeble half-smile, but said nothing more.

Seth realized Lloyd was going to have to come to terms with what he did in his own way.

Alys walked up and tapped Lloyd on the nose to get his attention. "Well I, for one, am glad to see you still alive."

Before he could respond she leaned forward and kissed him on the cheek. Lloyd's eyes went wide, his face turning a bright shade of scarlet.

Her eyes still glinting with amusement, Alys spun about and rubbed her hands together gleefully. "Did someone say dragon hoard?"

Seth loved teasing Lloyd almost as much as Glo. Feeling magnanimous, he stepped back and ushered her towards the open door. "Right this way."

They all filtered into the room and gazed about in awe. The amount of treasure stored in here was nothing short of staggering.

Kalyn's jaw hung down nearly to the ground. "This musta taken centuries to collect."

"Most likely," Glo agreed.

Seth realized it would be a daunting task to find the dracolich's phylactery in all this treasure. Having everyone pitch in might speed things up, but he also didn't want Jack to know what he was doing. Lloyd's previous comment about Penwick gave him an idea.

Pulling a portal bag from his belt, Seth uncinched it, and threw it on the ground in front of them. "Well, if you really want to collect some gold for Penwick, you can dump it in there. I'm going to take a look around at what else is stored here."

Catching Aksel's and Glo's eye, he nudged his head for them to follow. Seth then began to stride away, but paused to add, "Oh, and be careful what you touch. There's no way I can check out everything here, so I'm not responsible for any lost hands or fingers."

That elicited just the right amount of concern on the other's faces. On a whim, he pulled a second bag from his belt and threw it on the floor as well. "Just in case you do find something of interest, and it doesn't blow up in your face, you can throw it in there."

Satisfied that he'd made his point, Seth led Aksel and Glo away to search the cavern for the phylactery.

Lloyd took a seat on a nearby rock while the others roamed around gathering gold coins from the dragon's hoard. He supposed Alys was right—he should be glad to be alive. His body still needed a good long rest though before he'd fully recover.

Not wanting to think about what he'd done, the weary young man instead gazed around the cavern. There were many items that caught his interest scattered amidst the piles of gold, but he found himself drawn to a particularly daunting suit of armor.

That looks pretty sturdy, Jack whispered in his ear.

Lloyd groaned. The demon was the last person he wanted to talk to right now.

It's black, Lloyd responded flatly.

So what? If you'd been wearing that, the lich would never have beaten you, Jack pointed out in that smooth tone that typically meant he was up to something.

Lloyd should have known better by now, but he hesitated, nonetheless.

Sensing his indecisiveness, Jack continued to press him. *After all, it's not like your soul is lily white anymore.*

Lloyd grimaced, but did not deny it. Jack was not wrong. He was no longer a good person.

Slowly getting up, he went over to examine the armor. It was indeed very sturdy. There was even a matching helm to go with it. Perhaps he was being unfair about the color. Either way, he was a bit too sore to try it on now.

Carefully hoisting it, Lloyd carried the armor over to the second portal bag. Still feeling slightly self-conscious, he peered around to make sure no one was watching. Everyone else seemed more than preoccupied though, gathering gold coins and filling up the first bag.

Feeling somewhat foolish for worrying what the others might say, Lloyd dumped the armor into the bag. He then went back to sitting on his rock.

Alys had been relieved to find that Lloyd was still alive. Aside from the fact that he was like a brother to her, she wouldn't have been able to face Pallas or Thea if he had died on her watch. What would she have said to Andrella for that matter?

Either way, she needn't worry about that anymore. Lloyd now sat quietly resting his newly healed body while they gathered gold for their city.

Alys did her part in the collection, but paused at one point to admire a particularly handsome scimitar. It had a curved silver blade with a cross-guard that looked like a pair of wings, and a blue and silver hilt and pommel. A large blue gem had been inset into the guard where the blade met the hilt.

A set of elvish ruins were carved along the blade itself.

Alys attempted to translate them out loud. "L…I…L…T…Lilt."

The moment the word left her lips, the sword leapt from her hand. Alys watched in amazement as it danced about in the air before her. Now completely enthralled, she plucked the sword out of the air.

"Oh, I just have to have you!" She squealed with delight.

Scooping up a handful of coins to bring back with her, Alys covertly placed the sword in the second bag before making another deposit for Penwick.

A satisfied smile graced her lips as she went out for another haul. Her mind was no longer on gold, however. Instead she had begun to choreograph her next performance with her new dance partner.

Glo knew things were far from over. Though they managed to survive their encounter with the dracolich, they still had to return Phobas' body. After that, they needed to deal with the castle of undead that threatened Penwick. Only then could they get back to heading off the impending demon invasion. Seth had been right though to prioritize finding Jinkolothos' phylactery. The last thing they needed was for her to resurrect in the middle of their future struggles.

The real question was where to look. Finding the phylactery in all this treasure was like looking for the proverbial needle in a haystack.

Glo tried the spell to make magic items glow, but as he expected, half the things in the cavern lit up. Aksel then tried to sense the presence of evil. As one might have expected, there were more than one traces of evil in the undead dragon's hoard.

"Well, you two have been a lot of help," Seth griped. "I would have had just as much luck searching for it on my own."

Equally exasperated, Glo swept his arm around the large cavern. "Go ahead. Nobody's stopping you."

As per usual, Aksel interrupted them before their bickering went any further. "Come on, you two. Fighting amongst ourselves isn't going to solve anything."

Glo spread his lips into a flat line and nodded. "You're right. Sorry."

Seth folded his arms and looked away. "Yeah, whatever."

Glo knew that was the closest to an apology they were going to get.

"But that still doesn't get us any closer to finding the phylactery," Seth pointed out.

As luck would have it, Xellos happened around the edge of a nearby mountain of gold at that very moment. Three new bows were tucked under his arms—one crystal, one gold, and one that looked like a deer's antlers.

The three of them fell silent as the archer halted in his tracks. Xellos eyed them briefly before padding over to join them. Pulling down his hood, the redhaired youth leaned in close and whispered, "If you're looking for what I think you're looking for, then you might want to try that giant ice pillar in the middle of the cavern."

"At least, that's where I'd hide it," he added as an afterthought. With a slight nod, Xellos lifted his hood and strode off back towards the cavern entrance.

Glo, Seth, and Aksel all exchanged glances, then shifted their gaze towards the center of the cavern. As Xellos had pointed out, a huge ice pillar rose from the floor there, reaching all the way to the ceiling far above.

Seth shrugged. "It's worth a shot."

The three of them wound their way through the mounds of gold and other treasures until they reached the base of the pillar. While

Seth looked it over, both Glo and Aksel tried their spells once more. Sure enough, as Xellos surmised, something lit up inside the base of the pillar.

"There's definitely a trace of strong evil in there," Aksel confirmed a moment later.

Seth discovered an indentation in the ice and swiftly found a hidden lock similar to the one in the door to this cave. After fiddling with it for a short while, Glo heard a distinct *click*.

A small door in the side of the pillar swung outward revealing a recessed area beyond. Inside sat two small chests and one slightly larger box.

Deep creases formed across Aksel's brow as he scanned all three. After a half minute or so he pointed to the larger box. "The trace of evil is coming from there."

Never one to pass up a hidden chest, Seth pulled both of them out and laid them aside for now. He then took a closer look at the box.

"I'm not seeing any physical traps, but I don't like it," he declared after a thorough examination.

Glo had learned to trust the halfling's instincts. Leaning in, he peered beyond the physical plane and noted a thick layer of mana enveloping the box.

"There's definitely some kind of strong magic around this thing," he murmured as he tried to identify it. After a bit more scrutiny he figured it out.

"Well that's clever," he noted with a mixture of amusement and respect.

"Want to share with the rest of us?" Seth prompted him.

"Oh, yes," Glo half laughed, realizing he had been talking absently to himself. "It's a nice little teleportation spell. If you fail to dispel it, the box will be transported right out of your hands to somewhere else."

"That's cute," Seth admitted. "So, are you going to dispel it, or what?"

"Allow me," Aksel said, stepping forth.

The little cleric traced a familiar symbol through the air and invoked it with the words, *"Nullam Depelle."*

Glo could feel the mana drain from the area inside the pillar where the box still sat.

As Aksel stepped back, Seth moved in and unlocked the box in a matter of seconds. As he lifted the lid, a glow emanated outward from a large blue soul gem similar to the one Lloyd destroyed back in the cloud plane.

"I'd say we found it," Glo said with a sigh of relief.

Seth snorted. "Yeah, but more importantly, how do we keep this away from Jack?"

"I could take it to Sirus," Aksel offered. "She could dispose of it just as easily as us—probably better, in fact."

Seth shrugged once again. "Fine by me."

"I agree," Glo concurred. They had more than enough on their plates right now. That would be one less thing for them to worry about.

Seth lifted the melon-sized gem out of the pillar while Aksel pulled out his own portal bag. After he drew it open, Seth placed the gem inside. Before he could close it, the halfling held up a staying hand and motioned to the two chests he'd put aside earlier. "Take these as well. We can check them out later."

Aksel shrugged and continued to hold the bag open as Seth loaded the chests into it. Once he was finished, Aksel finally drew the drawstrings of the bag shut. As soon as he closed it, however, the entire cavern started to shake.

Seth glared accusingly at Glo. "Did you check the gem for enchantments?"

Glo's mouth hung open wide. "No, I don't think it's an enchantment. I think Jinkolothos created this place and now that the last trace of her is gone it's collapsing."

Seth put his hands on his hips and glowered at the wizard. "Well why didn't you warn us ahead of time?"

Glo threw his hands up into the air in exasperation. "Why must I be the one to think of everything?"

The pair stood there glaring at each other until Aksel stepped in and berated them both. "This is no time to argue. We've got to get back to the others and get out of here before this whole place comes down on our heads."

The trio swiftly retraced their steps, dodging and stepping around chunks of ice that fell from the ceiling along the way. By the time they made it back to the entrance, parts of the cavern behind them had already collapsed.

Lloyd, Alys, Xellos, Martan, Kalyn, Decon, and Daer all huddled together in the doorway between the caverns. Glo, Seth, and Aksel nestled in next to them as close as they could.

"What happened?" Lloyd cried over the din of the shaking caverns.

"Why'd everything suddenly start falling apart?" Alys asked as she held on tightly to Lloyd's arm.

Peering past them Glo saw the other cavern had started to cave in as well.

"Jinkolothos must've created this entire plane! It must be a delayed reaction to her demise," he yelled over the sounds of crashing ice around them. That first part was true at least, though he lied about the rest.

"Either way, we need to get out of here now!" Aksel shouted.

They all gathered around Xellos, this time interlocking arms so as not to inadvertently break the circle. The rumbling grew worse as the young man once again invoked his *boots of the gods*.

Mere seconds after they all disappeared, the entire roof gave in burying both caverns and everything in them.

23
MASTER OF THE UNDEAD

You don't think that measly vampire stole the lich's castle from her,
do you?

Alys breathed a heavy sigh as they reappeared on the plane of clouds. That had been a bit too close for comfort. A few more seconds and they all might have been flattened, even before Jinkolothos' personal plane winked out of existence. They'd only survived by the grace of the gods thanks to Phobas' boots.

Though thankful to be alive, one thing still bothered her—Lloyd just didn't seem himself. After his near death ordeal, she would expect him to be exhausted, but this was something else entirely. He seemed far more subdued than usual, his normal brash confidence all but gone.

Perhaps his loss to the dracolich had dampened his spirit, but Alys somehow doubted it. She'd seen him lose time and again to Pallas back at the Stealle Academy, but it would usually make him that much more determined. Though not quite sure what it could be, she was determined to figure it out.

The four ghostly dragons still waited for them on the main platform next to the remains of Phobas. The one who they'd spoken to before addressed them as they reappeared. "You have returned. What of Jinkolothos?"

That was a potentially loaded question if Alys ever heard one. Though Jinkolothos had bound these dragons here, they did not know the extent of their relationship to her. The last thing they needed now was another altercation.

Alys stepped forth before anyone else could reply, keeping her demeanor and tone as solemn as possible. "Regrettably, she had to be defeated and most likely will not return."

The dragons shifted about uncomfortably as they exchanged glances with one another. Alys tried to discern their reactions, but their expressions were unreadable. She did her best to remain contrite until the one dragon finally spoke again.

"That is unfortunate, but perhaps just as well. She has not been the same since Argazephari's passing."

A momentary wave of sympathy washed over Alys. She wasn't quite sure how she would react if she were to lose Pallas. Yet, Jinkolothos had taken it too far, unnaturally extending her life beyond death.

"That must have been hard on her," Alys replied with genuine compassion. She paused a moment before gently adding, "Still, there is a natural order to things. To defy them would change anyone."

The dragon cocked its head to one side as if mulling over her response. Alys maintained her solemn demeanor while silently wondering if she'd overstepped herself.

After a short pause, the dragon finally responded. "There is truth in your words and your understanding is appreciated."

A dulcet smile spread across Alys' lips. She had not offended them after all.

"It's the least we can do," she replied as another thought occurred to her. Her brow furrowed as she voiced it. "Tell me, was it Argazephari then that she was trying to bring back?"

The ghostly dragon slowly shook its head. "Alas, no. He has passed well beyond her reach and now sits with the celestials."

That caught Alys by surprise. If it wasn't her mate, then that would leave…

Before she could finish her thought, Lloyd interrupted them with a strained cry. "Then whose soul was it?"

The ghostly dragon turned its gaze upon the anxious young man. "That belonged to her son. The Dragon Thrall Master captured his soul and placed it into that gem to hold over his parents."

All the color drained from Lloyd's face. Without warning, he turned and ran off across the platform away from them all.

Alys stared after him, too shocked to speak at first. When her voice finally did come back, she called after him "Lloyd, wait!"

The dragon peered after him as well though its expression was still unreadable. "Is your friend alright?"

Alys shook her head. "I don't know." She glanced back up at the dragon with a strained smile. "I'm sorry, but I should probably go find out."

"That would probably be for the best," the dragon agreed.

As Alys went to follow after Lloyd, Glo intercepted her. "Wait, there's something you should know first."

Her concern mounting, Alys halted and vented her frustration on the poor elf. "Well, what is it then?"

Glo grimaced, perhaps from her biting tone or maybe from what he wanted to tell her. Either way, she felt remorse for snapping at him.

"Sorry," Alys apologized.

Glo merely nodded, his voice dropping to a whisper. "I understand, but let's talk on the way." He motioned for her to follow him in the direction Lloyd had gone.

Now more concerned than ever, Alys fell in next to the tall elf as they chased after their missing friend.

Lloyd felt as if his insides were going to tear themselves apart. He had helped to end the life of the dracolich's son. No wonder she had gone insane. He had thought her the monster, but in reality, it was him instead—and all because he had listened to that damn demon.

The tortured young man ran towards the edge of the huge platform, tears streaming from the corners of his eyes as he struggled with this latest revelation. As soon as he reached the edge, he pulled the great black sword from his back and held it out over the cloudy void.

Give me one good reason why I shouldn't just throw you off now, he thought at the blade.

Because you need me, Jack responded confidently.

Need you? For what? Lloyd railed. *So, you can trick me into feeding you more innocent souls?*

Jack's voice took on a hurt tone. *Now, now. I needed the strength—or did you want the lich killing your friends?*

Lloyd grimaced, his insides still churning.

There had to be another way, he responded, though his resolve had begun to weaken.

If you think she was tough, wait until you take on the Undead Thrall Master, Jack chided him.

A wave of confusion passed over the torn young man. *What do you mean?*

Jack laughed. It was a cold hollow sound. *You don't think that measly vampire stole the lich's castle from her, do you? It was his master that took it from her.*

Lloyd's thoughts flashed back to their very first encounter with Jinkolothos and what she had told them about the vampire lord. *He was once my servant, but he betrayed me. He now serves another, one more powerful than I.*

Lloyd gulped, his arm holding the sword out over the void dropping to his side. If they were going to save his city, he and his friends would have to face one of the most powerful mages of all time. They would need every ounce of power they could muster in order to survive.

Damn you, he cursed at the demon.

Feeling utterly defeated, Lloyd dropped the blade on the platform next to him, then sat down on the edge and buried his face in his hands. All the while, the demon's cold laugh continued to echo through his mind.

Aksel watched with trepidation as Glo and Alys went after Lloyd. Though he'd healed the young man's body, Aksel had sensed something else was amiss with him. Glo and Seth later told Aksel what had happened with the soul gem. That dreadful act was against everything Lloyd believed in. He could only imagine how it must be weighing on his friend's soul.

Seth had been right to hide Jinkolothos' phylactery. The last thing Lloyd needed right now was any more of Jack's influence. They were going to have to do something about that demon before he led their friend too far down a dark path.

For now, though, Aksel needed to fulfill his promise to the spectral dragons. He'd require the power of the staff to break the potent binding spell Jinkolothos had placed on them. Yet, Aksel had only been able to wield the staff before with help from the Soldenar. Thinking ahead though, they'd have to return to the plane of shadows to save Penwick. Once there, he couldn't count on his goddess's direct intervention.

Firming his resolve, Aksel turned to the rest of their little company and motioned for them all to "stand back."

He then fixed his gaze upon the spectral dragons. Holding the staff aloft before him, he told them to, "Prepare yourselves."

The ghostly dragons gathered closer then laid down as Aksel began to pray. Divine power built up around him, the air practically humming with it. The amount of energy swirling about him was so vast that he nearly lost control.

Beads of sweat formed on Aksel's brow as he concentrated on keeping the magic in check. His struggle was rewarded as it finally bent to his will. Tingling all over from the immense amount of power, Aksel finally released the spell with the words, *"Nullam Finis."*

The head of the staff flared to life as it had before, a brilliant blue-white. That light flared outward illuminating the translucent dragons in an unearthly glow. A thick set of chains became visible binding each dragon to the platform below it.

As Aksel watched, the light enveloped those chains making them glow brighter and brighter. All at once, the chains shattered, disappearing in their entirety into the ether. The light then faded and everything went back to normal.

A wave of dizziness momentarily overcame Aksel. He leaned heavily on the staff until a pair of extra hands came to bolster him.

Seth stood there wearing a thick smirk.

"Piece of cake, huh?" The halfling's comment practically dripped with sarcasm.

Aksel managed a weak smile. "Sure. Can't wait to try that again."

Seth nudged his head towards the dragons. "Don't look now, but I think you've got yourself a following."

Aksel peered up to see the four dragons with their heads bowed down before him. The lead dragon spoke once again. "Thank you for freeing us, noble one. We are in your debt."

Not quite sure how to respond, Aksel merely said, "You're welcome."

Still feeling a bit overwhelmed, he whispered to Seth, "What am I supposed to do with four dragons?"

A wicked grin crossed Seth's lips. "I could think of a few things."

Alys had been stunned by the story Glo related to her. Lloyd, her little Lloyd, had done that? He helped end an innocent life? It just didn't make any sense. That was the exact opposite of everything the Stealles believed in.

After the initial shock wore off, however, Alys realized she could see it after all. Good-natured as Lloyd was, he was also extremely trusting—too trusting, in fact. If he'd been led to believe it was to save the rest of them, she could see him sacrificing some unknown soul, and damaging his own in the process.

In fact, the more Alys thought about it, the more she realized it was very Lloyd-like. It definitely explained his sullen mood. He'd probably been beating himself up on the inside this entire time. It also explained why he ran when he found out the true identity of the soul in that gem. She just hoped he wouldn't do anything foolish before they found him.

Alys and Glo finally caught up with Lloyd a few minutes later. They found him sitting on the edge of the platform, the demon sword cast to one side. His head buried in his hands, deep sobs wracked the young man's body.

He looked so forlorn that Alys' heart went out to him. Glo nudged her forward, while he stood back a few paces.

Alys intrinsically understood the wizard's unspoken message. In the state he was in, she was perhaps the only one who could reach him.

Burying her own scattered emotions, Alys took a deep breath and assumed the role of the caring sister. She then went to sit next to Lloyd and placed a gentle hand on his shoulder.

"Is there anything I can do?" she asked in a soothing voice.

Lloyd stopped sobbing and peered up at her. Her heart nearly leapt into her throat when she saw the black circles under his eyes.

Something passed between them at that moment—an innate recognition of who they were and where they came from. The hollow look in Lloyd's eyes disappeared, replaced instead with a faint spark of that old Stealle self-confidence.

"No," he slowly shook his head. "I brought this on myself and I have to face it."

Alys wanted to hug him so bad right then and there, but she knew it was not what he needed. Maintaining her calm air, she asked , "And how do you plan on doing that?"

Lloyd sat up straighter and rubbed the remaining moisture from his eyes. "I just have to do what all Stealles do. I took on this burden and I have to continue to shoulder it."

A thin smile spread across Alys' lips. Glo had been right to let her talk to him alone. Her very presence seemed to have brought out his old self.

Alys gently rubbed her hand on his back. "Just remember, you're not in this alone. Even your parents have each other to depend on."

Lloyd grasped her hand, the hint of a smile forming at the corners of his mouth. "That's true. Even Pallas needed your help back at Redune."

Alys smiled in earnest as she thought back to that fateful encounter with the pirate captain and the witch of the sea.

"Indeed, he did!" she agreed fervently.

Straightening his shoulders, Lloyd rose to his feet, and offered Alys his hand. "No more time for sulking then. People are counting on us."

Alys took his hand and nodded. "Yes, they are, and we won't fail them."

Walking up to join the pair, Glo motioned towards the black sword laying on the ground. "What are you going to do with that?"

Lloyd let out a short sigh, then stooped to pick it up. "Unfortunately, we're still going to need it."

Lloyd proceeded to explain what Jack had told him about the master of the undead. The thought sent shivers up Alys' spine, but Glo seemed more surprised than worried.

"I think that remains to be seen," the tall elf responded with one eyebrow raised.

Alys' nerves calmed measurably as she realized the wizard was right. She fixed both of them with an impish smile. "After all, it's not like a demon has *ever* been known to lie before."

"Fair point," Lloyd agreed.

Satisfied that things had been set right for the moment, Alys laced her arms around both man's and elf's elbows. "Shall we, gentlemen?"

She then led the bemused pair back to rejoin the others.

The night sky was just brightening to the east as the companions appeared on the roof of the Inn of the Three Sisters. Xellos had used every last bit of mana in his boots shifting them all, not to mention the four dragons and the remains of the dead god.

Seth thought it foolish to try and jump them all at once, but Aksel was adamant that they all come back together. He finally gave up arguing with the stubborn cleric, but not before saying, "If we all end up dead, I'm going to haunt you from here to eternity."

Off to the west, the castle of undead still hovered over the city cemetery. When they left, it had been semi-transparent, but now it looked almost completely solid. Seth wondered what would happen to the mausoleums and gravestones once it did. He imagined they would all be squished.

Aksel's normally serene face filled with anger as he stared at the castle. "It's time somebody did something about that," he declared fervently.

"Tsk," Seth clicked his tongue. "Last time you used that staff you nearly keeled over."

Aksel grimaced, but did not deny it. "Maybe, but if we wait any longer, that thing will be a permanent fixture."

Seth had another scathing retort on the tip of his tongue, but Glo stepped in before he could say it. "Though I can't use the staff the way Aksel does, maybe I can lend him what magical reserves I have."

Seth shook his head in disbelief at the two eggheads. "Great, then we can pick both of you up off the floor."

Aksel then did the one thing Seth hated—he used logic. The gnome placed a hand on Seth's shoulder. "I know you're just worried about us, but don't. With Glo's help we can definitely do this."

Seth really was worried about them, but he'd be damned if he admitted out loud. Instead, he pushed Aksel's hand away and folded his arms across his chest. "Hey, it's your funerals."

Seth refused to say anything more after that.

Aksel traded a glance with Glo, then shook his head.

"Are you sure it's safe?" Lloyd interjected.

Now Seth knew that everyone had gone crazy. Lloyd was making more sense than any of them.

"We'll be fine," Aksel assured him. "While Glo and I do this, why don't you and the others figure on how we're going to get Phobas remains back where they belong?"

Like Seth, Lloyd didn't look all that convinced. Still, he merely shrugged and wished them, "Good luck."

Seth planted himself on the parapet surrounding the roof, silently watching as the two casters strode to the western edge of the building. Once there Glo knelt down next to Aksel and grabbed onto the staff with both hands.

Aksel nodded and they began casting whatever spell they had chosen. Whatever it was Seth could feel the buildup of mana all the way over here.

They're nuts, he thought to himself, *and they're way too close to that edge.*

Abruptly realizing the danger that posed, Seth leapt to his feet and bolted after the duo. Unfortunately, he was just a few steps too late. The two idiots released the spell before he could quite get to them.

A blinding flash erupted from the staff forcing Seth to shield his eyes. The magic released was so potent that it washed over him like a physical rush of air.

A loud clap of thunder boomed from just overhead and a hole formed in the clouds above. Blue skies and the first rays of the morning sun peeked through as the hole widened ever faster.

The opening swiftly spread across the sky until every last cloud in sight had disappeared from view. Over the graveyard, the dark castle began to fade. In just under a few seconds it completely vanished from sight.

Cheers erupted from the rooftop and from the surrounding city. Meanwhile, as Seth had predicted, both Aksel and Glo collapsed. Luckily, he and Lloyd reached them in time to keep them from falling over the edge.

When Aksel finally came to, he stared up at Seth with glazed eyes. "Did we do it?"

"Yeah, yeah. You did it," Seth assured him. "Now shut up and go back to sleep," he admonished his dopey friend.

"Soft bed..." Aksel murmured before drifting off again.

Seth didn't relish the idea of carrying Aksel all the way down to his room, but he couldn't just leave him here either. As he prepared to hoist him up, help arrived from an unexpected source.

"We can take em'," Kalyn offered.

Seth peered up to see the backwoods archer standing over them while pointing a thumb at an obviously uncomfortable Martan. When Martan remained silent, she elbowed him in the side.

"Yes, of course we can," Martin chimed in after the rough prompting.

Alys stood beside the pair wearing a mischievous grin.

"And I can show them to their rooms," the songstress added brightly. "I'm sure you two would be much better than us at thinking of what to do with those ghost dragons and Phobas' body."

"Gee, thanks," Seth drawled. Still, he rose to his feet and let the trio take the sleeping casters off their hands.

"Better you than me," Kalyn snickered as they walked off with the passed out pair. "Dragons fly, but I got no idea how to move that giant body."

The backwoods archer's flippant remake sparked an idea in Seth's mind. *Dragons fly,* Seth thought, his mind racing. *Sure, these were ghost dragons, but what if…*

Lloyd eyed him curiously. "I know that look. What are you thinking?"

Seth shrugged. "Maybe nothing, or maybe the solution to all our problems." He motioned to the tall man, "Follow me and we'll find out."

With the crazy idea still fresh in his mind, Seth strode across the rooftop over to the lead dragon. Staring up at it, he asked, "Any chance you guys can interact with physical objects?"

The dragon hesitated a moment before answering. "It is difficult, but yes we can for short periods of time."

Seth narrowed his gaze at the dragon. "How short?"

The dragon cocked its head to one side before answering. "Hmm, maybe twenty minutes at most."

Seth rubbed his hands together. This could definitely work.

"Perfect," he told the dragon. "Two of you take Phobas here, and the rest of us will ride with the others."

Lloyd frowned at him. "Where are we going?"

"To the temple, of course," Seth said glibly. "I can't wait to see Sirus' face when we show up on her lawn with a dead god and four ghost dragons."

Glo's eyes slowly fluttered open, but for some reason they seemed to have a hard time focusing. Laying prone, he rose to his elbows and glanced around. For the second time in as many days he found himself surrounded by nothing but grayness.

The wizard sat up and scratched his head. He appeared to be back in that eerie gray void once again.

Did I die this time? He wondered to himself.

No, my love, you are just in a deep sleep, a familiar voice answered his unspoken question.

Glo turned about to find Elistra sitting beside him, that same whimsical look in her violet eyes. The sight of the beautiful seeress improved his mood immensely, although he still felt somewhat confused.

"How exactly does that work?" he asked, taking her hand in his.

"It's simple, really," she responded, that knowing smile forming upon her lips. "Once you've been here it's easy to return, especially in dreams."

Glo thought that over briefly, then shrugged. "If you say so. For now, I'm just going to take advantage of the moment."

Elistra's eyes widened ever so slightly. "Oh really? Is that all you're going to take advantage of?"

"Not entirely," Glo murmured as he leaned in and kissed her.

"Good," she managed between kisses.

Out of the corner of his eye, Glo noticed a white tent had sprung up around them. He pulled back a moment and eyed the seeress curiously. "Did you do that?"

An impish smile lit up her face. "I thought we could use a bit more privacy."

Glo had no idea who could see them in all this grayness. Still, he forgot all about it as the beautiful seeress wrapped her arms around his neck, then pulled him down on top of her.

The star-crossed lovers lost themselves in the throes of passionate bliss. Once their desires for each other had been sated, they lay there quietly in each other's arms for a time. Unfortunately, it could not last forever.

Elistra eventually pushed herself up onto one elbow and stared down at him, her expression now serious. "You know I originally came to warn you."

Still in a playful mood, Glo reached up and touched the tip of her nose. "I could use more warnings like this."

A brief smile crossed her face as she grabbed his hand and kissed his fingers. Yet her expression swiftly grew somber once again. "I'm serious."

Glo sighed, then also rose up onto his elbow. "Oh, very well. What crisis is it this time?"

Elistra's expression didn't change, but grew even more grim if possible. "I'm afraid that demon was not lying to young Lloyd. Vanalor has indeed returned to Castle Ravenar."

Glo sat up straight, all other thoughts suddenly vanquished from his mind. "When you say Vanalor, you mean the undead Thrall Master, right? Not the holy knight from the group that led an assault on the Planes of Shaddonon."

"They are one and the same," Elistra replied, her gaze holding his unflinching.

Glo paused to wrap his head around that revelation. The name Vanalor was not all that common, but he never imagined a holy knight turning in the Master of the Undead. After what happened to Alana and Sir Craven though, he might have guessed if he gave it some thought.

Glo narrowed an eye at the beautiful seeress. "So let me get this straight—the Undead Thrall Master, who is actually Vanalor, has returned to Ravenar, the castle that can shift between planes."

"Yes," Elistra affirmed with a brief nod.

"And you think it's only a matter of time until he launches a full scale assault on the City of Penwick?" Glo continued.

"Yes," Elistra nodded again. "He has made a pact with demon kind to retrieve the staff."

Glo rose to his feet, pulling Elistra up with him. "Then I think I should go warn the others."

"Yes, you should," she agreed, her eyes misting over as she said it.

Glo peered down at her, his heart melting once again. Their time together was always far too brief. He forced himself to smile. "When this is all over…"

She reached up and put a finger on his lips before he could finish. "Do not jinx it. What will be, will be. Just know that no matter what, I will love you forever."

Glo's heart nearly burst with joy at hearing those words, even though they were bittersweet.

"As I will you," he told her softly.

The tall elf bent down and kissed the immortal seeress with all the tenderness of his fractured heart.

24
WAR COUNCIL

Andrella felt totally refreshed after a few hours in the Chamber of Arenor. It had been pleasant getting to know Lara and Kratos better, but afterwards she'd been raring to get back into the thick of things. Her future in-laws seemed to share the same mindset which definitely boded well for her impending marriage.

Andrella felt equally worried and annoyed when she found the others had left without her. *How could they leave me behind? What if they didn't come back? What if he didn't come back?* Those thoughts continued to plague her until her friends finally reappeared the following dawn.

Her reunion with Lloyd was blissful. It had been less than a day, but she already missed the feel of his arms around her. Lagerie had Andrella and the Stealles back to the fortress where Lloyd filled them in on what happened with the dracolich. It sounded like everything turned out alright, but something about Lloyd felt off to her. He seemed a bit more restrained than usual.

Once Lloyd finished his story, the conversation turned to what was going on in the city. "Though the castle is gone for the moment, no one is being allowed to return to their homes just yet," Lagerie told them.

"Lara and I have contacted Caverinus," Kratos continued. "We've asked for a meeting of the council to discuss our next steps."

Andrella wanted to be at that meeting. Before she could ask, Lara leaned in and placed a hand on her arm. "Of course, you and your friends are invited, dear. After all, the entire town is referring to you as the *New Protectors*."

Andrella liked the sound of that. She had never been counted as one of the *Heroes of Ravenford*, but being a *Protector* sounded far cooler.

As it turned out, Caverinus declined to have a meeting of the Penwick Council. With Carenna and Taliana gone, he felt it 'improper until their positions could be filled.' He did, however, authorize Lagerie to hold a 'war council' without him. Rumor had it Caverinus refused to leave the keep until all danger had passed.

After discussing it with Sirus, they decided to have the 'war council' at the temple. With so much unrest and the bulk of the city's displaced population to look after, the high priestess felt it best to not leave her post for too long. Thus, that evening, all possible participants gathered in Sirus' office.

Aside from the high priestess herself, Lagerie, Kratos and Lara attended. So did Lloyd, Glo, Aksel, Seth, and Xellos. Kalyn even came and dragged a reluctant Martan with her. Alys was there as well along with a handsome stranger with silver hair and silver eyes that Andrella had never seen before.

Even with all those present, Andrella wondered about some important folks who seemed to be missing. She addressed her concerns to Lara and Kratos. "What of Uncle Aillinn and your brother, Argus?"

Lara wore a look of derision upon her face. "My brother is apparently 'too busy' preparing for the next assault."

Andrella arched an eyebrow, a subconscious habit she had picked up from her mentor. "What does he think we're doing here?"

"Precisely," Lara responded, her tone dripping with acid.

Seeing his wife so obviously annoyed, Kratos stepped in to answer the rest of her question. "As for Aillinn, Caverinus temporarily appointed him to head up the *Protectors* and the castle guard in Carenna's stead."

"Well then all the more reason he should be here," Andrella insisted.

A pained expression crossed her future father in-law's face. "Trust me, if it were up to Aillinn, he would be here. He is, however, under strict orders not to leave his post, but I'm to inform him of any 'recommendations' this council has."

Andrella found this all rather incredulous. The more she heard about her Uncle Caverinus, the more she realized the extent of his cowardice.

"Has anyone contacted Kennig Lisink?" Lloyd interjected.

Lara let out a loud snort. "Kennig is apparently also 'too busy' fending off undead attacks in the countryside."

Andrella found that rather surprising. "I thought we'd taken care of most of them here in the city?"

This time Lagerie fielded her question. "We did. Kennig claims some random groups escaped from Three Forks to harass his lands. We have yet to verify any such thing."

The frustration in all their voices was obvious. Andrella found the lack of leadership in this city appalling. If this were Ravenford, heads would have rolled by now for dereliction of duty to their people.

Gazing about the room, Andrella noticed one other important head was missing. She turned to Alys. "What of your father?"

Alys rolled her eyes to the heavens. "Apparently"—there was that word again—"the Baron is in too much distress for my father to leave his side. Therefore, he asked me to attend in his stead."

Andrella had a few choice words for the delinquent Master of Coin, but chose to keep them to herself. Instead, she simply smiled at Alys. "Well at least he was good enough to send a capable stand in."

"One does one's best," Alys responded with a dip of her chin and an impish smile.

"Ahem," Sirus stood and cleared her throat, attracting everyone's attention to her. "I'd like to introduce our final attendee." She motioned towards the silver-haired gentlemen. "This is Banri, one of the dragons rescued from the cloud plane."

Andrella's brow rose with keen interest. Judging from the dragons they'd met before, this Banri must be a silver dragon.

Banri stood and executed a polite bow. "Your magnanimous head priestess here was good enough to resurrect me and my compatriots. We are thus in your debt and at your disposal in this war against the undead."

Andrella exchanged a pleased look with Glo. A group of adult silver dragons on their side would definitely help in any forthcoming battles.

Once Banri sat back down, Sirus leaned forward and placed both hands on her desk. "Now to business. The dracolich threat is gone, and thanks to you all," she nodded to Lloyd and the others, "we have more than enough gold to repair what has been destroyed."

"This council will make certain that the money from the dragon hoard gets used to fix up the city," Lara interjected firmly.

"I second that," Kratos agreed.

"And I third that," Lagerie chimed in.

Alys stood. "As stand in for the Master of Coin, I fourth and finalize that decision."

"Here, here," a round of cheers went up around the room.

"Thank you," Alys said with a smile and a brief curtsey. She then sat back down.

At the same time, Aksel now stood and addressed Sirus. "Pardon, your holiness, but what of Phobas body?"

Sirus gave him a warm smile. "Thanks to you, Phobas remains have been returned to his tomb. Some wards have been put up in place as protection, though obviously not any as good as with the staff."

Aksel started to say more, but Sirus raised a hand signifying she wasn't quite finished. "There is obviously need of the staff elsewhere at the moment. When all is said and done, we will return it to its rightful place."

A look of relief passed over Aksel's face. "Thank you, your holiness." He, too, then sat back down.

Sirus gave him a perfunctory nod then swept her eyes across the room. "Is there anything else anyone wants to share before discussing our next steps?"

Lloyd stood and repeated the demon's words about the Undead Thrall Master's return. Andrella already knew as he had told both her and his parents earlier. She was surprised, however, when Glo confirmed his story through Elistra.

"She also told me the castle hasn't moved from its current spot," Glo went on to say. "Thus, we can expect its reappearance soon."

Andrella felt a sense of dread creep up her spine. From the looks on the faces of the others around the room, she could tell they felt the same.

Lloyd shot out of his seat again, his tone vehement. "I think what we need to do is clear. We need to go back to the castle and take the fight to them before anyone else gets hurt."

While Andrella agreed with him wholeheartedly, Lloyd seemed particularly agitated. She knew there had been casualties, but his heated declaration sounded almost personal.

Kratos stood and placed a hand on his son's shoulder. "Now hold on there, Lloyd. You do realize we're talking about an actual Thrall Master here?"

Lloyd's reaction was totally out of character. He pushed his father's hand away, his voice filled with irritation. "I know that, dad, but we can't just sit around and wait for them to destroy more lives."

Andrella rose from her seat and grabbed Lloyd by the arm. "Woah there. I don't think your father's saying we shouldn't go. I believe he's merely trying to point out that we need to think things through first."

"Exactly," Kratos concurred, giving Andrella a grateful nod.

Lloyd shifted his gaze between the pair, his face reddening. His hand went to the back of his neck.

"Sorry," he mumbled beneath his breath.

Still seated with his hands steepled in front of him, Glo chimed in. "I believe the most prudent course of action is for those to go who are most familiar with the castle and the Plane of Shadows."

"That makes sense," Kratos agreed, though it was obvious he still held reservations.

Kalyn's hand shot up from where she sat. "Martan and I will go too. We've worked pretty good with these folks before."

Kalyn looked determined but Martan had turned deathly pale. "We will?" he stammered at Kalyn.

She slapped him on the arm. "Yes, we will. Now hush."

"I think that would work," Aksel agreed.

"I'll go as well." Banri rose from his seat and swept his silver eyes around the room. "If you'll have me."

Aksel gave him a grateful nod. "Of course. Your presence would be most welcome."

It appeared as if Kratos might have more objections, but Lagerie cut him off before he could voice them. "Now that we've established whose going, how do you intend to outfit yourselves? To Kratos' point, you may be facing one of the most powerful mages this world has ever seen."

Andrella had to admit it was a fair question. To be honest, the idea of coming face-to-face with the Master of the Undead had sent chills up her spine.

Glo met Lagerie's gaze evenly. "Aside from the Staff of Law, we have a number of other powerful artifacts that we borrowed from Phobas' tomb. Furthermore, we found a few more rare items and artifacts in Jinkolothos' hoard."

His words intrigued everyone there, but no one so much as Lara. The high wizard sat forward in her seat, her eyebrows twitching with interest. "What exactly did you find in the dracolich's hoard?"

This was also the first Andrella had heard of them bringing back anything from their last mission. Lloyd hadn't mentioned it and she had to admit to being almost as curious as Lara.

Glo's eyes shifted upward as if doing a quick inventory in his mind. "Well, without getting into too much detail, there were a few rare bows—including a Bow of Light, a Sphere of Annihilation, and the legendary dagger, Carnwen."

Lara's jaw nearly dropped to the floor. The rest of the gathering showed either similar signs of astonishment or appeared totally mystified. Andrella had to admit to feeling a bit of both.

"What in Dunwynn's undies is a Bow of Light?" Kalyn gaffed.

She immediately covered her mouth after she said it, her face paling from embarrassment.

Andrella found herself hard pressed not to burst out laughing. She felt better about it when Sirus let out a soft chuckle.

"It's a magical bow that fires arrows of pure light," the high priestess explained. "It can be quite destructive when dealing with undead or other evil creatures."

"What about this Carnwen?" Seth spoke up for the first time since the meeting started. The halfling had been slouched down on the couch at the back of the room this entire time.

It did not surprise Andrella in the slightest when Alys answered his question. The girl seemed to be a fount of knowledge. "It's the fabled dagger of the Kings of Lanfor. According to legend, the blade is sentient and is so sharp that it can cut the head off a man in a single swipe."

"Cool," Seth responded with a glint in his eye. It was obvious the dagger had sparked his interest.

In the meantime, Lara had finally found her voice. "A Sphere of Annihilation?" she emphasized each word individually, the expression on her face incredulous.

Andrella definitely heard the term before. If memory served her correctly, it was a ball of darkness that destroyed anything with which it came in contact. Now that she thought of it though, how would anyone store such an object?

As if reading her mind, Lara rose to her feet and blurted, "Are you insane? Where in the devil are you keeping such a dangerous thing?"

Glo winced, completely taken aback by her reaction. Seeing his friend's distress, Aksel stepped in and answered for him in a calm tone. "It was stored in an anti-magic chest and inactive when we found it…"

"…and that chest is now in turn stored in my own personal portal chest," Glo finished after finding his voice again, though he still sounded a tad defensive.

A wave of relief flooded over Andrella. She had just recently learned of portal chests from her mentor. Unlike portal bags, the chest itself would be stored in another dimension. A highly enough trained wizard could then shift the chest away to hide it and recall it when needed. It was a great way to handle dangerous objects like the one in question.

"Phew." Lara let out a huge sigh mimicking Andrella's feelings. She must have only then noticed the hurt look on Glo's face. "Sorry, Glolindir. I should have known you'd handle it better than that, but all I could picture is the entire city disappearing in a giant ball of darkness."

Kratos let out a soft whistle. "That bad?"

Lara met his gaze with a nod and a tilt of her head. "That bad."

"It would be our 'ace in the hole'," Aksel explained further, "only to be used if there is no other option."

Kratos looked from Aksel to Glo and finally to Lloyd. "Very impressive. My apologies then, son. You and your friends seem to be prepared for just about anything."

"I'd still like it better if we had a map of the place," Aksel murmured softly.

"I thought you'd never ask," Alys declared brightly. The clever songstress waved her hand and produced a parchment out of thin air. She then walked over and stood in front of Sirus desk.

"May I?" she asked the high priestess.

Sirus stood and ushered her forth. "By all means."

Everyone gathered around as Alys rolled out the parchment across the desktop. Andrella drew next to her and scanned what appeared to be a detailed floor plan of the entire castle. The title across the top of the parchment read *Castle Ravenar.*

From what Andrella recalled, that is the name Alys referred to when they first discovered the castle's existence. The layout before her matched what she remembered from their fateful mission to the castle in the shadow planes.

Andrella gazed at Alys with a mixture of curiosity and awe. "Where in Thac did you get these?"

Alys responded with a sly wink. "There's a great library in the midst of the old Thrushin Hall, if you know where to look. I spent much of my younger days there reading everything I could about myths and legends, heroic tales, and other such stories. If one knows where to look, one can find almost anything there."

Andrella was duly impressed.

Across from them, Aksel stood over the parchment, gingerly rubbing his chin. "This will most certainly help." He peered up at Alys and gave her an appreciative nod. "Thank you for this."

Alys responded with a dimpled smile.

Lagerie waved for everyone to gather around the desk. "Well then, how about we talk strategy."

About an hour later, the group had come up with a basic mission plan and some backup ones just in case. Andrella stood and stretched her back after leaning over Sirus' desk for so long.

"Alright then," Sirus said, sweeping her eyes around the room.

"Give us a list of anything else you think you might need and we will have it ready for you first thing in the morning. Otherwise, I suggest those who are going get a good night's rest. The rest of us will stay and discuss what we can do here in the meantime."

Those of the group who would be going on the mission rose from their seats and began shuffling out of the room. Andrella held Lloyd by the arm and tried to catch his eye, but his gaze seemed to be somewhere far off in the distance.

"Oh, and one last thing before you go," Sirus called from behind them. "May Arenor be with you."

Here ends Book Four of
Rise of the Thrall Lord
the story continues in Book Five
Children of the Baleful Moon

ABOUT THE AUTHOR

F.P. Spirit writes high fantasy fiction inspired by the likes of Tolkien, Eddings, Brooks, and Piers Anthony. An avid science fiction fan, he became hooked on fantasy the moment he cracked open the Lord of the Rings in high school. When he is not writing, F.P. is either spending time with his wife and sons, gaming, doing yoga, Tai Chi, or walking their dog.

A long-time lover of fantasy and the surreal, he hopes you enjoy his fun contributions to the world of fantasy and magic.

You can learn more about F.P. Spirit by visiting his website at:
Fpspirit.com